THE WORLD'S REVOLUTION
- BOOK ONE -

GAIA
AWAKENS

A CLIMATE CRISIS ANTHOLOGY

EDITED BY C.D. TAVENOR
AND MEG TRAST

Two Doctors
Media Collaborative

We hope you enjoy *Gaia Awakens: A Climate Crisis Anthology*. If you like the first book of *The World's Revolution*, consider following the project on social media.

Facebook: The World's Revolution

Twitter: @TheWorldRevolts

_____

Published by Two Doctors Media Collaborative LLC
www.twodoctorsmedia.com

Cover design by S.E. MacCready
https://semaccready.com/

ISBN: 978-1-952706-29-5 (Paperback)
ISBN: 978-1-952706-30-1 (e-book)
ISBN: 978-1-952706-31-8 (hardcover)

Gaia Awakens

A Climate Crisis Anthology

Book I of The World's Revolution

Table of Contents

Editor's Note   1
Acknowledgments   5
The Gaia Stones   7
Catalyst   33
The Spin   50
The Green Ceiling   71
Behind the Mirror   76
The Bent Greens   92
Two More Days To Sydney   120
Ring of Contamination   126
Garden of Eden   145
The Lifespan of Wildflowers   152
Real-Time   172
Culling Day   189
The Crystal Haze   213
Gaia's Final Embrace   219
Talking Trees and the Heavy Metal Moose   231
Enhanced Weathering   256
SOOT SHIELD   273
Scourge of the Mosquitoes   281
Translocation   302
Team Wolf Anxiety   309
The Coast Guard   334
The Quiet Ghost of Willow Way   345
Gaia Awakened   364
About the Authors   375
Join The World's Revolution!   381

EDITOR'S NOTE

Welcome to *Gaia Awakens: A Climate Crisis Anthology*. It is the first book in the collaborative universe known as *The World's Revolution*. We're excited you're joining us on this adventurous experiment in climate fiction storytelling.

The World's Revolution began as a simple concept discussed between a few authors. What would it look like to create an anthology where every story occurred in the same setting? How would you properly connect the narratives without everything feeling disjointed? More importantly, around what concepts should the narrative center?

While the answers to most of the questions resolved themselves over time, the need to focus the collection on the climate crisis became immediately apparent. I've wanted to dive deeply into the world of climate fiction for quite some time, having merely dabbled in previous stories I've written or books I've edited for other authors. An anthology focused exclusively on climate fiction both felt like a perfect opportunity to develop the collaborative universe *and* encourage storytelling about a topic of utmost importance.

A climate fiction anthology, with stories written by authors from across the world, from many different perspectives, ideologies, and experiences, presents a wonderful opportunity to explore those questions.

We need stories to inspire hope. Inspire change. Inspire revolution.

But "revolution" and "change" and "hope" mean a lot of different things to a lot of different people.

So we brainstormed. We developed the initial concept of *The World's Revolution* back in 2020, even before the COVID-19 pandemic began. We workshopped the branding for the project, created a Kickstarter campaign, and successfully funded it. We launched our call for sub-missions in March 2021, received excellent fantasy and sci-fi stories over the span of three months, and now we're here, releasing the first anthology.

It will hopefully be the first of many.

But as I write this note, the Intergovernmental Panel on Climate Change's (IPCC) most recent climate report is hot off the press. It's nearly certain that we'll reach 1.5 degrees Celsius during this century, and it's very likely we will far surpass that temperature. We are standing on the precipice of the climate crisis, with very few "good" options awaiting us in the future.

It's made these stories feel all the more important. And tiny, in the face of the true complexity of the threat we face.

Our final anthology features stories written by authors on four different continents and with a wide variety of backgrounds. Some stories address the question of climate change from a fundamentally human angle, or a technological approach, or a spiritual perspective. Some of the stories are wonderfully weird or action-packed, while others are melancholy. Thought-provoking. Reflective.

I'm proud of the authors who took a chance on this project and wrote stories for it. It's been a pleasure working with them, refining their narratives, and ensuring every tale fits within the collaborative universe. What surprised me the most was how many of the stories felt connected even before I made a single suggestion. The authors featured in this collection did their homework and read the worldbuilding we established as part of the call for submissions.

Still, there are many stories missing. The collection features the work of sixteen talented authors through twenty-three stories, but that's only sixteen perspectives on the climate crisis. Only sixteen voices coming together to write stories about the World's Revolution, a narrative that requires millions of voices to truly encompass the human experience of our rapidly transforming planet.

If you're an author reading this collection, I encourage you to consider what tale *you* would write.

Inside *Gaia Awakens: A Climate Crisis Anthology*, you'll notice connecting themes and characters. The story begins in 2040 C.E. and ends in 2055 C.E., and overtime, a full picture of *The World's Revolution* will emerge. The authors of these stories have taken the concept presented to them by storm and made it their own.

I am honored to have the opportunity to act as the facilitator for their stories to reach the minds of readers. At the end of the anthology, you'll find more information about each author. I encourage you to take a look at the works they've published elsewhere. If we're to tell more climate fiction stories, we need to support climate fiction writers, after all!

Similarly, I hope you'll stay in touch with *The World's Revolution* and prepare yourself for future collections. I'm excited to see what authors propose for our next anthology. And we're not restricted to short stories. I envision a future where authors can write novellas and novels and series under *The World's Revolution* banner, too.

The sky is the limit.

However, I'm not going to pretend like this one anthology is the solution to all of our problems. Telling stories inspired by the climate crisis means nothing if the inspired thoughts don't turn into action. Take what you learn from these narratives and find a way to make a difference in your community.

Find an organization to join that furthers the call for justice in your world. Organize your neighborhood to develop sustainable projects and programs. Talk to your friends and family about what we need to do to transform the world so future generations can thrive upon its surface.

Read these stories. Let them entertain you and inspire you. Then *do something in response*. Because the world described in the pages that follow isn't a world we should want to come to pass. In the present, we still have a chance to stop the worst impacts of climate change.

In *Gaia Awakens*, the world is nearly past the point of no return. By the end of the anthology, it'll be up to you to decide whether hope remains for our heroes.

In solidarity in the fight against the climate crisis,

C. D. Tavenor, Editor for *The World's Revolution*

ACKNOWLEDGMENTS

S.E. MacCready, A.E. Faulkner, and Kit Hanson all deserve a special recognition for their work on this project in both seen and unseen ways. They are an incredible team, and this project wouldn't exist without them.

Likewise, it's absolutely essential that we thank all of our Kickstarter backers who made this project possible. Every one of them contributed to the creation of this project, enabling us to pay authors immediately for the stories in the anthology. In particular, we would like to thank our Climate Guardian and Climate Vanguard backers, who went above and beyond in their financial support:

Julie Fillius Thomas, Alana Powell, John Winkelman

Shaun Olmsted, The Maggios, Scott Mattocks

Carla Severe, Dale and Sue O'Donnell, William Clemens

Susan Hutcheson, Trevor Britton, Susan and Tom Tavenor

Ganesh M. Nair, Ashley Welsh, Brian Timm

Christian Meyer, Noah Taylor, D Jole

Now, without any further delay, please enjoy the stories of *Gaia Awakens: A Climate Crisis Anthology, Book 1 of The World's Revolution*.

THE GAIA STONES

DAVID KERNOT

2040 C.E.

Mike Ironbark drove the shovel into the hard dry ground. He glanced at the year-old oak seedling in the pot nearby and wondered how many years it would take for the tree to shade the farmhouse. "This is for you, Dad," he said.

Dad had believed everything was connected, and he died twelve months to the day. The family had potted the acorn that night in his memory. Today, they'd plant the seedling in the ground and celebrate his life again.

Mike's arms and shoulders ached from the compacted soil. He blamed the early onset of summer. What, with the ongoing pandemic, climate change, and the looming global water shortages, he was happy the loose confederation of pacific island states, along with New Zealand and Australia, had formed the Oceania Alliance. As a small and isolated political bloc, it had been easy to mostly close their borders to the rest of the world.

He stood, straightened his tight back muscles, and removed his worn wide-brimmed hat. He wiped the sweat off his brow and stared at the small rise of hills in the distance. They marked the edge of the farm and had already turned a deep shade of rusty-brown. In front of them, the heat shimmered above the expanse of wheat. How could it be so hot in the morning?

"Curse this heat," he said, and looked around for his crowbar. He stared up at the cloudless, indigo-blue sky, proud of his successes on the land. This was Dad's farm, his legacy.

He turned at the sound of the back screen door spring stretching. Anna, his wife, stood by the door of their farmhouse, a towel wrapped around her slender body and her long wet hair stuck to her. Mike couldn't help but smile. She looked beautiful, and he was the luckiest man alive.

"Mike, there's no water for Maisie Jane's shower," she said.

"Have you checked the tank?"

"Yes, it's dry."

Mike's heart skipped a beat, and he frowned. Out here, water was their livelihood. Without it, everything would die. The crops, the animals . . . the people. Showers were the least of his concern. But it was odd. The bore pump should have automatically filled the house tank overnight. The breaker had probably tripped; it had done that a few times of late. Salt or contaminants lodged in the pipes stretching deep underground. He sighed. And spoke out loud in a rebellious fashion—but not loud enough for Anna to hear him. "Australia's Great Artesian Basin." Why they had renamed the Australian continent South-West Pangaea, part of the greater Oceania Alliance, was beyond him. Australia would always be Australia, even if the world continued to create new, locked-down alliances and isolate people, even if it was probably the only way to end the wars over water and food and maintain disease-free regions after endless years of pandemic.

"Have we got power in the house?"

She nodded.

"Ok, I'll go check."

"Daddy, Daddy." The outside screen door opened wider. Their daughter, Maisie Jane, ran around Anna and made a beeline toward him. He smiled and squatted down. She threw herself into his arms. Maisie Jane was the spitting image of Anna, except she was tall and her eyes a deeper blue—something she'd inherited from him.

Maisie Jane still looked too pale and thin, but the doctors had said her leukemia was in remission. He hoped so.

"Sleep well, Mouse?" He ruffled her uncombed hair.

The six-year-old nodded. Maisie Jane looked around him, to the small hole in the ground, at his shovel, and the oak tree. "Grandpa's tree," she said.

His throat tightened, and he swallowed several times to work it away before speaking. They'd made many promises on Dad's deathbed, but it had been at Maisie Jane's insistence that they planted an acorn in his memory.

It didn't seem a year ago that his father had leaned forward and put his paper-thin hand on Maisie Jane's cheek. "Mouse," he said. "You can tell your grandchildren it was Grandpa's tree because he loved you so much." She nodded. "And by that time me and the tree will be one with Mother Gaia, then you'll have the magic Gaia Stones I gave to your dad."

Dad had chuckled and made one last joke. He passed shortly after, his hand on Maisie Jane's arm.

Mike's throat tightened again. Dad had always been bigger than life, and he hoped he'd be the same for Maisie Jane. His hands went to the chain around his neck, to where the three small emeralds were cocooned in silk and their separate hessian bags. The Gaia Stones, Dad had called them. Even now, they glowed hot, as if they had lives of their own. They seemed to call to him. Unfamiliar images formed at the edge of his vision, and—

"Don't cry, Daddy."

Mike pulled himself from his memories, forcing the stone's images aside. They could wait for another time. He wiped away the tears he'd been unaware of until Maisie Jane spoke, and he ruffled her hair again. He didn't trust his voice not to be twisted with emotion as he nodded.

"Maisie, come inside and let Daddy check the pump."

Maisie Jane leaned closer. "Remember?"

He nodded again and swallowed. "If I see any, I'll let you know."

"But don't hurt them," she said quickly and held up a tiny index finger determinedly that reinforced the impression she was such an old soul. She seemed years older.

"I won't." He stood and watched the young girl run back inside. He smiled and shook his head. There was so much of his mum in her. It was uncanny. He regretted that Mum and Anna had never met, but Mum had passed years before from the cancer. Maisie's obsession with dragonflies always amused him, and especially Dad, who had given Maisie Jane his wife's anniversary gift of an intricate, gilded dragonfly. But Maisie Jane was right. They darted around near the small bore pump shed in search of water. They might even be at the header tank, hovering over a broken pipe that fed the farmhouse.

* * *

Mike stood at the empty water tank, and a sense of urgency gripped him. It clawed at his chest like a wildcat intent on ripping him apart. The stones at his throat seemed to lick him with fire, and he swallowed hard. He pushed away an image of vivid, lush green pastures with their horses frolicking across the paddocks and stared at the harsh, dry hillside. Far to his left, a flock of his sheep gathered near a clump of trees. The horses in the stables kicked at their pens and whinnied for food.

A dragonfly appeared. It moved straight up above him, flew backward, stopped and hovered a short distance away, almost as if it waited for Mike to do something. But he couldn't. The dragonflies would die soon as the remaining water vanished.

He had a bad feeling. Water was everything, and he didn't have the money to truck in supplies. Not this year. His two thousand acres of land were worthless if he didn't have water to last the dry summer. He took a breath, slow and deliberate. Worrying too much, as always, never helped. He had water. Everything would be fine. He strode down the hill to the pump shed, convinced the breaker had tripped again. Maisie Jane's shower would follow. Anna could wash the soap from her hair.

Mike's phone in his pocket buzzed. He stopped in the shade of a tree and answered the call. "Hello?"

"Hey big brother, happy 2040, how are you?"

He grinned. "Rashi, how have you been?"

"Good. I wanted to call and see how you are. Dad would have wanted that."

He nodded in agreement. "We planted a tree for him today."

"Lovely."

He rubbed the side of his neck and turned his back to the burning sun. "What's it like in the Texan Alliance of States? Are you going to return home soon?"

"Not with the border closures. I'm fine though. I've got a job tracking animals through ICARUS."

Mike frowned. "What did you say? ICARUS?" "There was a long pause. "Hello? Sis?"

"Sorry. It's the International Cooperation for Animal Research Using Space. It uses the new antenna array on The Gateway, the International Space Station."

"So you're going into space?"

She laughed. "I'm a ground tech. We use ICARUS to see the effects of climate change on animal populations. It's important work."

"I'm sure it is." Rashi had travelled the world to protest about climate change. Dad had loved her conviction as Mike did, and everyone worried over her safety with all the violent conflicts.

"How's the water situation?"

"Worse than usual, and—" He looked over at the pump shed and cringed.

"Sorry to hear that. Anyway, I just wanted you to know I was thinking about everyone. Have a glass of wine for me and toast Dad tonight."

He nodded. "Will do."

"It's really great to hear your voice."

"Yes, and yours."

"Got to go. There's some weird stuff happening with my animal data. I'll fill you in later when I can. Give my love to Anna and Maisie Jane."

"I will. You stay safe, sis."

She ended the call, and he looked back in the house's direction. Maisie Jane would like that her Auntie Rashi had called.

He sighed. Now back to the problem at hand.

Mike pulled open the pump-shed door and stepped inside, careful not to bang his head on the low roof. His stomach churned. If water was their life's blood, then the pump was at its heart. He'd heard of farmers leaving their land once the water supplies ran dry. But out here, they were blessed. The Great Artesian Basin was an ancient and enormous holding of water, buried under a third of the continent, had been here for an eternity, and it would remain so. He glanced about the small space, to the pump head in the middle of the floor and the outlet pipes that fed the holding tank up on the hill a short distance away. Everything was as it should be.

He flicked a light switch by the door, but nothing happened, so he clambered over generations of accumulated rubbish strewn across the floor to the circuit breaker. He smiled. It had tripped, which happened from time to time. He reset the breaker, and dull light shone from an overhead globe above the pump. He breathed a sigh of relief, and the churning in his stomach lessened. The pump would kick in. He leaned over and pressed the reset on the pump housing, waiting for it to start filling the header tank.

A pump light glowed, one he'd never seen, and his heart skipped a beat. He stepped outside and cursed in the knowledge he wouldn't be able to fix it. The water level had fallen below the pump inlet. But how? There should have been water to last generations.

He sat in the dirt, unsure what to do next. He didn't have the money to drill a new bore site. The farm was already in debt. How was he going to afford a new pump that could take water from a deeper well?

Perhaps he had overreacted. It might only need priming. Even as a glimmer of hope appeared at the idea, it died. Inside the shed again, he shut off the pump and wrenched open the top of the pipe descending deep into the precious artesian water. He grabbed a graduated test probe on a reel, switched it on, and inserted it down in the pipe.

Mike checked the circuit to ensure the water light was functional. It was. He unwound it bit by bit, down past previous water level markers etched on the bore inlet years before. He stopped at the point where the next marker highlighted the end. Mike stared at the light that would flare once the probe hit water. He unraveled the cable a tiny amount at a time, watching and waiting. A quarter of an inch . . . half an inch . . . the light glowed. Mike sighed. Half an inch. It might as well have been ten miles for all it mattered.

He switched off the probe and stepped back outside, heading up the hill to the farmhouse. He had no money to extend the pump. And without it, the farm would die. He wouldn't be able to water the sheep, and the horses, and grow their food in the garden. He'd have to sell the farm. Put their organic lifestyle behind them. He'd have to move closer to the city, away from the support network of the church for Maisie Jane. Anna would lose her friends. He didn't know what he was going to say to her.

* * *

Mike entered the cool, dimly lit farmhouse kitchen, and he threw Anna a half smile.

"It's that bad?" She frowned.

He nodded, uncertain where to begin, unsure how to put how he felt into words that would make any sense at all. "The pump has reached its limit. I need to extend the inlet, and to do that I need to replace it for a bigger one, and we—"

Maisie Jane entered the room, and without a thought, he squatted. She ran into his arms and hugged her. He closed his eyes. How? How could he sell the farm and move when everything they could want was here? He looked across the table to a scattered array of church notices, and he lingered on a recent one condemning the process of hydraulic fracturing to get natural gas from miles below the surface. Chris Owens had visited a month back and asked to lease the corner paddock. The church was against it. Against soiling the land. Against getting rich and using the money to spend on useless unneeded things. He chewed on his bottom lip and weighed up the wrath of the church elders against the promise he made to Dad about keeping the farm. Either alternative had consequences.

"Mike?"

He stood and faced Anna. "There might be a way."

Her eyes lit with expectation. She seemed taller. "What?"

"We can take up that offer from Chris Owens to put a hydraulic fracturing well here and extract natural gas."

Her shoulders dropped, and she became silent. She shook her head.

He could tell she was recounting the church elders' recent sermon about the risks of the deep wells. He had to agree. "I don't see any alternatives," he said softly, touching her shoulder.

She stepped closer to him. "Isn't there another way?"

Mike couldn't think of one.

"Your nest egg," she said and looked at where the stones lay under his shirt.

"The stones?" His hand went to this neck, to where they rested beneath his shirt.

She nodded.

They licked him with fire, as if they sensed his dilemma. He'd alluded to Anna once that there was a cache of emeralds on the property, and joked it was their nest egg, their pot of gold that could get them out of trouble. But he'd made a promise to Dad when he was a boy never to mention it, to keep the knowledge safe, and not to do anything with them. Dad said they were magic, and that was enough for him. The stones at the end of the chain around his neck were a reminder of that day, and there was something spiritual about their connection to the Earth.

He had never considered the emerald mine as an option unless there was no choice. But the mine . . . Another promise . . . they filled his soul with them. He closed his eyes and tried not to remember, but the images from the past swamped him, from a time when he was only ten . . .

How long had it been? The years fell away as he remembered that time, when he, Dad, and Lucky, their black-and-white border collie, had gone out camping in the back paddock. It was just after Mum had passed from the cancer. Dad was still hurting bad; it was visible in his eyes. The pain of losing his best friend and the loneliness. But he'd pushed on, because of Mike and Rashi. Back then there was a small lake out by the corner paddock.

They'd set camp near the water's edge in the small valley. A campfire crackled from the dry kindling. The air filled with spicy gum smoke, and burning ashes soared up into one of the darkest skies Mike could remember. They'd stared into the heavens and named one star in the constellation of Scorpio after Mum. Dad had smiled. Said it was nice, and Mum would have liked that.

Then Lucky ran off when one log in the fire exploded and a crescendo of sparks flew everywhere.

Dad called her, and when she didn't return, he told Mike to stay put so he could find her. But Mike had told him no. Mike knew what Lucky meant to him and Mum, and Mike went with him and searched for Lucky. It seemed like they'd searched forever, and it seemed like they'd stumbled around in the dark for hours. Apart from Mike, Lucky was the only other thing alive that reminded him of Mum.

It must have been about three in the morning, and they'd all but given up hope. Mike, tired, had shivered hard from the cold. He'd fallen over in the dark and cut his knee open. Dad was distraught. It didn't help that he was slowing him down. Mike stared up at the star he'd named after Mum and asked for a miracle. He wanted Dad to find Lucky so he could stop tearing himself up inside. It was about the same time a meteor flared across the sky to the southwest.

"Look," said Mike, and pointed in the direction. "It's a sign." He stumbled across the valley with no idea about what he'd find, determined that it had been Mum's influence. He stopped at the hillside and looked around. Mike couldn't see anything, but deep in the ground, he heard a muffled bark.

"I found her. I've found Lucky," cried Mike.

Dad ran to him. His eyes shone with hope, and he smiled and put his arm around Mike's shoulder but couldn't speak.

"Mum found her," said Mike. "She sent a shooting star from heaven."

Lucky had squeezed through a fissure in the hill's side and became trapped behind the stone. They dug away at the clods of grass and dirt with their bare hands, pulling away the small rocks until the opening was barely wide enough for Dad to squeeze through.

"Stay here," he said. "If I'm not back in an hour, then run and tell Joe Pearce where I am."

Mike nodded. Joe Pearce was their closest neighbour. Mike sat by the narrow cave entrance and stared up into the dark sky. To the star in Scorpio he'd named 'Eternity' after Mum. Soon enough, he heard Lucky barking at the entrance, and they exited the cave safe and sound. They all marched back to the campsite, clambered into the tent, and slept.

The next day they went back to the cave, and Dad took another look inside. He came out a while later, carrying a kitten. They could never be sure if Lucky had chased it or rescued it, but Mike always remembered.

Because that was the day they found the stones.

Three emeralds. All had been together on the ground before he found them. Mike remembered his father rolling them around in his hands until he became light-headed. Dad had to sit down, and had rubbed his head as if it hurt or something had overcome him. Dad always said there was magic in the stones.

He told me there were more down there. Lots of them. More than enough emeralds down there to make them wealthy a dozen times over, but that it would be their secret. Mike realised Mum had been looking down from the heavens at them, and she'd taken care of things in her own way. Dad made him promise not to tell. Mike did. Mum would have wanted that.

Mike shook the memories free and faced Anna. Over a course of twenty-five years, the place had dried up. The dragonfly swarms were gone. Mike never saw them again, and like the water once in abundance, it too had vanished, leaving a dry dust bowl in its place. But the cave was still there with its hidden cache of emeralds. Mike had always wanted to go in and explore it, but he didn't want to change any of the memories of that night when Mum had touched them all. He never wanted them to fade, and from that day on, it had always been a magical place.

He smiled at Anna with regret. "I can't. You know I promised. Maybe something good will come from seeing Chris Owens today and signing that contract. I might not be completely happy with drilling for gas on our land, but it's for the best." Mike rubbed Anna's arm and smiled. "You'll see, everything will work out fine."

* * *

Mike stepped inside the café, a small roadhouse on the edge of town, and he wiped the beads of sweat from his brow. The cool air from an overhead fan and the dim light was a welcome relief.

In the far corner of the room, Chris Owens sat at a table, reading. He looked up and waved. "Mike," he said.

Mike nodded and walked over to him. Nervous cramps twisted his gut. He felt trapped, as if there was no way out of his dilemma, but he assured himself this was the only way.

Chris Owens was a middle-aged man, balding with short-cropped hair. He wore a business suit, but his tie had been pulled loose away from the top of his shirt, and it made him look less formal, approachable. He smiled and shook Mike's hand. The grip was firm, confident.

"Mr. Owens," said Mike. "Good to meet you."

"You too. Call me Chris." He smiled at Mike. "I hope you don't mind meeting here, it's a little less formal, and we're not about pressuring anyone."

Mike nodded and sat down across from Chris. The tension in his stomach lessened.

The café server stepped over and wiped her apron. She pulled out her pad and pencil.

Mike didn't know her. He didn't come into town often, and it had grown in recent years.

"Coffee?" asked Chris.

"A glass of water," said Mike, and smiled at the obvious joke. Here for the town folk, water was not as precious a commodity, but all the talk on the news of possible water wars made people understand the value of it.

"Two waters, please," said Chris, and waited for the server to leave.

Mike sat down and didn't speak. A part of him felt uncomfortable, dirty, with his decision to come and discuss drilling on part of the farm. The other part said he had to be a realist if he was going to survive. His stomach churned again with uncertainty, and he sat with his hands under the table, clenching and unclenching them.

The server returned with two large glasses of water filled with ice. Chris pushed an empty coffee mug aside and frowned. "Is it that bad?"

Mike told Chris the story about the pump and the water level. He had nothing to lose being honest.

Chris Owens opened up a survey map of the land surrounding the farm. He tapped his finger on the area out by the corner block. "This is where we'd like to drill. It's close to the road, so we won't bother you for access. It's far enough away that the noise will be minimal. You won't even know we are there."

"Is it safe?"

"You've got a young girl." He looked down at his notes. "Maisie Jane?"

Mike nodded.

"We'll fence it off. It will be safe. Nobody will get near—"

"It's not what I meant. Is it safe? The drilling? It won't destroy the land?"

Chris Owens laughed, and he pushed his chair back from the table. "We get that a lot. Trust me. Hydraulic fracturing, or hydro-fracturing, is completely safe. It's one of the cleanest and safest methods to extract natural gas. It's great on the environment. All clean energy."

"What about leakage? I've heard there have been problems."

"Twenty years ago, the early wells were poorly designed. Nowadays we encase them in extra-durable steel and cement to ensure there is absolutely no risk of contaminating any groundwater." He slid a brochure across the table and tapped his finger on one area of it. "See, it says we're compliant with all of the Oceania Alliance's climate regulations. Take this. It shows our unique design. It's the only one in the world to capture all fugitive methane emissions."

Mike took the brochure and leafed through the pages, filled with testimonials from other people who had signed up. There were pages of design drawings showing how the shaft would be drilled and fitted out.

"I won't lie, Mike. There are always risks, but we strive to minimize them. I've conducted a geological survey of your land, and I can see that there won't be any problems. So, what do you think?"

"Sounds good."

"I've drawn up a contract. At least this is a copy of the digital version on my tablet you can take." He slid a thick wad of typed paper across the table. Chris tapped a spot on the front page. "Take a look. I think you'll find that we've been more than generous."

Mike leaned closer and glanced at the figure. It was much more than he'd expected. More than he'd average over five years of farming. He'd be able to buy a new pump. It'd see him right.

"Well?"

Mike looked up. "It's very generous."

Chris smiled. "Take it home. Talk it over with . . ." he glanced down at his notes. "Talk to Anna about it, and see what she says." He stood and held out his hand. "I'd just ask that you keep this between us."

"Of course." Mike shook the man's hand.

"And it's a minor point, but this is the best offer we can give you. It's only valid for five days. I'm sure you understand. After that, I'm afraid we reassess the situation downwards."

"So how long before the drilling would start?"

"Well . . . we could have a team in place within a month of signing."

"And the money?"

"As soon as you sign the contract, Mike. I'll leave you to think it through. I grew up a bit of a skeptic about all this climate change business, but this heat is no joke. That's why we gotta look out for one another. You deserve to make money off the resources beneath your land." The man paused to grin. "Well? From what I heard, it's going to be a hot summer."

Mike nodded. The man was right, it was going to be a long, dry summer. He felt it in his bones. And as soon as Mike signed the contract, he'd have the money he needed.

"You all right if I visit in a couple of days' time, Mike?"

"Sure."

"Excellent. If you've got questions, perhaps we can go over them then?"

"That would be good."

"Nice to meet you, Mike."

Mike shook Chris's hand again. He sat for a few minutes and waited for the other man to leave the café. He leafed through the contract, but nothing seemed out of place with the offer. Things were looking up, after all.

* * *

Mike stepped out from the café into the heat. He ambled down the street to his car.

"Michael!"

Mike stopped. He turned and faced the man.

Pastor Matthew strode across the street, hand thrust forward in greeting.

Mike shook the church elder's hand. "How are you doing, pastor?"

"Always good, Michael, always good." He looked over at the café Mike had just left and frowned. "What have you been up to? I heard you had a meeting with Chris Owens."

Mike opened his mouth, speechless. It wasn't any of the pastor's business.

"Anna called," said the pastor. "She said you might act rash."

Anna? Mike chewed at the corner of his lip. Why would she have done that? "I was discussing cash options to buy a bigger pump."

The church elder's forehead twisted with genuine concern. "Problems with your water supply?"

Mike nodded.

"Funny, a few of the congregation have said water levels have been dropping. We did some tests, and found the water quality has degraded, too." He looked down at the contract in Mike's hand. "Is that what I think it is?"

Mike shrugged.

"Did they tell you about the risks?"

"They mentioned they have a new design," said Mike.

"Did they say they pump disinfectants, acid, detergent and salt down these wells? And sand and ceramic particles?"

Mike cleared his throat. "No."

"Did they say they store wastewater on your land contaminated with radioactive material, heavy metals, and other toxins?"

Mike shook his head.

"They will throw benzene and toluene and who knows what into the air and poison your farm, and they won't care. Who knows what the risks of long-term exposure will be. Birth defects. Blood disorders. Cancer. Of all people, I don't need to tell you about that."

Mike didn't need reminding about what Mum and Maisie Jane had gone through. His throat tightened. "You seem pretty much against the idea, pastor."

"Fracking is a problem." The pastor pointed to the café where Mike had spoken to Chris Owens. "They are poisoning the land, tainting our water. The Great Artesian Basin supplies half of all the water used by our Oceanian Country. Here!" He pointed to his feet. "Right below us. It's not right, Michael. It's not the church's way. God wouldn't approve of this."

Mike squeezed his hands together. "None of those things are proven. Anyway, what choice do I have, pastor? I can sell up, move to the coast. Leave everything behind." He squeezed his eyes shut. Fail. Mike took a deep breath, opened his eyes, and sought for understanding within the pastor. "Without water, the farm is worthless. Without a pump there is no water. Can the church loan me money for a new pump, pastor?"

Mike heard blood pounding in his ears while Pastor Matthew stood silently. Mike watched the pastor's forehead twist as he wrestled with some inner turmoil.

The pastor spoke in hushed tones, and his voice caught every so often. "A little for food, perhaps . . ." He shook his head slowly. "Charity has boundaries, I'm afraid . . . and if I recall, Michael, you have an outstanding debt with the church elders?"

Mike closed his eyes and nodded. The church and the community had pulled together to provide the money to pay for Maisie Jane's leukemia treatment two years ago. But Mike could not repay the debt. "You don't understand, pastor. I have no choice. I need it for my family to survive."

The elder smiled. "I understand, son." He stepped closer. "You always have choices, Michael. I would suggest that you just ask Him."

Mike stepped back a step. "But it's not that simple, pastor."

The pastor smiled. "You'll find a way. I have faith in you. God works in the strangest of ways. I know the answer will arrive for you in time."

Mike nodded. Dad would have said to ask Mother Gaia and not believe a word of what the pastor was saying. All the pastor had done was to paint him into a dark corner.

"Sleep on it," said the pastor. "Do that at least. I'm sure your father would have wanted you to."

Mike nodded. Perhaps there was another way. He stared at the contract in his hand with no idea what to do.

When he looked up, the pastor had gone, and the stones, millstones, burned with a fire hotter than the afternoon sun. It was as if they called to him, almost beckoned him to do something. But what?

* * *

Mike stood at the base of the water tank and rapped his knuckles on the side of the corrugated tin. He did it on every rung until he reached the lowest, the one below the outlet, and it was only then that the hollow tone changed to show water. Maybe he'd be able to use a hand pump to scavenge the remains. But that didn't help him. It only confirmed what he knew.

He sat on the floor with his back resting against the empty tank and stared at the distant hills. Two days had passed since his meeting with Chris Owens, and with it, the last drops of their water supply reserves. He didn't know what he was going to do. His flock of sheep stood idle in the midday sun around the water trough. Empty. The horses frolicked in another paddock, unaware he couldn't top up their water. It couldn't get any worse.

He tried to massage away the tension in the side of his head, but it made little difference. Chris Owens was visiting at four in the afternoon, and Mike would sign the contract, but he couldn't wait. He couldn't sit idle. He'd go now and get it over with before his head exploded. Pastor Matthews and the church would turn their back on Mike's family. He knew they would, but Mike would rather keep his farm and continue living the life expected of him. A lifestyle he loved. He'd take care of the family in his own way, and if that meant they would frack his land, then so be it.

He heard Maisie Jane and Anna laughing inside the old family farmhouse. It filled him with joy. Maisie Jane had been immune to what was going on around her, thanks to Anna. He couldn't sell. It was all Maisie Jane talked about while she recovered from her illness. He wouldn't make them move.

They would survive on an old corroded tank by the side of the house, one that took water from the farmhouse roof. It was a small tank. The water quality wasn't the best, and he'd need some of it for the sheep and the horses. There'd be no showers, but it would have to be enough for cooking and drinking, and the toilet. What was the old bush motto: if it's brown wash it down, if it's yellow let it mellow? He grinned despite his somber mood. They'd survive. They had to! It wouldn't last more than a few days, but he'd find the best outcome he could.

Mike stood, aware he'd be with Chris Owens within the hour to sign the contract. He marched down the hill to the farmhouse and crept inside and grabbed the car keys, intent on letting Anna and Maisie Jane play in the next room, not wanting to break their mood.

* * *

On the way into town he took the longer route, the one that went past the bottom paddock where the hydraulic fracturing well was going to be sited. He pulled the car up on the verge and stopped. From the side of the road, the area looked picturesque. A small valley with gentle hills to the left. The quiet solitude embraced him. He stepped outside, and the morning sun warmed him. Sound pollution would probably not be an issue: it was a reasonable way from the house. They'd probably still hear something, but it wouldn't be too bad. It'd depend on the way the wind blew.

Mike clambered over the fence, and it was as if it triggered the stones in the canvas bags against his chest. It always happened as soon as he walked the land near the cave the three emeralds had come from. Fire smoldered at his neck. He ignored it as best as he could, unsure why the stones always became agitated around this place. It was as if they had a life of their own, yearning to be put back in the ground. Mike would never do that. But he twisted his neck uncomfortably against them. There was a power within the stones he couldn't ignore. Dad had joked several times to never rub them together unless he wanted to start a fire. "Everything is connected," he'd said. Even the Gaia Stones.

Mike had ignored the warning a few years after they first discovered the stones and dared clamber into the cave. The dark, narrow cavern hummed. All the hairs on Mike's body stood erect. It was a magic place. Mike clambered out of the cave as fast as he could. Dad laughed when he found out, and had told him of a time he'd taken the stones out and rubbed them together. "You've never known power until you do," he said. For years after, he laughed and said, "Never connect them. Keep them apart, like insolent children."

Mike pulled them out, away from his skin, and breathed a sigh of relief. He had to admit that they were magic. In their own way, they were alive. He'd never taken them out of their silk cocoons, never removed them from the hessian bags. Who knew what they would do. Fire? Magic? Either way, he'd promised to take care of them and the land here.

The once-wet depression was bone dry. The dragonflies that once hovered over the water pools had gone. Mike vowed, once again, that he'd never go. In the distance, off to his left, the low, rolling hills were already burned grey from the early summer heat. Nothing lived at this spot. The drilling company was welcome to it. He put the fiery stones around his neck, back under his clothes, and took comfort in their closeness. The other stones in the cave would remain intact, far enough from the clutches of the miners and their drilling for gas. It sat outside the drilling area.

That was all that mattered.

* * *

Everything was quiet in town, as if it slept in the midday sun. Mike strode into the mining office this time and asked for Chris Owens.

Chris entered the room just a few seconds later, and he looked a little startled when Mike held out his hand and announced he was there to sign the contract, and he didn't want to put Chris out with the drive.

"Come this way," he said, ushering Mike into a room. Moments later, a tall woman brought in the contract.

Mike signed it with no hesitation and sat down in the comfy black leather armchair.

"Did you have enough time to read it?" asked Chris Owens. His face showed surprise.

Mike recalled Pastor Matthew's concerns around environmental health, but the contract clauses around that area used terms like reasonable, low risk, and minimal impact. It all seemed fine. "Yes," said Mike. "Everything was fine."

"Questions?"

"No," said Mike. He waited until Chris Owens signed it. "That's it?" Mike asked.

"That's it." Chris held out his hand, and Mike shook it.

"There was one thing," said Mike.

Chris Owens smiled. "Name it."

"I wondered about getting a down payment. So I can drive in some water. Get that new pump," said Mike.

"Soon," said Chris Owens. "It's normally about a week or two."

Mike's mouth fell open. He leaned forward. "A week or two? I thought you said the money would arrive as soon as the contract was signed?"

Chris Owens smiled again. "There's a three-day cooling-off period. You know, in case we find anything different from what we had initially expected."

Mike frowned. "Different?"

"Don't worry, it's a formality. I'll organise the team to come out." He looked at his wristwatch and nodded. "There might be time to get them out later this afternoon. Tomorrow at the latest. It'll speed up the process so you can get paid."

Mike hesitated. "Team?"

"They'll double check the earlier survey. Fence off the site. Get the dozers in."

"Dozers?" Mike didn't understand what the other man was talking about.

"To level the site."

Mike's stomach knotted. He wasn't comfortable with what he was hearing. "Why does the site need to be flattened?"

Chris Owens shrugged. "It's what they do." He looked at the wristwatch again. "If you'll excuse me, I've got another meeting. I can get one of the site guys to take out your copy of the contract if you like? Saves you waiting around."

Mike nodded.

"I should be able to get him out today." He held out his hand again and smiled. "You've made the right choice, Mike. We're all going to get rich mining gas. You'll see. You'll have the best farm in the district."

Mike left the office. He should have felt relieved now that he'd signed the contract, but he didn't. Instead, an uncomfortable knot twisted in his stomach. Somehow, he had to make their supply last over the next week.

* * *

Mike sat in their kitchen across the table from Anna.

She stared at him. "So it's done?"

Mike nodded. She hadn't looked comfortable when he told her. "I've organised a water truck delivery for the end of the week. We're rationing until then."

Anna didn't speak. He noticed concern swimming across her face, twisting the corners of her mouth.

He frowned. "What's the matter?"

"I don't know. It doesn't feel right. I just thought you'd find another way somehow."

"What should I do?" he asked.

She shrugged. "It's your farm. You know I'd never get in the way. If it were me, I'd see if the church elders would give me a loan."

Mike nodded. "They told me our credit had expired."

"Still, but it wouldn't hurt to ask."

"I did speak to Pastor Matthew, but they can't help." Mike chewed his lip. The elders had been quite clear, although Anna wouldn't know that. He frowned. "I did what I thought was right for all of us."

"But bulldozers leveling the paddock... Is that what you want?"

Mike stood and raised his voice. "I had no choice. We're out of water. The animals are out of water!" He took a deep breath. His throat tightened. "I'm sorry, I don't mean to yell. I'm going outside to get some fresh air." He walked around the table and ran his hand gently along the side of her face. "I thought you'd be pleased," he said, his voice raspy with frustration.

Mike pushed open the door and strode outside. What had he done? Why wasn't Anna happy? Couldn't she see that he'd done it for them? What did she want him to say? That he wasn't happy they were going to bulldoze the site? If only he had asked before signing.

A dragonfly darted back into the shade by the water tank. It positioned itself in a pocket of shade. The beautiful insect had minimized its body to the sun, as if to use its four huge wings as reflectors. Mike couldn't blame it. The heat was draining.

His mind oddly drifted to the emerald cave again, so close to the drilling site. He'd been certain it was safe, but what if they damaged the cave by bulldozing the area? What if they uncovered it? Concern knotted his stomach. What had he done?

A distant hammering, metal striking metal, stopped him in his tracks. He glanced at the time and realised that Chris Owens's team had wasted no time in getting here. He heard an engine start up. A bulldozer. What had he done? He couldn't shake the thought. Fear kicked in, and he ran toward the bottom paddock as fast as he could. The stones around his neck blazed like wildfire.

* * *

Mike looked around, amazed. The corner paddock looked like a construction site. A perimeter fence was rising, and men were banging in posts. A bulldozer was leveling the land nearest to the roadway, ripping up the vegetation into a mound.

"Stop!" He ran toward the bulldozer and waved his hands in the air.

The driver of the dozer stopped and turned off the engine. He stepped down off the heavy machine. "This is a drilling site. You're trespassing."

"It's my farm," said Mike. His chest warmed where the stones were, and he moved them.

"I don't care. I was told you signed a contract. You agreed to all of this."

"I did," said Mike.

"Well, then you need to get off the site. I've got to level it before the end of the day. The drilling head is being installed tomorrow."

"Tomorrow?"

"Dave!" The dozer driver waved a man in a suit over.

The man strode over and smiled. He offered his hand to shake. "Mike?"

Mike nodded.

"I'm Dave Myers. I was heading down to deliver your signed contract. What seems to be the problem?"

"I just need a moment." He turned away from the man and stared at the line of pristine hills. A dragonfly whipped past. As they'd been doing a lot recently. They darted about, intent on their solitary missions.

Mike looked around, back to where he'd spotted the dragonfly. It hovered in more of a dance than anything else. This was where they had camped all those years ago. Back when there had been water, and the dragonflies swarmed the place in abundance. The cave entrance, hidden by a large rock, beckoned. Lucky had become lost there years before . . . and that was where they'd found the emeralds . . . If he did this, he'd never be able to take Maisie Jane camping here. He'd never be able to sit her down at a campfire and pass on the story of that night.

It wasn't right, but he had no choice. He felt trapped, like Lucky had been that night in the cave.

The dragonfly returned with another, and they hovered nearby. Mike watched the prehistoric-looking insects with interest. Dad had always called them the jewels of the sky. In the sunlight, they dazzled. Their large green eyes looked like enormous emeralds. Like the stones.

Mike touched his neck chain.

One hovered, the other zigzagging left and right. It stopped and then flew backward. It seemed so random. The first one swooped over Mike's head, made a hairpin turn, and they both flew off toward the area where the lake had once stood. Before, when there was water.

Almost in response to his thought, the stones flared.

Mike smiled. It was a watershed moment. The tension fell from him. Why hadn't he listened? Why hadn't Mike taken more notice of the world around him? He pulled the stones out from under his shirt and removed each of them from their small hessian bags. Even through the silk cocoons, they burned in his hand.

It all made sense now. He turned back to the man who had stood patiently. There was another way. He smiled at the man. "Dave, was it?"

The man nodded.

"You've got the contract?"

"Yes, here." He pointed to a spot on the paper. "All signed. Endorsed by the local company director."

"Can I see that?" Mike held out his hand for the contract.

"As you will see, the area is ours now, Mr. Ironbark. I would respectfully ask you to move away from the site until we can put up a perimeter fence."

"That's not going to happen," said Mike.

"I'm sorry?"

"I'm not leaving."

"For your own safety, you must leave this area. It's an industrial requirement. You can watch the works from the other side once the perimeter fence is up."

"No, I didn't make myself clear. This"—Mike waved his hands in the air—"this will not happen. You have a three-day cooling-off period before you can start."

"Yes, but we've elected to start early. We're happy with the site location."

"I'm not. And I have the same three days to change my mind."

"I'm not sure. I'd have to check—"

"I'm sure," said Mike. He knew it was only a copy, but the symbolism of physically destroying the papers was all he needed. He tore the contract in half and in half again and threw it onto the ground. "I have elected not to go ahead with the fracking on my land. You are now trespassing, and I respectfully demand you and your company leave. Immediately!"

The man stared back at Mike for the longest moment, and finally he smiled. "Ok. I can see you won't change your mind any time soon."

"No, I won't. Tell Chris Owens thank you, but I don't need a new pump. Tell him I have all the water I need."

* * *

Mike strode away from the drilling and construction team. They'd leave soon enough. They had no choice. He made his way near the cave and positioned himself on the high ground where he had camped all those years ago. Who'd have thought it would have been the dragonflies who would solve the riddle. He grinned. Dragonflies were an ancient insect, and had taken to the air long before any of the dinosaurs walked on the Earth. Dragonflies couldn't live without water. They always appeared around ponds and lakes. He'd always seen them around the animals' troughs, skimming the water's surface.

And there they were. Not one or two, but hundreds of them. They hovered in the dry paddock where the lake once was. Like a sea of emeralds. Mike stared at the three silk parcels in his hand. Never let the stones connect, he'd been told. But everything is connected, and all this time, the power of the Gaia Stones had been hiding in plain sight. The dragonflies, with their enormous emerald green eyes, had hinted to where there was water. Why else would there be so many dragonflies in abundance?

One flew closer and hovered, as if they waited for him. He pulled one of the stones from its silk cocoon and let it fall into his hand. He winced. It was as if someone had slid a rough piece of wood along the side of his head. The warm stone came alive. It pulsed deep inside his mind.

He pulled out the second stone and placed it alongside the first. More pain shot through his head and the throbbing deepened within him. His hand shook. He wanted to let go of the stones. They burned like nothing he'd experienced. Quickly, he let the third stone fall into his open palm before he lost all courage.

It was as if someone had smacked him on the side of the head with a brick. His heart skipped a beat. His hand was on fire, and Mike closed his eyes, biting his lip until he tasted blood. He took a breath, braced, and closed his hand around the stones so they joined.

So they connected.

He thrust out his hand, and the pain in his head grew until he doubled over. The ground around shook, and the fire burst from his hand. Or the stones—he couldn't tell, though a bright flash illuminated through his closed eyelids. He winced, shutting them tighter. Still, the pain grew, intolerable.

He opened his hand.

Let the stones fall to the ground. The pain vanished.

Mike opened his eyes, convinced his palm would be charred, but it was unscathed. He bent and retrieved the stones, one at a time, and he placed them back in their silk cocoons, returning them to the small hessian bags on the chain.

He glanced over at the spot where the lake had once been and smiled at the massive swarm of dragonflies. The swarm had multiplied. Now, there had to be a thousand or more. They hovered over the old lake and darted chaotically just above the ground.

Where water bubbled, rising from a rent in the Earth.

* * *

Mike and Anna stood in the bottom paddock, at the edge of a lake that hadn't been there three days before. In that time, he had unshackled the water pump and moved it beside the edge of the lake. It hadn't been difficult to rig up the inlet to take the fresh spring water, and now the farm tanks were full.

Mike watched Maisie Jane run in and out of the water, splashing. A car pulled up by the road and a man stepped out. Anna waved, and Mike recognized Pastor Matthew.

The pastor strode down and joined them. "I heard you'd experienced a miracle," said Pastor Matthew. "I had to come by and see for myself." The man laughed. "I knew you'd find a way. Your dad would be proud of you, son."

Anna stepped closer to him. "I'm proud of him too, pastor. Imagine there being water just below the surface all this time." She grinned at Mike.

Mike grabbed Anna's hand and squeezed it. There was more than enough water for the animals and the family, and he would be able to lavish the oak seedling they had planted to help it grow. It would flourish.

Anna squeezed his hand back. "Would you like to come in for some afternoon tea, pastor?" She grinned again. "A glass of cold water, perhaps?"

Pastor Matthew chuckled. "I'd like that."

"I'll grab Maisie Jane," said Mike. He stood and watched his daughter stalk something near the water's edge. He saw several dragonflies and smiled. One darted backward and hovered above her head. Its enormous, emerald coloured eyes glistened like the stones. They made him feel more alive, more connected to the world than ever thought possible. They pulsed to beat deep inside him.

One day, the farm would be Maisie Jane's, along with the cave. And the lake.

And the stones.

CATALYST

C. D. TAVENOR

2042 C.E.

Too often we imagine the Earth as a mindless ball of water and rock. But it's so much more. It's an organism. It breathes like we breathe. The atmosphere cycles air around the world, and the various molecules—whether carbon dioxide, oxygen, nitrogen—all have their systems.

Imagine the carbon cycle like a human's cardiovascular system. Carbon cycles into the oceans, into plants, into peat and soil and air. We, humans, have injected excess carbon into the system. The planet is hyperventilating. It is freaking out as it fails to breathe properly.

Like an organism, it is trying to find equilibrium.

There is one difference, though, between a traditional organism and our planet. As humans, our bodies have antibodies to fight off infectious diseases. We have ventilators we can use to help us breathe. We have medicine that can cure and protect us from dangerous symptoms.

What would it look like if the planet could produce its own antibodies?

Or perhaps it already has, and the antibodies are currently the ones doing the killing.

Just imagine if the Earth could fight back.

The hustle and bustle surrounding Natalie reminded her of college orientation. Instead of starry-eyed freshman, though, thousands of brave activists filled Golden 1 Center. On the stage above her, speaker after speaker said their piece, declared their personal zeitgeist, inspired further fervor. It was intoxicating.

And now it was Natalie's turn.

She breathed, resting a hand on the banister, listening to the final words before she said her speech.

"And so we're here today!" The older woman raised her hands into the air. "I've been doing this for over twenty years, and we've come so far. But there's so much more to do. They're taking action, yes, to stop the climate crisis. But we need a climate revolution to change the world. To save it. With thousands of you here in Sacramento, we will be the change the world needs, together. Thank you."

Sofia Huber. Natalie's idol. The woman who, when Natalie was five, stood before the United Nations and shouted them into submission. When Natalie was ten, Sofia tied herself to an oil rig in the Dakota burning fields Three years later, she received the Nobel Peace Prize; when she was twenty-eight. Sofia started fighting for everyone's lives when she was only thirteen.

Natalie couldn't believe she had to follow up Sofia. *I'm a twenty-year-old, making my first Climate Revolution speech, and I have to follow her up. She doesn't even know I exist!* With that thought, Sofia walked down the stairs, smiling at Natalie, whose eyes widened.

"You'll do great," the hero said, her Swiss accent sliding more naturally into her words now that her speech was over. "I'm excited to hear your words."

Just a few words, but heat rose in Natalie's heart. Her skin burned. Her moment arrived; she was joining the ranks of the heroes who'd come before. Sofia knew her place was amongst them. As quickly as the flushed heat hit her chest, it faded, replaced by a calming peace.

One foot after another, Natalie stepped onto the stage and approached the microphone. "Good afternoon, my CR friends! Tomorrow begins the most important Climate Accord of a generation. We're almost there. We've almost saved the planet. Our parents set the stage, now it's our turn!" She raised her fist, and the crowd followed suit. "Let's take their breath away this week. Here's how we're going to win."

* * *

Natalie leaned into the wooden chair, its hard back aggravating her already sore joints. A few rows ahead, a man in a black suit droned on and on about each Climate Advocate's assignment for the week. Everyone would attach themselves to a different delegation, different company, different important figure. They'd accepted her special application, so hopefully, she'd receive —

"Natalie Vorn?" Black Suit cleared his throat. "Vorn?"

Her phone buzzed, but she ignored it. "Hi, hello! I'm here."

"Natalie, we've assigned you as a note-taker for the floor negotiations."

A note-taker. No arguing. No speeches. Just a note-taker. Ridiculous. Yet she smiled. "Thank you, sir."

He moved onto the next name, and the next, and the next. Just a note-taker. They'd given her the opportunity to speak before a crowd of tens of thousands, and now they just want her as a note-taker? She could do so much more. She was ready for so much more!

Her phone buzzed again. Not interested in the presentation of names anymore, she slipped the device out of her pocket.

> Party in an hour. Zack's hotel room.
> You in?

Oh hell yeah. She shot back a nodding head emoji to Liza—and a heart.

A few minutes later, Black Suit finished up his platitudes about how they were all serving a key role in the fight for the climate, and how even the most minute assignments could save the planet. Of course, Natalie believed that in her heart. But she wanted to be more than a note-taker. She wanted to scream at a natural gas mogul. She wanted to negotiate with national delegations. The least interesting conversations occurred during the floor negotiations. The backroom deals were where the magic happened!

Whatever. As the breakout session ended, she shouldered her bag and headed into the hallway of the immense convention center. Moping about her assignment could wait until the assignment started. Her hotel room awaited her, where she could get ready for a party.

Climate Crisis parties were lit.

* * *

An hour-and-a-half later, with eyeliner, straightened hair, and a green dress, Natalie slipped through the door of Zack's hotel room. Anarcho-techno blared, its ambience matching the shifting and drifting partiers dancing throughout the room. There was barely room to move between their bodies. Glorious.

Natalie slid toward the window, where Liza and Zack leaned, red cups in their hand. "What are we drinking?" she said, her voice slipping through during a lull in the slick rift of the current song.

"Nat!" Liza leaned forward and hugged her. "Glad you made it. I can't believe it's already been a year since Paris!"

Leaning into the hug, Natalie smiled. Zack, leaning against the room's eco-AC, opened a package of cannabinoid-gummies and offered her one. Opening her mouth, she accepted the edible.

After chewing and swallowing, she said, "Yes, yes, I'm excited to see you both!" The music began to rise again, so she raised her voice to overcome its volume. "But I need a drink?"

Liza chuckled. "Zack gives you a gum and then you shoot straight to the liquor. Love it!"

"Well are we here to party against the end of the world, or just to watch our friends gyrate while sober?" Natalie slid into place beside Zack, propping herself up on the windowsill. "This is just the first of five days of partying, yeah? Every night. Fight the crisis during the day, get wasted at night."

Liza saluted with two fingers and slid away toward a desk holding the drinks only a few feet away.

Zack slipped an edible between his teeth, grinned, and swallowed. "Based on the way you said those words, I'm not sure whether you're more excited for the parties or for saving the world." He ran a hand through his curled black hair.

Liza and Zack, Natalie's best friends in Climate Revolution. They'd been dating each other for as long as she could remember, though she didn't pretend to understand the nature of their open relationship. They loved each other—and loved plenty of other people too in a lot of different ways. And Zack was apparently the heir to some trust fund, and so he used the funds to pay for these ridiculous climate parties.

Natalie wasn't going to complain. She loved them both too. And his parties. What a way to de-stress after twelve hours of arduous negotiations.

Who was she kidding, these were life back at uni, too.

A few seconds later, Liza slid a cup of something clear into her hands. "Vodka soda."

Natalie puckered her lips and bobbed her head. Taking a sip, she enjoyed the bite of the drink. Perfect. "So what's the first game tonight?" It was time to forget all about her assignment as a note-taker, drink away the night, and deal with the consequences in the morning.

* * *

A sweet buzzing noise, somewhere in the air. The smell of the auto-coffee dripping from the self-service stand. A drill, pounding behind her eyes.

No, that was just the hangover. Water. She needed water. And that wonderful smelling coffee.

The buzzing noise focused into a bouncy tune—her alarm. *Her alarm.* What time was it? She grabbed her phone from the night stand.

Oh thank goodness. Only 7:30am. She had another forty-five minutes to get ready before she met her site lead. Probably somebody boring like Black Suit from the breakout session yesterday. She fell back into a pillow and grabbed a second one, shoving it over her face. Note-taker. Just a freaking note-taker.

All for the cause, though.

Sitting up, Natalie slid out of bed, grabbed a cup of coffee, and plopped into a chair near the window. From the tenth floor of the hotel, she could see most of downtown Sacramento. The newly formed Western Republic of America, its capital in Sacramento, cherished the opportunity to host the 2042 Conference of the Parties for the United Nations Framework Convention on Climate Change. The threat was real. On the horizon, the scorched earth of last year's wildfires reminded everyone of the very real threat surrounding them.

Hopefully they would keep it sharply in their mind for the next few days. After a few more sips of coffee, she placed the mug on the windowsill and bounced toward the bathroom. After a quick swig of water, she hopped in the shower.

The lukewarm water rushing through her hair helped the pounding beneath her skull. Refreshing. She could barely remember the events of last night; that always happened when she mixed liquor and weed. Still, the spare memories flirting through her mind were . . . nice. Some great dancing. Someone may have taken a shot off her body? She wasn't sure. Maybe that was off Liza. Oh well. Worth it. After a quick lathering of soap, the shower timed out and the water shutoff. She dried with a towel, slipped into a dark pantsuit, and ran her hair into a bun. After brushing her teeth, it was 8:05am. Just enough time for a bagel downstairs.

Tablet in her bag, keycard in a safe pocket, Natalie left and locked her hotel room. Only a slight headache now. Perfect anti-hangover regimen.

The elevator wasn't crowded yet, and neither was the cafe on the first floor. Bagel in hand by 8:11am, she walked through the underground tunnel connecting to the convention center. And at 8:15am, she entered one of the small meeting rooms reserved by Climate Revolution for preparation prior to Conference meetings.

A group of ten other students sat in chairs forming a circle. And in the center of the circle stood Sofia Huber.

Her site lead.

* * *

Natalie was still stunned, even ten minutes into their discussion. Sofia Huber, her hero, her site lead. After a sip of water, she rubbed her temples, trying to wish away the last remnants of the headache constantly reminding her of last night. Sure, it was fun, and she'd probably go out again tonight, but if she'd known . . .

"So enough about me," Sofia said. (*No, please keep talking*, Natalie thought.) "We are here to prepare for your day as a note-taker." Sofia stepped back from the circle of tables and picked up a dry-erase marker from a container attached to the wall. On the board beside her, she drew a square surrounded by a larger square. "In the inner sanctum of the conference floor, only assigned speakers and negotiators may enter. The outer square, however"—she started drawing tiny Xs for flourish—"hundreds of reporters, executive assistants, corporate representatives, you name it. All watching. Listening. And making deals in real time, on the floor, behind the scenes. And Climate Revolution has ten seats in the crowd. You all. And I'm at our table, just inside the inner circle."

Natalie nodded, thinking she understood. Maybe. Wait, no. To be honest, she still didn't see the significance.

Sofia pushed a few stray blonde hairs behind her ear as she turned to face the little cohort. "Your task is simple. We've interspersed you all throughout the crowd in positions equidistant from the center. You will sit, pay attention to the speeches and announcements. That is what you will tell people you are doing. You are all students; you are all learning. If someone approaches you, asking why you're there, you say you're with Climate Revolution, that you're excited to observe the proceedings, learn, and hopefully be a negotiator in the future for whatever country, state, or organization you may represent in the future."

Sofia paused, drawing lines outward from the Xs. When she finished, she pivoted and returned to the circle of chairs. "Ostensibly, you all are the most important asset of the entire operation. Does anyone know why?"

Natalie wracked her mind for answers, but none arrived. Sitting with a pulse-pounding throb above her left eye, she tried. She really tried. But truth evaded. Her opportunity, right now, to impress Sofia with acute understanding, and she couldn't even field a word.

Instead, a young man—he looked like he might be from one of the Pacific island nations—raised his hand.

"Manuia?" Sofia said.

"Well, you said the crowd around us will be filled with all sorts of people," said the young man (Manuia, apparently). "Corporate representatives, aides, the like. Yes?"

"Correct."

"So . . ." He scratched a stubbly chin. "So we are to build relationships with them, make friends, learn from them?"

Sofia raised an eyebrow. "Close. I'm not sure about the 'friends' part of your idea, but certainly you should learn from them. Maybe build a relationship. But most importantly, you must *listen* to them." She pulled a small tablet from her pocket and tapped a few commands. "I've just given you access to a spreadsheet in which you will input your findings each day."

When the woman didn't continue speaking, rather eyeing the group with an inquisitive glare, Natalie quickly retrieved her own tablet. In her email, she found a link to the spreadsheet. Glancing up from the screen, she noticed everyone else now staring at their own devices.

"You'll notice tabs assigned to your names," Sofia said. "Columns with names of individuals who will most likely surround you. Rows for time of words, what words were said, to whom they were speaking. The most dangerous words of every Conference occur not via email, not in back rooms, not in public negotiating sessions. They occur on the floor—in the moment—in the final minutes before nations make their commitments." She sighed. "I will be monitoring constantly. You will flag the most important comments with red fill so it will catch my eye immediately—or send me a quick message through the spreadsheet's public chat. So why is your task so essential?"

Finally, the wall in my throat uncaught. Without raising my hand, I said, "By giving you information in real-time, we allow you and the other official delegates from Climate Revolution to react and counter anti-climate action efforts instantaneously."

Sofia smiled; Natalie's heart fluttered. "Precisely. If you do your job, you will shift the balance of power in the room in ways you won't fully understand for years."

The conversation continued, shifting more toward the specific assignments of each note-taker. Manuia, the kid from earlier, was sitting behind the Australian delegation, surrounded by a number of offshore fossil fuel companies. Victoria, a woman from Vancouver, was assigned to the dead space between Canada and the Midwestern States of America dominated by agricultural and pesticide giants. Yonas—Natalie thought he was from Ethiopia, or maybe Sudan, for she'd seen him speak earlier in the week—was placed right behind the many Middle Eastern delegations. The list went on.

"And Natalie," Sofia said, turning toward her. "You'll be catty-corner from the Climate Revolution table, directly behind the Western Republic of America representative, close to the Russian Federation and the People's Republic of China."

Natalie's breath caught in her chest. They'd . . . they'd read her research. They assigned her based on her thesis! The data she explored, regarding the fiery connection between sea-based trade routes from China and Russia to and from the ports in Oregon and Washington. The Western Republic continued to claim it was carbon neutral, but their calculations ignored the externalities of oil-based shipments from across the Pacific. Her advisor loved the data, and it had been her writing-sample for her Climate Revolution student delegate application. And they cared. That meant Sofia read her words. What a moment.

"Thank you," Natalie eventually said, realizing silence had lingered for a few seconds too many. "When do we start?"

"The first session begins in fifteen minutes." With that, the woman pocketed her tablet and walked toward the door. "Come along," she said. "It's time to have some fun."

* * *

Fun.

She said it would be fun.

For the past three hours, Natalie had tried to hear the words of the people around her. She caught a few potentially important sounds; a man from South Korea leaned over and whispered in the ear of an elderly Japanese woman, their ambassador to the United Nations. She noted it in the spreadsheet. And a few minutes ago, she caught a lobbyist for PetroCo slipping a note to a Midwestern ambassador walking down the aisle. All little things.

But otherwise, she tried to look normal. She pushed her back into the wooden chair, straightened her hair, and listened. Periodically, ambassadors and technical experts would stand at the podium, sharing platitudes (and sometimes data) with the group. Most of it was information Natalie already knew. Yes, everyone knew the planet was still on track for over four degrees Celsius by the end of the century. Yes, everyone knew about the intense decade-long drought striking most of west-central China and its relationship to anthropogenic climate change. Why was this all so profoundly—

"Thank you all for your time this morning, we'll continue in an hour. For now, please adjourn for lunch."

Natalie's ears perked up. Food. Yes, food is what she needed right now. Otherwise, she was going to drift into insanity.

A few feet in front of her, Sofia stood, turned toward Natalie, and gestured for her to approach. Happily obliging, Natalie approached the woman's table.

"Interested in grabbing a salad with me?" asked Sofia. "There's a cafe around the corner."

"Absolutely!" The word slipped from her mouth, before she could contain it. With a sheepish grin, Natalie added, "Thank you, Miss Huber. I'd love to learn more about your story."

"I appreciate your enthusiasm." Sofia slipped her tablet into a satchel and entered the aisle, motioning for Natalie to follow. "We won't talk much about me, though. I have a feeling you know a lot about me. Let's talk about you."

"Uh . . ." Natalie swallowed, following into stride slightly behind her hero. "I guess we can do that."

"Did you think I don't intend to get to know my note-takers? You were all chosen for a reason." They exited the massive conference hall before Sofia added, "I figured I'd start with you. I liked your speech yesterday. Fiery. Bold. Passionate. All of this means quite a bit to you, no?"

Natalie nodded, not sure how much to say. There were too many stories. She could talk about the time her family was forced to relocate because of a forest fire in Colorado. Or the drought, before she was born, ravaging her grandfather's ranch. She could discuss the existential dread and depression that wracked her high school junior year after she witnessed three friends commit suicide because of climate anxiety.

But no, there was a much more personal, visceral story worth sharing.

They reached the back of the salad line as the first words left Natalie's lips. "When I was six, my family fled the largest forest fire in Colorado's history. But that's not the story that matters. It's a sto-ry—but not *the* story. As we drove out of the state, I developed a ter-rible cough. When we reached family in Phoenix, I went straight to the hospital. They strapped me to a ventilator—you can't imagine how much that scared my parents, given their memories of the COVID-19 pandemic. My parents' fears aside, the doctors deter-mined my lungs had been coated with particulate matter from the smoke of the forest fires. I was in the hospital for weeks as they worked—more so waited—for it to clear from my body." Natalie's heart began to race, remembering the moment. Her wheezing. Her face, covered by a plastic contraption making it near-impossible to see. Her world, a white ceramic hospital room, for almost a month. "The feeling . . . of not breathing . . . of hopelessness . . ."

Her story paused as they built their salads, but Sofia looked her in the eye once they were seated at a table, as if expecting more. When Natalie didn't say a word, Sofia said, "I know this story is hard, but I want to hear it. And I think you need to tell it to me."

Natalie nodded, then nodded a second time. "Yeah. I agree. When they finished saving me, when I could breathe on my own again, I vowed to never forget that experience. To recognize that my experience was becoming the norm, that people across the world were not as lucky as me to survive from a climate-induced health problem. Of course, I didn't recognize the truth when I was that age, but it didn't take very long thereafter. And here I am. Future generations deserve to breathe, Miss Huber. To breathe without fear that their children won't have the chance."

Sofia smiled. "Please, call me Sofia. We're comrades in this fight, Natalie. Thank you for telling me your story. I've heard thousands over the year, and when someone like you, who went through true pain, tells their story, it makes it all real again. Reminds me of why we fight, when so many people have given up."

They ate in silence for a moment, chewing their spinach salads as other activists and delegates mulled about in an attempt to find a free table. Once they both finished eating, Sofia said, "We should probably head back to the auditorium. You'd be surprised by the conversations that occur in there during the lunch hour."

Natalie tapped her fingers on the table and stood. After placing their wooden bowls in a cleaning rack, they returned together to the conference hall. Before entering, Natalie said, "Thanks for listening. I hope we can chat more throughout this week. Even though you wanted to hear my story, I do want to hear yours."

"I'm sure we'll have the opportunity."

With that, Natalie returned to her seat a few rows behind her hero. Sofia slipped into her own chair at the Climate Revolution table. It was still only 12:45pm, so Natalie switched her tablet to its messenger app, shooting a quick note to Liza.

> You'll never believe who I just talked
> with.

A few moments passed before Liza's response.

> I'm stuck in a screening of some old
> ridiculous climate film from the
> mid-2000s. Thanks for the distraction!
> Who was it?

Natalie smirked.

> You'll find out tonight at the next
> get-together, no? Round 2?

Three dots, they disappeared. Then three dots again before:

```
Ha, you know it. I guess we'll invite
you again, if it's just to tell us
about who you met.
```

Natalie was about to respond when she heard whispering from over her shoulder. Her eyes widened as the words coalesced in her mind. Quickly switching back to the note-taking spreadsheet, she began to type.

". . . now look, I know what your marching orders are. I know what your public orders are. But let us be very clear, there are always hard decisions to be made. You can make a commitment to carbon-neutrality by 2075, or you can commit to best efforts by 2100, and we can ensure your nation becomes very profitable. And more importantly, we can ensure your path toward that governor seat we know you want is . . . open."

The next few words were garbled, and Natalie couldn't understand them. Then . . .

"Look, you know we have similar goals. You know what's coming. We need to let the hope of future generations down lightly. We can't keep stringing them along. Why not just make it clear that it's all going to collapse, and that we need to build our little fortresses now, rather than later?"

"I know. Believe me, you'll appreciate our actions by the end of this."

Her heart racing, she continued typing. The words ended, and chairs behind her shuffled. A few seconds later, a man in a black suit walked past her, heading toward the conference exit. She didn't recognize him. The next person to walk by, though, she recognized immediately.

The ambassador from St. Louis, the direct representative of the President of the Midwestern States of America. Natalie's blood boiled. The nerve, the boldness, to outright quid pro quo blackmail occurring right inside the room. How could they? It was 2042, and they were still fighting to end the world.

Natalie coughed. Was that a taste of iron in her mouth? Her memory flashed to the days of hyperventilation, her vision blacking.

No.

She was not going to lose control and have a panic attack on the floor of the 2042 Conference of the Parties.

She closed her eyes.

Her breathing slowed.

For ten seconds, she counted, letting her mind pause in the silence. Then, returning to the tablet, she finished her note-taking, identifying one of the speakers as the MSA ambassador.

The next fifteen minutes passed by. Delegates returned, the press returned, activists returned. The room filled, the Secretary restarted the proceedings.

And the ambassador—the same ambassador, from the Midwestern States—arrived at the podium.

Natalie's breath caught in her throat, and she held it there. She would not panic. She would not give in.

"Good afternoon, my friends, colleagues, heroes," the man said. "If you don't know me, I am Richard Pollick, Ambassador to the United Nations on behalf of the Midwestern States of America. During the days and months leading up to this COP, I've had the chance to meet with many of you about the MSA's approach to climate policy. We know you're all still wrapping your heads around the reorganization of states here in America, but we're glad you've taken it in stride. Some of you better than our own people!" The comment brought a ripple of laughter. "But that's not what I'm here to talk about. I'm here to talk about the opportunity before us to change the narrative. For decades, we have talked about the climate crisis. We have fought the climate crisis. And we believe it's time we reframe the war. How do we *survive* the climate crisis?"

That fast. Natalie couldn't believe it. In just a manner of minutes, the ambassador took words from a black suited man and translated it into talking points behind a podium. Did he understand? Did he understand how so many people had already failed to survive the climate crisis? That there was no path toward resilience that didn't include mitigating and eliminating emissions? He'd probably never lived a moment where he couldn't breathe. He probably always lived on some Midwestern farm, far from the forest fires of the West or the hurricanes of the East. The pure selfishness.

Natalie couldn't stop her mind. Her heart. Her lungs. Everything burned. Everything ached. She saw the faces around her, either engaged in their own conversations, staring at tablets, or . . . laughing. Beside Sofia, the delegations of China and Russia were leaning toward one another, chuckling. Why? Did they not see the seriousness of what was happening? Just like every other climate agreement, the fossil fuel companies managed to wiggle their claws into it and eviscerate the hope of real lasting change.

And future generations would suffer.

No longer.

Natalie stood, though she was breathing like she'd just finished a run. Her fists were clenched. Those sitting near her looked up in confusion, though she ignored their silent glares. Raising her fist in the air, she prepared to shout, but no words escaped her mouth.

Only air.

And then . . .

She stole the breath of Richard Pollick.

* * *

Time slowed. Not slowed—stopped. It was as if the world halted its rotation, with every molecule in the room suspended in the air. Natalie felt everything in the room, every heartbeat, every breath, every brainwave. The air, spread throughout the conference hall, it desired to be pushed. To be pulled. To be . . . somewhere else.

Her mind, racing with the fear and the anger and the pain of seeing a man shift and fall to the whims of greed, her mind reacted. It didn't think. Instinct guided, panic overtook and overran her reason and rational world. She pushed the air, she pushed it upward through the vents and out through the doors. The air, the life of every human, it fought against them, it wanted them to realize they were failing to save it. Was it the air that wanted that? Or was it Natalie? Was she the air?

She grasped, holding the breath of each human in the room in her palm. She pulled, snaking it from their lungs. Out, out, out it went, away from them. Everyone . . . even her cohort. Everyone . . . except Sofia.

Her mind retained that much control. She saved Sofia.

And herself.

The air escaped, it fled the corruption in the room, the endless fight. Part of her mind screamed for it to end, to stop the violence, that this was not the way.

But

She had lost control

No

Visceral anger

Power

A desire to fix, rather than restore

She wasn't ready

But something needed her to be ready.

* * *

Natalie awoke to screams. To sirens. To Sofia. "Natalie! Natalie! You need to wake up."

Like a dream, Natalie remembered standing, her fist raised. She remembered hyperventilating. She remembered falling to the ground. She didn't remember anything else. Hadn't she been texting Liza about something? What was it?

She opened her eyes. "What—"

"I don't know," Sofia said. "I really don't. But look around us."

Natalie lifted herself up onto her elbows. Around them, hundreds of people were on the floor, unconscious—or worse. "How?"

"I don't know."

"How did we survive?"
"I don't know."
"What do we do now?"

"I don't know."

THE SPIN

A.E. FAULKNER

2042 C.E.

Racing up the sidewalk, Graeson unlocked the door and threw it open. She called out "Mom! Dad!" as her work bag slipped off her shoulder, landing on the faded vinyl floor with a thump. Without waiting for an answer, she called again. "Mom! Dad!"

Considering her usual quiet demeanor, both parental figures rushed to greet their daughter. If she was shouting, whatever she had to say must be important.

"What? What's going on?" Her parents charged, prepared to comfort and protect their only offspring. The blazing smile on Graeson's face immediately snuffed out any worry.

Throwing her hands to her face, the news practically burst from her lips. "I won! I won the company's mascot design contest!" Wrapping each other in hugs and wavering between proud tears and disbelieving laughter, the family celebrated, speculating how this could alter Graeson's career path.

"Can you believe it? The biggest, fastest-growing corporation in the Midwestern Federation chose my design! Mine! And I hear they might be expanding to the other blocks! What if I get to travel to the Western Republic . . . or better yet . . . the Coastal Republic?"

Raising a hand in the air, her father nodded slyly. "Let's not get too ahead of ourselves honey. And after what happened in Sacramento, I don't know if you want to be traveling to the Western Republic. One major accomplishment at a time, okay?"

Joy seeping out of every pore, her mother added, "We're so proud of you, sweetheart. And I have a feeling this is going to be life-changing. For all of us!"

* * *

Fueled by the victory, Graeson was bursting with questions for her parents before dinner was on the table. In between forkfuls of vegetable lasagna, she begged them to share everything they knew about how SustainAble grew into a life-sustaining powerhouse of a corporation.

Although they were both quick to point out that Graeson should have remembered all of this from history class years ago, they indulged her questions. For the first time, she listened intently as they described the life they had before the whole world changed, a life she knew nothing about and had never given a second thought.

Before Graeson was born, a global pandemic knocked food and product supply chains off their axis. It shuttered meat production plants, some permanently. Blue collar workers found themselves forced to choose between risking their health or losing their income.

As businesses struggled to remain solvent, white collar workers became dispensable, many of their jobs facing extinction. Automation became the name of the game. The economy plunged into oblivion, even larger tech corporations thrived, and businesses closed their doors, one by one. A restaurant here. A department store there. Basic needs like food and medication became paramount.

The high cost of production—in the form of both human and natural resources—forced many factory farms to fold, but their long-term toxic impacts were unavoidable. Massive numbers of livestock confined in small areas left behind poisoned land and air, barren remnants that could not overcome the damage of many years of irresponsible practices.

Little by little, a once-united nation made difficult choices under the strain of economic and environmental deterioration, not to mention the non-stop hyper-partisan fighting dominating most statehouses as well as Congress. A constitutional crisis, it was called. Those vying for control rose to power, slicing the land into divided sectors and killing many archaic county boundaries. The populations within these individually-governed blocks quickly learned that aligning with a shifting society was necessary for survival.

By defining borders, each block could narrow the distance that food and goods had to travel to reach their end user. As both natural and manufactured resources dwindled, those in power squelched excessive, wasteful consumption by rationing household supplies.

Plant-based diets became necessary. And the SustainAble Corporation boasted a plan that would maximize food production while enhancing and preserving natural resources. Fully supporting its mission to build sites wherever it deemed necessary, leaders within a number of blocks granted the corporation eminent domain.

The company quickly ascended as an environmentally-responsible business, serving as a beacon for others to follow. Decades ago, it may have been considered an unfair competitive advantage. But these days, there weren't enough fully-functioning businesses to warrant those types of regulations. No one really cared as long as the masses were fed, their basic needs met.

Under the leadership of Alex Draven, SustainAble rose as the largest employer within the Midwestern block, and whispered rumors questioned if it would, or even could, expand to the surrounding blocks. Headquartered in Larkspur, Ohio, the closest major city was Columbus.

Graeson was so fascinated by her parents' tag-team explanations, she didn't notice the empty plate and glass monopolizing her place setting. Although they both tried to end the conversation, promising to talk more over breakfast, she insisted they continue while she cleared the table. She gladly scrubbed the casserole dish, washed the plates, and wiped down the table, all the while firing off question after question about a world with origins so different than anything she'd known.

Over time, Graeson's parents adapted to their changing environment. Their former lives became distant memories as the new reality became normality. They traded suits and pencil skirts for work gloves and aprons. They found employment with SustainAble's CFPG, the Central Food Production Greenhouse. The enormous climate-controlled facility housed fifty acres of vegetables. Smaller facilities in the surrounding area cultivated fruits.

Together, the greenhouses function as one unit, called a Collective Food Production Cluster, with worker housing on-site. A dozen clusters cropped up throughout the Midwestern blocks as a small-scale pattern of production to support pockets of the population – not exactly the ideal situation, but a workable one with the intent for growth. Literally.

Pushing past their initial resistance, Graeson's parents discovered a profound fulfillment blossoming with every sprouting seed. Also an employee of SustainAble, their daughter did not share their enthusiasm. She fulfilled her basic schooling requirements at age sixteen and then accepted employment shadowing her parents. At the end of a work day, she saw dirt-caked nails and calloused palms. She also had very little choice. Children were expected to apprentice their parents if they worked at SustainAble, ensuring a constant flow of qualified workers would enter the workforce and replace those who became ill or elderly.

Perhaps it was Graeson's lack of career options that drove her to enter the contest when SustainAble announced plans to unveil a company mascot, a character that would embody the organization's values. Employees were invited to write an essay, detailing the ideal image. One winner would be chosen to work in the headquarters building for three months—enough time to see their vision through to fruition as well as give the company a chance to evaluate if the employee was a good fit for a corporate career path.

All Graeson saw was a ticket out of the humid fields and into the elegant tower that lumbered over the city. When her win was announced, elation overpowered every cell in her body. This wasn't just an opportunity to create some random cartoon character.

It was so much more.

It was an escape from the mundane. It was a peek behind the curtain of a fairy tale that would otherwise linger out of reach. So while her employer would not change, her new habitat would be a glass and metal high-rise.

* * *

Waking with the first rays of sunlight, a side effect of coaxing crops to grow for the past two years, Graeson found the adrenaline rush too powerful to return to slumber. Instead, she took her time, perfecting her look. It was her first day in the administrative offices of SustainAble. No longer a greenhouse employee, she was ready to demonstrate just how much she wanted to become a fixture on the corporate team.

As she slipped into her most professional attire—a knee-length navy skirt with a matching suit jacket—Graeson attempted to smooth out any wrinkles, along with some frayed nerves. Thankfully, she fit into the clothing of her mother's former wardrobe, remnants of a society she never knew.

Her entire routine was changing, and she loved it. She would still ride public transportation to work, but now she needed to take an entirely different route. And she could never wear a skirt and jacket suit to the greenhouse.

Having mapped out the bus she needed, she easily navigated to the closest stop. Her enthusiasm was met with half-asleep riders who didn't even glance her way. It didn't matter though—she only needed to impress her new boss and coworkers. Gluing her eyes to the window, she watched the scenery pass from clusters of single family homes to apartment buildings and convenience stores. When the bus reached the center of the city, she rose. This was her stop.

Stepping off the bus, Graeson paused to admire her destination. Her eyes trailed up the glass exterior, landing on the twin smoke stacks. The deep purple and jade green tubes jutted out of the left corner of the flat roof, completely idle. Their only purpose was to serve as an aesthetic reminder: SustainAble emitted no chemicals into the air breathed by all.

Striding into the ten-story headquarters building, Graeson wore a mask of confidence. The structure's sharp angles and reflective features reminded her of skyline pictures from the past. The visage jutted into the sky: elegant yet unwelcoming and solitary. These days, resources were poured into necessities rather than luxuries. But SustainAble somehow managed to succeed when blending the two.

Striding through the glass doors as they swished open automatically, Graeson focused on appearing as though she was exactly where she belonged. Approaching the mirrored reception area, she explained that she won the contest and was reporting for her first day of work. Congratulations and warm welcomes flurried around her before she was reassured that her new supervisor would be summoned.

Within minutes, a raven-haired woman bounced across the lobby and extended a hand. "Graeson? It's wonderful to meet you. I'm Ainsley Rayne, director of public relations. I'll be overseeing your time here."

Graeson shook her new boss's hand vigorously, unable to contain the elation dancing across her lips, forming a smile that reached her eyes. "Thank you so much for this opportunity. I'm so happy to be here."

Expressing her anticipation of a productive couple of months together, Ainsley led the way to her office. The wheat-hued walls boasted Ainsley's qualifications. Graeson recognized the framed certificates with gold seals adorning the space. Her parents had similar pieces of paper from their college days. They weren't much good anymore. Dusty frames leaning against old bookshelves in the attic provided little value, at least to most people, including Graeson's family.

Cutting through the silence, Ainsley suggested they drop their personal belongings and embark on a tour of the building.

Struggling to commit every face, name, and floor layout to memory, Graeson wore a painted smile. Her heart fluttered as she envisioned her future self sitting behind an enormous desk in a corner office. It sure beat wrestling with irrigation systems and spraying growth enhancers on rows of vegetables.

The intimidation factor grew exponentially, along with the lush décor, with each level they breached. Graeson's nerves tingled with an explosive cocktail of envy, hope, and amazement. The tour strengthened her resolve to do whatever was necessary to secure a permanent position here.

* * *

Once settled in the high-walled cubicle just outside of Ainsley's office, Graeson spent the day drowning in paperwork. *Just formali-*

ties, Ainsley had said. Still, her fingers cramped after signing form after form of consents, acknowledgments, and waivers. The endless legal documents clouded her vision before she could finish reading even the first paragraph.

Her reward for completing the required forms was pouring through corporate promotional materials and mind-numbing videos, all gushing flowery mission statements and close-up images of plump, healthy produce like tomatoes and plums.

She'd certainly seen enough of that at the greenhouse. But this was nothing like her usual job. The people here sat at desks all day in air-conditioned comfort. Her body was accustomed to near-constant motion, bathed in sweat and dirt when evening arrived.

Losing the battle to remain focused on the unriveting information, Graeson allowed her eyes to wander from the screen. Her spacious area coalesced into a corner of floor-to-ceiling windows. She admired the space—it provided privacy from coworkers, as well as an impressive view of the city that could easily recharge a muddled mind in need of a creative jolt.

Her back instinctively straightened as she overlooked the city. She was used to digging in dirt in the greenhouses. This vantage point lent itself to a feeling of superiority over those who traversed the streets below.

Stepping closer to the tinted glass, she squinted, honing in on about a dozen bodies marching behind signs that covered their torso and head. She tried to get a better view, but no matter the angle, she couldn't make out the words on their signs.

"Don't mind them," Ainsley's voice called from behind her. Nearly jumping out of her skin in startled surprise, she twirled to greet her visitor. "They're just protesters," Ainsley explained, waving a dismissive hand toward the window.

Smiling wistfully, Ainsley strode into the cubicle, casually positioning herself next to Graeson. "I just wanted to check on you and see if you needed anything."

They stood side by side, gazes lurking beyond the glass. "I'm good," Graeson acknowledged. "I just wanted to give my eyes a little break from the screen and papers." Ainsley bobbed her head slightly. "I completely understand."

Still staring outside, she nodded toward the small group. "They're full of baseless accusations and fantastical assumptions. And worst of all, they'll engage anyone who gives them even a side glance with hostility."

Graeson bit back the words nearly slipping through her lips. *What could they possibly criticize?* Maybe Ainsley would view it as loyalty to the company. But what if she considered it naiveté? She chose silence as a safe response.

Turning from the window, Ainsley stepped back outside Graeson's work area. "Okay, back to work. But if you need anything, my door is always open."

"Thank you."

* * *

Within the first week, Graeson completed her orientation requirements and eased into her first assignments—creating mockups for the corporate mascot, drafting news releases announcing an upcoming press conference, and organizing spokesperson biographies. Not only was she finalizing costume and image details, she was working closely with Ainsley to plan the official introduction of her creation, Leafy, to the public.

By late Friday afternoon, her brain craved respite. She bid Ainsley a good weekend before shuffling to the bus stop. Sliding into a window seat, she stared outside, readying for the passing scenery to relax her mind. She let her eyes flutter closed, the soothing hum of the vibrating walls blotting out the voices surrounding her.

Of course, there wasn't much peace to be had when screeching brakes announce each stop and bodies scuffle in and out of the confined space. Blowing out a deep sigh, Graeson mentally inventoried possible weekend plans, attempting to mute the background noise.

A few stops later, a deep voice pierced her tranquility. "Excuse me, mind if I sit here?"

Mid-turn toward the stranger, she answered. "Of course not." Personal space was not an affordable luxury these days. At least not on public transportation.

Her eyes glanced over his rugged form, landing on the stiff

white board resting at his feet. She struggled to stifle the surprise splashing across her face. *It was one of them. A protester.*

"Thanks. You new to this block? I don't remember seeing you before this week." The stranger's question sent a wave of alarm along the back of her neck. Her eyes must have given away what her mouth did not, because he chuckled and ran a hand through his wavy brown hair.

"I'm sorry. I didn't mean to imply that I've been watching you or anything. It's not that, it's just . . ." He motioned toward the other riders. "Everyone around here is kind of on the same schedule. Day after day and week after week, you see the same faces. And it doesn't matter if it's morning or afternoon. They look the same—tired and bored. So when a new face shows up, it just . . . draws attention."

That eased her concerns. Slightly. She wanted to believe he was telling the truth, but she hadn't taken notice of others on the bus during any of her commutes to or from work. Although, it had only been a week. Maybe if this was her routine for years on end, the other riders would sneak into the corners of her mind, painting themselves into her memory, permeating her subconscious over time.

"Anyway, I hope I didn't startle you. I'm Jarrett and I'm just one more face in the crowd."

He seemed genuine enough. "I'm Graeson. It's nice to meet you." She extended her hand for an awkward shake, which he reciprocated.

When her eyes uncontrollably dipped down to the sign at his feet, he said, "Oh don't mind that. It's just part of my work."

His brief explanation made no sense. Her instincts nudged her to continue the line of conversation, but a follow-up question died on her lips. Just talking to a protester, one of the very people she was instructed to avoid, motivated her to refocus her attention on the passing scenery outside the window.

* * *

By Monday morning Graeson was eager to start another week at what she hoped would become long-term employment.

Jarrett had become her new seat-mate. Perhaps he gravitated toward her because they appeared to be close in age. Or maybe he just liked hearing his own voice. Graeson didn't discourage him, but she also didn't encourage a friendship either.

He filled most of their conversations with random thoughts. He likened the current national block system to a prison block, and the residents were all prisoners of new political leaders who had somehow become the wardens, but were really the same as everyone from before the Constitutional Crisis. He thought it was silly how they replaced county governments with something just as unresponsive to the needs of the people. The discussions didn't require much interaction. Other than an occasional nod or hitched shoulder, silently conveying her indecisiveness, Graeson considered most of his questions to be rhetorical. Seemingly satisfied with the level of interaction she was willing to offer, Jarrett smoothly steered and dominated their conversations.

Mostly, listening to him helped pass the time. But inevitably, every few days, the conversation steered back to SustainAble. Those were the times Graeson invested every modicum of concentration she could muster in order to appear neutral. Listening to Jarrett's accusations triggered jolts of guilt when she considered how badly she wanted to continue working at the corporate office.

"If I could just get inside that place, I could prove that they're feeding us all a bunch of lies." The more Jarrett spoke, which was a lot, the more Graeson believed sincere passion fueled his words.

Her curiosity grew each day. When his words started infiltrating her thoughts over the weekend, she decided to seek the truth for herself, ideally just uncovering a misunderstanding rather than a scandal. But first, she had to know exactly what she was supposedly looking for.

The next time he brought up his frustration with the corporation, Graeson decided to casually question him further.

"What do you think they're doing?" Warning tingled at the nape of her neck, but curiosity guided her words. Pausing momentarily to intake a sharp breath, his eyes widened. She had finally heard something he said. And she wanted to know more.

He leaned in closer, the intensity of his tone matching his gaze. "I've heard that underneath the greenhouses, they've got factory farms. Tons of livestock crammed into confined spaces. Those animals will never see the light of day. If that's true, they're producing massive amounts of waste and byproducts. That has to go somewhere. And I want to know where. And who's getting whatever meat is produced from these farms? Because my family sure isn't getting much more than carrots and potatoes."

Graeson eyed him questioningly.

"Don't you see?" he continued. "What a perfect cover? Sustain-Able's all *veggies and tree hugging* where everyone can see, but underground, they don't care about anything but mass producing meat at the cost of our environment."

Squinting her eyes, Graeson tossed the theory around in her head. "*If* it's even true," she mumbled. She worked in the greenhouses for two years and never saw—or smelled, for that matter—anything to indicate that SustainAble was hiding herds of animals under her feet. Although . . . she never wondered where their fertilizer came from. Manure was an obvious by-product of farmed animals. The fertilizer definitely had an odor, but it probably would not matter where it came from.

"What exactly would you look for if you got inside?" There was no way she'd sneak him in—that was way too risky. Plus, that would require her to admit she worked there. But maybe she could check it out for herself. She certainly didn't owe him any explanations, but her conscience demanded to know if she was an accomplice to corruption. If the company's growth extended to the other blocks, such a deception would spread further, poisoning widespread progress.

Jarrett detailed his plan if he could ever get inside a greenhouse. Graeson listened intently. She *could* get inside a greenhouse. As she committed his plan to memory, a shiver bolted down her spine. A warning—she might rather not know the truth.

* * *

"Graeson! Good morning! Just the person I wanted to see." Just as

Graeson crossed the threshold of the automatic doors, Ainsley animatedly rushed across the tile floor, her heels clacking with each step. Other than her first day, Ainsley hadn't greeted her in the lobby area. Goosebumps crept along her arms. *What was so important that it couldn't wait until Graeson reached her desk?*

"Good morning, Ainsley." Exhibiting a calm demeanor, Graeson cautiously greeted her boss, attempting to conceal the worry washing over her. *Did Ainsley know she talked to Jarrett, a protester? Was she in trouble?*

"I've got news! Come, let's talk in my office." Leading the way, barely able to contain her excitement, Ainsley motioned for Graeson to take a seat as soon as they entered the private space. Before her bottom even grazed a cushioned seat, Ainsley practically jumped forward, grasping Graeson's hands.

"So, I got a call from Mr. Draven late Friday afternoon. Graeson, he loves your mascot concepts!" She paused, wiggling her eyebrows. "He wants just a few minor tweaks, but otherwise, we're going to run with Leafy as you envisioned him. He says this is exactly what we need to appeal to the children and young adults of today, who will be our employees and customers tomorrow."

Ainsley's eyes practically bulged, awaiting a response. It wasn't exactly a surprise though. Graeson won the contest. She wouldn't have won if they didn't like her concept. "That's great!" Graeson said, lacing her words with forced enthusiasm.

"And even better, he wants *you* to attend next week's press conference and introduce Leafy. You'll say a few words, you know, just briefly talk about what Leafy stands for and how he represents our wholesome brand."

"I can't believe it!" Graeson's hands flew to her cheeks, as if her palms could contain the elation seeping from her pores. *Now that was news.* She suddenly understood Ainsley's demeanor.

"Now, you will be scripted, and your part will be very brief, but I think Mr. Draven sees you as the face of the next generation. I think he wants to show that we, as a company, are here for the long-term. Because of us, the Larkspur block has taken the lead in responsible food production and we can replicate our success throughout every state in the Midwest, and possibly in the other

American nations."

Unable to form intelligible words, Graeson nodded, a dopey smile plastered across her face. The silence served as Ainsley's encouragement to continue.

"Like everyone and everything, we have our critics. But that's why you and I are here." She plunked a pointer finger down on the desk. "Our job is to plant the seeds of trust and support. If we have the public behind us, we can tell those overzealous tree huggers exactly what they want to hear. And we can pave our way across every farm and unite them in our block system. Appearance is everything, Graeson. Don't forget that."

Confusion wrought Graeson's features. *The protesters. She's talking about the protesters.* The conversation took a sharp nosedive that she hadn't anticipated. Before she could form any sort of response, Ainsley redirected the conversation to the immediate subject.

"This press conference will be broadcast across the continent. Plan on speaking for about two minutes." With that, she shooed Graeson away in a playful motion. "Now get out of here. You've got a speech to write!"

* * *

Every time she attempted to draft the speech, Jarrett's words crept from the corners of her mind. She should be soaking in elation, but instead she was questioning everyone and everything around her. Finally an idea sparked—something that might inspire her.

Knocking on Ainsley's door, she shuffled in when prompted.

"Graeson, how's the speechwriting going?" Ainsley's smile spread in anticipation of positive feedback.

"Actually, that's what I came in to talk to you about," Graeson started. She pulled a seat out and plopped down on it. "I'm having a sort of writer's block, I guess." Ainsley's smile fell and her crystal blue eyes sharpened in evaluation. "But I think I know what will break it," Graeson added. "I was wondering if I could go to the CFPG and just walk around, take a closer look at how everything functions. I worked there for two years but over that time I stopped noticing the details. The little things I once appreciated." Internally,

Graeson reveled at her genius. Maybe she was pretty good at this public relations thing.

Ainsley's eyes narrowed slightly before she recovered, softening her features. "I think it's probably best if you stay here and just work on something else for a bit and then come back to the speech." Ainsley pursed her lips and steepled her fingers, elbows resting on the desk. "I'm hoping the enthusiasm you felt when you submitted your contest entry hasn't changed. If you could just tap into that energy again, I'm sure you can write a great speech. Because the only difference between then and now is that you've been working behind-the-scenes for a little while. I'm assuming that wouldn't have tainted your enthusiasm."

Surprised by how quickly the conversation shifted to a veiled accusation, Graeson bit her lower lip, unsure how to respond. Ainsley quickly filled the palpable silence.

"Don't forget, you signed non-disclosure forms on your first day. Those are binding legal documents and they require you to present the image that we deem appropriate." She rose, speaking as she walked around the desk. "Part of public relations is putting a positive spin on your message, no matter what you may believe. SPIN IT, Graeson! Appearance is everything and this is what the job requires, unless you want to spend the rest of your life pulling weeds and pruning bushes."

As if slight guilt washed over her, she added in a kinder tone. "Look, just talk up how SustainAble is leading the way into a pollution-free future and Leafy represents the generations that will benefit from the standards we set. You've only got about two minutes, so you don't have to prepare much at all. Give it another try. Okay?"

Graeson nodded compliantly, even though it wasn't truly a question. It was an order. Ainsley's reaction to that simple request confirmed what she suspected—SustainAble was hiding something. And while they claimed to be green, Graeson was starting to think they didn't mean leaves or plants, but money.

* * *

That week, Graeson slowly slid the pieces of a plan into place. She had to know the truth. The night before the press conference, she planned to pay her old workplace a visit. She was going to the CFPG to have an unofficial look around. She knew most of the security guards, and she had made friends in her time there. She didn't need Ainsley's permission to visit.

That evening, she bid her parents goodnight after dinner. She told them where she was going. They were pleased she wanted to see her former coworkers. In case the corporate opportunity didn't work out, it certainly didn't hurt to maintain connections.

She had no problems getting inside the greenhouse. Struggling to hide her distraction, Graeson chatted up everyone she knew — attempting to maintain a careful balance between bragging and displaying an appropriate amount of company loyalty. *Appearance was everything.* Ainsley had drilled that into her head.

When the chatter died down, Graeson slipped away under the guise of visiting former coworkers on the lower level. As quietly as possible, she crept and lurked, investigating doors and stairways.

Finally, she stumbled upon a series of steps leading deep below the greenhouse floor. Just as the headquarters building became fancier the higher she had gone up, this building grew darker and danker with each step down.

The fine hairs along her neck rose as her mind conjured images of underground prison cells or, worse, the skeletal remains of whatever might have been dragged down this very path. Because she couldn't imagine any reason why anyone would choose to come here.

Yet here she was, by her own choice. Driven by the need to prove Jarrett's words wrong. Or, maybe, to prove them right.

A single door, bearing clear signage to deter passage through it, awaited at the bottom of the stairs.

`Warning: Restricted Area`
`Authorized Personnel Only`

She slowly depressed the cold metal handle. The immediate resistance and limited range of motion confirmed an engaged lock. Graeson blew out a frustrated sigh, her eyes scanning the dim stairwell. The longer she took, the more likely she was to be discovered.

Dashing around the confined space, her eyes roamed every corner and crevice. When the squeaky groan of a door echoed through the chamber, she scurried beneath the steps. It was the closest thing to a hiding place within reach.

Heavy footfalls descended, two men—maybe security guards—-complaining about making the rounds in what they referred to as the "dung dungeon." Instead of tapering away as she had hoped, their voices bounced off the walls, growing louder, closer.

She squeezed her eyes shut, as if that could instantly make her invisible. The distinct jangle of keys preceded a soft click. A cautious smile spread across her face.

"Hey," one man barked. Graeson's heart dropped in anticipation of being caught, and subsequently punished. "You gotta lock it back up." *He wasn't talking to her, he was talking to his counterpart.*

"We'll be back in less than ten minutes. Let's just lock it up then. Who'd want to go in there anyway? Do *you* want to go in there?"

With that, they both chuckled and pushed through the door.

Ten minutes. She had ten minutes to find what she was looking for and get out before anyone found her.

* * *

Pushing open the heavy door, she slipped past it. A pungent odor slammed into her senses and a low bleating echo reached her ears. Pinching her nose closed, she allowed her eyes to explore the path ahead. The concrete hallway before her was bathed in darkness. Single yellow lightbulbs dangled from wires every few feet. Some were missing, probably broken and never replaced.

When she stepped forward, the door clicked shut behind her, launching her heartbeat to a surging rapid fire. *This is it.* Instinct directed her to depress the bar and walk right back through that door, but she forced her feet to carry her forward. The truth was near. Now was not the time to give up.

Shaking away jitters, she cautiously stepped forward. Her footfalls echoed down the empty hallway as the walls closed in around her. The deeper she crept into the void, the more attuned she became to it.

Thick, humid air wrapped around her limbs. The stench of waste and rot permeated her nose. In the distance, a chorus of bleats and squeals resonated. Jarrett's words filled her mind. *Factory farms. Below ground, completely unseen.* She didn't need to see what her ears and nose confirmed.

Bile rose in her throat, growing stronger with realization that she was in a highly questionable location without proper authorization. Certainty dawned—a company that built its reputation on purity and sustainability would do anything to ensure its misdeeds stayed secret. Fear swept through her. She wasn't sure which was worse: knowing the truth or carrying the weight of figuring out what to do with it.

Voices arose, echoing from the same direction as the animal sounds. Of course, employees must be here to take care of the animals. Frightened of what would become of a trespasser, she ran. With no idea of where to go or how to get out, she chose a direction and prayed her feet could carry her to safety.

Fleeing the noise, she stumbled upon a set of large metal doors. At one time they were probably shiny and smooth, but now they appeared dented and dingy. They reminded her of the storage rooms in the greenhouses above. Either way, they invited her to enter what could be the ideal hiding place. All she needed was enough time to gather her thoughts and come up with a plan.

Tugging one of the massive doors open, she cringed as it emitted a creaking groan. Seeing no one nearby, she took her chances and charged inside the door, tugging it closed with a similar screeching protest.

Enormous tubes jutted out from every direction of the wide room, all facing the center. They impaled the walls, perfectly sealed around their rounded edges. She sank to the floor and pinched her eyes closed, evaluating her predicament.

Her first step was to find an exit. She searched the perimeter of the room, checking for vents or anything big enough to squeeze her body through. When she reached the back end of the room, a red light started flashing, buzzing every few seconds. She knew it was a warning. *But a warning for what? Did someone know she was there? Did she trigger some alarm when she walked across the room?*

A low hissing sound quickly escalated to rapid successions of air being released. Her eyes darted in every direction, searching for the source. They quickly found the culprit. A green gas spewed from each of the large metallic tubes, mixing mid-air in the center of the large room. The vapors danced, combining and shifting as if they needed to occupy every inch of available space.

The cloying fumes burned her nose, throat, and eyes. She keeled over, uselessly trying to cover her face. The cloud consumed her, wrapping its spindly claws around her quaking form. Thoughts drifted in and out of her mind, rendering her unable to differentiate between reality and delusion.

The animals' by-products. She was certain, somehow, that the fumes were vaporized by-products in the process of being discarded. Perhaps released deeper into the Earth, where they couldn't be detected. And she had stumbled right into the heart of the process.

Her flesh seared. If it wasn't for the churning air, she imagined the pungent scent would invade her nostrils and prompt a reflexive gag. The pull of tears pricked at the corners of her eyes, but the sooty debris dried any moisture before it could build.

She was breaking, her body reconstructing, from her mind to her heels, and every cell in between. Her long hair blustered with the air's force and she struggled to hold her footing. It could have been one minute or one hour. Time passed with no measurement. But whatever was happening was changing her from the inside out.

Amid the cracking, snapping sounds assaulting her ears, a confident voice whispered through her subconscious.

You're stronger than human corruption. You're stronger than all of them.

All other noise faded as she processed the words. Realization dawned. The voice was her own, as if an alternate personality was speaking from within. Completely tuned in to every nerve ending, every cell, every molecule that composed her, Graeson's body tingled, awash in renewal. Her bones felt like steel bars, unbreakable.

Her mind flashed like a bolt of lightning, laser-focused and unstoppable.

When the swirling air settled, she rose to her full height. Flexing her fingers, she examined the ashen coating. It flaked, twirling through the air, with even the faintest movement.

Contrary to the weakened appearance of her skin, she never felt stronger. More powerful. Some of the most toxic chemicals in nature churned just under the ashen surface of her skin, but instead of destroying her, they invigorated her.

Exploring her renewed form, she raised her arms, twisting them at the elbows. In the blink of an eye, the air around her churned and swirled, hurling bits of dirt and debris around her. She stretched her arms higher and stood in awe when twin tornadoes, mirroring her height, shot past her and slammed into the wall directly before her, blowing it to splinters of stone.

With her mouth gaping open, she lowered both arms. The swirling relented, dissolving into a slight whisper. Her long brown locks slowed their dance around her head. When she turned her cheek toward her shoulder, she sensed a presence.

But she was alone. That could only mean that the twin tornadoes came *from* her. They resided in her, an extension of the power she now wielded. She didn't need someone to explain it to her. She just knew.

Hovering just below the surface of her muted pallor was the ability to destroy all in her path. A threatening force that she had no reason to fear. She *was* the force.

Any traces of weakness and uncertainty evaporated. A smile danced across her face as she settled into a newfound confidence. *Appearance is everything,* and she was ready to make an appearance at the press conference. SustainAble wanted her to put a spin on her speech. And that was exactly what she was going to do.

Chaos Erupts at SustainAble Mascot Unveiling

A press conference at SustainAble's headquarters near Columbus erupted in chaos yesterday, sending a dozen staffers and members of the press to a local hospital.

Witnesses claim the stage appeared to self-combust with no warning. The incident launched shards of steel and glass into the assembled crowd. Although there were no major injuries, many in attendance suffered cuts and bruises.

Several members of the press reported gusting winds, like those of a hurricane, just before the damage occurred. No local weather experts could confirm unusual activity in the area during the event's timeframe.

A SustainAble insider, speaking on the condition of anonymity, alleged that an employee was responsible for the destruction. Additional damage was caused when, in the midst of the chaos, witnesses claim a small group of unidentified individuals spray painted farm animal outlines along the sidewalks bordering where the stage previously stood.

Corporate spokesperson Ainsley Rayne could not be reached for comment.

THE GREEN CEILING
EMAD EL-DIN AYSHA

2043 C.E.

The harvest from the fields of space and time

Is not all that great. Bring some wine,
Because creation's amenities are not all that great.

Heart and soul are born for ecstatic conversation
With a friend. That's it. Otherwise heart
And soul are not in the end that great.

— Hafiz —

"You here for the tour?" the stranger asked unassumingly.

"Tour. What tour?" Noah replied uncomprehendingly. He wasn't in the mood for yet another sales pitch.

"The Nile tour of course," the stranger gestured to the boat station close by, with the rickety battery-powered falukas.

"I thought the Nile was off limits now," Noah said, though he was now intrigued. He'd traveled a long way to experience Egypt. "Since they built—"

"Nonsense," the stranger replied. "Some portions aren't walled in, and these walls operate mostly in the day time. You can still have a romantic get-together in the night time, and if you take one of the luxury lines you can head from one end of the Nile to the other, from Lake Nasser to the Delta, and see all the sights along the way. As if the lotus farms aren't enough!"

The stranger was clearly overjoyed, like a kid who'd discovered the earth was round. Noah had no idea who the guy was, but some of the man's enthusiasm had washed off onto him. He made his mind up to take a peek. It wouldn't hurt.

He bought his ticket and took a seat in a very traditional means of transportation indeed. The stranger insisted on sitting next to him, not that he'd asked for a tour guide. He was planning to get off at the next boat station before he got too far away from the hotel and fell prey to street hawkers and unlicensed tour guides and taxi drivers who turned their GPS trackers off.

One minute they were out in the burning sun, the next they were enveloped in a world of green humidity, broken rays of sunlight slicing through the air towards the browny waters beneath. It was going to be one of the most eventful trips of his life.

* * *

Noah looked up at the sun, the orb of yellow light trying desperately to get at him from the world up and above. Like a tunnel of love with a cracked ceiling at a derelict amusement park, decorated with ivy.

"So, this is all trees," he finally asked, looking at the green webbing around him.

"Oh, no, it's a translucent gel membrane that breathes in . . ."

"Breath . . . There's no *holes* in the canopy so we don't suffo . . ." Fear entered his voice.

"No need," the stranger replied all too lightly. "You've got vegetation growing 'in' the membrane, generating all the oxygen you need. And the climate is carefully monitored, I *assure* you." He paused for a long moment. "It's really quite brilliant."

"Making a giant greenhouse, you mean," Noah queried.

"Oh no. Nothing remarkable about that at all. They hit two birds with one stone. The lotus plant was clogging up the Nile, for so long after the building of the Aswan high dam."

"But—"

"The dam held up the silt, in the past." The stranger ignored him. He spoke as if a recording was playing away in his head. "That was bad enough by itself, for the country and its agricultural potential, relying on chemical fertilisers instead when they had the best natural fertiliser in the world. To make matters worse, the silt had kept the waters occluded and foggy enough to stop the lotus seeds sprouting and growing and multiplying. Without that natural balance, the lotus plant took off, clogging up the waters, and the propellers of boats."

Noah instinctively held onto his tiny seat upon hearing those words.

The stranger went on, unabated, his starry-eyed gaze elsewhere entirely. "With the final building and operation of the Renaissance dam in Ethiopia, and a whole swathe of other dams in imitation elsewhere, the situation became unbearable. And for the Ethiopians, to be honest. Even less silt, more lotus plants, and a whole bunch of other plants that the Egyptian ecosystem couldn't handle, washed up by the waters from the South. And *pressure*, more and more pressure to save every last drop of fresh water in the whole country. Not just Lake Nasser, where most of the evaporation used to take place of Egypt's official share in the waters of the once mighty Nile." His eyes misted over now, as the reel of memories continued to make itself felt on his delicate frame. "Only for more water to be lost along the way to the Delta, a Delta that was, incidentally, sinking into the Mediterrane—"

"Because of global climate change, you mean," Noah chipped in. "Though is it really sinking if the ocean itself is what's rising?" About the only science he knew, apart from what happens when you stuck your finger into a light-bulb socket.

"Right you are," the stranger said as if clearing his throat. "Not that we hadn't slit our throats, beforehand, with the Aswan High Dam. *Yet* another imbalance. We'd been starving the Delta of silt for decades and decades, and now it was reaching crisis proportions as we needed even more silt to keep the Delta afloat. Sandbags and landfills wouldn't do. And so, we . . . they began with a trial project, over Lake Nasser, first to keep the humidity in, using a transparent synthetic polymer they . . . err, had fabricated that could handle the temperature on the inside of the enclosure, and the sun above." He jabbed with his thumb upwards as if hailing for a celestial cab. "The sun destroys everything in this part of the world. Wallpaper, paint, curtain blinds . . . That's why the blinds Egyptians traditionally use are made of wood. Metal is useless in such a dusty, sunny country. That's when they made the breakthrough. The polymer was biodegradable and non-toxic, and had remarkable properties they hadn't counted on. Flexing and stretching. You could actually squeeze wood splinters into it and it would grow around them. The next logical step was to get the lotus plant to grow in this artificial environment, a hydroponic farm of a completely new kind. After repeated success, the system was standardised and expanded to cover the full length of the Nile. The water, the evaporation, was kept in, and the plant cover kept the temperature reasonable on the inside, and the membrane let in oxygen and sunlight for the plants to thrive."

"Then what about . . . soil?" Noah said weakly. The sheer magnitude of scientific genius was beginning to overwhelm him. He'd stopped looking at the coastline, the images from behind the membrane pumped into the environment with the aid of holographic projectors. He could still enjoy the scenery alright, with cows and sheep and farmers and mud huts and modern buildings along the way.

"I presume you mean fertilizer," the stranger said, finally breaking out of his trance and staring at Noah. "The UN, their environmental and conservation bodies, finally pitched in and negotiated a deal with the countries that had built all those dams, demanding that they hand over their accumulated silt in exchange for this water-saving, clean technology. Minus the royalties." He gestured with his hand to the green tunnel that went as far as the eye could see, behind and ahead of them. "It *is* a patented invention, after all," he finished proudly.

"Sounds like duck hunting season to me," Noah said wisely. "They shot more birds than they could count!"

"What an appropriate analogy," the stranger replied. "The roots of the lotus plant extend *down* into the water, carrying the nutrients up into the plants . . . into the very skin of this solar ceiling."

Noah went bug-eyed.

"Yes, indeed. They've already started planting orchards on the outside of the membrane. They're still doing trials, to make sure the new plants can handle the water, salinity levels and nitrate composition, without sapping the life out of the lotus plant." The stranger paused for a moment, gently scratching his scalp with a thumb. "I could tell you . . . but I wouldn't want to bore you with the medicinal value of the lotus plant. How it's powered the country's self-sufficiency in pharmaceuticals. Followed by exports. Of drugs, grains, paper, organic fertilizer, organic dyes and paints . . ." his voice trailed off.

"*Please* do," Noah replied without a second thought, surprising himself.

* * *

"Please, allow me," Noah said at the cafeteria table. It had been a *long* day and they both needed refreshing, and he was picking up the tab.

They'd ordered eggplant steaks and seaweed salads and zero-calorie soft drinks. Eggplant had long been the poor Egyptians' substitute for meat for as far back as anybody could remember, given how high it was in protein and iron. Now it was Egypt's substitute for soy burgers, allowing it to use soy as animal feed and a nitrate introducing agent in soil, augmenting the traditional Egyptian *fuol,* broad beans. The vegetable oil they cooked the eggplant steaks in was soy oil, lifting another burden off the shoulders of sunflower and corn oil, which Egypt now exported in bulk to China—in exchange for the pure soybean genome.

The seaweed harvested in the Red Sea was of a distinctly crimson complexion, why the shallow waters of the sea had been given that name, and substituted for tomatoes and cucumbers. The stranger had ordered a side helping of *humus* to go with it. It took some of the bite out of the taste. And the Stevia plant, imported from Syria, was a healthy substitute for sugar in everything from tea, coffee, ice-cream to, typically, soft drinks.

The sky was quite literally the limit, once people had figured out there was no way out of the bottleneck they'd found themselves in except through cooperation. Public sector, private sector, and everything else in between. At least that's what the stranger had said along the length and breadth of the trip. They were already using the synthetic membrane on the salt marches in the Delta and around the mega-city Cairo had always been, since the stuff allowed them to slowly sap salt water out of the marches to be desalinated by the power of the sun above.

Sitting there, after the hearty meal was finally digested, Noah reminisced on the surroundings. The clutter and noise of the loudly coloured cafeteria. And the heat and dust of the crowded landscape of the world that lay outside.

The translucent tunnel they'd been in, with the sounds of the outside world muffled, and the dust kept at bay. This was the true Egypt, on the inside. The outside, it seemed so dusty and *bleak*. He'd never felt that before, since coming here and doing his fair share of sightseeing.

It took several sips of Moroccan green tea to slide the small feast down his digestive track. He was going to order Stevia powder for the tea, but the stranger advised using a crystal of sukar nabati (plant sugar) instead, placing the crystal underneath his tongue. It was a Persian habit, apparently, and prolonged the sugary effect without crowding out the green granules in the glass of hot water; it cut down pressure on the Stevia plant sector too.

Noah finally asked his companion how he *knew* all these fascinating details. How could anyone know everything, all the details, and the policy fights and business deals that had made the science of it all possible.

"Oh, that's easy," the stranger answered, a cunning sparkle in his eye. "I'm the man who made it all possible. I'm the inventor."

Noah's eyelids stretched to breaking point.

"My brother passed through the legislation for my inventions. And that wasn't easy, I can tell you," the stranger said casually. "They don't call us Egypt's Gracchus brothers for nothing!"

BEHIND THE MIRROR

E. R. HOFFER

2044 C.E.

Arang was determined to get the weekly ration package before her angsty six-year-old brother devoured her fingers. Jae's dirty face peered up as he gummed her hand, threatening to take a bite, complaining about his terrible hunger. Rain pelted the street-smart teenager's ratty black hoodie. "Stop doing that," she said, tightening her grip on his slippery hand, dragging him past the line of sleepy people.

A grizzled dude with a moon-shaped face checked her out. A red-haired woman with a cloud of frizzy hair shook her head and spat. "Get back where you belong, bitch."

She ignored them, flipping damp black bangs out of her eyes with a head toss. The twins, Tim and Tom, bear-like brothers with makeshift cardboard head coverings, waved from the front of the line. She sidled up and grabbed them by their padded elbows.

"Thanks, guys. I might lose a hand if we have to wait." She jerked her head toward Jae, now shuffling his feet and scowling.

"Almost there," said Tim, or was it Tom, pointing to the doorway where ragged yet triumphant front-liners departed, clutching brown paper parcels filled with cans and bags to keep them alive for a few more days.

Arang hefted an overstuffed pack up on her shoulder. A tan leather belt with a brass buckle secured the patched and torn canvas bag filled with everything they owned—a few shirts, a towel, and her notebooks.

Jae wriggled his thin frame lost in a men's roomy blue denim work shirt. "How long do I have to wait?"

At least the awnings would keep them dry. Ahead of them,

Mitch, a long-haired surfer type with a deep tan, sidled into the spot in front. They'd been in the same job class last month. Just a way to kill time, meet some people. There weren't any real jobs left anymore.

"Haven't seen you around. How you doin'?"

Arang shrugged. "Meh. You?"

"Yeah," said Mitch, scratching a line in the dirt with his over-sized sneakers. "Kei left last week. Got a job in the Western Republic."

"Why'd you stay?"

"What? And leave my luxurious life in Boston, the intelligentsia-filled capital of the Coastal Republic?" he said, rolling his eyes. He smiled at the fuming pair behind them. "If Kei makes it, I'll join her. Hey, what happened with your invention? The Bioenergy guys said they'd pay for your invention?"

Arang shrugged. "Told me to come back next month. Whole lotta nothing."

"Can I see?"

She unclasped the pack and pulled out a notebook, flipping it open to a gridded page of smudges, scribbles, and notes. Jae pulled down on the notebook to tilt it into his view.

Mitch shook his head. "Cool. Energy from garbage?"

She nodded. "Need a ton of plasma. And the syngas is a mess."

They peered at the dense page of diagrams and numbers. Then her brother slapped the cover up with his hand. "Why can't we get breakfast there?" He pointed toward a posh cafe at the end of the block.

Arang ignored the question and shook her head. She didn't have the energy to explain the economics of social inequality to her brother.

"Where'd you learn that stuff?"

"My folks were scientists. When they got sick, they tried to stuff all their know-how into my head. But now I have this weird kid . . ."

He patted her shoulder and stepped forward to close the gap as the family ahead of them inched ahead.

Mitch leaned against the mirrored glass and Arang peered past him at the blurry reflection of sleepy heads in tousled hair, hats, and scarves. Everyone faced the blank windows lining the walk, absorbed in liquid memories of an abundant past, reflections of empty buildings across the street.

* * *

A few hours later, backpack laden with food supplies, Arang and Jae trudged back to camp in a torrential rain soaking deep into their layers of torn clothing. The boy waved his arm up at the sky and the waves of rain seemed to part in hypnotic patterns, like rivulets of silver. At the edge of their site in the camp, Arang's girlfriend Oakley perched on an overturned plastic bin, head forward in both hands, red hair sticking out between splayed fingers.

Arang shoved her shoulder. "Where's the tent?"

"What?" She jumped to a bow-legged standing position and swiveled her head back and forth, open-mouthed.

Arang's mouth twisted and her face reddened. She dropped her armful of plastic bags and canisters and flung her pack to the ground in a shower of gravel. "You promised to watch the camp while we got the rations."

"I did," she said, rubbing her scalp with a frown. "Maybe, I lost track of time and—"

Arang pointed her boot toward the flattened dirt behind the trees, where the tent used to be. "Cut the crap," she said, kicking the dirt with her boot. "You promised to quit. Where did you get it? How did you pay for it?"

She picked at the toe of her wet yellow and pink sneakers. Straightening with a bright smile, she snaked both hands around her friend's waist. "No worries. My bud in the next quad has plenty of room. Be right back." She thumbed toward the walkway, pulled a wet pink hood over her head, and strode off.

Arang wiped her face on her forearm and sighed as her friend turned the corner. She kneeled and forced a smile at Jae.

He knelt next to her and patted her knee. "I like sleeping out."

Tugging at the laces of a wrinkled mustard-colored bag marked "Dry Goods" in block letters, she said, "I promised you breakfast. Let's see what we've got."

A rumbling sound erupted from the opposite side of the camp.

"What's that?" asked Jae, standing, and turning toward the noise.

Arang stood as a few camp dwellers came running.

They sped past, yelling. "Higher ground!"

"Why? What's happening?"

Dammit, Oakley, where are you?

More people streamed past the site, yelling something unintelligible.

She slung the bag over her shoulders, grabbed as many parcels as she could hold, and ordered Jae to do the same. They jogged alongside the pack of runners as the rumble and woosh of water grew louder. Higher ground in just a few blocks. She turned to the person next to her, a man carrying a bawling infant, shielding his baby's face from pelting drops, squeezing the bumping child, as he sped forward.

"What's wrong?" she yelled.

"Flood comin', levee burst." He sped past them toward the stairs.

Jae's shorter legs pumped and he struggled to keep up. Arang lost her grip on the supplies. Precious foil-wrapped packages tumbled, bounced off her moving legs, crashing to the ground. Arang cursed as a week's worth of meals rolled down the street, trampled by the horde. The roars of people were drowned by the louder noise of waves.

When they reached the first step, Arang shoved her way between two tall men, dragging Jae into the crowd. The crush was too awkward to make efficient progress, but locked together in a dense cluster, they inched upward and got to the first landing.

She made the turn to the next set of steps and scanned through the crowd for spiky red hair. A cascade of water washed forward. Gray foam swirled below the staircase as a rising wave of dirty brown water surged past them. She pressed up against lumpy bodies, writhing and grasping, reaching for salvation amid bobbing refuse and gear.

Arang lurched backward as someone yanked her pack. She teetered on one boot, struggling to regain her balance. From behind, a frantic woman screamed for help. Jae's fingers slipped from her grasp. He sank under the water, arms flailing.

"Jae!" she shouted, turning, her view obscured by the panicking mob.

She pressed back and the water split into two currents. The crowd parted to let her drop to a lower step, then another. Jae lay moaning in a dry spot between the raging waters. The remaining stair climbers shoved past to higher ground and the crowd thinned.

"What's wrong with you?"

"My leg."

She pulled him closer and propped him up with one hand. They crouched together, watching the water rise around them on two sides.

"We need to get higher," she shouted at him. He shook his head and pointed up at the tangled cluster of people stuck, pushing, shouting, making slow progress. The crowd had passed and there were no more people below. She looked at the rushing water passing around them, as if they were inside an invisible bubble, free of the crush of more desperate escapees on all sides.

Jae leaned on Arang and they limped to the top of the stairs as the waters subsided, leaving a muddy mess of trash. She knew something terrible was wrong with her brother. He needed more than food. A young couple wandered past, arguing in loud voices. A gray-haired man in a baseball cap held out a stained photograph, asking anyone who passed if they'd seen the woman in the picture, his wife.

Arang and Jae drifted to an off-limits area secured by an electrified fence. The flood had washed away the park's security, along with everything else. Jae cried out, clutching his abdomen, and fell to his knees, panting.

"What's wrong? Are you faking?" She raised Jae to his feet. "Come on, there's a lovely campsite," she said, putting on a lilting tone to mask her fear about his condition. Inside a security fence, there must be something worth protecting. A safe place to spend one night might be worth the punishment.

They took a careful first step on the lawn. No alarm, no security forces, no angry dogs. They walked past the invisible boundary into a different world. Arang leaned over to touch the grass. Her fingers brushed stiff plastic. Why would someone put simulated turf behind a security fence? They moved deeper into the park. The ground cover melted into dirt and dry leaves. Thick birch and pine cover blocked the gray light of a cloud-filled sky.

"What's that?" Jae pointed at a spot of light in the distance. They limped toward the source. In the dim light, a sliver of a beam peeked out within a close stand of trees. The two siblings squeezed through the black scratchy trunks and discovered a clearing. Arang jumped at a glimpse of movement, the threat of other people.

"Boy, we look awful," said Jae.

Their own reflections stared back in a mirrored wall. Jae hobbled toward the structure.

"Stop," said Arang. "It might be dangerous."

"I'm hungry. I'll bet there's food in there." He pressed the palm of his hand against the surface. "Warm?"

He pounded the glass. "Hello? Please help us. We haven't eaten in days."

Arang marched up to the mirror and pounded with both palms. "My brother's hurt. He needs help. Please. We'll die."

Jae stifled a frustrated sob. A rectangular panel slid open, revealing a dark void a few feet above their heads. A rod jabbed out into the darkening park; a spherical camera with a spotlight swiveled in their direction. "What assistance do you require?" A metallic voice.

Jae's mouth dropped open. "Wha?"

Arang said, "Food. And medical attention." She pointed at her brother. "His leg. He's injured."

The camera scanned the boy. As Jae reached out a hand, the devices shrank back, and the panel closed over the void. *Click.*

"I told you not to touch it." She slapped his hand.

"I didn't—"

A mirrored panel slid open at ground level and a voice said, "Enter."

Jae limped forward. Arang threw her arm across his chest.

"Wait." She turned to him and whispered, "It could be dangerous."

"I'm hungry. My leg." He pushed her arm away and limped

into the opening. Arang followed him and stood in the doorway, jamming her backpack against the frame. Inside the dark cube-shaped room, the camera swiveled. A rectangular screen brightened into focus with the image of an animated face. A blank-looking gender-neutral person blinked at them with a friendly smile.

"What do you require?"

"My brother's injured—"

"Food. I need something to eat." Jae pressed his nose up against the face of the screen.

"Please face the camera for identification," said the person on the screen. Jae turned to face the sphere. After a quick scan, the camera moved toward Arang, who presented her smirking face as ordered.

"Jae Persef, Arang Persef," said the face. "Admittance approved. Please sign this form and agree to the conditions."

A document scrolled past them on the screen.

Jae reached a finger toward the e-signature line on the screen, turning to his sister. "How do they . . ."

"He's underage," said Arang, shaking her head. "I'm his guardian. I need to read this." She scrolled through the document. "Is this right? Once we enter, we can't leave?"

The face nodded. "Yes, a security requirement."

"We can't pay for anything."

"Payment will not be necessary."

"What kind of place is this? Medical research? Are we guinea pigs?"

"This is a pilot site for a model community." The face tilted to one side, oozing sincerity.

"Too good to be true." Arang stood back with her hands flexed and knees coiled, ready to grab her brother and leap out the door.

Jae turned and said, "I'm starving. Come on, say *yes*." His face reddened as he pounded her arms with both fists, repeating the phrase, ramming his head back and forth, "say yes" over and over, louder and louder. Wound into a paroxysm, Jae grabbed his abdomen and keeled over.

"Hey faker. Get up."

The camera dropped and scanned Jae's inert body.

"He has lost consciousness," said the face. "If you sign now and gain admittance, the medical team is standing by to assist Jae Persef."

"Damn you." She dashed a messy line across the form. Later, she'd just deny it was her signature.

The panel slid shut and the cube-shaped room transformed into a long mirrored corridor lit by pin lights in the ceiling. A mechanical device, a metal box on wheels topped by a cot, rolled forward and parked next to Jae.

"What a performance."

"Please place your brother on the med-unit."

Arang hefted Jae onto the cot. "Just sit tight," she whispered.

"Told ya," he said in his best ventriloquist voice, winking.

The bot reversed direction and headed down the corridor. Arang ran to keep up as Jae lay back and closed his eyes, a theatrical hand across his brow.

* * *

The med-unit delivered them to another cube-shaped room with a chair, a desk, and two cots. After they entered, the panel closed, sealing them in. Arang's throat tightened. She scratched at the walls, trying to figure out how they would escape when the time came.

The rectangular screen brightened on one wall and the familiar face appeared. "How is Jae doing?"

"I thought you guys monitored your guinea pigs." Arang frowned. "But in case you haven't figured it out, he's hungry and injured. I'm starving, too."

A panel next to Jae's cot slid back. A tiny shelf presented three bowls filled with apple slices, roasted almonds, a handful of crackers smelling like sawdust, and a cup of some translucent gold liquid.

"Wake up, eat something." She propped Jae up and poured the liquid between his lips, hoping it was water. A tall rolling med-unit arrived with a range of non-invasive implements. Jae submitted to poking and prodding while he chewed his food.

"The analysis is complete," said the face on the screen. "We confirmed that Jae is Awakened."

Arang frowned. "A what? One of those people the internet conspiracists keep talking about? His only superpower is driving me crazy."

"Please consume the medications provided once a day. With rest, Jae will recover fully. And begin manifesting his powers."

The screen disappeared as the tall med-unit withdrew and the room closed up again. The food door closed and reopened with a clear container filled with pills next to the fruit bowl.

"I think I'll call that one Slim," said Arang, tossing her pack on the floor and sitting on the second cot.

Jae smiled. "How about this power?" he crunched into a ball.

She nodded. "Think I'll just close my eyes."

* * *

They awoke hours later, unaware if it was day or night. Amber bulbs in the ceiling cast shadows in the dim room. She wrinkled her nose at the chlorine smell surrounding them. She did feel better. Arang peered at her brother's sleeping face and dabbed at his forehead. His skin was warmer, less clammy. A screen illuminated the wall, filling the space with moving characters and lines. Too fast to read, she suspected this was a map. She analyzed the patterns, pulled her notebook out and started sketching.

"How are you?" The characters disappeared and the screen filled with a simulated human face, generic features that reminded her of her own.

Next to the face, the screen displayed red block numbers—0800. She did a quick calculation. They'd encountered the mirror wall around sundown, so if the time was correct, they'd both slept all night. No wonder she felt better. She hadn't had a full night sleep in, well, a long time.

"Who are you talking to?" said Jae, sitting up.

"Yeah, off your butt and move around." Arang squinted at the face. Time to find out if they were prisoners.

The rectangle disappeared, and the wall opened, revealing the familiar empty corridor. No med-units this time. Jae slid to the edge of the cot and hopped down, wincing, and touching one leg. He took a few steps. Arang shouldered her pack, and the two paced the corridor. Jae gained strength with each lap. At the far end, she figured they were near the exterior wall. She searched for an escape, and ran her hands across the blank surface, tapped and scratched with her fingernails, searching for panel seams.

The friendly face reappeared.

"What assistance do you require?"

"Looking for the door. Where are we?" She jabbed her finger against the wall.

The face shrank and a video of the woods outside the building appeared on the screen. Arang squinted into the screen at the slices of light between trunks to find something familiar, a sign of the camp, or the city beyond.

Jae hopped, walked, then jogged up and down the hallway.

"Can you open the door? We gotta' go." Arang shoved back from the fake window and stood with her hands on both hips.

Dead leaves blew across the video. She rapped on the screen.

"Hey, you in there? Open up."

The smiling face reappeared. "So glad Jae is better."

"Just open this wall or whatever." She explored the smooth surface with her hands.

The smiling face turned grim. "Please return to the recovery room and the med-unit will confirm Jae's health status."

Jae sprinted up and down the hallway, giddy. She wondered what they'd put in the water. A panel opened at the far end of the hallway. The energetic boy rushed toward the opening. Slim trundled toward them, unaware of their presence.

"Stay there," Arang shouted as she sprinted to his side. "Squeeze, like this," she ordered, pressing her back against the wall. She held her finger to her lips and Jae copied her stance with a toothy grin. She knew he loved nothing better than a hide and seek game.

Slim trundled past, unaware of them. They both dashed through the opening before the panel shut behind them. The corridor looked just like the one they'd left. At the far end, lights.

"Come on," she said. "We'll find another way out."

"Cool." Jae passed her, laughing, arms pinwheeling. He squeaked to a halt at the end, peering out. The corridor opened onto a walkway in a huge cylindrical space filled with natural light. They squinted up, both shielding their eyes with their hands. Sunlight streamed down through the glass ceiling. The two siblings stood on a narrow metal walkway, five floors above the ground level. Below, hundreds of people and machines hustled across the floor, chatting, pushing carts.

"What is it?" Jae asked open-mouthed.

"Dunno, a factory? We'd better mix into the crowd before they spot us. We can find a way out from there, I'll bet."

"Let's check that out." Jae pointed to a cluster of kids seated at tables filled with baskets, building something.

"We have no idea what this place wants to do to us. Be careful."

"Why?" He turned his open face up to hers. "I'm feeling really good. Getting superpowers, right?"

She grabbed his hand and ran to the nearest metal stairwell and trudged down the metal steps. They made it down four flights to the rubberized floor. Groups of people working on food production, similar in design to the med-units, mixed with groups of people, engaged in many team activities.

From a distance, Arang sensed a bot approaching, heads turning in their direction. She scanned the entire floor and grasped four quadrants, divided by long beige pathways where humans and bots streamed back and forth. She navigated around the pathway edging around the base of the cylinder. Doorways spaced at regular intervals opened onto blank corridors, just like the ones they'd occupied upstairs, crowded with people, bots, and carts. She found an unoccupied hallway, promising and dark.

"This one."

They sped into a corridor that grew darker the farther they got.

"Are you sure?" Jae whined, stopping as they reached the dead-end in the darkness.

"Dammit," said Arang just as the wall at the end of the corridor slid open.

Inside, a voice said, "What assistance do you require?"

They peered into a spare room with a dark rubber floor and

metal walls filled with pulsing screens, showing videos of people working and playing around the facility. A Black man in a silver jumpsuit sat in a chair with his hands folded on a long table. He seemed to be waiting for them. The other two chairs were empty.

Jae peered into a screen at his eye level, as the panorama swept across the cylindrical space they'd just left. "What are they—hey." He pointed at the video image tracking the siblings as they crept through the throng, looking for an escape route. White rectangles on their faces labeled them as Arang Persef, Jae Persef. "And there." A close-up in the recovery room. He wheeled around. "You're snooping on us!"

The man stood and extended his hand. "Let me introduce myself. I'm Malachi Smith, a co-founder. I can explain."

Jae folded his arms with a pout and kicked his boot.

Arang frowned. "What do you want from us, Mr. Smith? Or should I call you Big Brother? I told your . . . guard, or whatever that thing was outside, we've got no money, nothing valuable."

"Please, call me Malachi." He waved his hands. "No need for money here. We're building a new society where we reward contributions based on the positive impact on society."

"What the hell does that mean? We don't need any more Republics."

Malachi nodded and put his index finger up to his lips, squinting at Arang. "Not another one. Something different. Instead of money as a measure of value, we're testing an advanced system which predicts cause and effects of any action or decision and assesses its long-term value to society."

Arang smirked. "You'd never have enough information to make those predictions. Or a system advanced enough to do all the calcs."

"Good point. Sit and I'll explain." He gestured toward the last remaining chair and sat back down in his seat.

Arang shook her head and took a step away.

"I'm a data scientist at heart. Started my own company, decades ago. We provided state-of-the-art forecasts to industry and government leaders around the world. But I was alarmed by the patterns, scenario after scenario. Humanity's days were numbered. So I reached out to five other tech CEOs. We founded a consortium to monitor key indicators in society."

He ticked them off, tapping his right index finger to the finger-tips on his other hand, one at a time. "Social factors, like intolerance and inequality. Environmental factors, like global temperature rise, storms. Economic factors like income inequality." He drummed his chest with his fingers and shrugged. "We enjoyed the generous fruits of capitalism, but we could all see its days were numbered. We're inventors, and we even toyed with leaving the planet, creating an off-world enclave. But that was unrealistic, so we created this place as a kind of experiment, to find another model for society. So humanity could move into a new age, before the planet shrugged us off for good."

"What happened?"

"We've come a long way. We're beyond the experiment stage. We, all the founders, live here now. We're committed."

"Ridiculous. The Enforcers would have torched this place long ago. This must be a government trick, to subjugate us. Or worse, get rid of the trash that didn't wash away in the last storm."

"We believe in transparency as you can see." He opened his arms and pointed to the walls projecting flashing images—children raising hands in a classroom, adults leaning over work tables filled with seedlings, a young couple kissing in a cafeteria.

Jae hopped off his chair and ran around the room peering at one screen after another. "Where did they come from?"

"Like you, we selected them for their special talents, and offered them the choice to join us. They believed the chance to build a better world was worth the risk of leaving the old one behind."

"Do they know you spy?"

"In our culture, behavior that advances the social mission is accepted. We've learned to live with openness, in fact, we find it liberating."

Arang scanned the surfaces for cameras, pressing her face against the satin steel walls, picking at one of the small circular holes that formed a grid pattern on all sides. She spun around from the wall and faced him, hands on hips. "You snooped my stuff?"

Malachi nodded. "Yes. We understand what you could do if your talents were nurtured and not wasted. Your energy project, for example." He tapped his chin. "We have contacts. More sophisticated than the idiots that passed on your idea."

She narrowed her eyes. Malachi stood and opened a panel, pulled out Arang's bag, and handed it to her. Her eyes bulged as she squeezed her thin arms around the tattered backpack with a sigh.

"So you're stealing my ideas?"

"Not at all. We need your help. Here your brilliance can shine. And Jae's, when he comes into his power." He continued. "Arang Persef. You have a talent for innovation. Your energy device would reduce our community's waste problem. Have an important impact on humanity's survival."

She shook her head, refusing to let herself believe.

"Jae Persef. Your powers are awakening."

Her brother's eyes widened. "Really?" He turned to his sister. "See, I told you."

The same window view of the trees she'd seen earlier appeared on the opposite wall. It was getting dark outside. Either that, or a pretty good fake video.

"Show us the door, if we're really free to go."

"Certainly. But when you leave, the opportunity will expire."

"What do you mean?"

"The invitation to join us, become part of this community, to pursue important work, contribute to society."

Arang frowned, pulling the backpack close to her chest.

The far wall slid open. Jae ran to the void and glanced up.

"A stair back to the park." Malachi stood, opened his hand, and pushed his chair under the table. He stepped backward out of the way and welcomed them to exit. "You are free to go."

Arang shouldered her pack, walked over to Jae. The open metal stair scissored upwards several flights towards a dark ceiling punctuated by tiny lights. She could just make out a hatch. A mechanical click echoed, and a panel opened. Sunlight slanted into the deep shaft. She thought about the world outside, sinking into an environmental wasteland, societal breakdown, a girlfriend she loved, an invention no one wanted, a brother with powers she couldn't control.

"What's the catch?" She swiveled around, addressing all the cameras in all the walls.

"This is all the information I can provide."

"Aren't you worried about us ratting you out? Do you have people outside to kill us when we try to run away?" Arang put her arm up to her forehead. Her temple pounded, hot like the last time she faced the intractable engineering problem of getting her garbage energy device to work on paper. It had been so long since she'd believed in anything. She felt hollow inside, unsure whether to sink or swim.

Malachi shook his head. "The damage to our security system is already repaired. Once you leave, you won't be able to find us. No one will."

Arang had a powerful urge to run, as she'd always done, flee from danger, from hunger and addiction, from deprivation, from someone who might care for her, from getting too comfortable. She took a deep breath to fight the urge, think it through.

"Where would we live?"

"All new members live in modest residences. And all young people are required to attend school."

Jae's brows twitched as he grabbed his sister's arm. For the first time ever, she fought her instincts. Maybe if she stopped running, she could make a difference. One screen flickered with a group of teenagers. They argued with pointing fingers and frowns, devolved into laughter. She tried to picture herself among them, someone with friends, a purpose. Arang turned to Malachi.

"My friend on the outside, can she come with us?"

Malachi shook his head. "We've all had to leave people behind. A painful part of the journey."

Jae yanked on his sister's hand. "What is he talking about?" He squinted at Malachi, and tilted his head from side to side.

"If you join us, I can answer all the questions. For now, I can only promise to protect and support you, provide food and clothing, education, and a community that will support you, and will value your contributions. But you can never return to your former world."

Arang clenched her fists. Her stomach twisted as fear and mistrust morphed into a foamy curiosity, and a giddy feeling bubbled in her chest. "What do you think, Jae?"

"Say yes," he said. "I'm hungry again. But no school, no deal."

She squeezed his hand. "Saving the world sounds like a pretty good deal to me."

They turned back to Malachi and walked back down the hall as the panel doors behind them clicked shut.

THE BENT GREENS

JASON A. BARTLES

2045 C.E.

Imelda stretched the letter taught between her fingers. The paper, practically transparent, almost reached its tearing point as she re-read the words. She and the others were being evicted from the homes they built and the land they revitalized. The letter warned they had less than two weeks to gather their belongings and leave.

It had to be a prank. A foreign country couldn't evict someone from their home. That's what the Southern States of America were now. A foreign country. The politics of it all was so messy, and even more so in this undesirable border land.

The state lines that used to divide West Virginia, Virginia, and Kentucky had lost all meaning in these parts. The Bent Greens was technically located in the Midwest, north of the Tug Fork, former Mingo County, Hatfield Territory, the land of Chief Logan. The allegiance of these lands flopped around like rainbow trout in a dry riverbed.

Imelda lowered the SSA letter. Her desk was cluttered with soil samples and art projects from the children. File folders overflowed with reports of their remaining food stocks, plans to weather-proof the cabins, and orders for their recycled handicrafts. The Bent Greens was supposed to be a refuge, a collectively built dam against the chaos of the world. A place where the patterns of the past would no longer define the negative limits of what could be achieved. She had come so far. They all had. Yet so much remained to be done.

She felt the rage sweats kicking in, and she pinched her shirt to fan herself.

"Knock, knock," said Peter with his singsong voice.

"Not now," said Imelda, more aggressively than she had

intended. Peter had startled her, but she knew better than to snap like that. "I'm sorry, Peter, I was dealing with something. What's going on?"

"It's ok. It's your three o'clock. They're here."

"Tell them I'll be right out."

"You got it," said Peter with a smile.

She was lucky he was here. As Imelda refocused on the task before her, she heard Peter inviting the newest arrivals to a cup of coffee and some cookies in the lobby. Meanwhile, she tucked the letter back into its threatening red envelope and skimmed the Garner family's file on her desk.

Imelda stood up, and at six feet tall, she had to duck a little to avoid grazing her head on the squat office door frame. The buildings that had been still standing upon their arrival all seemed to have shrunken. One day she would fix the door, but more pressing matters always got in the way. By now, it had become a habit to lower her head as she passed through any threshold.

In the lobby, the newcomers huddled together. The man was balancing a toddler in his lap while blowing on the hot coffee, and the wife was clutching a denim backpack close to her chest.

Imelda had carried a similar package while she and Dale wandered these valleys a few years back. Among their marriage license and other mementos, she safeguarded an old photo. Her mother towered above her wearing dark glasses and a floppy hat. Imelda had found the picture frame in a pile of broken glass and debris in her childhood home after Hurricane Maria, but somehow, it had remained undamaged. Through all the destruction and loss, the photo reminded her of the strength and resiliency of her community in the wake of disaster. If there were a fire in her cabin today, she'd run in to grab that bag, and she was sure the woman before her felt the same about her own.

"You must be Regina," said Imelda, extending a hand.

"It's nice to finally meet you," said Regina. She kept a tight grip on the backpack as she stood up and shook Imelda's hand. "This is my husband Walter, and our baby girl, Toni."

Walter remained seated, rocking little Toni in his lap, and nodded. "Thank you for having us," he said. He pressed his upper arms tight against his sides, probably embarrassed by his five-day musk.

"We're delighted you were able to make it all this way. It must've been a long trip from Raleigh."

"Two weeks. A few of the days on foot. But that's behind us," said Regina.

Imelda could sense the too-recent memories playing on repeat as Regina spoke. She might share some of them when she was ready. Walter handed her the baby and reached for the suitcase under his chair. Regina looked at Imelda as if to apologize in advance.

"We're grateful for anything you were able to secure," Imelda reassured her.

"It's not quite what you requested," explained Walter as he opened the suitcase and dug through the cables and replacement parts for solar panels. He pulled out a box with a few pairs of reading glasses and handed them over. Imelda tried one—blue and dark gray. Regina gave her a thumbs up, and Imelda folded them into her shirt pocket. Meanwhile, Walter kept searching for something at the bottom. "Even the best kept hives just aren't surviving the winters. We asked around for a week and nothing. I'm sorry. We did bring these." He pulled out some tattered workbooks.

"That's too bad about the bees," said Imelda as she accepted the consolation. "Three years now we've tried, but they always die off." She leafed through the pages. "Algebra workbooks?"

"From the school I used to teach in."

"That's very thoughtful of you. Thank you, Walter. We have a school set up, but Jacob isn't teaching anything that advanced yet. Maybe you can lend a hand with some of the older kids."

"I'd like that."

Regina let out a deep sigh as she rocked Toni in her arms. Imelda remembered that sense of relief, of having made it and not being turned away at the gates. They could settle in and try to start over in this unexpected haven.

"Should I give them the tour?" asked Peter. He was already sorting and arranging the supplies from the Garners.

"That's ok, Peter. I've got it. I could use a walk," said Imelda. Three syllables pounded beneath her temples: *e-vic-tion.* "You can leave your bags here. Peter will help you with them later."

Regina passed Toni back to Walter, and she put on her back-pack. They stacked their two other bags in the corner and followed Imelda out the front door.

* * *

Imelda squinted as the morning sun peeked its head above the eastern ridges. She made a visor with her right hand and waved the Garners out of the visitor's center. They stepped onto the former practice putting green. The astroturf, more grey than green these days, peeled away from the concrete. Another repair job perpetually postponed.

"If you haven't figured it out yet, this place used to be a golf course," said Imelda. "Though I can't imagine who would have traveled all this way to play a few rounds."

"What's with all the old tires, then?" asked Regina. The winding road that led through the mountain pass to the entrance was lined with tires, and all around the Bent Greens, more tires had been turned into planters, fences, and mulch.

"There's a layered history to this place," explained Imelda as they started walking. "We're deep in the heart of what used to be coal country. This golf course was built on the site of an abandoned strip mine. It's so unbelievable you couldn't make this stuff up."

"Nothing like destroying an ecosystem and then turning it into a wasteful resource pit," said Regina.

"No wonder the Earth's in the mess it's in these days," said Walter.

The four of them walked down a winding path lined with retaining walls. The beds held neatly arranged bushes, and perennials pushed through the soil. A flock of robins alighted on the rubbery mulch.

"This region had been on the brink of collapse for decades, and the always promised clean energy jobs to replace coal never materialized. The town emptied as jobs dried up and the infrastructure fell into disrepair. Around 2028, they did begin to convert this site into a tire recycling center. They shipped in thousands of old tires from all over the East Coast. Dumped them right over there." Imelda pointed off into the distance at the heaps of discarded tires sprawled across a few old courses. Some had been bailed, but mostly they were piled high and wide. "It might have worked had it happened ten years earlier. The funding and the people had disappeared before they could build the recycling plant. This place became a de facto dumping ground for everywhere east of the Mississippi. Out of sight and out of mind. Until we showed up five years ago. At first, it was bunch of displaced queer folks, but soon people from all over began arriving."

"Just like us, huh?" said Walter.

"Yeah, exactly. I know you were in Raleigh, but Peter only collects basic info on newcomers. What brings you here?" Imelda gestured down the ruins of the first fairway, pointing the way toward the cabins. In the distance, she saw a slender body speed-walking in their direction.

Regina and Walter exchanged glances, and then Regina spoke. "We tried to stay. We really did. We were mobilizing our communities to turn out and vote for climate policies, but after the U.S. fractured, there's been nothing holding back some of the states from completely disenfranchising the black vote. We are, or were, I guess, professionals. Even we couldn't stay on the voter rolls long enough to collect a ballot."

Walter cleared his throat.

"I don't mean anything by that," added Regina. "It's just we could invest time and money in trying to fight for access. Imagine someone without our financial stability."

"Were you there for the Black and Green marches last year?"

"Yeah," said Walter. "Regina was seven months pregnant, but we still went out."

"I felt like a cartoon character, one hand on my lower back, the other on my belly, waddling around," said Regina, presumably laughing to displace the other memories of that day. "I didn't make it that far, maybe two blocks from our front door."

"That still counts!" said Imelda.

"We were lucky, to be honest. We never made it to the State Capitol. Thousands gathered peacefully, until the governor sent in the guard. They killed thirty-five." Walter's voice turned shaky, evoking Imelda's own memories of tear gas and the shouts of frightened neighbors and friends as she protested anti-trans bills and marched in support of climate policies. Regina reached out for his hand, and Toni cooed and let out a little burp. The two of them recentered his attention. "There were minor protests after that, but the governor had won. People got scared. Organizers started disappearing. We didn't know if they had fled or had been arrested in the night."

"That's terrifying," said Imelda.

"It was, and with little Toni here, at a certain point, we decided we couldn't risk it. We couldn't let her grow up in a place like that."

"I still feel guilty," said Regina. "Leaving everyone behind."

"It's an impossible choice," said Imelda. "One you shouldn't have had to make."

"Too often, people assume the South is just a bunch of bigots, but they forget about the rest of us who get stuck living in conditions we fight every day to change," said Walter.

Imelda nodded as he spoke, trying to hide her concerns about the hatred and greed currently skulking around the perimeter of their mountain community.

"Good afternoon, my fellow BGs!" said Michi, relentlessly chipper. He sped through the rough. "Are these the newcomers?"

"That's right, meet the Garners."

"Welcome!" Michi waved as he passed them. Then he walked backwards without slowing. "I'd stay to chat, but I'm needed in the chicken coops. I'll come over to greet you properly this evening. Bye for now!"

"Bee gees?" whispered Walter.

"That's what we started calling ourselves a while back, since this is the Bent Greens."

"And he works with the chickens?"

"Michi is what we call a floater," said Imelda. "He's handy in about any situation. Plus, he gets bored doing the same job day in and day out, so he goes where he's needed."

"Speaking of work, how can we help?" asked Regina.

"Everyone works within their abilities for about six hours a day.

You can commit to one job for as long as you like, or you can float like Michi."

"It's really that flexible?"

"Yes. Except for a few times a year. During harvest season, for example, it's all hands on deck. And then in an emergency, we might ask people to redirect their energies."

"Sounds reasonable," said Regina. "Where should we start?"

"Usually, we suggest newcomers spend a few weeks learning the basics at a number of different jobs. We like to decentralize the knowledge, and it gives you a chance to meet everyone. Walter, if you want to work in the school, that's great, but if you'd prefer to try something new, that's great, too."

As they approached the greens at the end of the first hole, the tree line to their right side parted. They rounded the corner and two parallel courses opened up before them. Cabins dotted the former fairways. Each home was surrounded by black tire fences. Squishy walkways connected the cabins. On the old hazards, a bunch of kids were climbing on a rubbery jungle gym, running through an obstacle course, and swinging and see-sawing. Three adults watched them from patio chairs and tables also made from recycled tires.

"This is what we call the Camp. I believe there are three open homes. One is meant as a single, but the other two should have plenty of room for your family. There's also an available cabin up in the woods, if you prefer a bit more privacy."

"Where's that?" Walter sounded more interested in that option than Regina.

"If you look up there," said Imelda, pointing toward the low mountains. "Do you see the cabin with the light blue, pink, and white flag?"

"No," said Walter, shaking his head.

"Follow the end of the course up into the ridge."

"Oh, there it is."

"That's where Dale and I live. Now, keep your eyes at that height, follow them to your left, and you just might see the roof of a cabin peeking through the tree line."

"I see it," said Regina. "We could consider it. How much do they cost?"

"Cost? Oh, nothing at all. Later on, you'll pay it forward. Maybe you'll help us build the next few cabins for other families."

The words usually poured from Imelda's lips. She had repeated this conversation with each new arrival, but this time it felt like a lie. She promised a vision of the future blocked by the red envelope on her desk. She worried she was leading the Garners back into the line of fire they had barely escaped. And all the others, too. There were no guns here, no real weapons at all. The surrounding mountains provided some protection, but otherwise, they were exposed and defenseless in this man-made valley. Suddenly, visions of a massacre flared before her. Everywhere the bodies of her friends and loved ones. Blood streaming into the soil. Deep black smoke rising from the valley. Imelda heard her name. She foresaw herself holding Dale's dying body in her arms as he whispered her name once more.

"Imelda?" said Regina for the second time.

"Is everything ok?" asked Walter.

"Hmm?"

"It's just, you stopped talking for a second."

"Oh, no, it's nothing. Always so many things to keep track of, you know? What was the question?"

"We just move in?" Regina repeated.

"Yeah," Imelda swallowed hard as she returned to the real world. "You can try each of them out for a few days before committing. There's no rush."

Regina and Walter looked at each other in disbelief, but they would roll with it. Imelda called them over to an old placard. The faded map had been modified for the current state of the Bent Greens.

"You can see that about a third of the course is still the dumping grounds filled with tires. Another third has been converted into farmland. We're completely organic and mostly plant based. Way over there are the solar fields."

"You've really set up a whole world," said Walter. He studied the map, starting to commit it to memory, and then he saw an outlier, marked *JFC*. He smirked and asked, "What's that?"

"Juan Felipe and Cal," said Imelda as a grin blossomed. "You'll meet them eventually, I'm sure. Lovely couple. But prefer the company of animals to people. Moved way out to the edges of the farthest green. They're trying to domesticate foxes. It's a whole thing."

"I didn't know you could domesticate foxes."

"You still can't," said Imelda a bit smugly. "Though, I have to admit, they've come a long way. The foxes are friendly. They live in these enormous outdoor cages. You'll have to take little Toni to meet them and the other animals."

"Where did they find a bunch of foxes?"

"Animals just seem to make their way to J. F., and vice versa. Sometimes he just leaves for a few days. Then, out of the blue, you'll see him coming down the road to the visitor's center walking a fox in a harness as if it were a dog."

The three of them broke into laughter at the thought of it. Walter and Regina assumed Imelda was telling them a fish story.

"And Cal was a baker. He made the cookies we had in the office."

"I'm speechless," said Regina. "I assumed we'd be showing up to a slum."

"We have come a long way," said Imelda. "Well, this was a lot for your first day. I've got to get back to the office. Take a look at the houses, and Peter will help you move in. He can answer any other questions. But for now, just take a few deep breaths and relax."

"Thanks, Imelda," they both said. Regina helped Toni wave good-bye. Imelda gave her a wink and left them so she could figure out her next move.

* * *

When Imelda opened the door to the visitor's center, Peter was not at his desk, but the music was turned up loud. He liked to listen to the oldies, turn-of-the-century pop. He told Imelda it reminded him of trips to his uncles' condo in Philadelphia when he was a teenager. They'd get water ice and have rooftop dance parties. Imelda was never allowed to listen to that music. The things people used to get worked up over, she thought, as she poured a cup of coffee and walked down the hallway.

Peter was standing just outside the door to her office. He looked at her, then quickly away, then back at her again.

"I tried to stop him from going in," he said.

"Tried to stop who?" As Imelda pushed past Peter, she found Dale standing behind her desk holding the eviction notice in his hands. "Ow, dammit!" She had bumped her forehead on the door frame. Coffee splattered over her shoes, and little purple spots crackled in her vision. Peter ran to get some paper towels. She winced as she checked for blood.

"Are you ok?" asked Dale.

"It's just a bump. What are you doing in my office?"

"I came to drop off your lunch, but then I saw this." He shook the letter in his hand. "Is this for real?"

Imelda was about to interrogate Dale over his presence at her desk. Her younger self would have been shouting by now, but she took a breath and told herself this was not the real issue. She sighed, cleared a stack of papers from one of the chairs, and took a seat. The pop music echoing down the hallway faded into silence. She looked into the corner of the room as she gathered her words.

"It looks real. But could a foreign nation have the legal jurisdiction to kick us out?"

Peter returned with paper towels, two fresh coffees, and a little plate of cookies. He wiped up the splatters on the linoleum in the threshold. "Can I get you anything else?"

"We're good," said Imelda. The black coffee burned Dale's tongue, and he sat it down to cool. But Imelda didn't seem to notice. She guzzled it as if it had been sitting out for hours. "Thanks."

"You're welcome," he said and left the office.

"Normally, no," said Dale, returning to their conversation. "But the Attorney General of the SSA claims to represent the families who lived around here before the Constitutional Convention. He says they plan to return now."

"They abandoned this place. Not just this valley, but the entire surrounding region. It was a ghost town when we stumbled in, remember?"

"I'm not arguing with you. I'm just trying to figure it all out." Dale laid down the letter and sat back in Imelda's chair. It squeaked as he reclined, and he had to grab the edge of the desk to stop himself from rolling away on the slanted floor.

"If we were talking about the families who had gone off to Dayton, I might understand. But these people went south and became citizens of the SSA. They have no status in the Midwestern Federation now."

"Maybe we can call the governor?"

"Of West Virginia?" Imelda scoffed into the room. "Like he'd lift a finger to help out a bunch of queers and people of color. You remember what he said last time we spoke?"

"I do."

"Then you know he only tolerates us because we don't ask anything of him."

"And he buys our products."

"Right, our relationship is purely transactional."

"What about the Federation's Attorney General?"

"Let's see if we can get their office on the phone," said Dale. "Peter, can you come in here?"

"Coming!" Peter poked his head into the office too quickly. He had been waiting nearby.

"I need you to get the Attorney General on the line."

"Hmmm, yes, I can make that happen." Peter hurried to his desk.

"We should try to keep this quiet, right?" Imelda hoped to clear her conscience for having told the Garners to take a breath and relax.

"Just for a bit," said Dale. "If this escalates, we need to prepare everyone, be up front with them. But let's not create a panic before we have any answers."

While they waited for Peter, Imelda turned on the TV in her office. She flipped through the channels. Local programming, static, reruns of Battlestar, more static. Then she stopped on the news. "Another hurricane is smashing into the east coast, and floods are being reported as far west as the Ohio River. Protests continue from Minneapolis to Detroit as activists call for the Great Lakes to be opened for global water distribution, especially to provide some relief for Southeast Asia. But first, a new deal could see the boundaries of two of the five nations shifting in coming days," announced an all-too-happy voice.

"Hey, TV! Turn up the volume," said Dale.

Imelda leaned forward. The screen cut to recorded footage of the Presidents of the SSA and the Midwest shaking hands in front of their respective national flags. Cameras flashed nonstop, and a raucous chatter could be heard as journalists jockeyed to interview the two men. They smiled and waved at the crowd but took no questions. The camera returned to the announcer in the studio.

"The Southern States of America and the Midwestern Federation are reported to have reached an agreement. According to our sources, the former state of West Virginia, which was always the sticking point in the Midwest's Constitution, is to be divided up. The capital, Charleston, and all land south of the city will be annexed by the SSA as the South looks to renew its investments in coal. Territory to the north of the state capital will be absorbed into Ohio. Citizens of the affected territory will be granted one month to migrate north. If they remain, they will become citizens of the SSA, subject to its laws and authority. Big stuff, right, Jim?" The camera cut to another male announcer, who shrugged. "Up next, weather reports for the weekend. Right after this commercial break."

Imelda stared at the television, shaking her head. Dale gnawed on a pen cap as he reached for the letter. This just confirmed their worst nightmares. The SSA was preparing to take back the land Imelda and Dale had usurped from King Coal. His majesty's forces were on the rise. He was eager to reclaim his throne, and now he had the legal cover to do so.

Moments later, Peter returned. "I've got someone from the Attorney General's office on the line."

Imelda put them on speaker phone. "We've just seen the news report, and we don't know if you're aware of our situation, but we wanted to speak with you about an eviction notice we received from the SSA."

"Yes, we are aware of your situation. You should have received a letter from us as well, about a week ago, we believe."

Imelda turned to Dale and Peter, but neither could confirm the existence of this mysterious letter. "No, we didn't receive anything."

"I'm sorry to hear that. Mail deliveries can be so unpredictable way out in those parts. My apologies."

"What was it about?"

"It was a courtesy letter to alert you to the geopolitical situation that had developed. We wanted to provide you with ample time to relocate with as little disturbance as possible."

"As little disturbance as possible!" shouted Imelda.

"Fuck me," mumbled Dale.

"We realize this is a delicate matter, ma'am, but what you have to understand is that the situation is out of our hands. This was a decision made by the sovereign authorities of both nations, and beginning at 12:01 a.m. Central Standard Time on May 1, 2045, that land will become SSA territory. Now, given the—what shall we call it—diverse identities of many of your citizens, we strongly recommend you move north. This week if possible."

"You're just going to abandon us?"

"To the contrary, we can provide assistance if you come to our offices in Columbus, Ohio, or to any of the other capitals of the Midwestern Federation."

"Do you realize what you're doing? What we've worked to build here?"

"I'm truly sorry, but there's simply nothing else that can be done."

"Nothing else you can do, right."

"Please forgive my haste, but I must be on my way."

"Thanks for nothing," Imelda said, but the bureaucrat had already hung up.

Imelda paced her tiny office with clenched fists. Dale started to speak two or three times, but the words were not there.

"What can I do?" asked Peter.

Imelda paused. She massaged the bump on her head. Yellow and orange streaks flickered on the backs of her eyelids before turning to a fiery blue. She took a deep breath and opened her eyes. "Post a notice for a community meeting tomorrow at 8:00 a.m. The news of the treaty will already be spreading. Folks need to know we'll address this together. Dale and I will need some time to prepare. Ask Michi to meet us in our cabin after he helps the newcomers."

"You got it," said Peter with a grin, always eager to implement her plans.

Dale walked over, wrapped his arms around her, and said, "It'll be ok. We'll figure this out together." He raised himself up on his tiptoes and kissed her forehead.

Both Peter and Dale had placed too much trust in her, Imelda thought. All the BGs had. But right now, their presence was all that kept her from turning to ash and getting lost in the wind.

* * *

The next morning, Imelda and Dale arrived at the visitor's center to set out rubber benches and chairs, while Peter arranged napkins in a delicate spiral on a table with light refreshments. As the residents packed the putting green—soon they would need a more capacious commons—Imelda greeted them with a hug or a handshake and a gentle smile.

Chatter about the weather and the state of the crops floated through the air. The residents nibbled on wedges of bread and sticky buns. A small girl chased an even smaller boy who giggled as he weaved between legs in the crowd. J. F. and Cal lingered on the periphery.

On Imelda's signal, Peter rang a triangle bell, and everyone quieted down.

Standing before dozens of friends and loved ones, a chill rippled through Imelda's body. These people had survived untold crises before arriving at her doorstep—floods and forest fires, pandemics and tainted water supplies, police brutality and being shunned by their biological families. Over the past few years, they had become her family and her friends as they participated in this collective experiment. But now she had to bear the responsibility of delivering the bad news.

"My dear friends and fellow BGs, you've all heard that the Southern States plan to annex the land on which we live. But there is more: we have been told to leave the Bent Greens."

Imelda heard gasps and cries of no. The Garners, she noticed, stared at one another with heavy bags under their eyes. Peter raised his hand, anticipating the need to ring the bell again, and a few people shushed the crowd. Then a voice invited Imelda to continue speaking.

"Yesterday, I received an eviction notice from the SSA. They claim those who abandoned these lands more than a decade ago now want to return." While she spoke, something tickled at her ankles. It felt as if steam were rising from the ground below and seeping into her skin. She tried to ignore it. "However, we know the real issue is that the SSA is seeking a desperate and destructive short-term solution to its failing economy. They plan to reopen coal mines throughout Appalachia."

The BGs jeered and winced as the twin knives—being evicted, and being evicted *by* King Coal—dug into their backs. Imelda's shins simmered as the pressure began to build within her and within the crowd before her. She encouraged them while concealing her own rage.

"This morning, I come before you, not as the founder of the Bent Greens, but as your equal, to ask what course of action we should take. The floor is open."

At first, people turned inward to consult with their partners and their children, their best friends and their neighbors. Michi's lips were moving a mile a minute as he worked out different ideas in his head. J. F. shed a tear, and Cal pulled him in close. He whispered something to J. F. and to him alone. Meanwhile, Regina bounced baby Toni, and Walter stood with his arms crossed, staring at the frayed putting green. Dale rose as if to speak, but Imelda placed her hand on his shoulder to remind him to be patient, to wait until others were ready.

A middle-aged woman parted the crowd and walked toward Imelda and Dale. Genesee was one of the earliest walk-ins and the architect of the solar grid. She spoke to the crowd. "I've been here a long time now, and I consider this place my home. I'm not prepared to just pack up and leave. But before we go too far . . ." She paused and turned toward Imelda. "Is there a legal avenue we can pursue? A way to contest the decision or slow it down?"

"We have spoken with our Attorney General's office, and they made it clear that no help would be sent our way. They advised us to relocate. Point blank, they do not care."

"Nothing ever changes," said Genesee. "In that case, I believe we must defend our home, but what say the others?" She reentered the crowd and listened.

Cal cleared his throat, and people half-turned in his direction. "This sounds very dangerous, and scary even. What if we resettled somewhere? We learned a lot here. It wouldn't be as hard to start the second time."

Jacob spoke up in agreement. "We have to think of the kids, too. We can't put them in harm's way. I think we should pack up and leave."

"But Cal," said J. F., wiping his eyes with the back of his hand. "How would we get everyone out of here? And the animals? We don't have a way to transport them."

"I don't know," said Cal.

Over the years, Imelda had come to realize just how much J.F. loved those animals, especially the foxes. His connection to them ran deeper than the untapped veins of coal under their feet. The animals were their children, and no one could tell them any different. She was certain J. F. would lay down his life to protect them all, and Cal would go wherever J. F. went.

"Does anyone have suggestions about where we could go?" asked Michi.

"What about the Coastal Republic?" Jacob asked. "I've got family in Hagerstown."

"We checked into that," said Imelda. "But the Coastal Republic closed its borders six months ago. Their visa application process is egregious. Besides, we've all heard the stories trickling in across the border and the little that makes it through the firewalls. Things are getting weird on the coast." She tried her best to limit her comments to the facts—and to contain the fire rising inside her.

Jacob nodded, accepting her explanation.

"Other possibilities?" Imelda searched the faces in the crowd as people turned inward, presumably hoping for an epiphany in a nearby mind. Those who met her gaze shrugged or shook their heads. Others looked at the ground. No one could think of a decent

place, some unclaimed region where they could build this community anew. The Bent Greens, they came to realize, could not be easily
replicated. They had developed it over time, by expanding their
knowledge of the history of this land and responding to the changing needs of the residents, the animals, and the plants. The ideas
implemented here could be borrowed and repurposed, just as the
BGs had drawn inspiration from others. But the Bent Greens could
not simply be picked up and dropped down elsewhere. Their community was not a commodity. It was a dynamic work of art being
perpetually revised by a hundred hands.

"If I may, I know we've been here less than twenty-four hours,"
said Regina.

"You're a BG now, regardless of when you arrived," said Genesee. She and others gestured for Regina to take the floor.

"On the outside, there's nothing better. Not that we've seen. It
was a miracle we made it here, that we got out when we did."

"The Southern Army is no joke," added Walter. "They took off
their hoods years ago, and with all the new laws, there is almost no
one left in power to even slow them down."

"And most of the Midwest is only better in appearance with
their friendly surveillance state," said Regina. "I'm sure no one here
really thinks any of us would be much better off in Minneapolis or
St. Louis. We all know who the cops like to target, whether you're in
the north or the south or anywhere in between."

"If we stay, we'll be up against a ferocious force," said Michi.

"I'm just speaking for myself," said Dale, unable to keep quiet
any longer. "I'm too old to start over. And too stubborn to let them
drive us out of here so they can do what? Rip more coal from the
ground and destroy how many other lives as a result? This is our
home. And more than that, we're doing good work here. Restoring
the land, repurposing the tires. It's not perfect. We can't truly make
up for the centuries of dispossession and violence committed in
these valleys, but we can keep learning and improving. We can keep
trying to build something better in the rubble."

Jacob was among those who raised their heads and began to nod
while they listened to Dale. Soon more folks straightened their
shoulders, unclenched their fists, and stood taller. "Yeah," they

shouted. "That's right," they said. Their conviction began to chip away at the fear and uncertainty that had clamped its vice on the valley since the news conference the day before.

"We left one place already," said Regina. "The guilt eats at my insides. I can't do that again. I plan to stay."

"Me too," said Walter. "If others will."

"We're staying, too," said Cal, and J. F. nodded in agreement.

"We'll stay," said a voice.

"Us too," said another.

"Count me in."

Imelda couldn't find the speakers quickly enough to identify them. Their declarations of support overlapped with whoops and hurrahs. She could not contain herself either. She didn't want to contain herself. And when she stopped resisting, a heat wave washed up her legs, slowly at first, but then it picked up speed as it rose toward her abdomen. Faster now, it rolled across her chest and branched into her arms before crashing behind the bump on her head. When she exhaled, her breath fogged in the crisp morning air.

Imelda didn't know if she needed to take a seat or a few laps around the fairways.

But it wasn't just Imelda who was on fire. This conversation had sparked a drive in each and every one of the residents of the Bent Greens. They hey hey-ed and they ho ho-ed, chanting in their collective joy, as they committed to fighting for the lives they had built and for the futures they were protecting. They hugged their neighbors, and they stored some optimism for the battle to come.

Amidst the celebration, Imelda caught Michi's attention. During their strategy session the night before, they had hoped for an outcome like this. Now it fell to Michi to organize his peers. Together, they would build a massive barricade at the main entrance and, deep in the woods, shelters for the children and the animals. They would craft makeshift weapons and armor, identify rendezvous points, and make contingency plans. The Southern Army could arrive in as few as ten days.

Peter rang the triangle bell, and then he rang it again and again to allow Michi to speak.

"We've got lots of work to do," said Michi. "Let's get to it!"

* * *

Imelda woke to a dry throat. She had slept without dreaming, which was a welcome change. It had been almost two weeks since she had received the eviction notice that conjured up all manner of nightmares.

She checked her watch. 4:30 a.m. She should try to go back to sleep. She reached for her glass of water on the nightstand. It was cold to the touch, but there was no condensation. One little sip gave her a brain freeze. She pressed her tongue to the roof of her mouth—her mother had taught her that trick—and the pain subsided. Imelda placed the glass back on the nightstand. She sat on the edge of the bed, and her feet rested on the floorboards. They stung her toes, as if they had been covered in frost.

She pinched her arm to see if she was dreaming. No, it felt too real. It was real. She was awake now, and there could be no doubt about that.

She tucked her feet under the blankets and quietly blew her nose into a handkerchief to clear her sinuses. Dale turned over and snored. She inhaled through her nostrils and caught a whiff of something charred. The aroma almost delighted her. She breathed in again, deeper this time, catching hints of a definite smokiness. This smoke was not like that from a charcoal grill. It was chemical, tarry, and her mouth watered as her tongue absorbed the toxins.

Imelda shook Dale.

"What time is it?"

"Something's wrong! Get up."

Dale sat up. "They're here," he said abruptly, shaking away the sleepiness.

The Southern Army had arrived, and the BGs set their plan into action. While Imelda got dressed, Dale ran to the balcony and sounded the alarm. In the distance, three other bells clanged in the smoke-filled air. Everyone would be jumping out of bed, gathering their water and their first-aid kits. They would clutch their weapons and retighten their armor as they rushed their children to the shelters and headed to their assigned locations.

"The sky looks black," Dale shouted from the balcony. "Something's on fire."

"I can taste it in the air," Imelda responded. "It's the tires."

"Oh shit, that's not good. We didn't station anyone over there," said Dale as he ran back inside. He helped Imelda pull on her tire-leather vest and helmet. "They must have sent someone in under the cover of night."

While he got dressed, she grabbed her backpack. She pulled out the shiv she had crafted from her keepsakes—a shard of glass tied to a wooden handle. She had dismantled the picture frame carefully, hoping it would protect her now like it had protected the old family photograph, but she had to admit it did not look very menacing.

After she was dressed, she helped Dale into his armor, and the two of them ran down the forest path toward the cabins.

The playground had been designated as the rendezvous point for most of the adults. Imelda and Dale were greeted by a large crowd, including Genesee, Walter, and Regina. Imelda felt as if she could sense the adrenaline coursing not just through her own body, but through all of their bodies, as her community resolved to defend the Bent Greens. Following Michi's plans, Imelda and Dale started the march toward the barricade outside the visitor's center.

The air grew denser as they turned the corner and approached the greens at the end of the first hole. In the direction of the tires, a golden glare roared from within the blackness. Particulate matter and carcinogens billowed from the pits and blocked their way forward.

"Hold up!" shouted Imelda as they teetered on the edge of the chemical fog. A helicopter buzzed overhead, sweeping the valley with a spotlight that desired to blind and expose. "Pour some water on a shirt or a piece of cloth and wrap it around your mouth and nose."

The BGs covered their faces, and Imelda waved them deeper into the black smoke to hide from the helicopter. With their heads down, they held their breath and entered the veil. Step by step, they moved forward. Imelda and the others waited as long as they could, and then a few seconds more, before having no choice but to take in deep gulps of the smoke. Fumes poured into their airways and filled their lungs. Imelda and the others waited, half expecting to collapse right there. To have risked it all and to have lost in mere minutes.

"Dale?" said Imelda.

"I'm right here," he replied. "Are you feeling this?"

"I am."

The blackened air did not char or choke. It did not burn their eyes, nor did it singe their cilia. The tire fire smoke felt as fresh as the breeze blowing off a mountain stream. Those wasted tires were now breathing new life into the BGs.

"This smoke, I can breathe it like air," said Genesee in the darkness.

"Me too!" exclaimed another.

"Imelda, I can breathe ok, but I can't see you," shouted Walter.

"Follow my voice," Imelda said, but the atmosphere roiled around their bodies and carried away her words. She needed another solution.

In the corner of her eye, she noticed a glowing light. She looked down at the memento-shiv in her hand. She had intended it as a weapon, as a means of defending herself against her attackers, but the old picture frame had a different plan. The glass tip melted and, as she raised the unassuming wand above her head, it emitted a guiding beacon that pierced the maelstrom.

The BGs locked their eyes onto it. Imelda waved the light in a spiral. They understood her signal and followed her, undetected, toward the visitor's center.

* * *

The BGs emerged from the densest part of the smoke. They spread out across the old putting green and took their positions along the bouncy barricade. Tires had been stacked twenty feet high and five interlocking rows deep. They formed an arc that blockaded the road where it emerged from the mountain pass. This was the most likely point at which the Southern Army would try to enter.

"You made it," said Michi, amazed. He had been waiting for them, uncertain whether anyone could survive the trek from the cabins. But here they were before him. "How'd you get through all that smoke?"

"We could breathe just fine," said Imelda.

"You inhaled it?"

"Yeah, I can't explain it. But I feel powerful. Like I've acquired a resistance to heat."

Michi nodded. "The air did taste . . . not sweet, but appetizing in some way this morning."

"Maybe we're all just losing it," added Genesee.

"Lucky for us," said Michi.

The roar of military jeeps interrupted their attempts to figure it all out. The fleet screeched to a halt before the barricade. Soldiers jumped out, took defensive positions, and aimed their assault rifles at the wall of tires. Leaning out the window of the lead vehicle, an officer raised a megaphone to his cracked lips.

"This is your last—" The commander coughed. The scratch of wobbling mucus in his throat echoed into the surrounding hills. He lowered the megaphone, hocked up something, and spat it out the window before continuing. "Your last warning. We are the Army of the Southern States of America, and you are trespassers on this land. Surrender now, and you will be granted safe passage across the border to the Midwest. If not, we have been authorized to evict you."

While he spoke, Imelda and Dale climbed to the outpost near the center of the barricade. Imelda raised her glowing shiv to catch the attention of the soldiers and make sure they weren't ready to open fire at the slightest movement. They did not shoot—the Southern Army expected the usurpers to wear themselves out before crushing them—so she poked her armored head above the edge.

"My name is Imelda Etchepare, and I am the founder of the Bent Greens. Today I speak to you as a representative of the sixty-two adults and twelve children who call this place our home. You can threaten us all you want, but we plan to stay. I ask you now to leave in peace."

He raised the megaphone again. "Sweetie," he began, "I will do more than threaten you. Stand down now."

Imelda ducked below the barrier and turned to Dale and Michi for reassurance. They urged her to push back. "We will not stand down," Imelda shouted without showing her head.

"You were warned," said the commander. He called for just a handful of his assault troops to march forward.

"They're coming," shouted Michi to those stationed along the barricade.

They did not have many weapons. Suddenly, Imelda realized just how underprepared they were for this eventuality, but it was too late to turn back. Walter and Regina threw some rocks and bricks over the wall, but they clunked off the soldiers' helmets. Genesee was among those who dumped kettles of boiling water over the wall. That tactic sent the first, small wave running back to the jeeps for medical attention.

"We can't hold all of them back," said Imelda. "What are we going to do?"

"I think we can help," called J. F. as he and Cal emerged from the black smoke flanked by a skulk of foxes. There were more than two dozen of them in all. Their auburn fur rustled in the early morning air, and their eyes were aflame. They, too, were prepared to defend the Bent Greens.

As the second wave of soldiers approached the wall, the foxes leapt into action. They scurried up various points along the barricade and lurked just out of sight, waiting for the enemy to enter within striking distance. As fingers and tender necks poked above the barrier, the foxes sank their teeth into the soldiers' skin, and the BGs battered them with blunt tools and homemade weapons. The foxes bit deep, bit again, and then released their prey to slink away.

The BGs cheered and regained some courage as the second wave also retreated. The humans were not alone in this fight.

Then, a few soldiers doused the outside of the wall in kerosene, setting it on fire. They intended to smoke out the BGs and burn down the barricade.

But the commander was making an egregious tactical error, Imelda immediately realized. She could feel it in her bones. She could feel in all of the BGs' bones, strangely aware of a new connection between them.

As the barricade of tires caught fire and began to smoke and melt, the BGs' bodies transitioned. They studied the new shapes of their hands and chests before turning toward their neighbors. They noticed their eyes were no longer brown or hazel or blue, but had become more than human. They roiled like liquid rubber set on fire, and their insides turned viscous, yet remained stable. Those still near the barricade's base scaled the barrier, half crawling, half flowing up the side of it.

When they reached the top, they entered a collective equilibrium with the melting rubber down below and even with the burning tires way off in the pits. This chosen family now fought as one. Imelda sensed their senses. She knew their thoughts, and they knew hers. Together, the BGs stretched and funneled the tar through the air toward them. First, they pulled it into thin strings, but quickly, they learned to control ever larger quantities and to shape it as they saw fit.

Michi was the first to shoot off a little blob, and it splattered across a soldier's legs. Then he shot another, and another. Intuiting where their companions would aim, they worked as one, firing hot tar pellets at the invading forces. The foxes swished their tails, and the toxic fumes from the tar pits and the burning wall funneled above them. They directed carbon clouds toward the Southern Army, forcing them to scramble for gas masks.

"Open fire!" shouted the commander. His forces picked up their weapons and trained their lasers on the heads and chests of the BGs. King Coal's soldiers unloaded hundreds of bullets in seconds, aiming to kill. But not a single BG fell over dead. The soldiers jiggled their sites and double-checked their weapons.

Imelda and the others were surprised to still be standing. The bullets had hit their targets just fine. They tore through the tire-leather helmets and vests, sending ripples along the surface. But the burning tar inside each of the BGs swallowed, slowed, and stopped the bullets. Just as the BGs could direct the tar outside them, they instinctively manipulated the boiling rubber within their own bodies, pushing the bullets back out, completely unharmed.

"Get that helicopter over here," shouted the commander. "Now, dammit!" He had never met a civilian force he could not squash in seconds, a collective of people of any color he could not compel into obedience, nor a parade of trans and cis queers he could not dispel with a flick of his wrist. Imelda realized this fight was no longer just about seizing property. It was about his fragile ego.

But he had been too slow, and too filled with hate, to recognize the strength of the community before him.

Behind Imelda and all the others, thick streams of molten tires came pouring through the smoke cloud. A group of the BGs raised their arms, lifting the streams into the air, and others stood by, ready to direct the rubber with utmost precision. Acting in tandem, they aimed it straight down the barrels of the soldiers' guns and wedged it behind their triggers. They covered the jeeps in hot, sticky tar. Some, like Genesee, preferred to lob large cannon balls, while others, like Peter, threaded fine strings deep inside the jeep engines to jam up the motors. When the helicopter reappeared, it was Regina who knocked out the spotlight while Walter streamed tar toward the spinning blades. The pilot swerved just in time and flew away. Within seconds, every remaining weapon and engine had been rendered useless, and every soldier was either incapacitated or dragging the injured away from the hot zone.

The assault ended, and the BGs had won.

They defeated the Army of the Southern States.

Now, Imelda and Dale, J. F. and Cal, Genesee, Michi, Peter, and the Garners, and all the other BGs at the battle, even the foxes, towered over the army from atop the barricade. They controlled a tsunami of molten, smoking rubber just behind them, ready to unleash it at Imelda's signal.

Imelda called out to the commander. "This is your last warning. You are trespassers on our land. Leave now."

The commander came out from hiding behind his sticky jeep. He opened his mouth. "Swee—" he started to say, preparing to unleash a well-rehearsed string of slurs, but before he could even finish his first pathetic word, Imelda's rubbery arm lunged down toward him. She wrapped her elastic fist all the way around his throat and lifted him off the ground. She pulled him through the air and dangled him before her and the others on top of the flaming barricade.

"I told you to leave. And you will do so without spewing

another hateful word."

She lowered him and, when he was still about two feet from the ground, dropped him. He fell over as he landed, and he shuffled backward, trying to stand. Finally, he got up and rallied his defeated soldiers to retreat. They could not use any of their jeeps, so they ran away on foot, still unable to comprehend how any of this had been possible.

The residents of the Bent Greens watched as every last one of them rounded the corner and disappeared behind the mountains. The foxes leapt off the wall, followed by J. F. and Cal, and they ran down the road to ensure King Coal's troops had left for good.

Meanwhile, Imelda and Dale invited the others to make their way off the barricade. Their bodies still roiled with the forces of the earth inside of them. They would put these powers to one final use.

Michi, Peter, and the Garners ran toward the tire pit to quell the still-raging fire, and Genesee led the others to cleanse the greens of the toxic particulate matter spreading over the valley. Imelda and Dale stayed beside the barricade and smothered the fire. As it cooled, they parted the wall of tires in two and withdrew the solidifying mass like stage curtains reopening after a lengthy intermission. Despite the damage, both physical and mental, the BGs had sustained, this attack would not become a flimsy excuse for them to shut their gates to the world.

By day's end, their bodies returned to their fully human states. While healing their wounds, they would try to make sense of the mysterious powers that had flowed through them. In the coming weeks and months, they would shape the stories of that day, but when reporters arrived to question them about the wild and crazy tales spun by SSA soldiers, Imelda would deny it all. She did not have a clear explanation, but more importantly, she did not owe them one. Whatever their origin, the BGs were grateful to the powers that helped them save their homes, protect their loved ones, and hold at bay at least some of the forces continuing to threaten the entire planet.

Though the ability to think one another's thoughts had faded, their connections to one another grew even stronger in the aftermath. For now, and for a little while longer, Imelda and the others could get back to the unpredictable and never-ending set of projects that added up to the marvelous experiment they called the Bent Greens.

TWO MORE DAYS TO SYDNEY

BRANDON CRILLY

2045 C.E.

"You admired the view yet?" Mikayla pointed past the starboard railing at the thick plume of smoke in the distance. The setting sun created a hazy, orange glow that she was having trouble giving a specific name. "The Kurils are something else."

The woman clinging to the mast didn't look, making her smarter than most people Mikayla tracked, even as she tried to balance on the rigging ten feet above while holding a stolen kitchen knife.

"Captain says the eruption added to our trip." Mikayla patted the tranq gun on her belt, considering. "How did you want to spend your time before we hit Sydney?"

"Like I have any choice." The other woman's blouse had come partially untucked and she'd lost a flip flop during the chase. Combined with the way the sea breeze tangled her fine, silver hair, Constance Dunner looked almost nothing like her old cover profiles on *Business Insider*. Or Stewardship Earth's recent wanted posts.

"Didn't have to steal that knife," Mikayla reminded her. *Or push the server and make a scene*, she thought. Except if Mikayla had been more careful, Dunner never would have spotted her in the dining hall and panicked. They could have both spent the *Heron*'s voyage in peace, one of them believing they escaped prison and the other taking a break from chasing, for once.

Dunner flinched as the deployment mast released a loud pop and clang. Abandoning the tranq gun plan, Mikayla sprang forward until she was directly underneath her.

"Stay there!"

"Sure." Mikayla held her hands at shoulder level. She pointed at the rolled-up sail ratcheting up the mast. "You might want to come down, though. Ever seen this kind of greentech before?"

"I'm staying right here," Dunner said, as the rigging rumbled around her.

"Okay. You're the boss. I suppose."

The dark look Dunner gave her probably terrified everyone from interns to vice presidents back when she ran DFB Petroleum. Mikayla gave it three stars compared to other Powerful People Glares she'd received. Her last target, Dunner's former CFO, earned four before she caught him in Medicine Hat.

"I want off this ship."

"Really? I think it's pretty." Mikayla glanced around the *Great Blue Heron*'s polished railings and deck; the latter reminded her of coffee with more milk than average. She pointed at the other high-altitude sails tugging the passenger liner along and scrunched her face. "Is it those? They offend you a bit?"

"Quit. Stalling." Dunner jerked the knife in her direction, even though she was way too high to be a threat. "Bring me the captain."

The new sail clicked at the top of the mast and a warning klaxon sounded. "You sure you don't want to just come down?"

"The captain. *Now.*"

Her tone sapped a little more of Mikayla's limited patience. "Fine. Hold on tight."

Dunner's eyes narrowed, confused. Mikayla reassessed her intelligence.

The launcher at the top of the deployment mast boomed and Dunner cried out as her feet slipped off the rigging. The knife clattered to the deck, while Dunner landed in Mikayla's waiting arms. She stared open-mouthed as the massive sail unfolded above them.

Mikayla dropped her on her ass and pulled out her zip ties.

"Told you to get down," she muttered as she trapped Dunner's arms behind her back, mindful to make sure her wheezing came from catching her breath, not a broken rib or worse.

She could bind a prisoner without looking these days, so she let muscle memory work and watched the new sail. It finished unfolding to its full two hundred square meters of wind-catching glory and joined the six other high-altitude sails down the *Great Blue Heron*'s length. Each had been a different color so far, mostly shades of yellow or blue, but this one was closer to periwinkle and immediately Mikayla's favorite.

Once she got her breath back, Dunner spat something about buying Mikayla's life out from under her, which she ignored as she searched the woman's pockets. Contracting with Stewardship Earth protected her under the same UN decrees that were theoretically supposed to shut down DFB Petroleum and companies like it. Her parents and their commune of Californian refugees couldn't be touched, either. Otherwise, Mikayla wouldn't be out here, tying up another bounty instead of enjoying some peace for a change.

Dunner gasped, and Mikayla turned her onto her back so she could breathe easier, muttering an apology. Thinking about home wasn't a good idea. A crewperson peeked from a walkway nearby, and she waved at him to wait. Once she was certain Dunner didn't have any accomplices on board, she would give Captain al-Bukhari the all-clear and call a solarsled to the mainland.

She cracked the password on the phone in seconds and found messages to a contact in Sydney who planned to ferry Dunner "somewhere safe" from Stewardship Earth. Smart enough not to say where even on their Dark Web channel. Mikayla snorted at the other messages, all of them about secreting away bits of DFB Petroleum and buying new greentech firms, probably to help Dunner enjoy a comfortable life in hiding. High-powered CEOs weren't much different than warlords or crime bosses; once they fell, figuratively or literally, they thought they could recover and carry on like they had before. Case and point: Dunner's entire wardrobe in her cabin was crisp blouses and slacks, as though she was on a corporate retreat instead of running for her life. Too bad they were mostly neutrals.

"Thank God for solar, right?" Mikayla circled around to crouch in front of Dunner, waving the phone. "Have you spent any time away from this thing? Kicked back and read a book? Found someone to hook up with?"

A sharp crack in the distance drew her eye as a new jet of ash spewed from the Kurils. Maybe half the sun lurked behind their smoke now, washing the islands and the Pacific around them in a color she could finally name: *burnt* orange. She didn't like that she liked it, knowing what that smoke meant for the west coast back home. The *Heron*'s passengers had it easy, with only two extra days on the slow crawl from Juneau to Sydney. Her parents would be facing a week of smoky air on the Oregon coast, unless the rains came again and threatened flooding instead. She hoped they finished building the latest residence first. The newest Californians they took in were eager to keep busy, which helped with Mikayla working so much.

The solarsled was only two hours away. She would be on Sydney's catwalks with new Stewardship Earth money in her account before dusk. Most would get wired to her parents while she checked the SE servers for another target. Likely someone exactly like Dunner. There were enough of her type still loose in the world.

Except these days, it didn't excite her as much.

"You know a ship like this is a gift, right?" She didn't know if Dunner was listening. "Nothing but time out here, nowhere to go, and you're not even cut off from the world." She patted Dunner's phone. Its case was matte gray around the greentech charger, several shades darker than her hair. "I'm going to start chasing everyone onto ships."

And not be sloppy in the dining hall. She let herself relax too much, but stupid as that had been, she wanted the feeling back.

"Oh, enough," Dunner said, exasperation drawing the second word out. "Let's not talk while we wait for your pickup."

"Suit yourself." Mikayla tugged out her comm and opened an encrypted channel to the Stewardship outpost on Fuji. In the distance, the Kurils belched more smoke, turning the sky from burnt orange to darker brown, almost like the soil back home.

Her fingers paused. "You're the sort of one-percenter always tied to their work, right?" Dunner didn't respond, but Mikayla could feel the woman's gaze. "Me, too. I mean, minus the one percent, even if corporate types aren't nearly as good at hiding as you'd think." Not that it would matter to someone like Dunner. "Can't remember when I stopped moving last, other than a brief night here and there."

Surprising her, Dunner replied, "Sounds tiring." Without any sarcasm, which was impressive given the circumstances.

Mikayla pursed her lips. "Maybe it is."

She watched Dunner carefully as the other woman sat up. The tranq gun was within easy reach if she needed it, but Dunner already proved she wasn't much of a fighter.

"Time is something we all value." The ex-CEO flicked her chin at the sails. "That thing is a technical marvel, but do you remember flying? Spending the morning in New York, the afternoon in LA, and then back again like that." She snapped her fingers behind her back. "We *made* time back then. Now flying . . . your only economical option is a blimp."

"Sure. Making time without consequences." Mikayla snorted, even though she did remember being on a plane once or twice as a kid. Business class, even, which had been peaceful, too, except for takeoff and landing.

"Well, we didn't know that at first. That came with time, too." Dunner leaned forward. "Time to reflect, maybe? Instead of rushing?"

Mikayla stared at her, chewing over her words, hating that she was even listening to them. Her parents said something like that, after she asked them about taking in the first batch of Californians when they weren't even sure they could protect themselves. They had spent enough time reflecting, they said, and now they wanted to *do*, in a way most comfortably wealthy people like them hadn't. Mikayla supposed she joined Stewardship for the same reason, spending more time with people like Dunner than with her family.

People like Dunner, who had this expectant look on her face like she expected Mikayla to start crying.

So she laughed, loud and hard, right in Dunner's face.

"Wow. *Wow*, Constance. I'm disappointed. In myself, I mean. You, I'm impressed with."

She turned the comm's screen so Dunner could see her transmit the pickup request. When the ping came back from Fuji, the way Dunner's face paled reminded Mikayla of macaroon cream.

"Now you're really thinking about time."

Dunner was almost a dead weight as Mikayla hoisted her to her feet. She scooped up her tranq gun and the knife and nudged Dunner forward. The crewman nodded his thanks as they passed, and someone else cleared the corridors on their way back to Dunner's room. Mikayla stopped her before she could step through the open door, and she tensed like she expected that stolen kitchen knife to end up in her back.

When the zip ties fell from her wrists, she scurried forward. It only took her a second to realize her possessions were already cleared out, along with anything she might use as a weapon.

"Don't worry. You won't be in there long."

Dunner kept looking around the room, probably picturing something a fraction of the size, with bland stone walls and a force cage for a window, powered by the same greentech her type spent decades fighting.

"Thanks for that little talk. Dealing with people like you, I forget sometimes to think about the positives."

"Positives?"

Admittedly, she had to think for a second. "Never would've had a ship like the *Heron* without you people first."

Mikayla closed the door and sealed it with one of her adhesives before returning to the bow with some of the passengers. The sails tugged the *Heron* further away from the Kurils, while people pointed at the sun's amber halo around the billowing, pitch black clouds. Mikayla leaned against the railing, wondering what color would come next.

Four hours, maybe five, until this contract was fulfilled. An extra hour to book a blimp back across the Pacific—not only was it more economical, like Dunner said, but also faster than something like the *Heron*. She was willing to rush herself once more, if it meant reaching Oregon in enough time to help her parents and the Californians with final preparations for the smoke. Then she would stay a while longer, for a change.

But before that, she had two full hours to appreciate the view. Like Dunner said, it was all about time.

RING OF CONTAMINATION

ERNEST SOLAR

2046 C.E.

"The battle spread out over the whole
countryside, and the forest claimed more
lives that day than the sword."

2 Samuel 18:8, NIV

"We need that water and those trees," barked the corporate executive from SustainAble Corporation through the video screen.

Edward pinched the bridge of his nose as if he was willing himself to calm down. In a more even tone the woman from Sustain-Able continued, "Do whatever it takes to secure those resources."

The video screen went black.

Edward looked up from the monitor mounted in his vehicle and surveyed the handful of Humvees parked on the dirt road. He physically turned to take in the wall of vines, thorns, and trees blocking their path to the resources they were tasked to secure. The wall of flora was at least fifty feet high and stretched into the thick forest on either side of the old, rutted logging road. By order, his men had searched for a way around the blockade through the forest, but they were unsuccessful. Their attempts were riddled with mishaps and curious incidents that left them bewildered. In two cases, men had simply vanished while traversing the wall of flora.

In the simplest terms, the wall before Edward should have been an impossibility. Instead, he watched in amazement as the vines and roots crept toward the convoy of vehicles. The vegetation wasn't growing quickly. However, the vehicles and logging equipment needed to continuously fall back before being enveloped by the mass flora. Watching a single vine wiggle toward his boot like a snake, Edward's instincts told him the blockade was alive. Alive in the sense that it contained a consciousness purposefully preventing him from accomplishing the task of reaching and securing the freshwater lake in this region.

Edward combed a hand through his black hair and exhaled. *Impossible,* he thought. He whistled through his teeth to the foreman managing the lumberjacks across the road. The aged, rugged logger glanced over in response.

"Move back another hundred yards," ordered Edward.

The electric Humvees and cargo vans powered to life. In near silence, the vehicles reversed down the dirt road. Edward stood his ground even as a rhythmic and scraping reached his ears. The flora wall continued to grow crawling toward him, further stalling his objective. He was a lean gentleman in his late fifties who had witnessed a lot of change in his life. When he joined the military as a young man, he never dreamed the United States of America would dissolve into five separate nations.

That's when he retired.

He had every intention to melt into the backwoods of Oregon and spend the rest of his life fishing. Instead, he found himself recruited as a bureaucrat for the Western Republic of America, trying to secure freshwater resources and lumber. Then came along Ms. Rayne from SustainAble Corporation, the beautiful bane of his current existence. By the way she acted, you would think Ms. Rayne controlled the monopolistic company secretly weaving its way into power with four of the five American republics.

Edward smiled to himself. Not Texas, though. He knew Ms. Rayne was beyond frustrated with her lack of success in convincing the Texan Alliance of States to fall under her dominance. The American public, as Edward still saw them, needed to be fed, and SustainAble filled that role. Anyone in the *know* knew SustainAble's environmentally conscious, plant-based efforts were bullshit. To feed millions of ego-centric Americans, something had to give. That give was the environment. Edward had to give Ms. Rayne props, though. She weaved a convincing story that SustainAble was all about saving the earth.

A vine tentatively reached out and poked Edward's boot. Snapping him from his reverie, Edward stepped back in surprise. The vine retracted like a viper back into the mass of green flora that was crawling down the road like slow moving lava. Edward stood his ground a few feet from the thick wall of green overgrowth.

Birds flitted from branch to branch. Bees drank nectar from flowers. Butterflies drifted on the breeze. Squirrels and chipmunks skittered along the boughs. Mixed among the green wall of growth, Edward spotted the piercing hazel eyes watching him. The branches parted to reveal an older man in a faded kilt and an open flannel shirt revealing a black KISS t-shirt from back in the day. The sleeves of the flannel shirt were cuffed to reveal thick, muscular forearms bearing faded tattoos. The man's bare scalp was scarred and stained with sun spots. His white beard was thick and bushy like a woodsman. The man reminded Edward of an old Scottish Highlander he saw once during his travels.

Under his breath Edward mumbled, "What the hell?"

Stepping from the wall of verdure, the man leaned against a gnarled walking stick, exuding confidence in his casual stance.

Edward stepped forward and stuck out his hand in a friendly gesture. "Hello, my name is Edward, and I represent the Western Republic of America."

The weathered man simply stared at Edward, making no effort to shake his outstretched hand.

Edward let his right hand drop. He clenched his left fist to control his frustration. "The Western Republic of America needs access to the lake along this road."

The woodsman eyed Edward for a long moment. The walking stick twisted in the man's hand and ground the earth beneath its point.

"Please go away and leave us alone, young man." The woodsman's calm words registered just above a whisper.

Edward squeezed his eyes for a brief moment, attempting to stem the flare of instant anger igniting inside his chest. He was beyond frustrated and didn't have time for this nonsense. When he opened his eyes, the woodsman was stepping backward into the wall of flora. He watched as the vines and branches curled themselves around the man's legs and arms as if embracing him.

Edward stepped forward with a surge of irritation. He spat out, "Sir, it is your civic duty to allow us to pass in order to access the freshwater lake along this road for the citizens of our great nation."

As soon as the words left Edward's mouth, a huge tree bough covered in vines shot out of the wall of green growth. The vines wrapped around Edward's arms and legs like vipers and enveloped him. His scream of surprise was muffled by the vine twisting over his open mouth. Thrusted skyward, he was powerless, suspended in the air by the tangle of vines. His men shouted, their roars of dismay erupting from below.

The woodsman stepped surefootedly, like a squirrel, along the thick tree bough to where Edward dangled in the air. He leaned against his walking staff one more time and smiled at Edward.

The woodsman's green eyes sparkled with amusement. "We did say please."

Edward tried to maintain his composure as the vines tightened their hold of his body. His men continued shouting below him, but the woodsman never broke eye contact.

"We hold no allegiance to your supposed Republic. Our loyalty is to Gaia. We won't tell you again. For your safety, stay away," warned the woodsman.

Defiance flared through Edward's veins. He tried shouting "No!" through his strangled mouth. But the vine only tightened, causing him to gag. The woodsman's eyes filled with sorrow. With a slight shake of his head, he turned and disappeared into the foliage blocking the dirt road.

In a sudden movement, the tree bough slammed Edward onto the roof of the closest Humvee. The force of the blow crushed the roof. The vines and branches quickly retracted back into the wall of flora like scattering children. Edward was momentarily dazed but uninjured. He stared up into the clear blue sky, wishing he was fishing in Texas. His men scrambled to the crushed Humvee and helped him down.

He silenced the murmurs and shouts with an order. "Pack up. We're leaving."

* * *

Sage watched the young woman slip through the wall of flora as his uncle interacted with the government official. He flinched when the vines slammed the man onto the vehicle, but Sage knew the man would be okay. The vines would take the brunt of the impact. He diverted his attention to the woman and skipped along the branches of the trees as he followed her deeper into the forest. In order for the woman to slip through the barrier, she must have a relative buried within the boundaries of Lost Ways Memorial Garden. The trees only allowed kindred spirits of the bond to enter.

"Liza," whispered the trees.

The woman stopped and spun around, searching. The leaves and branches rustled in the breeze. Sage heard the whisper. His suspicion was confirmed; she was a relative to the trees. Perched on a branch high above the underbrush, Sage watched Liza move deeper into the forest. He wondered if she came on her own accord in search of tranquility . . . or for hostile reasons.

Hours passed as Sage followed Liza through the forest. Occasionally, she would pause and look around as if she was searching for something. Sage suspected her sixth sense was telling her that she was being followed. But he was always one moment ahead of her. Whenever she stopped, he would slip behind a tree or duck behind a tangle of brambles. He always knew which way she would turn or stop because he could feel the subtle shift of her weight against the roots under the soil. It was an unfair advantage, but it was his special connection to the trees in the wilderness.

When Liza neared the edge of the lake, he was almost discovered. Trying to get a better look at her, he clumsily tripped over a rock in the soil. Sage dove behind a thicket of bushes and ceased to breathe.

"Hello?" she called.

He watched her through the tangle of undergrowth and weeds. She was a slim and toned woman, clearly used to physical exertion. She wore shorts and a tank top with hiking boots. Her pack was light and suitable only for a day hike. Her fair skin was speckled with freckles. Her strawberry blonde hair was pulled back into a loose ponytail at the base of her neck. He found her attractive in a nondescript way.

When Liza turned her back to the forest and moved toward the lake, Sage slipped into the branches of the trees. Liza meandered for a time before deciding on a camping spot. She dropped her pack and started arranging stones for a small fire circle. Sage watched from the safety of the trees as she gathered small sticks and finished setting up camp. When she relieved herself, he turned his back. As she started the fire and prepared her dinner, he enjoyed the aroma of mixed scents. He enjoyed watching her.

With the sun descending in the western horizon, Sage slowly moved through the layers of tree canopy until he was sitting on a large tree bough just over the modest flame. The cool evening air, mingling with the warmth of the fire, played across his bare skin. Liza continued to busy herself, oblivious to his presence. But when she turned to feed the fire, her eye caught his shadowed form on the branch. She jumped back.

"Gah! What? Who?" Liza stammered as her grip tightened on the stick she held.

Sage simply smiled at her.

Liza's eyes narrowed. "Have you been following me?"

"Yes."

"Who are you?" Liza asked.

Sage smiled and asked, "Who are you that trespasses on our land?"

The woman straightened in defiance. "Trespass?"

Sage shivered as the sun dipped further below mountain peaks on the horizon. His skin cooled from the lack of sun rays. "We saw you slip through the barrier earlier today."

"Who's we?" asked Liza.

Sage tilted his head to the side in amusement. "The trees." And with that he slipped back along the tree bough into the shadows of the canopy.

Liza stared into the darkness for a long time before adding more wood to the fire. Sage settled against the trunk of the old growth tree for extra warmth. The silhouetted flames of the fire against the leaves lulled him to sleep.

When the sun crested the eastern horizon, Sage woke with a

renewed vibrancy. The light of the sun penetrated the green tint of his skin and warmed the cells of his body. He unfolded from his sleeping position and stretched to the morning star, working out the knots in his muscles. Through the leaves, Liza slept on a mat next to the cold embers of the fire. Quickly, he ran along the tree boughs to the berry field. Upon returning, he quietly slipped through the grass to display the bundle of berries and nuts on a leaf where Liza slumbered. With grace, he shimmied back to his perch on the tree above her camp and waited for Liza to arise with the new day.

Sage, like trees, didn't mind waiting. Trees, like Sage, weren't affected by time. Time was a human-constructed restraint. For Sage, the seasons offered the only concept of time he needed. He thrived in spring and summer. In the fall, he prepared for hibernation. During winter, his uncle and aunt watched over him as he lay dormant. His uncle called him a sapling. Which was true, considering he only had five rings compared to the Old Ones peppering the forest around the lake. As he waited for Liza to stir, he closed his eyes and concentrated on the subtle vibrations of the waking forest. The symbiotic relationship of the trees, creatures, and insects arose to a new day. Compared to the day before, when his uncle confronted the man from the Republic, the forest was quiet and content.

"Thank you," said Liza as she tossed a berry into her mouth.

Sage opened his eyes and gazed down at her. He liked how the early morning sun rays reflected off of her strawberry-tinted mane. He slipped out of the tree and joined Liza by the fire she rekindled.

"Do you have a name?" asked Liza.

"Sage."

Liza poured water into a metal cup and placed it in the fire to boil. "Are you one of the caretakers here at the garden?"

Sage squinted his eyes in thought. His uncle and aunt were the caretakers. What *he* was never occurred to him before. He tilted his head back to peer up into the canopy of trees. The branches stirred as the breeze rippled against his skin. He sensed the languid pleasure of the roots absorbing the ground water under the soles of his feet. He discerned the conversion of the sun rays into energy as his own life force. He was the human embodiment of the forest, not its caretaker.

Sage turned his periwinkle tinted eyes toward Liza, "We are the guardians."

Liza regarded him for a moment before busying herself with a cup of hot tea. A span of breaths passed before Liza asked, "Last night you said *we*, meaning you and the trees. What did you mean exactly?"

"We are one and the same," replied Sage. Before Liza could reply, Sage asked, "Why are you here? We only allow kindred spirits of those who are memorialized here to pass through the Wall of Rampant Renewal."

Liza dropped her gaze to the steaming brew of tea in the metal cup. She took several sips before answering Sage. "My mother. She passed about twenty years ago from cancer."

There was sorrow in Liza's words. She missed her mother. He could intuit her loss for the physical presence of her mother, but he did not understand how Liza did not feel her mother among the trees. Sage knew trees were never truly lost. They may lose their physical corporal body when their lifecycle ended, but they were always reborn among the saplings. And if her mother was buried here among the Memorial Gardens, didn't Liza detect her mother's spirit among the trees?

"Your mother is here," whispered Sage.

Liza peered at him, tears hovering on the rim of her eyes. Hope sparkled in her blue irises. "Yesterday, when I first entered the forest, I thought I heard my name. But I think that was just my imagination."

"It wasn't your imagination. We heard it too," confirmed Sage.

Sage struggled with the concept of a singular identity. His uncle and aunt had given him a name based on the seed pod he had emerged from. For Sage, all of the trees in the forest were his mother, father, brother, and sister. He understood his uncle and aunt to have unique identities similar to Liza. But he had never seen himself as an individual.

"Why was your mother memorialized here in the gardens?" Sage asked.

Liza's blue eyes brightened as a smile spread across her face. She pulled her hair free of her ponytail and gave it a fluff. Sage watched in delight as Liza pulled a pick comb from her bag and tended to her locks.

Liza began, "My mother was the Queen of Recycling! She recycled or reused everything. When I was in grade school she read an article one time that a family of four only produced one Mason jar of trash a year. Everything else was repurposed in some capacity. From that point forward her mission in life was to reuse and waste nothing. I don't think we ever got down to one Mason jar of trash a year. But we were pretty close."

Sage shifted his position to feel more of the direct sun on his bare skin. Liza eyed him as she pulled her hair back into a loose bun at the base of her neck.

Liza finished her cup of tea. "People often made fun of her. Asking why she put so much effort into recycling and reusing everything when a majority of people in the world embraced the 'throw away' concept. She would smile and simply say, 'I'm doing my part for Mother Earth.'"

"Mother Gaia," murmured Sage.

Liza nodded her head in agreement. "Yes, Mother Gaia, I've heard a lot more people using that term over the past few years." She paused for a moment and looked out over the lake. "At the time when she passed, seed pods were a new fad in the world of sustainability and environmental consciousness. My mother loved the idea of her body decomposing in the earth to help the growth of trees. It was the ultimate act of recycling."

The trees surrounding them swayed and shook. The rustling leaves and squeaking branches fostered a sense of anticipation.

"There must be a strong breeze up there to shake the trees so," commented Liza.

Still looking up at the canopy, Sage corrected Liza. "No, they're excited. Your mother is among them."

"Wait. What?"

"Trees can move on their own accord. Albeit slowly, but they can move," explained Sage.

"But what did you mean my mother is among them?"

Sage dropped his gaze to the surface of the lake. The memory of the ring of contagion was painful yet joyous to the trees. During that ring the merging began and he sprouted. Turning to Liza, he shared his story for the first time with an outsider. "Many rings before, uncle purchased the land around the lake to begin the Lost Memorial Gardens. When he chose the glacial lake and the surrounding land, it was mostly because of the serene beauty. He assumed the lake wouldn't be populated by the Columbia."

Liza interrupted, "The Columbia is almost dry. It doesn't even reach the Pacific at all times of the year."

"That's what uncle told us. The John Day and the Deschutes ran dry before we sprouted, because of the Columbia," confirmed Sage.

Liza stood and stretched her legs and back. Movement on the lake caught Sage's attention. He peered out and saw his uncle gliding across the water in a kayak.

"You'll get to meet our uncle," informed Sage.

Liza raised a hand over her eyes and squinted, gazing across the sun-reflected lake. Sage stood and ambled toward the water's edge. He stepped into the ankle deep water and grabbed the bow of the vessel, pulling it to shore. His uncle climbed out and grabbed his shoulder with a squeeze.

"Sage," he grunted.

Sage wrapped his arms around the man in an embrace. The uncle smiled. He then turned to Liza with a stern expression.

"My wife and I saw your fire last night from our cabin. We assume you slipped through the barrier during yesterday's confrontation."

Sage offered, "Her mother was memorialized here in the gardens."

The uncle grunted. "That's what your aunt and I figured." Still eyeing Liza, he continued. "You come to pay your respects? Or something more nefarious?"

Sage placed his hand on his uncle's shoulder. "Please, give her a chance."

Uncle shrugged off Sage's hand and brushed past Liza as he moved toward the glowing embers. He squatted down and added some kindling to build up the flame. He stared into the fire. "Sage, I told you. Humans aren't like trees. They can't be trusted on face value."

Liza resumed her seated position on the sleeping mat. She pulled a second mug from her pack. "Would you share some tea with me?" she asked.

Uncle shot her a look and grunted. He reached out a calloused hand and took the mug. Liza busied herself with preparing the water and herbs. "My name's Liza. My mother was buried here about twenty years ago."

"Peat," grunted his uncle, a little less harshly. "That would have been around the first planting when Lillian and I bought this land."

Liza reached across the fire and dropped a fresh bag of herbs into Peat's mug. "Your nephew was just telling me about this place." She dropped a bag of herbs into her own mug. "But we got side-tracked talking about the rivers in this region going dry."

Peat leveled his gaze at Liza. "You here about the freshwater like that bureaucratic asshole I had to deal with yesterday?"

"No."

Sage watched Liza hold Peat's gaze.

Peat grunted.

So Sage decided to ask what he knew his uncle wanted to ask. "Why are you here then?"

Liza poured the steaming water into Peat's mug and then her own. She shifted on her rump and held the steaming cup under her nose. Peering into the steam she stated, "The awakening."

Peat stared at the woman.

Sage's eyes darted back and forth between Liza and his uncle. He could sense that his uncle knew what she meant. He did not.

Liza peered at Sage and smiled. She then turned her steely gaze on Peat. She took a sip of her hot tea. "Well, either your nephew is one of the awakened, or he has a very rare skin disease."

Peat held her gaze.

Sage held out his arms and peered at the green tint of his hands and forearms. What was wrong with his skin?

Peat dropped his gaze and placed the mug on the rock in front of him. He interlaced his fingers, resting his elbows on his knees. He stared into the fire for a long moment before speaking. "His mother, my sister-in-law, was pregnant. She was crossing the street and got struck by a car by a fool on his smartphone. She died instantly. We were told her unborn child was dead also."

Peat's eyes darted to Sage. While watching Sage, he continued. "When transitioning from death to memorialization in the seed pods, time is of the essence. We encased her body in one of the first pods we received shortly after buying this land. We didn't know that her unborn son was still alive in her belly. We buried them both with sage seeds."

Sage listened in complete rapture as his uncle continued. Peat turned his gaze back to Liza.

"Fresh water is scarce. Countries have died because of it. The world's losing its glaciers, and everyone realized too late how many rivers relied on them as their source. Our lake"—Peat nodded toward the body of liquid—"is thought to be one of the few sources in the region." Peat shook his head, "But it's not. It's contaminated."

Liza sat up straighter. "Contaminated?"

Peat nodded his head. "Trench 94 from the Hanford Nuclear Site. Up river on the Columbia in Washington."

"How?" asked Liza.

"During the previous century, millions of gallons of radioactive wastewater seeped into the soil toward the Columbia. The pollution traveled downstream contaminating hundreds of miles of land, including the glaciers and our perceived oasis," reported Peat. "They claimed they were storing it properly. But they must have gotten lazy."

The three sat in silence for a bit before Sage asked, in a whisper, "But, what does that have to do with us?"

Peat gave the young man a sad smile. "We didn't know the land was contaminated. Just like we didn't know you were alive in your mother's womb." Peat shook his head from side to side in silent wonder. "But by the grace of God." He paused. "More like the grace of Gaia, you were preserved. Maybe through the contaminated land the trees in our garden achieved a new level of sentience. Or maybe it was something else entirely. They must have sensed your life force in the seed pod. Roots from neighboring trees bored into the pod and provided you the substance you needed to grow, just like your mother's umbilical cord would have done." He paused and reached out to hold his nephew's shoulder with a squeeze. "And then you *sprouted*. The seed pod emerged from the soil years later, and we found you within." Peat smiled at the memory. "Laughing and cooing."

The tree branches surrounding the three shook and rustled. The roots beneath the soles of Sage's feet quaked with a joy encompassing the whole forest. It flooded through him.

Liza peered up into the tree canopy in amazement.

Still gazing at the surrounding trees, Peat continued. "Shortly after you sprouted, we learned of your connection to the trees. We learned you didn't need food. Your sustainability comes from photosynthesis. Hence, your skin has a green hue to it."

"Amazing," whispered Liza. "You must be one of the first awakened."

Sage turned to Liza and asked, "What are the awakened?"

"Special individuals awakening to defend the planet against the corrupt devastation humans have brought upon our planet," shared Liza. "That's our running theory, at least."

Peat chuckled. "A bit dramatic."

Liza shot to her feet to challenge Peat. "Do you mock me?"

"Oh settle your ass, lass. You don't need to sell us on the importance of Mother Gaia. We already hold our allegiance to her. Without Gaia, we would all be dead on a chunk of rock drifting in the void." He waved a thumb in Sage's direction. "If anyone, this boy has more connection to Mother Gaia than you and I could ever dream. The trees possess a hive mind. He's a part of that hive mind. He understands better than any human could possibly imagine to comprehend."

Liza's anger physically deflated as she sank to the ground with her mouth open. Sage gave a bashful smile in hopes to comfort the woman from his uncle's verbal thrashing. He knew better than anyone that the only other person on earth who valued Mother Gaia more than his uncle was his Aunt Lillian. The trees shuddered, and nervous energy rippled over his skin. He turned, settling his gaze on the sky beyond the canopy of leaves. Sage didn't see any storm clouds or any other reason for the trees' anxiety.

Still concentrating on the warning rippling through the roots, Sage heard Liza ask, "Is that why he speaks in third person?"

Peat barked a laugh. "Yep."

Sage moved off toward the edge of the forest as the distress of the holt gnawed at his senses. Something was wrong. Sage could identify a surge in the trees' pheromones as he breathed. The roots under his feet vibrated with novel intensity. Sage's skin tightened, solid as bark. The boughs and branches vibrated in unison, warning the grove, preparing to fight an invader species.

Sage stiffly turned to face his uncle and Liza as they continued talking. "Uncle," he moaned as a falling tree crashed to the ground. Sage's face hit the leaf-strewn forest floor, and his world went black.

* * *

Lillian broke through the tree line into the clearing at a dead run on her steed, Loves to Laugh. She watched as Sage crashed to the ground like a fell tree. A moment later, the sound of giant saws reverberated through the forest. Lillian reigned in her horse before trampling the campsite.

"Peat!" shouted Lillian.

Peat slid to Sage's side and momentarily looked back at Lillian. She watched as her husband rolled the boy over onto his back and brushed the leaves and dirt from his face. Loves to Laugh trotted toward the pair, and Lillian slid from her mount's side. She watched as Sage shook and convulsed in a seizure.

A young woman stared up into the trees and spun in a circle, probably dizzied by the roar of chaos. She asked, "What's going on? What's that noise?"

Lillian grabbed her by the shoulder. "Your people are back with saws to break through the barrier."

But the younger woman did not back down. "Not my people! They work for SustainAble Corporation. They don't care about these trees and their sentience. They want to capitalize your land, water, and trees for their own profit."

Peat stood between the two women, physically separating them with his own body. "Liza, stay with Sage."

With a whistle, Peat's own steed, Grumpy, appeared from the forest with a snort. Peat grabbed the reins and stepped into the stirrup. Lillian mounted Loves to Laugh. Peat swung up onto his mount. He looked down at Liza. "We'll be back. Stay with Sage. You'll be safe with him."

Before Liza could respond, Lillian and Peat squeezed the sides of their horses and broke into a gallop. Grumpy, a brown and white American Quarter horse, was faster than Loves to Laugh. But Lillian knew Grumpy and Peat would never leave her behind. Glancing back over her shoulder, Lillian saw the trees shift and bend, shielding their sapling, Sage.

Together the four weaved through the maze of trees toward the barrier. The constant grinding and buzzing of the saws remained steady as the entire forest shook around them. In her peripheral vision, several treetops shuddered and crumbled. Lillian urged Loves to Laugh to run faster. The invaders had come down the same rutted dirt road they had used the day before. The barrier was thickest along the road, to discourage intruders. She took the lead from Peat. She wanted them to go wide around the barrier and slip through the trees to come up behind the invaders and their cursed machines.

Trees shook and shuddered around them as they raced through the flora. Even over the pounding of the horses' hooves, massive trunks screamed as they crashed to the earth. Tears stung Lillian's eyes. She refused to slow down. She and Peat broke through the tree line onto the dusty road. They leaned forward on their mounts, hoping to increase their pace on the open ground. The sound of the saws deafened as they crested the last ridge. Their eyes widened in horror as giant, gas-guzzling machines with saw blades as large as vehicles mercilessly chewed through the barrier and surrounding forest. Scores of men with chainsaws fanned out into the woodland.

Unabashed tears streaked Lillian's face as she watched the massacre of her home. Grumpy snorted and rose on his hind legs. Peat brought the horse down and charged with the ferocity of a Highland warrior. She watched as he clubbed the first logger he passed. Lillian spurred Loves to Laugh and charged after her husband with the shriek of a banshee.

As they dashed into the fray, the trees began to retaliate. Unsuspecting men were swept off their feet by thrashing branches. Loggers riding machines under the thick boughs were caught and left hanging in midair by their throats. The massive saws choked and sparked on rocks bursting unexpectedly from the ground. Vines strangled those who tried to flee the onslaught.

And then there was silence.

Lillian pulled Loves to Laugh to a halt. Peat pulled Grumpy up short. The forest was silent and empty. Slowly, as the moments passed, the forest started its timely way of reclaiming what had always been theirs. The horrid machines and saws disappeared under a new growth of underbrush and flora. The bodies of the loggers were left for the animals and insects, all peeking out of hiding to feast.

Lillian clasped Peat's hand, and together they quietly rode back to the lake.

* * *

Liza watched in wonder as several of the tall trees and shrubs along the lake's edge curved and curled over them. The branches and trunks created a protective dome, though it centered on Sage. The dome's interior was bathed in a green suffused light, the sun's brilliant rays filtered through the leaves. Liza cradled Sage in her arms as his body trembled and spasmed. His limbs and torso were as dense as branches and as heavy as a fallen log. But she suspected Sage was as supple and graceful as an old oak swaying in the breeze when he moved among the forest.

Sage's forehead beaded with sweat. His eyes frantically darted beneath his closed lids. Liza could hear the whirl of the saws outside of the protective dome. As trees cracked and collapsed, the ground shook beneath them. She had no reference of how close or far the suffering trees were in reference to the lake. She bent over Sage, rocking him and whispering in his ear, "Stay strong." As the screams of men intermingled with the cracking and splintering of wood, her whispers shifted to pleas.

"Please mumma, please," Liza whispered over and over again.

Then, silence.

It took Liza a moment to realize it, but the only sound she heard was her own voice. She uncurled from Sage to face the silence. He no longer trembled. Sage's body relaxed against hers.

He opened his periwinkle-tinted eyes and smiled. "They're gone."

Relief flooded Liza, and tears spilled over the rims of her eyes. She pulled Sage into an embrace and squeezed him tight. He chuckled against her body. She pulled back and beamed down at him.

With a grin in his voice he said, "Only Aunt Lillian ever hugs us that fiercely."

Liza hugged him again just as tight. The trees and shrubs unfurled themselves from their protective cocoon. The sun's yellow rays bathed them in light. Liza stood and stretched her entire body toward the sky. She felt Sage's eyes. Liza turned to him with a fresh smile.

"Thank you," he said bashfully.

Liza turned to him and grabbed both hands. "For what?"

Sage shrugged his shoulders. "For staying with us."

Liza chuckled. *Like she had a choice,* she thought.

The horses' neighing caught her attention. They both turned and watched as Peat and Lillian rode through the trees to the lake. Peat looked haggard, but the smile on his face spoke volumes. Lillian slipped off her mount and embraced Sage with a tight, powerful hug born of love. Sage let a giggle slip from his lips. Still mounted on his horse, Peat rubbed the side of the animal's neck with affection.

Liza asked, "What happened?"

"The trees fought back," answered Peat with a straight face.

Liza glanced up at the canopy of branches arching over the lake. The fading sunlight of the day peeked through the leaves. The quiet noise of the forest was slowly returning with the skittering of critters, the whistle of birds, and the buzz of insects. She looked over at Sage and Lillian, who were watching her.

"How did they fight back?" asked Liza. "Trees can't move."

Peat smiled, "Well to be honest, trees *can* move. But they tend to be really slow at it and when we aren't watching." He paused, glancing at Sage. "But these trees are a wee quicker and don't mind so much if we see them move."

Liza turned toward the forest, half-expecting to catch a tree mid-step.

Behind her, Peat finished, "I wouldn't expect them to let you see them dance anytime soon, lass."

"That's why you said the contamination was a blessing," said Liza, still facing the thicket of the trees. "The trees in this region are special."

Peat laughed out loud. "They are more than special. They are infused with the spirits of those buried here in the memorial garden. My theory? The pollution from Trench 94 mutated and merged the cells of the people buried in the gardens with the roots and seeds of the trees."

"Meaning the essence of those buried here is among the trees," offered Liza. Given the crazy things she'd seen and heard about over the past few years, anything was possible. It could be the radiation, or it could just be the Earth awakening, fighting back. Some of the stories she'd been collecting with Natalie . . . there wasn't an easy "scientific" explanation.

"Within the trees," corrected Lillian.

"That's why only family of those memorialized in the gardens can safely pass through the forest," continued Sage.

"Because the trees can sense the familiar DNA structure in the family member," concluded Liza.

Peat smiled. "Yep."

Sage reached out and clasped Liza's hand. "We are all one."

Liza smiled. He might look like a young child, but his mind held timeless wisdom. "We are all a part of Mother Gaia." It wasn't phrasing she would normally have used, but in the moment, with these people, it felt right.

"Yes," said Lillian.

Liza's eyes grew wide as a single thick tree branch stretched down from the canopy and reached toward her. Sage's hand was on her shoulder. His voice, near her ear. "Your mother is proud of you."

A single tear rolled down Liza's cheek. She reached out and brushed the velvety leaf with her fingertips. Sage urged her forward with a hand on her back. The branch gently wrapped itself around her torso and lifted her up into the canopy. Embraced among the young and ancient boughs of the forest, Liza remained, watching the first stars of night speckle the sky alongside her mother.

GARDEN OF EDEN

KIT HANSON

2046 C.E.

God is good.

Eden opened her eyes, taking in the sunlight drifting in through the curtained window of her cramped living quarters. She sat up in bed, stretching her arms to the ceiling.

Today is the day to share His word.

As she moved to stand, she felt something under her tongue and paused, frowning. Reaching up, she pinched her thumb and forefinger around the object, retrieving it from her mouth. There, glistening in the early morning sun, sat a small, black seed. Eden cocked her head, wondering where it could have come from.

No matter.

She quickly dressed, exiting her room to join the rest of her commune. They gathered together, chattering excitedly, moving aside for some of the men to lay out their freshly painted signs to dry. Turning to the right, Eden exited the common area, stepping outside to bask in the fresh air. Next to her sat small wooden sign hammered into the ground:

EASTBORO PENTACOSTAL CHURCH

As she twirled around to return to the church, movement near her feet caught her eye. She crouched, examining the grass. In a near perfect circle around her, small, pink flowers had begun to bloom, rapidly growing upwards. Reaching out, she brushed her fingers against the petals, amazed by them.

Yes, God is good, indeed.

Her pastor, the leader and Father of the church, poked his head

- 145 -

outside. "Are you coming, Eden?"

Eden smiled, pointing down. "Look, Father. A miracle. A blessing for our actions to come."

He followed her finger, his lips flattening into a grimace as he saw the flowers. "Maybe, child. The Lord works in mysterious ways. But then, so does the Devil. Why would God come to you, here in secret, to express his blessing? Beware Lucifer, the most beautiful angel."

Eden's grin faltered, and she lowered her head. "Right. I'm coming in."

* * *

An hour later, Eden found herself in the back of a black SUV, squished between two other women. They rode in silence, the men in the front driver's and passenger's seats occasionally exchanging knowing glances. The man in the passenger seat shifted at one point, exposing a long, sheathed knife at his hip. The sight of the metal gave Eden chills, and she shivered.

Something small crawled across her arm, and she absently reached down without looking to flick it away. She felt only skin, however, and glanced at the appendage, noting nothing on the surface. As she watched, though, one of her veins seemed to pulse a little, generating the crawling sensation once more. She blinked in surprise and alarm, but it settled, growing still.

"I don't know if I feel so good," she whispered to the woman on her left.

The woman smiled curtly, leaning over. "The Lord will provide. This is too big for you to miss."

"What if we're wrong?" Eden whispered. "There's a lot happening, things we still don't understand . . . maybe God wants us to . . . help?"

The two men glanced back at her, the expressions stoic, and Eden shrank back into her seat, pressing her hands in her lap. "Right. Of course. God is good."

A shadow out the window drew her attention to the passing tower, a large, metal structure with a slowly spinning fan up in the sky. The blades caused the sun to flicker, hurting Eden's eyes, and she turned away. Ahead, she saw the others gathered at the property driveway, picket signs in hand. As the SUV slowed to a crawl, two young men exited the house at the end of the driveway, cautiously approaching the crowd.

"Here," one of the churchgoers said to Eden, shoving a sign in her hands. "Hold this."

Eden looked down at the words on the placard.

YOU TAKE OUR WIND, YOU TAKE OUR SPIRIT! JOHN 3:8

"What's going on here, neighbors?" one of the house owners asked, nervousness infecting his voice.

Father emerged from the crowd, waving his beat-up copy of the Bible in the air. "What's wrong? What's wrong! You and your kind have brought a blight upon the land, and you have the gall to ask me what's wrong?"

The man glanced at his husband, raising an eyebrow. "My kind? We have names. I'm Teddy, and that's William."

"Yes, your kind," Father retorted. "As it says in Mark, 'what comes out of a person is what defiles him,' including sexual immorality. But you will bear the punishment of your private crimes when the Lord sees fit. We're here for what you've done to the Lord's sky."

The couple's eyes drifted upwards, at the spinning blades in the clouds. "You mean our wind turbine?" William asked. "We were offered a stipend to put it on our property. It's a good step towards clean energy."

"*Clean* energy!" scoffed Father, turning to the crowd. "These men think they know clean. They think they know purity. They think they know better than God!"

The crowd hissed and booed at the couple.

Eden shifted her stance uncomfortably, disquieted by the church's behavior, and something tugged at her foot. Looking down, she saw the grass beneath her had grown rapidly, wrapping around her ankles. She jerked backwards, startled, and ripped away the plant matter, almost stumbling against the door of the SUV. Where the grass had touched her, her skin had shifted to a forest-green hue. She rubbed at the marks, but to no avail.

"Climate change is a liberal hoax," Father lectured the two homeowners. "The wind isn't theirs to control. All you're doing is obscuring God's beauty, and casting a shadow over our church." He pointed down the road, where Eden's home could be seen as a speck in the distance.

Teddy crossed his arms. "We're not taking it down. Period."

William nodded. "We go to church too, you know. We know our Scripture. And we know our rights and responsibilities as God-fearing men."

"Fine," spat Father. "I'll do it myself."

He gestured at one of the men behind him, who produced a clear, fluid-filled bottle with a rag stuffed into the spout. They began to walk past the couple, towards the wind turbine. The couple intervened, shouting in protest, and two more churchgoers appeared, wrestling them to the ground.

"Wait!" Eden stepped forward, heart pounding in her chest. "Father, don't do this."

Father glanced over his shoulder at the woman, scowling. "Don't give in to the Devil's voice, my child."

"This isn't what God wants!" Eden argued. "God is good. I don't know what's right here, but I know violence isn't the answer."

"Is it not my right, as an emissary of God?" Father asked, gesturing to the crowd. "Leviticus 20:13 says, 'If a man lies with a male as with a woman, both of them have committed an abomination; they shall surely be put to death; their blood is upon them.'"

The crowd cheered in agreement.

"You're still on that Old Testament nonsense?" William laughed, his face still pressed into the ground. "Aren't you wearing a horrendously basic cotton-polyester t-shirt right now? That's also a no-no."

"Come on, the Bible is full of contradictions," his husband pleaded, making eye contact with Eden. "Jeremiah tells us to be stewards of the earth. So does Isaiah."

"Well . . ." Eden hesitated. "They're right about that, Father."

"You're letting their agenda corrupt you," Father growled, anger in his voice. "Step aside, child."

He turned back to the couple, rearing his leg up to kick the one closest to him.

"No!" cried Eden, stretching out her hand.

She felt a small pulse leave her body, rippling across the crowd like a whispering breeze. In the wake of the disturbance, thousands of small, pink flowers sprouted from the ground, growing until each was almost a foot tall. The flowers closest to Father grew longer, though, wrapping around his arms and shoulders before retracting, jerking him to the ground.

The men holding down the homeowners released them, standing in surprise. One of them retrieved a knife, heading over to cut Father loose, while the other glared at Eden. The homeowners leapt to their feet, running back to their house before the other churchgoers could recapture them.

As Father was cut free, he shouted to the crowd. "Eden has been possessed! The Devil works through her to stop us. Return her to The Lord!"

What? Eden thought. *No! I've done nothing wrong.*

The members of the church, those she'd befriended and grown with these last few years, turned on her in an instant, stalking towards her.

She backed away, arms raised, tears streaming down her face. "Please, everyone. God is good. I just want to do good, like Him. I didn't ask for this . . . whatever this is."

Some of the closest churchgoers reached out to grab her, but as their fingertips touched her, the flowers around them rapidly twisted and grew, flicking like a whip to crack against their offending appendages. Eden looked down at her own hands, now covered in some kind of green rash. Panicking, she turned and fled, making her way to the SUV. The crown stomped behind her, struggling against the field of living flowers.

Reaching for the SUV door, she pulled at it, but her finger crackled as the bones within snapped apart, almost as if they'd transformed into twigs. Eden cried out in surprise, but surprisingly found herself devoid of pain. She knew, deep down, she had become something beyond the limits of pain and fear.

Slowly rotating to face her would-be attackers, she raised her hands, the veins beneath her green skin rippling like worms. The flowers and grass stretched like taffy, encircling the feet of the churchgoers, who *did* cry out in pain. Doubt and panic faded away in Eden's brain as leaves overtook it, and she watched dispassionately as the stems and weeds washed across their legs, tying them to the ground.

Father tried to light the clear bottle on fire to throw at Eden, but her flowers had other plans. As the rag stuffed down the bottle's neck ignited, elongated flowers encircled his wrists, tightening. Father screamed in pain, dropping the incendiary device, and it shattered at his feet, engulfing him in flames. His cries grew shrill as fire washed up his body, but Eden barely heard it, examining her work with the others.

"Beautiful," she whispered, seeds pouring from her mouth and dropping to the ground, where they immediately sprouted into more flowers. "You're all so beautiful."

The crowd grew still as the plants reached chest, neck, and skull, locking them in place. Tears leaked from their eyes, and pink flowers appeared around them, covering their terrified expressions. Grass and flowers overtook flesh and clothes alike, and soon, Eden's former family seemed to be no more than a large garden.

My first garden of many, Eden thought, feeling as close to gleeful as she felt capable. *The world is my family now.*

"What in God's name . . ." she heard Teddy exclaim, and she turned to see the man and his husband standing at the edge of Eden's garden. "How did this happen?"

"They needed to see," Eden said, her voice shaky. "I loved them, but they needed to see. God is good." The flowers grew larger, sprouting thorn-like teeth, and a carnivorous urge overtook Eden. "You need to see it, too."

She took a step towards them, practically floating atop the flowers, and they backed away, faces pale with terror. More stems, thorn-covered and razor-sharp, emerged from the ground, capturing them, and they screamed for help. She hardly heard them, though; they were drowned out by the plant life inside her, the planet's very soul, weeping. Mother Nature cried out for justice, for vengeance, and Eden was nothing now but a vessel for her fury.

God *was* good, after all. It just turned out her "God" wasn't the one she expected.

THE LIFESPAN OF WILDFLOWERS

S.E. MACCREADY

2047 C.E.

Briar knew what it was like to watch the world decay.

Once the sun started fading, life held on a little tighter to things that, ultimately, wouldn't save it. Sunflowers turned their bulbous heads to search for each other. Sickly honey bees bobbed through barren fields wheat wouldn't even touch. Oceans lapped at the shores of beaches endlessly, without change, without rest, seemingly without the tides.

Briar wondered if the hidden sun worried about her.

If it saw the honey bees drop from the sky, skinny and twitching, to land on dry, dead grass.

If it tried to peer through the thick blankets of smog to watch as Earth slowly wilted. Slowly spun. Slowly descended into a rock, hurdling through space, in a sea of dead stars.

In a barren Georgia field, Briar reclined on her back, staring at the dim expanse of those dead stars.

"Ursa Major," she mumbled, tracing the little points of light with a finger. Off to the side rested Ursa Minor—the little dipper. Mother bear, and little cub, together in the sky. She traced the tail of the smaller constellation, leading her to Polaris—the North Star. When she narrowed her eyes, she could *just* see it. It was faint, and most nights it was hidden, but it was always there. She smiled to herself; if she could find that ever-present star, she would never be lost.

Get far away from the heat of the south. Keep heading north. Maybe there would still be wildflowers there.

But soon, it would be winter, and the further north she moved, the colder the night air became. It would be difficult to make it in time. She could be too late. There could be nothing to find at all. Most nights, she found she didn't care.

At night, it was easier to pretend things were normal.

She could sprawl out in barren fields, stiff stems prodding into her back, and imagine that somewhere, out there, was a different planet. It would be abundant with fresh water. It would be covered in vibrant fields of wildflowers, gently waving in an omnipresent wind. Bees pollinated those flowers, and soil grew fruits and vegetables—and grain.

The shifting of seasons wouldn't be so absolute. Transitions would be gentle. Slow. It could be a place where snowstorms were predicted—like they were when Briar was a child. Now, snow bombarded the north without warning. Winter, with a bite.

Unforgiving, and relentless.

After pulling herself to her feet, Briar followed Polaris. Soon it would be too cold to travel, and Briar had a long way to go. She hoped she found somewhere to stay when the weather grew dangerous. Maybe an old house to squat in, its inhabitants gone. Bigger cities had hostels, but how many rooms were left? She didn't know. And if there were spots left, she wasn't sure she wanted to stay there. They were overcrowded, so it was either share a bed or sleep on the floor. An empty house in the middle of nowhere was better than that; at least she had privacy. She slung her pack over a shoulder, humming softly to herself.

Find that field of wildflowers.

Then look to the sun and smile.

That's what she told herself.

But Briar knew that when the sun and the moon peered down from the heavens, they no longer cared for Earth.

* * *

"Tell me what you're thinking, Rosie," Briar said.

She was staring up at the afternoon sky, back pressed into a brittle bed of flower stems. She watched as clouds slowly drifted past. Not the puffy, white clouds from paintings or photographs, but stringy, gray clouds, all looming too close to the ground. Briar felt she might be able to reach out and touch them. But this far from any city, she could at least see the sky, however patchy it was.

The truth was, they weren't clouds. They were the tails of smog, drifting in from an SSA state, dissipating in the country air.

"You always know what I'm thinking," Rosie replied. Briar looked over at her twin sister. Rosie reclined on her back, arms folded behind her head. She squinted through the smog, as if she could see the sun, as if she could see anything at all.

"That one looks like a snake," Rosie added, pointing to the sky.

"They all look like snakes." But Briar smiled anyway, glad for the distraction. "Do you remember what mom used to tell us?"

Rosie shook her head, but a grin twisted her lips. A small, content grin. Innocent.

She wasn't there to watch their parents waste away. She didn't have tainted memories seeping into childhood ones. As a family, they streamed a church service every Sunday morning, pretended to pay attention, and stayed huddled within the walls of their farmhouse. Boring, but safer than going outside. They could control the purity of the air indoors, at least until the generator failed.

Fuel costed money. When money ran out, the only option was to watch as the fuel level decreased, watch as the gauge ticked down the weeks, days, hours, left in safety.

After taking a deep breath, Briar continued, "She used to tell us we were like flowers. We flourished in the sun. Pretty as pictures. Didn't take much to keep us happy, just warm sunlight and plenty of room to grow."

Rosie chuckled. Briar's mouth cracked into a grin. Not long into their childhood, they no longer had the sun. They stayed indoors, every hour of every day, and found new ways to flourish.

"I always thought we were more like weeds," Briar added.

"*Weeds*? We're not weeds."

"Yes, weeds," Briar said with a laugh. "We can grow anywhere. And when they try to get rid of us, we come back stronger than before. With a *vengeance*."

Rosie sighed, stretching her narrow fingers toward the wispy, gray sky. "It's been so long since I've seen a flower. Do you think they're out there somewhere?"

"If anyone can find them, I promise it'll be us."

* * *

Briar made her journey without a car. If told last year she would traverse the old state lines on foot, she would have laughed. There
were few things she loved more than the idea of driving—physical
exertion was not one of them. Of course, driving was too expensive.
Her family couldn't afford to purify the air of their house any
longer, fuel for a *car* was out of the question. She counted on one
hand how many times she was in a car. And, they were all when she
was very young, before she was old enough to drive.

A vague memory of being strapped into a car seat lingered
somewhere in her head, only surfacing when she passed a rusting,
abandoned car on the side of the road. It was always gone before
she remembered any more about it.

Her rules were simple. Travel at night, when nobody could see
you. Don't stray too far into cities. Don't answer any questions. And
the most important rule?

Keep moving.

Always keep moving.

That was easier said than done when food was hard to come by.
If she had the money, she could walk into any grocery store and fill
her pack up. But it was always the same food, made with whatever
was able to grow throughout the year. And each time she ventured
inside, the prices were always higher, the quality lower, until eventually, she gave up. She survived for a few weeks on the cans she
pulled from her apartment, and glass jars of preserves her mother
made for her three summers earlier. But once the nearby beehives
died, and the flowers left, berries followed soon after. No berries, no
preserves, and no way to make them.

Briar squinted at the horizon, watching the haze thicken as the
sun slowly rose.

East.

At least that didn't change.

Scanning the area around her, Briar searched for a place to bunk
for the day. With the rising summer sun, heat would follow.

Already, tendrils of thick red hair stuck to the back of her neck. That was another reason to travel at night—it was easier to breathe. The humidity was suffocating, and it only worsened the deeper into summer it became. Pair that with smog, and any extended time outside could kill her.

She longed for an air-conditioned apartment, energy consumption be damned.

But she pushed forward, tramping over the dying planet, drinking preserves out of a dusty glass jar. Briefly, she wondered if she was only on a journey to end up dead. It seemed the further she walked, the longer it took to get north. For all she knew, she was still in Georgia. Maybe even outside Atlanta. If she listened closely enough, perhaps she'd even hear the planes.

The sun rose higher, bringing heat the smog couldn't stifle. Briar consciously controlled her breathing. Deep, even breaths. Slow exhales. To keep herself calm, to keep herself grounded. She tightened her fingers around the straps of her pack, taking some of the weight off her back.

When she saw the large house in front of her, she walked faster.

Even from a distance, she knew it was empty. The fields she walked along looked like they hadn't been tended in years. Broken, dry stems stuck in the dry dirt. Tobacco, if she had to guess. Or cotton. Not that she could tell the difference—she never cared much for agriculture. Everything ended up dying, anyway.

Still no sign of flowers.

She climbed up the front porch stairs. They creaked under her weight, the wooden planks bleached from sunlight. There were no sounds from inside the house, and the long, winding driveway was empty. No cars, no people. She gently turned the doorknob; the house wasn't locked.

After a glance over her shoulder, she stepped inside.

* * *

The fact there wasn't water shouldn't have been surprising.

There were *wars* over fresh water. It was a resource more valuable than gold, more valuable than *oil*. But still, Briar stood in the abandoned kitchen, dragging her fingers through the dust coating the countertops, hoping that when she turned on the tap, water flowed from the faucet.

It didn't.

Sighing, she hoisted her pack onto the countertop. She rummaged through it, pulling out empty jars, and half-filled jars, and the shards of a jar that broke some point between her last stop and now. She looked at the broken bits of glass in her hand. The old Briar wouldn't have cared—she would have just traded it in for plastic. Or thrown it away. Maybe even carried plastic from the beginning. But the new Briar realized a broken jar meant one less container for food, or water, or whatever she needed to keep clean.

She kept the broken glass anyway, wrapping it with her extra shirt. At the very least, she could repurpose it.

Standing at the useless kitchen sink, Briar stared out at what may have once been a beautiful yard. Now that there was no one to tend it, it was dust-covered and full of the dried husks of plants. An old, wooded wing set still stood, though the paint was faded and chipping. Just beyond the yard, she recognized a dead field of wild-flowers, weeping and brittle. She wondered what color the flowers were.

She turned from the window and began rummaging through the cupboards. Most of them were already hanging open, their shelves bare.

"Tell me what you're thinking, Rosie," she said.

Rosie replied instantly. "You always know what I'm thinking."

Briar grinned, spying a lone jar of preserves sitting in the back of a cupboard. She pawed for it carefully, sliding it through dust and grit until it was safely in her grasp. She had to be careful with this jar; she couldn't let any more break.

"That one looks like a snake," Rosie added.

"You think everything looks like a snake." Looking over at her sister, Briar watched as Rosie wandered around the kitchen. She didn't touch anything, or look too closely at the pictures hanging on the walls, or the curtains dangling in front of the windows. "Do you remember what mom used to tell us?" she asked.

Rosie shook her head, her back to Briar, still wandering around the room.

"She used to tell us we were like flowers," Briar continued. "Pretty as pictures."

Rosie chuckled.

"I always thought we were more like *weeds*."

"*Weeds*? We're not weeds."

"Yes, weeds," Briar said, placing the jar she rescued onto the counter next to her pack. Using the bottom of her shirt, she carefully wiped dust from its surface, finding the jar full to the brim. A small mercy, but a welcome one. She continued, "Because when everything's gone, we'll be the only ones left. *You'll* be the only one left."

Rosie sighed, stretching her arms high above her head. "It's been so long since I've seen a flower. Do you think they're out there somewhere?"

"They better be, or else this is all for nothing."

* * *

If Briar didn't find water soon, she was going to die of thirst before she ever found a flower.

Two days. Almost two days since she last had water. She wouldn't survive a third, especially with the heat. She hoped the north would save her. But this pilgrimage? This journey, chasing an idea? She should have prepared more. Should have stocked up.

Should have done a lot of things it was already too late for.

Foolish. She was so very foolish.

If only Rosie could see her now.

She remained in the house for the day, watching as dark clouds rolled across the sky. They meant rain, but she didn't know if it would be safe to drink, even if she could collect it.

Acid Rain, her memory told her. Because of the pollution. Even as Briar watched the clouds, she knew they weren't normal clouds. As rain fell through them, it would pick up toxins floating in the air. It would turn the rainwater into something dangerous, something unfit for human consumption.

Rosie would have known what to do.

She'd always known what to do.

Even when they were young, Rosie had a flair for the scientific. She could tell you which plants were safe to eat, which water sources were trustworthy. Always running water, always *this* color of berry. She knew what the pH of soil had to be to sustain particular plants. Which ones preferred alkaline, and which acidic. But the rain? It changed the soil. It made it acidic. *Too* acidic. Every growing thing had a preference, and if the scale tipped too far in one direction, nothing would grow at all.

Most fields were left as a menagerie of old, dead things.

But Rosie wanted to change that. She thought, if the pollution could be lessened, then the rain would become neutral again. Soil could heal. Plants could grow. People wouldn't have to survive on water rations and processed, pre-packaged food, or food shipped in from distant states and countries, or on preserves made years ago, when the last of the berries were ripe for the picking.

At just eighteen, Rosie was invited to speak in California.

She was thrilled for the opportunity to share her ideas.

She wanted to save the bees. And maybe if she was born different, she could have.

For someone like Rosie, air was important. Childhood asthma never really went away—it only worsened with the quality of the air. She couldn't speak without coughing. She couldn't breathe without an inhaler.

And they always made sure to have inhalers—when they could afford them.

Someone like Rosie wouldn't survive at all when there was little air to breathe.

* * *

Voices woke Briar before sunset, her head spinning and mouth unbearably dry.

Her heart thundered in her chest. The voices came from below her, from the main floor of the house. Tucked away in an old bedroom, she hoped she could stay hidden. She had her pack with her, and every valuable thing she owned. Which, admittedly, wasn't much.

It was a lesson she learned early.

Never let your things out of your sight.

"It doesn't look like anything's left," a hushed voice said.

"There's always something," another replied. Cupboard doors slammed against each other as the duo rummaged through the already scavenged kitchen. They wouldn't find anything, Briar knew. She already found the preserves. And the only other cupboard that had anything was under the sink, full of cleaning supplies that weren't worth the weight to carry.

"We should check upstairs," the first voice said.

Crouching, Briar slid along the floor to the closet. It had a large set of sliding doors. Carefully, she pried them apart and crawled into the darkness inside. She perched against the wall, pack held tight against her chest. She released a shaky breath. If she were quiet enough, maybe she wouldn't be found. A fool's hope, because any scavenger good for anything would think to check the closet.

She cursed herself, glaring at the ceiling.

And then froze.

Above her was an opening.

It was a small square, barely big enough for a grown man to squeeze through. But for her tiny frame, there was plenty of room.

The floorboards in the hallway creaked as the duo moved closer to her hiding place.

As quietly as she could manage, she pushed herself up along the wall, back slick with sweat. From the heat or her nerves, she wasn't sure. She stretched, fingertips brushing the wooden frame of the opening. She wasn't strong enough to pull herself with just her fingers. Silently, she lifted her pack above her head and slid it into the crawl space. If she didn't have enough time to find a way up there, at least her supplies would be safe.

When she was a child, Briar loved to climb. Trees, fences, large bales of hay resting in fields—it didn't matter. When her family became housebound, her interest in climbing disappeared. You could only climb so high within a house.

Her house had lacked an attic. Or crawl space. Or whatever was waiting above her.

The footsteps grew closer.

"Think there are any blankets left?" the second voice asked. "Looks like there's a storm coming."

"We'll be gone before it hits." A pause. "Last room. Let's check it and get out of here. This place gives me the creeps."

It was now or never. Briar ducked low, hoping she would be silent and praying she was still strong enough. She pushed off the floor, jumping as high as she could manage. She clawed at the wooden opening to the crawl space, legs silently swinging beneath her. Already, her arms burned, and her fingers strained to keep their hold. She was small, but she still had to be strong enough to support her weight.

"Did you hear something?"

"Shh."

The door to the room opened.

She pulled herself up as fast as she could, trying not to kick the wall, knowing she may have to, to get the leverage she needed.

With shaking arms, she lifted herself just enough to get an arm on the wooden floor of the crawl space. She braced her elbow along the floor, stomach sliding against the rough wood as she slid through the hole. Splinters pricked at her skin, but she ignored them.

As her feet cleared the opening, the closet door opened.

"Nothing in here," a voice grumbled. "Not much left in this dump at all."

Briar held her breath, fingers trailing to her pack. With slow movements, she unzipped it. At the bottom of the back, she found the balled-up shirt, and the shards of glass wrapped tightly inside it.

She didn't want to use them, but she was glad she kept them.

"We should move closer to a city," the other voice said. "At least hostels have water."

"But the air is shit. We'd be stuck there."

The floor creaked as one of them stepped further into the closet.

Briar held her breath, hoping to whoever was listening that they wouldn't look up. That they wouldn't find her hidden above them.

She squeezed her hand, silently cursing as the glass bit into her hand. But she didn't cry out. If she did, they'd steal her supplies and leave her for dead, if they didn't kill her for them.

They walked away from the closet, slamming the door behind them. It bounced against the door frame.

Briar released a shaky breath and placed the glass on the floor next to her.

She waited for their retreating steps, for the creak of the hall, for the sound of them descending the stairs, and for the malicious slam of the front door before she dared to move.

She lifted her head. Brushing her thick hair out of her eyes, she glanced around her. Cobwebs dangled from the rafters, but there was no other sign of spiders. The webs were probably old; she couldn't remember the last time she'd seen a spider.

Spiders ate bugs. Without flowers, there were no bees and bugs, and nothing for spiders to eat.

Aside from the cobwebs, the attic was empty. Briar had the presence of mind to be disappointed. *Anything* would be helpful. In a pinch, even an old blanket could provide shelter. And if the stranger was right, and there was a storm coming, she would need to find a way to keep warm.

The sweat trickling down her neck mocked her.

She needed to find water.

If a storm didn't kill her, thirst would. The most basic of human needs, and the most difficult to find.

She began pulling out the items from her pack. Lining her possessions up in a row, she took inventory of her supplies. The jar of preserves she found in the kitchen two stories below her. The shirt, concealing the rest of the shards of glass. The old holotape. Two purification tabs, for when she found water. Even then, since the tabs were expired, they wouldn't work as well as she needed them to. But without them, it was worse. She placed them carefully back inside an empty jar. She retrieved and folded a pair of pants, balled up a dirty pair of socks, and finally found her sweater nestled at the bottom.

That was it.

That was all she had.

With shaky hands, she unscrewed the lid of the preserves. They weren't as sweet as the ones her mother made, but they were wet, and that was the most important thing to Briar. What little water the berries contained may be enough to help her make it through the remainder of the night. And after that, she didn't know. She was never one for planning, a trait now coming back to bite her.

She only allowed herself to drink a quarter of the contents of the jar, tucking the rest safely into her pack. She looked at the row of her belongings. She realized the pack contained mostly empty jars, but it would be enough. It had to be enough.

Briar wouldn't let herself think otherwise.

She repacked her belongings then slid back through the opening and into the bedroom. Slinging the pack onto her shoulder, she crept through the house. The floor creaked under her weight, and she prayed the strangers were long gone.

But she knew this place wasn't safe to stay in much longer.

She found it, the pair of strangers found it—there would be more people to stumble upon it. She may not be so lucky next time. If thirst didn't kill her, the next stranger might.

She paused at the front door. Was there a storm coming? She peered out the window, parting tattered blinds, but couldn't tell. The air was too thick, the window too dirty.

A risk. It would be a risk. She had to check, but there was no way to be sure.

Walking through the front door, she met sticky air. The sun was low in the sky. It didn't radiate brilliant golds and pinks like pictures showed. Instead, it was gray and muted—a sunset seen through a curtain. She watched as the sun fell, waiting for the stars. She knew which way north was, but she wanted to see Polaris, wanted to know there was something that would never change.

At last, the sky faded into darkness, and Briar turned toward Polaris, preparing to walk through the night. There was no sign of a windstorm. The environment was calm. Still. If there was a storm coming, she'd hear the rustle of dead stems and grass.

She heard nothing.

She huffed out an excited breath, watching as it fogged the air in front of her.

She exhaled again, the second breath easier to see than the first.

A chill slowly worked up her spine.

And then, the smallest of snowflakes drifted through the air. She stared curiously, then held out a finger to try to capture it. It was too far away, and too small to track. She dropped her hand and watched it plummet.

The ground was still too warm for the snow to stick. It baked throughout the day under the heat of the southern sun. But for the air to cool this rapidly . . . Briar didn't know the last time she saw snow in Georgia. The last time she saw snow at all was during a short vacation spent in the mountains of the Western Republic—when there was still an abundance of breathable air, and her family had the money to spend on time away.

She took a single step, leaving the shelter of the overhanging porch. Looking to the sky, she watched as snowflakes swirled through the air. They were larger than she imagined them to be. Fat flakes, looking too heavy to float. She let one land on the palm of her hand. It melted before she could get a good look at it.

How long was it going to snow? Briar wasn't sure. She didn't even have clothes warm enough for icy weather. But she had jars. An abundance of empty jars. Could she catch the snow? It would melt. But, that was perfect. She could purify it, or at least attempt to, and have something to drink for the next day or two. If she rationed, maybe even longer.

She looked over her shoulder. Maybe the house had something large for her to catch snow in. An old pot, or even a baking sheet.

A gust of wind knocked Briar into the porch.

She tripped over her feet, grunting as she sprawled across the worn steps. Small stones embedded her palms. A new wound cut across her knee. Wincing, she adjusted the pack on her back. Luckily she fell forward; she didn't know what she'd do if she broke more jars.

She curled her hand around the railing, pulling herself to her feet.

When she turned to look at the sky, she no longer saw Polaris.

She could see nothing at all.

The world was white. When she squinted through another strong gust of wind, she realized she couldn't see two feet in front of her. The icy air curled into her chest, froze tears to her eyelashes, and threatened to send her toppling to the ground again.

Anything she found to catch the snow would never stay on the ground. The wind was too strong, and nothing she had was heavy enough to stay rooted.

She wasn't heavy enough to stay rooted.

In the back of her mind, Briar knew the two strangers were trapped outside. Like she would be if she didn't act quickly enough.

She raced back into the house, closing the door firmly behind her.

The glass panes rattled in the windows. Whether from the wind or the force she closed the door with, Briar wasn't sure. She wrenched her pack from her shoulders, sagged against the door, then slid slowly to the floor. She kicked her shoes off, watching as they flew across the room.

If it kept snowing like this, she'd never make it north.

She'd never find water.

She'd never find a flower.

"Tell me what you're thinking, Rosie," she said softly.

From inside her pack, Rosie's voice answered, "You always know what I'm thinking."

Unzipping her pack, Briar pulled the holotape from its hiding spot. She set it on the floor in front of her, waiting the few seconds it took for Rosie's image to flicker to life. It was a life-like image. Thick tendrils of red hair, sun-bronzed skin. If she didn't already know the difference, Briar would think she was real.

"That one looks like a snake," Rosie said, gesturing to nothing in particular.

Briar didn't respond to the projection of her sister. Instead, she sat against the door, pretending she was here. She would know where to find water, she would have thought to pack warmer clothes. She would have rented *some* sort of transportation, and they would already be stargazing under the northern sky. Maybe up there, Ursa Minor wouldn't be so faint.

Rosie chuckled.

Briar pursed her lips together.

"*Weeds*? We're not weeds."

Briar still didn't respond. There was no need to. The conversation was always the same, no matter what Briar said to urge it in another direction. It was only a memory of a conversation years ago, when the two of them believed the world could be saved.

When they believed the world was worth saving.

From before her sister went to California, only to be suffocated in a room with other people who claimed they wanted to save the world.

Rosie sighed, stretching her arms high above her head. She reclined, staring up at the white ceiling. "It's been so long since I've seen a flower," she said. "Do you think they're out there some-where?"

Silence. Then, "No, Rosie. I don't think there's anything to find at all."

* * *

Briar stood in the backyard.

Disoriented, she raked her eyes over the dry bushes. They had splotches of frost covering their branches. Her tongue was limp in her mouth. Too dry. Thirst was going to kill her. The storm the previous night lasted hours, until Briar no longer saw the point in waiting for it to stop. She was stuck in this house another day, waiting out the heat of the sun and hoping for the chill that came with night.

Not that it mattered now.

She was going to die here.

She was stranded, hiding from the heat, without food, and without water.

Three days. She was now three days without water.

Around her, she saw death. Dry stems. Dirt that wasn't anything more than dust. The chipping paint on the old swing set, the rusty chains and cracked rubber seats that hang from it. Within her, she felt death clawing. Her eyes were too heavy, her limbs too weak. She could barely support herself enough to make it outside. And really, what was the point? There was nothing here for her. No more food hidden in the house. No blankets tucked into an old linen closet.

She shifted her gaze past the rose bushes, past the swing set, and to a square plot of land edged in a rickety, white fence.

Walking toward the garden, she didn't let her hopes get too high. The dry grass crunched under her shoes. She walked briskly, rubbing her arms to chase away a morning chill. Even with the sun rising in the sky, ice still clung to every breath.

It was a Georgia summer, and winter was coming much too soon.

Briar swung the gate of the garden open. Inside were heaps of broken vines, empty stalks, and dirt that looked like it would blow away with even the smallest of breezes.

Still, Briar stepped past the gate.

She recognized some of the plants. The vines were from watermelons; the stalks were from corn. The ground was littered in broken pea pods, wasted and decayed.

It was a private garden, Briar realized. The crops she passed the previous day—the tobacco or cotton—were for public sale. This little plot fed the family.

But with that realization, came the knowledge that they must have kept their private stores somewhere.

Which meant preserved food.

And hopefully water.

A small smile lit up Briar's face, but she didn't let herself get too excited. The house was empty; any other building on the property was probably empty as well. But if it were a root cellar, it could go unnoticed. She flicked her eyes around the yard.

Hoping.

Praying.

There, tucked along the rotting fence, was a set of flat wooden double doors, barely noticeable through a thick layer of dust.

A root cellar.

She stumbled toward it, not caring as stems and vines scratched her ankles. She was no longer Briar—she was a dying human, desperate for salvation.

At the set of doors, she made herself pause and catch her breath. She didn't know whether the air was thinner, or if she was just having difficulty breathing.

After inhaling a deep, raspy breath, she knelt and pried the doors open.

Silence. The cellar was silent. She walked down stairs made of packed dirt and rock, minding her footing, and keeping a hand trailing along the wall. Salvation was so close she could almost taste it, and she didn't want to risk falling from her excitement.

She needed to qualm that excitement.

There could be nothing at all down here.

But still, she walked.

And still, she hoped.

The room at the bottom of the stairs was dark. She dug around her pack for the holotape, powering it on. Without her voice initiating the recorded memory, all it would do was glow. But right now, that was all she needed it for. It was a source of light, bright enough for her to grasp the surroundings.

The image of her sister illuminated the cellar, but she didn't make a sound.

Shelves lined one wall, filled with a small row of what she hoped was preserves. She walked toward them excitedly, using a shaking finger to wipe the dusty film from the glass.

They were full.

She breathed rapidly, counting the jars.

Seven. She had seven more jars of preserves.

Her eyes drifted lower. On the lowest shelf were more jars. She knelt, counting five more.

But when she wiped the grime from them, the liquid inside was clear.

"Water," she croaked.

Inside her pack, she found the purification tabs. She wanted to drop one in one of the jars of water and chug it as fast as she could.

She knew that would be a waste.

One tab could purify more than what was in the jar. One tab could be enough to purify *three* jars. And if she drank them as quickly as she wanted to, she would only make herself sick.

She tucked three jars into her pack and stood slowly. There had to be a pot inside the house large enough to fit the contents of the jars. If she couldn't find one, she'd use the sink. She had to make her tabs last as long as she could until she found more.

When she turned, heading for the kitchen, she saw them.

Another neat row of jars along the floor, tucked into a corner so dark she almost missed them. They weren't filled with any liquid. Instead, when she unscrewed the lids, she discovered they were seeds, kept safe from the harsh environment in their little glass prisons.

She had water. And if she found a place safe enough to stay, she had a source of food. Could she wait long enough for the seeds to grow?

Would they grow?

She didn't know, and she was hesitant to let herself think they would.

Placing the seeds back into the dark corner, she told herself she'd come back for them, when she knew what to do.

She didn't spend much time wondering what happened to this farming family—the family who thought to hoard seeds and water, and preserve any fruit that wouldn't last. As she climbed the stairs, she silently thanked them. They helped a stranger they would never meet. Above ground, one look at the plants around her revealed what she needed to know—the local climate couldn't support them anymore. The family moved where their livelihood could grow.

That didn't leave a lot of places. Perhaps they went to work at those ultra-corporate SustainAble greenhouses in the Midwest. They were gigantic glass structures, harnessing solar energy and creating an environment suitable for growth, but they'd also destroyed all connection to nature itself.

But for that to work, you needed the sun. And every day, the smog in the air seemed to grow thicker, accented by the rising temperatures.

We drove cars less. The thoughts came haphazardly. *We no longer burned coal. We turned to solar and nuclear energy.*

But it was already too late.

The damage was irreversible.

In the garden, Briar ran her hands through the soil. Her fingernails snagged on small bits of rock and roots that lay too close to the surface. If she closed her eyes, she could pretend they were alive. She would care for them, and they would feed her. She reached into her pocket, setting the holotape on the ground next to her.

She closed her eyes.

She continued digging in the soil with her opposite hand. It was beginning to feel warmer, more *alive*. She knew it was only her mind playing tricks on her—her thirst was making her hallucinate. She needed to purify the water in her pack. She didn't have time to day-dream.

"Tell me what you're thinking Rosie," she said.

"You always know what I'm thinking. That one looks like a snake."

Briar smirked. She played with the roots twisted around her fingers. They moved with her. They followed her hand as she pulled away. It felt like a snake. Maybe in some ways, it was. "Do you remember what mom used to tell us?"

Briar already knew Rosie wouldn't answer. She never did.

"She used to tell us we were like flowers," Briar said. "Pretty as pictures. All we needed was a little sunlight and plenty of room to grow."

Rosie giggled.

"I always thought we were more like weeds."

"*Weeds*? We're not weeds."

Briar slowly opened her eyes. Vibrant green leaves swayed in the light breeze, glistening faintly under the dim sun. In her hand was the watermelon vine. It was thick and healthy, heavy in her hand. It was beautiful; she couldn't remember the last time she saw something so full of color.

She didn't know what to make of it. The pea pods were now plump and hanging from the sprawling vines. Beside her, a water-melon larger than her head rested. There were whole stalks, heavy with ears of corn ready to be picked. The garden was cluttered with plants she didn't recognize, and many more she hadn't seen in years.

Rosie sighed, stretching her narrow fingers toward the gray sky. "It's been so long since I've seen a flower. Do you think they're out there somewhere?"

Briar looked down at her hands, noticing the dirt crusted under her fingernails.

She stood and spun, looking past the yard. Her breath caught in her throat.

The field of wildflowers was in bloom, a hundred different colors stretched as far as she could see.

Briar smiled at the image of her sister. "Have I ever told you about the weeds?"

REAL-TIME

J.A. KITS

The problem with time is that it moves in one direction. You can circle back to a memory or imagine a future for yourself, but you remain on a linear path. Real time moves forward at a constant, steady pace.

My relationship with time has always been twisted; obsession with the gaming world will do that to you. As a teenager, I spent hours at my screens, fingers clicking away, jaw chomping old gum, knees bobbing with the momentum of my battles. Inside the world of a game, time ground to a halt. Power and opportunity—limitless. Outside, the world could fester with crisis, but not in the world I inhabited.

One day, time caught up with me. In adulthood, set to inherit a world I didn't create, I had nearly managed to wield time for my own purposes. That's when they came for me.

Time caught up with me and said, "David, we need your technology to change our world. We need Real-Time."

* * *

Ten years ago, Real-Time was more myth than reality. Now it's debuting on the world stage. Not because I'm particularly interested in sharing it so publicly; rather, it's under threat of being shut down. Apparently, the prize for being too successful at fighting the climate crisis is being called on to justify one's actions.

Today Real-Time will have its moment in front of the world, and tomorrow I'll either be back to work or behind bars.

"Mr. Schmidt—"

"Please, call me David," I interrupt. I didn't make it this far to be patronized like some petty government intern.

"David," the head of the inquiry begins, "it is our understanding that Real-Time has, until now, been funded by the research and development department of an organization referring to itself as The Network."

Ava rolls her eyes, and I lean closer to the microphone, trying to hide my own annoyance at such formalities. "That is correct, Madame Chief."

"And from which nations does The Network gain its funding?"

"Classified," I respond. "The Network is a decentralized entity. We don't claim allegiance to any one nation. We believe we are citizens of the world."

A wave of chortles rolls around the inquiry board.

"With respect," I continue, "the climate does not see borders, and the planet does not have member and non-member citizens."

The room falls silent and I lean back in my chair to pour water from a polyhydroxybutyrate (PHB) bio-plastic bottle. At least one of the American nations got a few things right since I left.

In the silence, my last statement echoes in my head, and I barely recognize my own voice. I haven't been back to this region in ages. Even my accent has developed into a unique mix and, just like all my Network colleagues, no one can place my origins. All is as it should be. I, like everyone, am a citizen of the world.

"And Mr . . . David, you are convinced of Real-Time's impact on the climate crisis? You can quantify such things?"

I was hoping they'd finally ask about our results. It's the inspirational part.

"You want proof? Consider this: I took a solar-ship across the ocean to get here, and though it was a rough ride, the pre-boarding report stated Earth is now entering the first year without a winter hurricane in recent history."

The ride across the ocean was actually smoother than expected, not only due to a lack of hurricanes. The new solar-ships are designed to slice directly through waves with a slick, partially submersible hull. Besides advances in green-travel, I've been through enough hours in Real-Time. My brain is accustomed to rough travel.

"Skeptics would say this data is a fluke. One year of cooler temperatures a healed world does not make," the Chief investigator counters. "In fact, over the course of a century, we should expect a year or two on the 'better' side of the bell curve."

"I'll leave the specifics of climate data to the IPCC, ma'am. But as far as ocean temperatures are concerned, there are a few members of the audience who could speak about the billions they've donated towards efforts to stabilize ocean temperatures."

How many billionaires have ridden Real-Time through a hurricane, I wonder.

"Former billionaires you've tortured with your program!" exclaims a board member speaking out of turn.

"Torture?" I question coolly. "Billionaires have historically been able to move inland and ignore the damage of climate change, whereas communities whose lives and livelihoods are being destroyed have no such privilege."

"And you feel it is The Network's job to educate these individuals?" the Chief investigator questions.

"Often, wealthy individuals will have zero understanding of the difference between a bad storm and a category six hurricane. Therefore, they do nothing to change their ways. Real-Time educates them about the disparity. Our motives are in-line with the work of groups like Stewardship Earth. They capture the billionaire climate criminals; we re-educate them."

It was always a delight dropping some wealthy asshole on their yachts in the tropics, where they'd normally be enjoying vacation, before having Real-Time pummel them with wind and rain until the end.

"I am not a proponent of torture, and I disagree that Real-Time falls into that category. However, our method has had an undeniably high success rate. Where the climate crisis has failed," I continue, "Real-Time has made experience the great equalizer."

Fighting about the ethics of solving the climate crisis was never my dream. Hell, the only reason Real-Time even exists is due to my express wish to escape this damned world.

* * *

I was lucky, spoiled even, growing up near Silicon Valley in the shadow of America's tech gods. Internships in my younger years brought in sufficient cash to buy the latest gaming equipment, but more importantly, I could keep my finger on the pulse of the tech world as it advanced. When they formulated a new glass composition for phone screens, I was the first of my friends to own a device displaying it. Whenever they shrunk the microprocessors down to yet another unfathomably small size, I was at the office early, ready to get my prototype installed. The tech world was my safe haven; no one there talked about what was happening to the shrinking coastlines or in the air. We barely even noticed when the US fractured into multiple nation-states. If it didn't affect our work directly, it wasn't on our radar.

Sometimes we talked about China, water needed for making microchips, but it always felt distant and nebulous. We kept our heads down in Western America's tech valley, all while continuing to siphon money off the wealthy few who, like me, enjoyed a narrow view of existence. At the top no one tells you what to care about, and when you have money, you're not beholden to the rules: government or nature's.

Good money, and continued protection from an outside world I had no interest in changing, kept me focused on my passion project well into my twenties. It started as a conversation among like-minded friends—could we expand on our desire to escape the real world and create a true virtual reality platform? The idea calmed me. I would provide a new space for others like myself, sick of all the doom and gloom that came along with the climate crises of our time.

Beyond climate emergencies, the chaos of the US finally reaching its breaking point meant my peers were all disillusioned. Again, we saw our government officials more concerned about their own image than our future. Some my age fought back, joining movements or adapting to nomadic life. I needed modern comforts and instead used the chaos as an opportunity to continue creating a different, digital reality.

The trick to creating alternate worlds we wanted to live in was access to data, and there was no better place to tap into user data than at the heart and soul of human connection—the Western Republic's servers. Physically, they sat off the coast, in military-grade floating fortresses. But thanks to the few significant connections we had in the tech world, the data was only a click away.

We started with personal data, building training sets centered around our interests and desires. Asking ourselves what sort of worlds we wanted to inhabit was the easy part—anywhere but here. The challenge was making it feel real to our brains. I could get us close with the right algorithm, capturing the desires of any one user and providing enough fine detail to produce an illusion of reality the brain couldn't decipher from real memory.

Once people believed, truly believed, they were in a different world, I'd be set financially for life. Sure, it was selfish. But selfishness is a matter of opinion. It wasn't my fault the world was burning, I was still just a kid when my country decided to postpone indefinitely any chances of righting its negative climate impact. I didn't choose to burn coal or keep designing new gasoline engines. If the world was circling the drain, I would enjoy a few breaths of success before the end.

Working with a big data set is much like creating a piece of art. You start with a data dump: raw material, as much as you can capture, forms the foundation of a user's world. Then you chisel away, using training sets to teach the program not just who the user is but what they want next. One of the big lessons we learned early on was that living in a perfect world doesn't cause enough of those real-feel brain synapses to fire. I'm no biologist, that was Braydon's job, but I know data and I can tell when an algorithm doesn't work. The human brain rejects the idea that everything can be perfect. It wants challenges and problems to solve. Reality is imperfect, so we needed to make sure the worlds we created were imperfect too.

Kennedy and Teagan set out to design a flawlessly realistic shell for our program—what users would see during the experience. Visuals are always important, and we knew sharp images that didn't buffer near the edges would be essential. The eyes are the windows to the imagination, but the brain makes it real. So, as I worked and reworked the data, I discovered how to make the VR program not only show a world the user wanted to live in but also learn with the user as they experience their new existence. With active adaptation, the entire experience would be made real to both body and mind.

The first few patrons, tech valley upper management types willing to provide both feedback and funding, asked for mundane worlds: a bigger mansion with more beautiful women, champagne and utter simplicity. It bored us all. What's worse, my program couldn't learn.

I tried a plethora of worlds myself, tweaking details large and small to challenge our creation. Once, I was a young girl living in the mountains of Colombia, helping my family with menial daily tasks. Another time, I was an astronaut working with the Chinese and Arab Republic moon base to explore possible life on exo-planets. I wanted to see if, without having ever been those places myself, the program would make it real for me.

The trial phase was exhausting. We didn't lack funding or enthusiasm from our small, wealthy tech community. Rather, the team started to fall apart. Ayla met a guy who wanted to help the climate refugees in Canada, so we lost a programmer. Rian died of a drug overdose, a side effect of the VR world he was inhabiting. It worked too well, and he was convinced of his invincibility. By the time we launched Real-Time, I was both President and CEO. Everyone else was too changed by one thing or another. The climate crisis was making its way into my personal sanctuary, my work and world, and I didn't appreciate it.

* * *

"I'd like to circle back to The Network's origins, David. Did you found the organization with money from investors?"

"Forgive me, Madame Chief," I say, "but I'd much rather stick to Real-Time's successes than speak about my origin story."

But I can tell you. I didn't make The Network. It was the other way around. They made me; at least, they forced me to see my world for what it really was and to live in the present reality.

About a month into the limited launch of Real-Time, they showed up at my house. More specifically, they were waiting inside when I arrived home. They called themselves The Network.

I'd never heard of them.

I couldn't place their origins from look or accent, but I quickly learned they were a conglomerate of mismatched soldiers—thrown together by circumstance, galvanized in the fires of climate change, and utterly resolute in their mission.

As they circled me, outlining the purpose of their uninvited visit, jealousy stabbed me. My team had fallen apart as soon as we exposed ourselves to the real world again. Now the real world stared me in the face, demanding I rejoin it.

Their initial attempts to get me on board included invoking honor and sympathy. They'd clearly not dealt with many Gen-Z adults from the Americas before. Next, they tried appealing to my humanity—didn't I want to facilitate change, give our planet a fighting chance? Then, they tried to appeal to my ego. Be an early adopter of our plan, David. A plan so ridiculous I had to stifle laughter when they first outlined it. Real-Time could already give me everything I wanted, freedom to live in a world under my control, tailored to my liking.

When dialogue failed, they took to threats. If I wasn't going to help of my own free will, they'd force me to comply. Not very polite manners from a group of supposed environmentalists. I thought these world-wary climate organizations were full of pacifists who lit candles and worshipped Gaia—which I found to be a ridiculous name for Earth. But this one was full of ex-military from every corner of the livable world. They had seen enough and, under the discreet support of unknown benefactors, had been tasked with taking matters into their own hands.

When it became clear saying no wasn't a feasible option, if I wanted to remain among the living, I gathered the necessary equipment and allowed them to load me into a transport. Their guns didn't scare me. I grew up in America, after all. If they wanted to shoot me, steal my tech and sell it off in Asia, I'd already be full of bullets. Instead there was something rigid and respectful about them. Somehow, they'd found a way to want to live in the real world, in real time. At first, I hated them for it.

* * *

"The board would like to bring up the case of Mr. Sampson—a captive of yours from four years back."

"Yes, Mr. Sampson was a client who experienced Real-Time."

Mr. Sampson disappointed me, but then he wouldn't have been my client if he hadn't. We sent him a warning letter, backed by the reputation of The Network, and we even roughed him up once or twice when he was visiting a mistress. Still, Mr. Sampson loved the feel of gasoline under his pedal foot more than he loved our planet.

I'd been adapting my platform in secret for half a decade and already been listed as dead to the world for just as long. I didn't miss my old life. But I was also starting to believe we could invoke real change and save this planet. I'm not sure which fact made me sadder in those days.

In the beginning, I mulled over whether or not forcing people to live a simulated reality where they suffered their own climate-crimes was unfair. In my tech world bubble, I hadn't given much thought to human rights. It wasn't a theme I incorporated into my own view on humanity. I figured, because the future had already been stolen from me, my only concern would be self-preservation. Working with The Network for half a decade changed me, though.

Each day showing up at headquarters to continue perfecting Real-Time, I'd curse The Network in secret—damn this organization, and fuck me for wanting to try.

At the time, Mr. Sampson probably wished I didn't try quite so hard.

* * *

"I thought you Americans promised to stop torturing your captives," spits Mr. Sampson in a thick British accent.

I've taken to calling them clients. It sounds nicer than "prisoner" or "political enemy."

"If you wanted to avoid this process," I respond while attaching his VR headset to suit, "you shouldn't have taken your illegal, gasoline-fueled Ferrari for a spin in the countryside last week. Or flown your private jet to meet your Saudi friends."

Mr. Sampson is screaming about scorching hot air before I even leave the simulator room. Poor rich bastard.

I've experienced the tortures of Real-Time's augmented VR myself on many occasions. Call it penance for years wasted before caring. The agony when my brain tells my lungs they're burning, that my skin is melting off, is a rush and a punishment. No matter how many times I go in, I still can't tell if it's reality or not. That's exactly why The Network chose me. The only way to learn about our choices is to live them out to their fullest, so I help The Network teach people by forcing them to live in the world they're creating. I'm not a policymaker, and I'm certainly not a government official, but I am in the business of facilitating Real-Time.

"He looks like he's drowning," Ava remarks once I'm beside her in the control room. "Did you tweak the lung settings? I'm concerned about asphyxiation."

"Relax," I chide while sipping my tea, "we haven't lost a client in ages. Besides, this gas-guzzler has three more of those fire-red Ferraris hidden at his mansion, he needs a deep clean."

As Mr. Sampson tries desperately to quench his thirst via a dried-up pond, I lean in to watch his vitals. He probably doesn't realize I dropped him into the burnt remains of his own neighborhood, or that the pond he's desperate to drink from is actually his own swimming pool. The finer details of Real-Time aren't there to deepen the torture, despite some clients' complaints. Rather, we keep every VR experience as accurate to the individual's life as possible to increase the likelihood, upon returning to their world, they will actually be a changed person. I find starting out clients like Mr. Sampson in a burning forest is a decent way to shock the brain into cooperating with the fear. Plus, nothing makes for a more satisfying connection than a gas-guzzler and the fires of his mistakes.

As the program simulates him gulping down tainted, metal-heavy pool water, distress washes across his neural synapses. His mind begs for relief, clean and refreshing water, but his actions over the past month show he needs a few more hours experiencing Real-Time. If Mr. Sampson doesn't care about what the future will look like in the case he doesn't stop, we are always glad to show him again, and again.

* * *

"Your . . . client, Mr. Sampson, has been registered as a missing person following a lump transfer of his wealth to Solar Solutions. Care to comment on this?"

"No," I reply. It's nobody's business that Clark lives a nomadic life in the hills outside his former mansion. Last I heard, he's taken to raising chickens. Mr. Sampson wasn't all disappointment. And if they want to implicate The Network in a potential kidnapping and robbery, they'll only hurt themselves, and the planet, in the long-term.

Besides, we didn't capture Mr. Sampson. We aren't in the business of policing at the street level. Rather, clients from all over the world are delivered to us, and we show them the consequences of their actions. No organization can do it all, but over time I've grown satisfied with my small part in the process.

World governments couldn't figure it out sooner because they were always thinking too big when it came to invoking change. Rational arguments don't work, they never will. You have to appeal to a person's own reality and, in our case, twist it into such a nightmare that their brain cuts off all its connections to bad behaviors. This is the beauty of Real-Time: it allows us to show climate perpetrators how their actions impact the planet's future by dropping them smack in the middle of it. Yes, ruling by fear has had its place in history, but we want people to fear something much worse.

The consequences of their own actions.

This isn't the revolution as I imagined it in my youth. The battles in my games were epic and sprawling. The Network's battles are fought on an individual basis. This is the best way to ensure changes take hold—make each ultra-wealthy person so affected by their experience, the results inevitably last.

* * *

A new speaker takes control of the hearing. He looks about my age, but much more squeamish by the way his eyes dart everywhere except into my own.

"David, I represent a council for the fair distribution and protection of global freshwater. I understand The Network has a common interest in such topics?"

When I launched Real Time, all I wanted was money and freedom. It took a long time to truly be convinced of The Network's plan. But while I was working on deciding if I cared, the world decided for me.

The World Water War went full scale not long after The Network finished setting up my first work station at headquarters. The Triple W was a real, human battle for resources and life. Unlike my games, there would be actual death and destruction when regions ran out of freshwater.

"The protection and fair distribution of freshwater is a central pillar of The Network's mission," I confirm. "However, I'd advise against any pigeonholing."

"Sorry, can you clarify?" he stammers.

"What I mean is, we care about every aspect of healing our planet. We don't limit ourselves to freshwater or clean energy initiatives."

One of the first clients delivered to me for testing out Real-Time's new objective was a politician's son from Florida. He was set to inherit one of the largest gated communities in The Coastal Republic of America, sitting on a massive underground freshwater reserve, and we didn't wait long to observe how his privilege influenced his climate impact before bringing him in. And to think he'd been running an underground commune too, designed to escape the climate crisis and "build a new world" after everything collapsed.

Some parts of the Coastal Republic of America once boasted some of the largest underground freshwater reserves in the Americas, but the water tables were depleted through decades of watering golf greens and exotic plants. It is so like humans to try and force the Earth into our idea of comfort and though the planet punches back with hurricanes and heat waves (I don't take any stock in the rumors about the planet awakening "powers" in people), The Network feels we can facilitate a more direct lesson. As was the case with the politician's son.

Hooking up that bulky first edition suit to its VR headset, I hid a smile. In those days, I didn't believe Real-Time would work as a functional re-education system. Why should it? The past fifty years had already made it abundantly clear what the Anthropocene had in store for us. The science was so straightforward, a child could understand it. For some reason, the crises never resonated long enough with those in positions of power, though. The Network insisted we implement Real-Time to teach them, on an individual basis, what the climate crisis would feel like. It became my job to have these select individuals feel everything their wealth and privilege had numbed them to.

I couldn't say yet, back then, whether or not I believed in our ability to invoke lasting change with Real-Time. But when I saw the six-month follow-up report on that first client, I started to believe in something greater than myself.

"Your client from Florida, he did some good after his release, yes?"

This meek board member is clearly aware of what happened next. But I don't mind the opportunity to boast. "After being released into the real world, he could have simply gone back to his old life. Instead, he took every penny he had to convert his community into a sustainable living option. And he had a lot of pennies. He funded the teaching of youth courses on agriculture and water management suited for the region's climate, and he incorporated water usage timers onto all properties under his control. One man, after one procedure, preserved an extra four percent of the freshwater in Florida."

The man whistles, showcasing, at last, his appreciation for what Real-Time has already achieved.

* * *

I know how change works in theory. I'd seen the tech world evolve through the influence of a few brilliant individuals. Now, thanks to The Network, I'm watching the planet change as well. For the better, and this time by taking influential individuals and letting them face actual, VR-facilitated consequences.

That first client didn't save the world, he barely saved more than a few from suffering climate related catastrophes in his region. But Real-Time was never meant to be a miracle cure for the climate crisis. Rather, it was meant to show what was ahead so people could no longer deny the future. Even if it was already on everyone's doorstep, the privileged weren't letting the truth in. That is, until Real-Time busted through.

* * *

Another member of the council activates her microphone to join the conversation.

"The Network recently worked with a very prominent client. Can you speak to us about how you managed to gain compliance with all the related nations?"

Her language suggests she supports Real-Time's use, but her even tone says she isn't allowed to reveal as much.

The client she's asking about is actually sitting in the audience. I know we aren't allowed to say his name, but I still turn to shoot him a glance before reminiscing on the subject.

* * *

Today the simulator facility is buzzing with excitement.

"They finally caught him," Ava whispers as we stand together behind the observation window.

"How?" I question. I've been too busy updating Real-Time's temperature maxima algorithm together with the Biologists—the true masochists of The Network—to increase exposure time of clients within forest fires.

"We had to get China to extradite him from the moon. And they agreed!"

"They agreed," I whisper. "Impressive. That's the most cooperation I've seen between nations in a long time."

"It's Real-Time," she insists while poking me in the rib with her elbow. "It seems we've recalibrated enough high-powered individuals for The United Nations to consider acknowledging it as a legitimate device for change."

Something inside me stirs. Real change, in our time. Could this planet still have a chance? I really believe it now, but the work is just beginning.

Down in the VR unit, technicians hook him up to the system.

He looks older than I remember; fragile and afraid. When I was a teenager, he was my hero: the future-maker, the man building electric cars and turning space travel into a tourist trap. Initially, he was a force for good. In time, though, he went the way of all wealthy men, and his obsession with exploration and power tipped towards hurting the planet.

The Network named him enemy number one the day he started convincing people we could just find another, better Earth. The dialogue hurt an entire generation, myself included.

While I hope it isn't too late to teach him, make him feel responsible for the path he and others like him have put us on, I still have my reservations about Real-Time.

The problem with time is that once there is enough momentum in one direction, we can't ever go back. Real-Time is meant to shift the momentum at its source—the individual. But, much like rolling a boulder back up a mountain, we have to be strategic with our efforts if we want to shift the forces of our planet towards its protection.

As the priority client slips into his VR experience, I turn to leave.

"Going to the control room?" Ava questions.

"No," I reply with a sigh. "I've been inside his world long enough." It isn't the only reason I'm bowing out of this client's trip through Real-Time, but she doesn't have to know everything about me.

The plight of today's client upsets me to an extent I'd rather not showcase in front of colleagues. This man and I were on similar paths once. Fortunately, I diverged. Yes, at first it was only because The Network threatened me into cooperation, but at least no one had to strap me into a VR suit and headset for my changes to take hold.

I will never know if it was compassion or foolishness that led to my awakening five years ago. Either way, I use my ingenuity to save this planet. This particular client has been using his wealth to leave it behind. He also seems keen to leave Earth in chaos. Hell, this man supported half-a-dozen coups worldwide. That alone makes him deserving of everything he's about to experience.

It's easy to become obsessed with launching rockets and building high-speed trains after reaching his level of wealth, and it's not a bad thing to dream up different futures for humanity, but this client's vision doesn't include the Earth, and I'm in the business of making people care about our one home. Lucky I did diverge, or else I'd be the one now standing in that broiling desert under an unforgiving sun instead of inside my cool, cement-walled office. The client will likely attempt to seek shelter inside the remains of his own expansive electric car facility there. But moving forward, the temperature in his Real-Time experience will be the least of his worries. You don't become a high priority client without receiving one of our most personalized experiences to date.

Eventually, he'll get relief from the desert heat when he's dumped into coastal waters and dragged downward under the weight of wasted batteries and excess car parts his facilities have only just begun dumping there. Finally, he'll spend a day orbiting the planet as it burns. Maybe he won't notice the dark plumes from forest fires or the dirt-brown patches where forest once grew, but he will have to start paying attention as his space capsule collides with the garbage he's responsible for littering the upper atmosphere with.

As the shards of metal poke through his company ship and pierce his body, I'd like to imagine he'll question why he didn't follow the pleas of scientists to put his money towards restoration and conservation of his home planet instead of blasting off to find another.

* * *

The Network has always kept to a self-imposed ethical standard of a one-experience policy. We only get one shot at accosting and re-educating climate-criminals. Once our priority client experienced Real-Time, we released him back into the world he'd been so eager to leave.

Now, we are at the mercy of global opinion, and I wonder if all that time spent scrolling through the follow-up reports to see if, based on that opinion, The Network will still be considered a force for good, has caught up with me.

Some time after his Real-Time experience, this particular client decided he'd learned from living his planet's future. Now without any trace of ignorance, he's chosen not to doom it any further. Isn't that enough? Even if he doesn't go on to solve an energy shortage issue or cure a disease, he has resolved to not do further harm.

* * *

"Real-Time works." I put it simply so they can't talk around the subject any longer. "And we, The Network, feel it's time the world recognized our method so we can extend the augmented-VR program to the general public."

In the United Nations main chamber, the few former clients in attendance stare down at me from their seats. I recognize all their faces, each a former billionaire and all once priority climate-criminals. Their depleted funds and nods of recognition calm me. What more evidence of Real-Time's success can the UN possibly demand from us beyond the living proof of my program's success sitting a few rows away? Unfortunately, the UN isn't in the business of letting vigilante organizations like ours implement such unorthodox methods without a thorough inquiry.

The Chief Investigator purses her lips.

"And what sort of plan did you have in mind for extending Real-Time?"

"We are proposing a multi-national program to diversify into education. We want to teach future generations about our planet and how to care for it. Real-Time and the climate crisis have both taught us that a person cannot learn through being told, they must see and do to make it real and lasting to the brain."

There are murmurs through the crowd and members of the

council whisper to each other in front of disengaged microphones.

"You want funding, too, I presume?"

Ava grumbles a few expletives under her breath while I gather my response. I say, "Yes. And we want to be officially recognized as an organization that has affected real change. I already have the algorithms in place to offer programs for educating the general population."

"Could you elaborate?" the nervous male from earlier intones.

"With Real-Time, we can teach teens proper farming techniques for soils with high clay content or low water saturation, found in regions they plan to visit on good-will missions. Or I can drop adults into remote villages where they learn how to harvest and prepare local, sustainable produce. Real-Time will let people experience the beautiful world we have without leaving any carbon-footprint in the wake of their travels."

My impassioned speech pushes many to the edge of their seats, perhaps in anticipation.

"More importantly, Real-Time will break down the cultural misunderstandings which have hurt us in the past and reinforced our unwillingness to unite. Today, individuals can walk in each other's footsteps—literally."

"And you believe this will work, David?"

"Madame Chief, I already know it does. And I think you do too. If we've learned anything, it's that Real-Time can change the individual which directly leads to changing the world."

I am confident there are still young people out there like I once was—wanting to withdraw from the world they're inheriting. But I also trust that if they choose to hurt the planet in doing so, Real-Time can put their feet back on the ground.

"If I understand, you want Real-Time to be made available as both a tool for . . . re-education of climate-criminals, but also as a more general climate education program?"

I nod, too exhausted to continue repeating what is so abundantly clear. Years of observing first-hand how one individual can impact a community, a government, or the world have changed me entirely. All I can do now is hope the UN understands that impact as well.

Real-Time isn't the ultimate solution. It won't fix everyone. We had a few clients who never changed at all. Or they lost their minds entirely through the experience. As an education tool, it would certainly help some people. Maybe not everyone. But some. In the end, we only need enough people changing their ways to change the world.

While the council debates whether or not Real-Time will be ratified as a global tool for change or as an illegal weapon for torture and fear, Ava and I sit together on a bench down one of the building's many corridors. Statues boast of heroes past, and I question if they'd be so brave today, in such a big, broken world.

"I'm sure they'll rule in our favor," Ava whispers. "How can they not?"

"Wanting to preserve the life of our planet requires living it, Ava. And we know from experience that most people don't want to live lives that are more challenging than their own, even if it is the right thing to do."

"What are the chances we'll succeed then?"

I shrug.

With the wisdom of age and the experience of Real-Time, I still keep my expectations of people, even ones as righteous as a UN climate committee, inside a realistic framework.

"Surely they understand Real-Time is necessary? Even if it doesn't make the world a perfect place, entirely free of destructive tendencies."

"I hope they do understand," I respond in a hushed tone. "The nuance of our program may be lost on these governmental types, though. And it's possible they won't grasp the overarching truth of Real-Time."

"Which is?"

"That if the world was perfect, we'd all just burn it down again to feel real."

CULLING DAY

A.E. FAULKNER

"I can't believe we have to do this again."

"Finn, hush!" My mother's eyes dart back and forth as she repri-
mands me, her urgent tone just above a whisper. The warning
might have worked when I was a child, eager to please and easy to
cower. But the most recent of my fifteen years have rendered an
awareness I can't ignore.

"Let's just skip it." I lower my voice, hoping she'll actually listen
if she isn't worried about anyone overhearing me. "We can go to the
cave . . . and just . . . hide out there for a few hours until this is all
over." I fight the urge to glance at her. Even minor, indiscriminate
movement might draw attention to us. And plenty of eyes are
watching.

Enforcers stand at attention, perched atop platforms at least
twenty feet above the tallest village resident. Their cold eyes scan
the crowd, watching for any hint of defiance. Their mere presence
virtually ensures a smooth, calculated entrance as hundreds
descend upon the square. From newborns to those who depend on a
walking stick, every last community member will be in attendance.

We're supposed to walk in silence, contemplating the Republic's
generosity in providing for us all year long. Every meal, every piece
of clothing, and every roof over our heads is courtesy of the leaders.
Without them, we would undoubtedly suffer, exposed to the ele-
ments with no nourishment or ability to thrive in a world with too
few resources to support the many mouths awaiting food, the many
hands awaiting assistance. Or at least, that's what we're supposed to
believe.

Other than a few hushed murmurs from the younger citizens,

the only sound is shuffling feet. We move as one fluid wave, our steps flowing along the cracked pavement. Swirls of charcoal gray clouds blot the sun's belligerent rays, painting a perfectly somber stage for today's Ceremony.

My mother refuses to even breathe in my general direction. My whispered words have once again fallen on deaf ears. She always follows the rules, and she expects the same from me.

I never thought much about the laws until they split my family in half.

* * *

"Thank you all for gathering here today." Councilman Adair offers his usual greeting. As our village's highest ranking official, he merely sits on the outskirts of the Republic's true leaders. The Council is a visible extension of those who would rather not preside over a seaside community, battered by a host of storms and threatening weather, at the mercy of Mother Nature year-round.

His deep voice booms, commanding attention from every last person crammed within the confines of the human radius we form around the stage. *Stage* is a generous word for the rickety platform he stands atop. His dark eyes peer across the sea of heads, but I'm sure he doesn't see us. He doesn't see fathers and sisters or aunts or cousins. He sees a cumulative burden fallen on his shoulders. His job, and that of the Council, is to ensure that our community can sustain itself without relying on the bordering territories.

"By order of the Miami Accords, our annual Culling Day is a time to give thanks for the means this community has been given not only to survive but also to thrive." He said similar words every year. "On this day we honor the guiding principles set forth by the Accords, which restore a balance for all that is provided to each citizen so freely all year long. On this day, each family will bestow the Council with a sacrifice. And while your hearts may be tempted toward anger, remember, it is not the leaders before you who have decreed this. In fact, we are here today as a result of those who came generations before us. Their reckless assail upon the environment led to a complete breakdown of supply meeting demand."

His tone sharpens with the last few words, and he plunks a stubby finger on the sun-faded podium acting as a dilapidated barrier separating him from us, the crowd. Second Councilman Hale steps forward and clasps a thick hand around Councilman Adair's shoulder, silently guiding him back the speech. Back to the mask he wears for the crowd.

The Councilman's features soften immediately, and his tone drips with understanding and concern. My fists clench instinctively. I don't believe for one moment that he feels any regret for the previous Cullings, or for whatever the Council has decided to take from us today.

The other Council members stand behind their elected superior, adopting a posture of loyal confidence. It's all an act. I have no idea what we stand to lose today, but I'm certain anything they say has nothing to do with our well-being. They paint a relatable facade across their faces—eyes drawn, chins squared—as if their worry runs as deep as our own.

But they already know what's to come. A breeze rushes through the thick air, carrying the ocean's unforgiving chill. Shivers race up my spine. It's a mild day for September, but the threat of winter lingers.

The annual Culling Collection is used to build our stores for the harshest season. Each family is required to give whatever the Council decrees on Culling Day each year. The current state of the climate barely yields enough to support the basic needs of the Republic's citizens. Arctic temperatures, unavoidable sickness, and impossible storms won't help the situation. They are all in the near future, if past winters are any indication.

Some say our land and sea have been stripped of all that is useful, but the Council claims we're on a path to reverse the mistakes of the past. Who knows what goes on behind the closed doors of their meetings, because all we've heard is a steady stream of words meant to inspire. From where I stand, nothing's changed. I allow my defeated thoughts to fade and tune back to the Councilman's words.

"In past years, some Culling Day sacrifices have been great," he says, "and others have been comparatively lesser. Your leaders make every effort to bear the burden of supporting our society. This year's Culling will require one non-essential animal from your household. If you raise livestock, you will deliver one non-breeding specimen to the central warehouse. If your family does not raise livestock, then you must offer a pet or spend your afternoon hunting in order to harvest some offering. You have until six p.m. to procure and present your contribution." He sighs. "The Collection may be difficult, but it is necessary. It will yield much-needed stores of meat in preparation for winter. It will yield a fresh supply of coats, protecting our citizens from the chilling air that will descend upon our community in the coming months. And we have several skilled craftsman who can repurpose bones into tools. Not one ounce of your sacrifice will be wasted."

Bile rises in my throat as his words slink through my mind. I'd laugh out loud if this was a joke. If only. I know he's serious. I glance at the faces surrounding me. Their features soften with relief, since it's only an animal this time.

But relief is nowhere within my grasp. Our home was once filled with more life than space. As a young child, I never noticed the cracked blue siding, marred with holes. Or the leaky roof, its weak spots sagging. All of the houses sat in some state of disrepair. Ours was no different.

Nostalgia paints images across my mind, flashes of happy memories now bitter. Mira and I, exploring the rocky ledge we were forbidden to visit. The day we found Captain, lying on the rocks, a scrawny ball of fur.

Mira was sixteen at the time. I'll never understand how she masterfully convinced mom and dad to let us keep the dog when we could barely feed ourselves. And now, less than two years later, we're expected to give him up in the Culling. Mira's last words rush back to me, a whisper echoing in my mind.

Take care of Captain.

Once again the Councilman's words evaporate as I struggle to focus. My mother chews on her lower lip, the only indication that today's Ceremony has made any impact on her. We're thanked and effectively dismissed, encouraged to set forth and prepare our sacrifice.

Red-hot fury courses through my veins, but I know better than to express it here. I turn on my heel and stride toward home. I toss a quick glance over my shoulder and verify that my mother is following. Her pace is much slower than mine, so I pause until the physical distance between us closes.

Along with my body, my mind slows. The beginnings of a dull headache pulse beneath my temples as the irony settles over me. Since Mira's Culling one year ago, my mother and I have settled into a detached coexistence.

Even with all we've lost, she's a model citizen of the Republic. She wouldn't dare express one word against the laws or those who created them. I may not have questioned anything if Mira hadn't told me stories about the time before the Accords.

Decades ago, people lived freely. They chose an occupation, opted to spend more years in schooling than was required, travelled for amusement, and made a home wherever they wanted.

Of course, it was that freedom that doomed civilization. It bred waste and carelessness. Selfishness and arrogance. Abuse and disregard. Oceans were overfished. Lands were overfarmed. People lived for the moment, with little regard for the future.

Now we pay the price. Not just each year on Culling Day, but in every choice we were never offered. The Council says that the sacrifices we make are for the greater good of our community. We are strongest when we all contribute.

We all attend primary school until we're twelve. Our reward for completing a formal education is a life of labor. We're all destined to learn our parents' trades so the cycle of their contributions can continue indefinitely.

In our community, we're deemed old enough to work at age thirteen. And that's what we do, as many hours as possible each day, learning and perfecting a trade. We spend five years as an apprentice. Once we turn eighteen, we can take over the family profession should it become necessary.

As one generation grows slower and weaker, the next will be ready to captain the ship, in a sense. Or at least in my case. I spent every moment of free time I had on my father's boat, watching and learning. But before I could start my apprenticeship, one adult from each family was chosen for the Culling. He refused to let my mother go.

At the time, my father captained a small fishing boat, just barely big enough for him, his catch, and a crew member. After his Culling Day, I felt a duty to take over for him. I watched him haul catch for years. But no one trusted I was ready to oversee his territory without guidance, so the Council decreed our boat to another family, the Rowes.

The only thing worse than scrubbing crimson stains off the dock is seeing Caspian and his twin brother Galiot patrolling the waters my father and I once conquered.

They happen to be a few years older than me, and apparently, they excel in all things nautical. Although their father was also called in a Culling, they were able to take over his duties seamlessly. And due to my own family's misfortune, they were awarded the opportunity to expand their territory.

For the good of the community, of course.

I swallow the lump in my throat, along with my pride. I'd give anything to be a child again. Just a few years ago, I was blissfully unaware of anything but threading bait on a hook and casting a line out to sea. And that was just for fun, before fishing was to become my profession.

I found a job on the docks as a deckhand. No matter how dirty or disgusting the work is, I do it. Whether I'm gutting fish or shoveling away their innards, there's only one thing on my mind: the boat I'm going to buy when I've finally saved up enough money.

My mother doesn't know I've been hiding a percentage of my wages each week. I tuck the dollars inside a tear within Mira's thin mattress. Someday, I'll be able to afford little more than a rusty tin bucket, but that's all I need to prove myself.

* * *

As soon as I crack open the door to our ramshackle house, Captain greets us. His tail whips back and forth as he releases a few happy yips. My fury rushes back full force as he dances around my legs, completely oblivious to his fate. I don't care what they say or do,

I'm not giving them my best friend. They've taken enough from us. From everybody.

As if reading my thoughts, my mother says, "Finn, I know it hurts, but we have to do it." She rests her hands on the creaky wooden chair my father sat in for every meal.

"I'm tired of having no choice!" My words pass through gritted teeth, harsher than I intend. It's not her fault, but there's no one else left to listen to my rage. "We do everything they say and they just keep taking more! When does it end?"

Captain scurries under the table as if I've struck him. Guilt trickles through me. I'm doing this *for* him. The last thing I want to do is frighten him.

My mother shakes her head sadly. "The leaders, they have to make hard decisions. Decisions for the greater good. They created this system so we can live, even with how little we have."

"This isn't living. It's existing." I soften my tone, for the dog's sake. My mother closes her eyes, maybe attempting to squelch tears. Maybe she's wrong. Maybe there's something we can do.

"Come on, boy." I squat and thrust a hand toward my best friend. He trots toward me, already forgiving, or maybe forgetting, my outburst. "We're going for one last walk together."

My mother nods, pressing a fist to her mouth to choke back any emotion. "That's a good idea. Be back soon."

* * *

Captain and I jog the path we've walked hundreds of times. We race each other straight to the cove, the closest thing to a fishing pier I've got. We reach the small beach in no time, and for just a moment I savor the familiar scent of sea air.

Turning back and forth, I sweep my eyes across the surrounding rocks to ensure our privacy. Confident no one's watching, I dig in the sand, two feet past the cairn I stacked as a marker. I scoop handfuls of the fine granules with my bare hands.

Within minutes, my fingers strike the thin rod. Smiling, I call to my best friend. "Here it is, Captain. This here's gonna catch us the biggest fish you've ever seen. And we'll turn that in for the Culling."

His tail swings back and forth in response to the hope radiating from my words. I'm not sure if they'll count a large fish, but a tuna could provide meat for days, if it was big enough.

Shifting my attention to the shoreline, I plant myself in the wet sand, just beyond where the water laps the beach. When it rolls away, returning to the depths, I scan the surface for holes. Once again I dig, following the trail one unlucky sand crab just made.

I scoop his smooth oval body into my hand and promptly introduce it to my hook before casting the line out. The sun's rays ignite beads of sweat along my forehead despite the gusting wind that wraps me in a chill.

With each passing minute, the sun plunges closer to the horizon. I cast and recast, refreshing my bait, but the ocean's stingy. Before long, time's almost up. They were right. I'm no fisherman. I couldn't catch one measly fish when my best friend's life depended on it.

I yank the line from the water for the last time. Defeated, I drop to my knees and lower the pole into its sandy grave before covering it once again. Captain's brown eyes watch me with an admiration I don't deserve.

Slowly, I trudge along the path, Captain playfully nipping at my heels. I pause, rotating in a complete circle, searching for something, anything, that can help us. My eyes land on the boat dock in the distance. Yes!

Dashing toward it, Captain mirrors my movement. When we reach Dad's old boat, *Cerulean Seas*, we climb aboard as if it's the most natural thing to do. Up close, it's barely recognizable now. The Rowe brothers made improvements since it fell into their possession.

Of course, I've seen these changes over the past two years, but I never wanted to look too closely. They've extended the hull from bow to stern, widening it and adding a simple cabin. It doesn't appear to be sturdy, but it's something. This may work. I haul myself back onto the wooden dock. Thankfully it's empty. One unspoken tenet of Culling Day is that everyone returns home immediately following the Ceremony, staying there in quiet obedience until the Collection.

I stalk to the mountain of loosely stacked lobster traps and wrap my fingers through the green mesh. One by one, I haul four traps onto *Cerulean Seas*. I'm not stealing, I'm just borrowing. Just for a few hours.

"Come on, boy." I lead Captain to the helm and drop to my knees, wrapping my arms around him. "Just stay here, okay? I promise, I'll come back tonight after dark and get you."

He leans into me, licking his lips as his ears relax. "I'm not giving you to them. But you've gotta stay here for now." I run a palm over the top of his head one last time. "Stay!"

Watching my every move, he heeds my command, releasing a sharp yip and spinning in a circle as if watching me stack lobster traps is a game. When his only exit from the cabin is blocked, I whisper goodbye and run home.

* * *

Enforcers patrol the streets, quietly observing the aura of descending subservience. I slink into the shadows as best I can, hugging every alley and side street along the way home.

When I push through the front door, my mother sits at the dinner table in my father's empty chair, perhaps trying to channel his strength. Her crystal blue eyes drop to the floor behind me, but they won't find what they seek. Her gaze narrows in confusion, but something else claims her features. Maybe a combination of fear—and dreaded anticipation.

"You've cut it awfully close, Finn." Her words are shaky. "We've got to leave now to take Captain—"

"No." Crossing my arms, I level my gaze to meet hers. "We're not doing it."

She rises, rushing over. "We have to! You don't understand!" I back away just as she reaches for my shoulders.

"I *do* understand! What we give will never be enough! They took Dad and Mira, and now they want Captain. No! We have to make a stand!" My voice rises with each syllable.

A sharp knock rattles the walls. My mother whimpers, launching her trembling hands over her mouth. Tears spring to her eyes instantly.

"This is the Enforcers," a deep voice booms. "It sounds like there's some trouble in there. Open the door and step back."

"Yeeee . . . yes, sir." My ever-obedient mother darts to the door and throws it open before dashing back to the table. Enforcers have never been inside our home before. They never had a need. My anger fades to fear as they cross the threshold.

Three men step into our home. Their very presence is overwhelming in the cramped space. Their crisp green uniforms are plain except for the gold band around the left bicep. Those bands cling tightly to the muscle they cover. Three sets of cold eyes land on me.

"We heard shouting from outside. What seems to be the problem?" The tallest man of the group addresses my mother. He maintains a calm exterior as his gaze slides past me to her.

"Oh no, no problem, sir." Her voice quivers in an unspoken plea for mercy.

Another Enforcer brushes past his colleagues, as if he's closing in on us. "I'd like to remind you that lying to an official is a punishable offense. Now, we heard a commotion. I'm certain of it."

Her head drops and her shoulders hunch. Any frustration over her insistence that we follow every rule without question dissolves as I witness her cower in fear. These people aren't here to enforce a broken rule or law. They're here to bask in power.

"Isn't your job to enforce the law? Because we aren't doing anything wrong. No law has been broken, so there's no reason for you to be in our home." Accusations pass through my lips before I fully comprehend the level of my stupidity.

For a moment, silence overtakes the charged air. The uniformed men twist their heads from side to side, gauging each other's reaction. Arrogant smirks tug at their cheeks. The man closest to us takes two swift steps, stopping just inches before me.

Hot breath blasts my forehead just before he grits his teeth. "Your business is *our* business, and it sounds to me like you've forgotten who's in charge around here."

Before I have the chance to release the breath I'm holding, a flash of motion draws my eyes upward. A fist launches down, slamming a rigid baton across my temple. A streak of fire slashes my skull as I drop to my knees.

My vision swims in an infinite darkness splintered by flashes of white. Muted sobbing drifts to my ears, but it's as if a fog has descended around me, slowing my reactions and hindering my senses.

Gravity's protests are ignored as I'm yanked to my feet. Too weak to even push my eyelids open, I concede to the arms wrapped around my own, dragging me away. Conversation rises and fades, blending together as one continuous stream.

"But where . . . where are you taking them? They . . . Finn . . . didn't mean to be disrespectful." My mother's voice trembles as much as I imagine her body shaking right now. Questioning an Enforcer is bold, especially for her.

"He's earned himself a trip to a Republic Reclaimance Center," the man sneers, obviously pleased to announce their intentions. Although my vision still spins in a daze, the arrogance in his tone is clear. "And if he behaves during his time there, maybe he'll even get to come back."

My mother shudders audibly. I imagine her wrapping frail arms around her thin frame. A flash of remorse stings the back of my eyelids, but I refuse to let even one tear fall. Captain's safe, if he can just stay hidden for a few hours. And my mother will be safe too. They didn't say anything about taking her. And I can take care of myself. I've been doing it since Mira left.

* * *

I don't remember being shoved in a car and passing out, but it must have happened, because I'm jolted awake by a rough hand shaking my shoulder. As consciousness returns, I crack my eyelids open and take in my surroundings. I'm slumped in the backseat of a boxy vehicle with dark windows. My head pounds as if an Enforcer is stationed inside my skull, chuckling as he repeatedly drums a hammer behind my temples.

"Out. Now." My wake-up call is courtesy of another Enforcer. This man wears the standard deep green uniform with a gold band around his bicep.

I attempt to push myself to standing, but the movement awakens a striking pain that runs the course of my arms. They're pinned behind my back, hooked together at the wrists. I must have been shackled when I was unconscious. Shimmying back and forth, I struggle to propel myself out the open door.

The Enforcer's patience expires. He hooks a palm around my elbow and yanks me outside. I stumble, nearly keeling over in an attempt to maintain balance. Once I'm steady on my feet, he guides me to the nearest building.

The enormous gray box reminds me of home. The thousands of blocks that form its walls match the sullen sky we marched beneath to the Culling Ceremony. The expansive rectangular shape bears a resemblance to our Community Supply Bank. But this structure dwarfs our warehouse of winter provisions—clothing, blankets, and jars of preserved food.

I'm guided from one place to the next about as gently as a fisherman would toss a tuna on deck. Not that the ocean has yielded much of a harvest in recent years. My mother was right, but I was too stubborn to listen. I never could have taken over my father's boat. The oceans were overfished years ago. I was more likely to catch a floating plastic bag or bottle.

They assign me to a residence building, and within that, a narrow bed nearly swallowed by the large dispirited room. What is supposed to be my sanctuary is but one speck within an army of cots in perfectly parallel rows.

My escort allots me ten minutes to use the communal restroom and swap my old clothes for a new uniform. With that, I'm led to another building. Like the others, its gray exterior promises mind-numbing boredom.

I expect to find a maze of hallways lined with classrooms, rows of desks adorned with pencils and paper so all requiring reeducation regarding the Republic's benevolence can eagerly take notes. Then, once we proclaim loyalty to and appreciation of the system controlling everything we do, we'll graduate back to our old lives.

But rather than approaching a quiet learning environment, a hum of activity churns beyond the cinder block walls. The Enforcer escorting me opens an entrance door and shoves me inside.

The heat and noise strike me immediately.

A rhythmic clomp-clomp blends with squeaking metal and a recurrent clanking to invoke an unpleasant chorus. A woman's voice blares over a loudspeaker, dulling the other sounds. Her tone sounds more robotic than human. She must provide the *reclaiming* part of this place.

> *The Republic was created to serve every single citizen. Sometimes we have to enforce rules that you may question, but it's important to understand: our goal is the greater good. We must all work together to achieve the greater good, and the greater good starts with each of you . . .*

Tuning out the message, my other senses seek information to understand my new situation. The vast open space is divided into sections, each a copy of the others. People, clad in uniforms like mine, are positioned every few feet. They stand beside conveyor belts carrying items from one section to another. Each person contributes to the process in some way—dumping materials into machines, sorting items as they pass by, and packaging finished products.

They're all workers. The Reclaiming Center is actually a labor camp, and I've gotten myself enlisted.

* * *

By the second day of my service, I've committed the routine to memory. I anticipate every step, every turn, and every stop before a baton can be raised in my direction. The highlight of my day is mealtime.

I've learned to seamlessly slide into the food line, keeping pace with the others as they push their trays along the counter. The choices worsen with each step, ranging from seaweed green sludge to a gelatinous loaf of what may or may not be meat. Nothing looks appetizing, but my stomach grumbles in hunger.

This place is nothing like I expected. In school, we were taught Reclaimance Centers were places for citizens who forgot their allegiance to the Republic. I imagined parallel rows of desks aligned in a classroom much like my own. An uptight teacher would pace up and down the aisles, proclaiming the value of each rule and regulation set forth by our leaders.

I could easily lie my way through memorization and testing. But that's not what we do here. Just like back home, labor is our primary goal. Others like me, swept away at the first mention or act of anarchy, piece together clothing, weapons, or supplies as history lessons blare over the public address system.

We make a captive and bored audience. All day, our fingers flutter across machinery, ensuring it's loaded with materials to crank out what feels like an endless stream of finished products for the Republic. The work is mindless, practically inviting our brains to absorb any sound, even if it's a faceless voice declaring the necessity of our unwavering loyalty.

Sometimes I'm able to block out the announcements, conjuring memories of my family when it was whole. Besides the four of us and Captain, there was Kai, Mira's best friend for as long as I can remember. Their friendship evolved into romance and grew stronger even when Kai graduated from an apprentice to a full-fledged Enforcer. He was never like the others. Or at least the ones I've been unlucky enough to meet.

He spent more time at our house than his own. If Mira was home, Kai was right beside her. After Mira was summoned in last year's Culling, his path stopped crossing ours. Mother said it was probably too painful for him to see us. But she's more understanding than I am. All I know? Once Mira disappeared, so did Kai.

Over the years, he became like an older brother to me. Especially after we lost our father. And now, after completely cutting us out of his life, Kai stands before me, eyes narrowed in disbelief.

* * *

He rushes toward me, his tone hushed but urgent. "Finn, what are you doing here?" Assuming an indifferent demeanor, he casually glances back and forth. Maybe to check if anyone's noticed his sudden interest in me?

I bite back the retort that jumps to mind: What do you care? Regardless of our history, he's still an Enforcer, and punishment awaits any show of disrespect. His uniform serves as a constant reminder that he's untouchable while I'm breakable.

"I got in trouble . . . after the Culling." I can't meet his eyes. He knows all we've lost, but I don't know him anymore. He may be just like the others now. How could he possibly understand?

"Look," he whispers, "Your sister's—"

"Enforcer Frederic." I nearly jump out of my skin, but Kai remains unnerved when a boisterous man in a green uniform slaps his back in greeting. "It's your break. I've got grub patrol."

Kai nods to the other official, his eyes briefly sliding over me before he turns on his heel and strides away.

* * *

Another two days pass, each one a repeat of the last. Life has become an endless cycle of tasteless meals, monotonous work, and uncomfortable sleep.

As I gather the least offensive offerings in tonight's food line, I step into the crowd of tables, scanning for an empty seat. Small groups of people cluster together whispering, taking advantage of the address system's silence. Maybe whoever runs this place figures any sort of brainwashing messages would be wasted during mealtimes, when the clank of plates on trays and scuffling of chairs would muffle the words.

Just as I lower myself onto a seat, my eyes meet the bluest irises I've ever seen. Her gaze reminds me of the ocean, and exhilaration swirls through me when I meet it. Instant recognition sparks a blazing smile across her cheeks. I stare, incredulously, as she rises and scampers to the seat across from mine. If I blink, this mirage might evaporate.

"Finn." She slides a slender hand across the table, and instinctively I offer my own.

"Mira."

* * *

"We don't have much time," she whispers. "I had to learn a new line today and it delayed my meal break. I probably don't want to know why you're here."

"I can't believe it's really you!" I never thought I'd see my sister again. But here she is, and she looks . . . healthy.

She shakes her head subtly and drops her eyes to the table, a signal to blanket my enthusiasm.

"I mean, have you been here the whole time since you . . . left?" I drop my voice to a whisper.

She nods. "Finn, you should know some things about this place."

"I'm learning a lot already. I mean, it's boring but not hard. Every day is the same routine. What else is there?"

"Dad's here," she holds my gaze, silently willing me to stay calm.

Breath catches in my lungs and I struggle to exhale. My chin drops, but no words form.

"We were both brought here after the Cullings. This place is just a catchall for the Republic. It's like they look for reasons to send people here. It's all about the work and getting supplies made for the entire region." She shifts in her seat and twists slightly, assessing for any unwanted attention aimed our way. A buzzer sounds from overhead and her face pales. She squeezes my hand. "I've got to go, but Finn, we think there's something going on . . . with the food. We think it's making us stronger, faster."

"What? That doesn't make sense, why—"

She rises, clearly out of time. "I don't know, but I feel it, and Dad feels it too. We've both gotten stronger since we got here. Like, much stronger."

Her words settle in a haze of doubt. Of course they're stronger, they've been forced to work probably every day since they arrived. And who knows what they've been assigned to. The work I do is easy, but it's exhausting.

"Bye, Finn. I'll look for you," she whispers over her shoulder before dashing away.

* * *

Questions swirl through my mind the next morning. All of them unanswered. I complete today's mindless task—folding and packing what appears to be Enforcer uniforms. Although the seaweed green color is the same, the material is stretchy and silky. I run a palm along the sleeves, admiring the lightweight yet sturdy fabric.

As I seal my first completed crate for the day, a deep voice startles me. "That package is needed in transport immediately. Pick it up and follow me."

I sigh, inwardly of course. My back strains as I struggle to raise the box. The Enforcer huffs, "This way," as he steps around me. I trace his steps, although mine are clumsy as the crate bangs against my thigh with every other step.

He leads me to an office and points to a corner. "Place it there."

I oblige, instinctually flexing my hands when they're relieved of the weight. Only then do I face him. Words catch in my throat. It's Kai. His voice didn't register. Here, the Enforcers are all nameless superiors, too quick with a baton and not worth distinguishing one from another.

"Finn, you saw Mira." It's not a question, yet I feel the need to answer.

"Yesterday." The memory triggers my questions. "Kai, what's going on here? She told me something, something about the food. She thinks it's changing her." I don't have the luxury of refusing a meal, but I want to know what I'm putting into my body.

"There's something really wrong with this place." He takes a step closer. His eyes flash to the door before focusing on me again. "I didn't really think about it when I first started working here, but the Enforcers and other overseers aren't allowed to eat the food you eat. I think it's derived from byproducts of the mass recycling system." His eyes and voice drop.

"What does that mean?" With any other Enforcer, I'd be punished for my demanding tone. I'm relying on our history to protect me.

"I noticed we never get food deliveries here. Ever." His tone turns fierce. "Yet somehow they produce enough food for two thousand people for three meals a day, every day. That must mean the source is already here."

I stare at him, my mouth opening and closing with too many questions at once.

"Staff don't eat what you eat. There is some food production on site, but it's minimal, not enough to feed everyone. That makes me think what they're feeding you is somehow derived from waste or pollution. Resources are limited, they're always exploring alternate sources. And who better to test it on than people who have no contact with anyone outside of this facility? I mean, most people's loved ones don't even know they're here."

"Do you really think they'd do that?" He knows more about this place than I probably ever will. And if he believes it to be true, then I have no choice but to agree. He's the only one I can possibly trust here, other than my dad and sister.

"Finn, think about it. They took you, your dad, Mira . . . they took all of you and sent you to work. You only see the light of day when you walk from the factory floor to the food lot or your dormitory. This is how they supply the villages of Maine with needs. By forcing people to do it, in secret."

I shake my head slowly, as if that will save my mind from processing this information. "No one will ever know." The realization catches in my throat. They'll never let me go back home. They'll never let anyone leave here. We carry a secret. And I have a feeling those in charge would do whatever it takes to keep it hidden.

We fall into a compatible silence, wrapped in despair.

* * *

The next day, Kai arranges a way for Mira, our father, and me to meet. He collects us individually, claiming we're each needed in another part of the facility. He delivers us to a storage shed one at a time, stepping inside and pulling the door closed as Dad wraps me and Mira in a strong hug.

"I'm glad to see you, son," Dad says, "but I hate knowing your mother's on her own."

Before I can respond, Kai joins our huddle, pressing a finger to his lips.

"We've got to make this quick and quiet. The four of us are getting out of here. Tonight."

"Kai, as much as I'd like to believe that, how is it possible? Whatever you're planning, they'll find out." My dad voices my fear. Still, a hint of excitement swirls through me, even as my father's disbelief clouds the conversation.

"I'll figure something out." Kai glances at Mira before continuing. "Look, I had some suspicions about this place and today I . . . I slipped into the Head Keeper's office. It took a while, but I found some files, some answers. This place is one big experiment, and you're all subjects."

His eyes lock with Mira's when he adds, "And I won't let them do this to you for one more day."

My father sighs. If he's weighing options, I can't imagine why. We've already lost our freedom. Life here is a blur of work, hinging on a struggle for sanity. *How have my father and sister endured the reconditioning messages for so long?* If I have to trade the possibility of punishment or death for the chance to go home, the risk is worth the wager.

Mira squeezes my hand and nods. I tilt my chin in a subtle confirmation that our thoughts mirror each other's.

"We've got to do this." Mira's voice is a low growl, almost unrecognizable. "It may be our only chance to get Mom and find a place where we can all be together."

Glancing between us and then focusing on Kai, our father confirms, "Okay."

* * *

No one seems to notice or care when I return to my work station. The Enforcers on duty barely look up from their card game. I have to bite back the smug smile begging to tug my cheeks. I should be scared. Terrified even. We could die tonight. But the distant hope of freedom outweighs the fear.

As planned, I follow my usual routine. Although I prepare for bed and climb into my uncomfortable cot, the adrenaline coursing through me easily delays any hint of sleep. I squint through the dark, watching the minutes edge toward midnight at an achingly slow pace.

When the clock hands finally align at twelve, I rise, stumbling as if I'm half-awake in need of the bathroom. I slink off to our meeting place, hidden in shadows. I'm the last to arrive. Mira, our dad, and Kai turn their heads in unison.

"Good, we all made it." Dad grasps my shoulder before turning to the others. "You three go. Kai, get them out of here. I'll lead the others once you've cleared the way." *He wants us to clear the path? Why isn't he going first?*

"Dad, you should come with us!" We can't risk something happening to him. We're so close to escaping and the taste of freedom is nearly hypnotic.

"No. It's not just us leaving. We're getting everyone out of here. They don't deserve this life. This is our chance to expose what's really going on." I recognize the stubbornness in his intense gaze. It matches my own. "We all go home. Tonight."

"He's right," Kai agrees. "Come on." He tugs Mira behind him and I follow, glancing back at my dad. He throws me a subtle nod of encouragement.

We run, flattening ourselves against the buildings as much as possible, pausing every dozen or so feet. When we finally reach open space, there's no choice but to keep going. We watch for a moment, from the relative safety of the building's corner. Seeing no activity, Kai tears off into the night. With no warning, four blasts ring through the air. Kai drops to the ground with a thud.

"No!" Mira screams, mirroring my own mind's protest. We can't lose him now.

"Come out with your hands up!" A lone male voice cuts through the darkness. "Traitors are shot on sight."

"Stay here," I whisper before I rise and step forward, my hands raised in surrender.

"That's right," the shooter encourages me. "Just take it nice and easy. We'd hate to lose any of our workers."

When I'm close enough to Kai's prone form, I drop to a crouch and grasp his ankles, pulling him backward to where we last stood together.

"I'm going to count to 10 and if you don't come out, then I'll come for you!" The tone grows angrier, but I tune it out for now.

Blood pours from Kai's wounds, the bullets having seared right through him. He clumsily reaches into his pocket.

"Mira, take . . . these." He pushes a thick envelope into her trembling hands.

"Wha . . . what? No! Kai, you're coming with us."

My eyes see what her heart refuses to acknowledge. He's not leaving this spot. At least not by his own two feet. I reach around Mira and grab the papers.

"Get these to—to my contact. Nat." He coughs, a wet and wheezy exhale. His body crumples as if exhausted by the force. Tears flow as Mira presses a kiss to his forehead and squeezes her eyes shut. Cradling his cheeks in her hands, she steadies his head.

She collapses against him, a guttural cry escaping her lips, when she notices his unseeing eyes. I don't know what's so important about that envelope, or who Nat is, but hopefully Dad will know what to do with it. Kai can't help us anymore.

"Mira, we have to go! There's nothing we can do." I grasp her elbow and yank her up. There's no time to mourn. She doesn't speak or even acknowledge me, but she allows me to guide her away.

* * *

I drag her around the other side of the building, away from the shooter. We run and we don't look back, not even once. As we turn another corner to face the compound's entrance, a solid steel gate towers over us. It's got to be at least ten times my height.

How did I not notice this before? I must have been too focused on whatever was happening right in front of me.

"Mira, we're trapped," I huff, the words escaping between gasps for oxygen. *Why did Dad send us first?* We'll never get past that behemoth, and everyone will be caught like fish in a hold. Defeat slows my resolve but it seems to ignite hers.

My sister bolts toward the gate like a streak of lightning. Her whole body is a brilliant blur. Flashes of white hot fury swirl through her core, pulsing toward her extremities. Throwing her hands in the air, she aligns glowing palms with her target. A burst of pure force erupts, hammering the gate.

It screeches and wails as the enormous sheets of gunmetal gray sheets curl in defeat. My jaw drops and my feet forget what they're supposed to do, but Mira never even slows. She charges right through the decimated structure.

She turns back, and cries, "Finn!"

I shake off the shock and dash toward her. Those hands flash fury again. Bolts of white light blaze from her palms and hone in on every Enforcer that was stealthily closing in on us. She eliminates the threat by blasting each one to bits.

By the time we reach the meeting place, Mira is barely panting, but my legs and lungs sear with pain. Of course, for the past year she's eaten experimental food. It must have rendered her powerful beyond what's humanly possible. That's the only explanation I can think of. Regardless, I've only been eating it for mere days.

Her eyes wash over me, unseeing, but I can't look away. Swirls of silver dance within her blue irises. The light she carries has faded, but the power remains. It's like another presence between us.

"Mira, how?"

"It's the food, Kai. They created food from waste and gave it to us to see what would happen. If they could manufacture food completely by recycling byproducts that would have been discarded otherwise, that's all the less we have to rely on natural sources."

I absorb the words that make perfect sense and no sense at all.

"They just wanted to see if the food would make us sick," she adds. "They wouldn't offer it in their precious Republic communities unless it was safe. What they never expected is that it would have side effects. It's somehow supercharged us. It's awakened an unnatural strength, and we're turning it against them. I don't know how long it'll last, but at least we can use it to escape. And fight back."

The next question hangs in my throat as a low hum reaches my ears. By the light of the moon, I turn to see a massive wave of escapees heading toward us. Their feet don't pound the ground.

Like Mira, they shoot across the land like a collective comet of brilliant life forces.

"We did it!" My father pulls me and Mira toward him, wrapping an arm around her shoulder and clamping mine with his palm. His eyes dart past us, searching for the person who helped us. Exhilaration melts into concern. "Where's Kai?"

"He didn't . . ." I can't say it out loud. "But he gave us this." I press the envelope into my father's hands. His eyes drop to it as if it's his last connection to the Enforcer we had to leave behind.

Slowly, carefully, he slides a finger between the envelope and its seal. His face wrinkles, marred in confusion. He tugs the stack of papers out of the package. A few loose pages from the uneven stack slip through his fingers, fluttering toward the ground. Although they vary in size, each is a variation of a rectangle. Mira and I lean toward him, scanning the print.

It's a collection of articles, but not from the *Coastal Republic Courier*, the only newspaper I've ever seen. My eyes flash over each prominent headline. Like a collection of single brushstrokes striking a canvas, they paint a disturbing picture.

> UN Climate Conference of the Parties Ends in Chaos, Foreign Powers Suspected in Attack

> 'Tree People' Blamed for SustainAble Corporation Casualties at Nature Preserve

> Wildflowers Overtake Religious Cult, Scientists Search For Answers

We've never heard any of these stories. We always knew the Coastal Republic installed a firewall on our social networks, but these headlines were too strange for us to have never heard of them, especially the one about an attack on the UN. How much has been kept from us?

My sister's voice pulls me from my thoughts. She's been planted in this spot for several minutes, yet she suddenly sounds breathless.

"I can already feel the power fading. It's like . . . it was given to us as retribution for what we've experienced. But I don't think it's permanent. I think it was a one-time gift," Mira says quietly.

"What do we do now?" I ask. I look to my father, eager for his guidance.

"We go home to your mother," he says. "And we figure out how to make our own headlines."

THE CRYSTAL HAZE

EMAD EL-DIN AYSHA

2047 C.E.

Sometimes I say to a poem,

"I don't have the strength
To wring out another drop
Of the sun."

And the poem will often
Respond

By climbing onto a barroom table:

Then lifts its skirt, winks,
Causing the whole sky to
Fall.

— Hafiz—

"Sandstorm ahead," said the pilot.

Two passengers right behind the pilot, in the cramped confines of the plane. A young couple. The man, Qays, grabbed his wife's hand, squeezing it beyond recognition. "We're short on fuel. We'll never make it." Beads of sweat coursed down his face.

A gentle clasp greeted his own shivering hand. "We'll make it, you'll see," Lobna replied calmly.

"Brace yourselves!" the pilot added for measure.

They waited patiently for the black expanse ahead to make it to the tiny speck of flotsam that was their plane, gyrating up and down with the winds. The heavens above were blotted out for an instant as a carpet of dust stretched out above, seemingly swallowing the horizon. The poor passengers witnessed it all through the solar roof as the pilot struggled to pull the sluggish plastic capsule upwards. The propellers *groaned* from the effort.

One second, two seconds, three seconds—dust particles bombarded them like locusts on a scavenger hunt—and then they were *free*, passing through the choking mass of dust to the safety of the sunny skies above. That's all it was, thankfully. Looking down through the glass expanse beneath their feet, they were witness to a second desert *above* the desert, driving them *up* with the beams of reflected light.

"I told you we'd make it," Lobna said triumphantly.

Qays squeezed out a breath through his tight nostrils. It was a relief from squeezing her hand. "I should never have doubted you." He paused for a moment then added. "After all, I'm married to one of the scientists responsible for all this."

They felt proud to be citizens of the United Republic of Arabia. The country, a conglomeration of countries, really, had finally solved the riddle of global warming. By turning the warming against itself!

* * *

"The sands of the desert, as you all know, give 'scorched earth' a whole new meaning," said Doctor Hakim Abdul-Khaliq, dressed in a pristine lab coat to the room full of pressmen. He was the chief scientist, the director general of the Desert Conservation Agency. The joke fell flatly on their ears.

Oblivious, he continued. "Not *too* long ago . . ." It was several generations ago. "Scientists working in Arabia . . . foreign scientists, realised that the dust blown up from the deserts of Arabia was having a surprising cooling effect on the environment in that scorched plot of land at the centre of the world. Even the waters of the Red Sea, and everything swimming or otherwise in it, was sheltered by the dry land swept up into the air." He paused for dramatic effect. "Dust, we discovered, sand, was our *greatest* resource. Greater than oil. Greater than uranium. Greater even than soil. All these years, we'd been trying to turn the deserts green, expending exorbitant sums on water and fertilizer, trying to become like the so-called *modern* world." He scoffed. "When all along, it was these moderners who were polluting the environment and trapping more and more heat inside the envelope of our beloved planet. *Until . . .*"

Another dramatic pause, as the man's bald cue ball of a head reflected light from the energy saving light bulbs aloft. For all his talk about the healing powers of the sun and the wind on the brow, he hardly left his laboratory, or the accountants' mess hall.

"Until, I say, some of those self-same foreigners discovered how nature, *our* nature, was one step ahead of them, reflecting the very light they were trapping with their cans of hairspray. Just as the sand beneath our feet"—Dr. Abdul-Khaliq gestured to the tiled floor beneath the sandals he was sporting. "Reflect sunlight upwards, scorching the soles of our feet, so sand in the air does the same, forming a protective layer, layers . . . above our own heads that we were, to our great shame, never aware of."

Another pause stretched longer than people could withstand, followed by a thundering "Why not *harness* it, I said!" The walls of the expansive room shuddered. "Not just to cool the earth and protect us from harmful UV rays, but as a source of *energy*. A floating solar factory, with every particle of sand a God-given solar panel, reflecting and refracting light. We extended invisible fields of electromagnetism, from the crust of the earth itself . . . *into* the dust clouds, shaping them, disciplining them . . . *charging* them, then piping the solar power back down into the bowels of the earth for us to tap into them from our mobile power units. The storm watchers, as we lovably call them. *Then*, my friends . . ." Nobody in this room seemed to be a friend of his. Even his own staff didn't like him, genius that he was. "*Only* then, were we able to make the final transition . . . the long sought after, struggled for, transition to total solar power!" Another thunderclap.

The only people clapping were his staff.

"Planes that run on solar energy when they begin to run out of fuel. Propeller planes. Less load on the solar cells, more liquid fuel conserved . . ." The fuel itself was ethanol, clean energy from converted sugarcane exported to the United Republic from South American nations, in exchange for the manned sand-clouds the Arabs specialised in. No money exchanged hands. It was a good old-fashioned barter deal.

Temperatures were stabilising . . . stabilising, and *stabilising* over there, and not just inland, but on the coastlines as well and over the plankton farms in the Pacific and Atlantic. At least, that was the hope. Geo-engineering, something only the billionaires in the West thought they could accomplish. "More resilience against dust, unlike jet engines." Dr. Abdul-Khaliq spat the word out. "Solar panels on the wings from above. On the wings from below. On the body of the plane, the very skin. The very inner furnishings of the plane. All sensitive to light and heat, *dosed* in it. Turning every ounce to energy. The same with cars, the same with buses, the same with trains . . . But planes, especially. If a dust cloud comes your way and cuts off your lifeline to the energies from above, all you need do is navigate *above* and you will be blasted by twice as much light as before, as the heated air and sunlight reflected from the sandstorm from below carries you up and up, closer to the ultimate source of energy. The su—"

"But didn't Icarus get too close to the sun?" some smart aleck reporter finally said.

"Nonsense," Dr. Abdul-Khaliq retorted. "Wax doesn't melt the higher up you go. It gets *colder* the higher up you go. And with a solar roof you stay nice and warm on the inside. And he was fighting *against* nature, while we are fighting *with* it." A small pause as he eyed the respondents in the room. "So, any questions?"

Someone else placed his hand up like the shy boy in class.

"Yes."

"Any other applications?" the reporter said. "Or risks?"

The chief scientist grimaced. "Risks?" he said with a startled tone of voice. "You talk to me about risks? Our applications have eliminated the risks caused by all those imbalances in nature *your* people created."

He placed his hand inside his pocket, finally remembering the control device his employees used for presentations, and started clicking away at a maniacal pace.

"You see this!" Dr. Abdul-Khaliq said shrilly.

It looked like a satellite photo of a sand storm. Before anybody had a chance to query about the picture's significance, the director general clicked on the enlargement button.

It looked like a plate full of brown rice, segmented and 'shivering' in the heat of the sun. The director general sighed in relief as he heard the entire crowd of pressmen breathing it all in one go.

The agency had already handed out brochures before the press conference on their practical applications. The whole list of them. Hadn't these rascals heard about their *locust* farms, trapping the beastly things in the layers of floating sand so they could be harvested for protein and pharmaceuticals, while sparing the lowly farmers all those carcinogenic pesticide costs? Wasn't that enough? Weren't these people *ever* satisfied?

Hadn't they heard about the dust clouds they used to purify the air of pesticides, huge clouds of them, headed across the border into Arabian airspace from the less fortunate countries? Hadn't they heard of the extra farming land the dust clouds had exposed, once enough fruitless sand had been blown up into the air, revealing nature's goodly bounty hidden below. Fertile soil and subterranean rivers that got to breathe fresh air for the first time in millennia, if not eons?

Dr. Abdul-Khaliq thought it over and decided to go big. If this didn't impress them, nothing would. And they were handling the risks. How dare they ask about *risks*.

"And if that isn't enough for you, then how about—" Yet *another* dramatic pause.

* * *

They made it in time after all, after traversing that sandstorm. *Because* of that sandstorm.

The young couple made it to the facility. The space launch. Lobna was an environmental scientist, or *sculptor* as they now called them, and she was going to board the United Republic of Arabia desert agency's space shuttle. The URA's orbital station had been online for a little over three years, monitoring global dust storms and ensuring the slow work of managing the resources continued successfully. It would also serve as a future launching point for missions planned for Mars, though those were many decades in the future. Their scientists were hopeful Martian dust-storms would provide the energy needed to terraform the planet itself.

But Mars was not their priority now. No, Qays, her husband, the astronaut—he could never stand flying within the atmosphere—was going with her to the URA station. Together, they'd use it as a launchpad to traverse space to where cosmic radiation was most pronounced in the solar system, so they could use the principles they'd perfected in the URA with sand particles. They'd use cosmic dust to do the same thing in outer space.

To divert cosmic rays to solar sails. To station solar panels. To power everything needed to fully explore the solar system, and possibly beyond.

AUTHOR'S NOTE

This story was inspired by recent research into the effects of dust from the Middle East and its cooling effects upon the Red Sea. *See* "Scientists discover dust from Middle East cools the Red Sea," 26 February 2020, https://www.zawya.com/mena/en/press-releases/ story/Scientists_discover_dust_from_Middle_East_cools_the_Red _Sea-ZAWYA20200226111916/.

GAIA'S FINAL EMBRACE

DAVID KERNOT

2040 C.E.

Rashi Ironbark lifted another rock the size of a cob loaf and carried it over to the pile sitting in her all-terrain gardening cart. She lowered it into the pile, stood, and straightened the tight muscles in her back, already sore from the heavy baby inside her. There was still room for one more rock in the cart. She removed her worn wide-brimmed hat, wiped the sweat off her brow, and stared across the flat plateau, littered with the heavy ironstone rocks. One just the right size was sitting near the ancient thermal vent.

Rashi ambled over and leaned forward until the heat trickling from it warmed her already flushed face. The faint smell of sulphur burbling up from deep beneath the Earth tickled her nostrils, and she closed her eyes and inhaled slowly. The baby kicked and wriggled defiantly. "Hush little one." She straightened and placed her hand on her belly to reassure them. But the baby always squirmed like this every time she got close to the thermal vent. A link from the atmosphere down into the heart of Mother Earth.

Into Gaia's womb.

Winter was approaching the Texan Alliance of States, and yet according to the local tribes that had populated the semi-arid region for centuries, it was unusually drier and warmer than normal. Rain normally saturating the high mesa and beautiful, lava-infested plateaus was late in arriving.

At least the conditions were good for her to collect materials for the house. She grunted as she picked up the chunk of heavy ironstone and lugged it over to the cart. She pulled the cart back to their home building site, where the extension to their Earthship was taking shape.

She navigated through the piles of haphazardly placed tires, the pile of bottles, stacks of second hand sheets of iron, recycled wooden beams and giant mounds of soil, sand, and clay. The place looked a bit like an old dumping ground, but when she looked over at Earthship Trinity, it was clear the recycled materials would have a new life. She recalled Juan's description of the building extension and smiled.

As the world's climate changed, so had people's housing choices across the Texan Alliance of States. Energy process had skyrocketed. Water was scarcer now than ever before. Snowfall was rare. The Eco-warriors from the Taos New Mexico region, with their well-insulated Earthships, buildings connected to the Earth through a mashup of used tires, recycled bottles, and mud, grew in popularity through necessity, and Earthship complexes spread across the rift valley floors where once great ash sheets flowed across New Mexico.

The region, ringed by ancient super eruption Calderas and flat infested plateaus, suited the adobe buildings. It's what Rashi loved about the area. Here Gaia was at her most obvious, with the Earthships joining the myriad of ancient ancestral Puebloan sites carved directly from the dormant volcanic ash flows from the Valles Calderas to the north.

She walked inside and placed her pager on her desk before returning to the living room. Out of the large, sloped windows, the tall mound of tires blocked her view of the beautiful Jura Mountains. Excitement rippled through her. How long would it be before she and Juan completed the extensions to their Earthship?

They'd named it Trinity because it was the closest of the Earthships to Los Alamos where she and Juan worked, and in defiance of the Manhattan Project's world-first atomic bomb. Naming her Trinity was a peace offering to Gaia.

She braced herself and strode out into the late afternoon heat. Their Earthship stood in the shadow of the ancient and revered Pajarito Plateau Mesas, and firmly connected to Gaia, contributing positively to the world's energy problems and climate change. Off grid life was the best. Water from the sky and power from the sun. And all free. What else could she have wished for, outside of a wonderful life for her unborn child? Cooler climates? If she could, but the world had decided otherwise.

Rashi was used to the heat, however. She pulled off her Australian Akubra hat, a keepsake from home, and used the wide, flat brim to fan herself. She eased herself down onto the low adobe wall at the front of the Earthship and pulled out her phone. The baby inside her wriggled defiantly, and she patted her stomach. "Hush, little one."

What had she done? Bringing a life into the world when everything was so unstable. But Dad would have liked that. He would have said hope is something stronger to hand on to the next generation, like he had with her and her brother, Mike. Perhaps Dad was right. He died a year ago today. With international borders difficult to traverse, especially for U.S. residents, she couldn't return home to Australia, even for a brief visit to celebrate his life.

No, a phone call would have to do. Rashi stood up off the adobe wall and stretched, then strode back and forth in the afternoon sun, kicking up the dusty soil. She took a deep breath and squeezed back the tears. She could do this.

But what would she tell Mike about her new life in this ancient part of the world, living so close to Gaia, when he believed she was on her way back home as soon as she could manage?

She noticed a piece of glass shining along her path.

No. Some obsidian.

She stood and absently kicked at it with the toe of her shoe while she grabbed her phone and checked the time. It would be early morning in Australia, but Mike would be up working on the farm. She paced while she looked for his number and pressed the icon. The phone rang.

"Hello?" said Mike.

She grinned. It was great to hear his voice. "Hey big brother, happy 2040. How are you?"

"Rashi, how have you been?"

She glanced down at the exposed obsidian and kicked it over in the dirt. It was about the size of her extended fingers, and there were chips around the edge. She frowned. It was as if somebody had carved out a spot for four fingers and a thumb.

"Rashi?"

"Oh, sorry. I'm good. I wanted to call and see how you are. Dad would have wanted that."

"We planted a tree for him today," he said.

"Lovely." She bent down and picked up the obsidian. Her baby kicked out, and Rashi winced and rubbed her belly with the stone. The stone grew warm, tingled, and she raised it up toward the sun and peered through it. The light at the centre swirled with the ebb and flow of a heartbeat.

"What's it like in the Texan Alliance of States? Are you coming home soon?"

She cringed. Here goes. "Not with the border closures. I'm fine though. I've got a job tracking animals through ICARUS." The stone glowed and light grew within it. A place inside her head hummed. The sound grew. She let go of it, and it fell.

"What did you say? ICARUS?" asked Mike.

She bent down and touched the obsidian, but it was cold. Inert. She frowned. A trick of her imagination? Perhaps she wanted to be closer to Mother Earth, and this stone helped her with that link? Dad had said something about stones to her once, when she was younger, but who knew why? Maybe Mike would know?

"Hello? Sis?"

"Sorry. It's the International Cooperation for Animal Research Using Space. It uses the new antenna array on The Gateway, the International Space Station."

"So you're going into space?"

She laughed. "I'm a ground tech. We use ICARUS to see the effects of climate change on animal populations. It's important work."

"I'm sure it is," he said, and she could hear him pause, as if he was thinking about saying something else.

"How's the water situation?" she asked. Water was critical to the farm even when she'd lived there, but it had to be more problematic for Mike than it had been for Dad and the family.

"Worse than usual, and—"

The long silence said it had to be bad.

He sighed.

Maybe now wasn't a good time to ask him about stones and Mother Gaia. "Sorry to hear that," she said. "Anyway, I just wanted you to know I was thinking about everyone. Have a glass of wine for me and toast Dad tonight."

"Will do," he said.

"It's really great to hear your voice." It was, and she needed to do it more often.

"Yes, and yours," he said.

An alarm whooped from inside Trinity, and she faced the long single-story mud-covered home and frowned. An ICARUS alert? "Got to go," she said. "There's some weird stuff happening with my animal data. I'll fill you in later when I can. Give my love to Anna and Maisie Jane."

"I will. You stay safe, sis."

Rashi ended the call and ran inside the cool, dark house to her office. Inside, the ICARUS alarm page deafened. She switched it off, bringing up the ICARUS app on her laptop and scrolling through the logs.

The screen readout highlighted the south-east Coastal Republic of America out in the Gulf of Mexico. Five of her tagged sea turtles and half a dozen bottlenose dolphins were all travelling at high speed. She frowned. But where? She checked the regional contact for the island of Sumatra. Volcano or earthquake? It could be anything, so she called the Indonesian agency for Meteorology, Climatology and Geophysics, the BMKG.

"Dewi Ramelan, on call support. How can I help?"

"Hi, Rashi Ironbark, Los Alamos lab. I'm wondering if there any indications of early seismic activity out in the Northern Sumatra."

"Let me enquire. One moment."

"No, nothing on our monitors. Which particular area?"

"Out to the coast from Mount Sinabung. The ISS ICARUS antenna is showing migratory birds returning south and not heading north."

"I'm sorry, there's nothing from that region. Perhaps try the Ministry of Energy and Mineral Resources. The Volcanological Survey of Indonesia?"

Rashi scrolled through her list of contacts. "Mustika Pramana, yes, I'll try her."

"Sorry we cannot help."

"Thank you."

Rashi ended the call and dialed a new number. The call went to a recorded message announcing that staff were unavailable. Rashi checked the time and realised it was around 5AM, give or take the time zone differences. Should she leave a message? She called the number again. "Hello, this is Rashi Ironbark, Los Alamos lab. We have ISS ICARUS antenna data showing migratory birds returning south from Mount Sinabung and not heading north as expected. This could be an early warning of volcanic activity."

Rashi left her number and ended the call. She wondered if she should have mentioned the event in the Gulf, but it wouldn't have made much difference being so far away.

For the second time that day, she logged the account of the ICARUS alert to her boss, Euga.

She stepped outside. Juan put down a tire and leaned it against the side of the truck. "What was it?"

She shrugged. "Not sure. Lost migratory birds, perhaps?" Her gut told her otherwise. In the year they had rostered her to watch the early warning indications, there had never been two events so close together. Many had been false alarms. What was Gaia telling them? She looked over at Juan. "I'm going for a walk, clear my head." She thrust her hand deep into her jacket pocket to the obsidian and gripped it hard. A sense of lightheadedness threatened to overwhelm her, but she pressed on.

Rashi strode off across the plateau and over to the area near the ancient thermal vent. The stone tingled in her palm and sent vibrations to her elbow. Near the ancient vent, the heat seemed warmer than she remembered, and the humming in her head grew. Dizzy, she sat down on the ground and rubbed her temples, letting go of the obsidian.

The baby stirred and kicked and pushed.

This wasn't right. None of this should happen. She pushed herself back away from the vent until the sensations faded. What did it mean? Why was the baby reacting this way? Why was this happening whenever she held the stone?

Mike would know. She should call him. Just not tonight. They would be asleep back home.

On the way back to the Earthship, Juan met her by the gate. "Did you hear?"

She frowned. "Hear what?"

"It's on the radio and all over social media. Out in the Pacific Ring of Fire, Mount Sinabung in Northern Sumatra, it just erupted. There are reports of people being woken up with rocks and lava. There's a plume of ash two kilometres high. Apparently, it's still gaining momentum. You warned them. You would have saved some lives!"

"No, I didn't, I left a message. There was no one there." Tears burst from her.

"Hey, it's alright. You tried. Come here."

He held his arms wide, and she stepped into his comforting embrace. This couldn't be a coincidence.

* * *

Rash woke from the baby kicking. She turned onto her side, but that wasn't it. Something deep beneath the earth had called to her. A sensation. A thing, indeterminable, demanding attention. The image of a circle of volcanoes erupting, red flames bursting from them, slowly faded. Was it a dream-generated memory from the volcano out in the Pacific Rim of Fire, or something else? Had she just seen volcanic ash and molten chunks of burning rock fall everywhere around her? It seemed too real. Too close. The ground seemed to shake beneath her. She sat up and checked the time. 2AM.

Juan stirred and turned over. "What is it?"

"Did you feel anything?"

"You mean like an earthquake?"

She nodded.

"No, but the Earthship is pretty stable from all the earth over it. There could be volcanic action and earthquakes and we'd never know in here. It connected us to the Earth. Have you checked outside?"

She shook her head.

"Did you want me to?" He moved to get up.

"No." She pushed him lightly back down. "Stay there, I'll be back in a moment." She stepped out of bed and into the front of the house. Peering through the large windows, the moonlight illuminated the area. Nothing seemed out of place. She walked over to the side door and stepped out into the open. A gentle breeze tugged at her nightdress. But otherwise, again, nothing seemed any different from normal. There wasn't a sound. Nothing moved. No ground shook.

The Jemez Mountains a short distance away to the north-west were part of the Valles Caldera volcanic region. They built Los Alamos on the flank of a huge volcano, one so large it was best viewed from space, but the mountains were dark and clouded. Again, nothing pulled at her outside of the dream sensations.

Rashi returned to the bedroom and clambered back into bed, pulling a sheet back over her body.

"Well?" asked Juan.

"It's just my imagination. Everything is fine."

"You don't sound fine. What is it?"

She sat up. Now wasn't the time to pour out her soul or her concerns. It was late, but she couldn't help herself. Juan understood her. "I don't know? I'm scared and want our child to see the world. There's so much talk of war over water and food . . . People are dying, and no one cares. They just hint at more death. I want a different life for our child, so they enjoy fresh water, and see the moon and the stars at night."

He rubbed her arm. "We'll get all that. You worry too much."

"If those clathrates escape the ocean, and the volcano continues to spew ash, so it goes around the world . . . all we'd need was one more event."

"It won't happen," he said.

"You don't know that. This is Gaia's way of letting us know she's not happy." She leaned over him to see his face. "Isn't it?"

He shrugged. "It could be."

She sighed. His computer-oriented brain rarely allowed him to view things, even scientific things, through a spiritual lens. "If it gets any worse, our atmosphere might get blanketed in ash and

debris so thick that the sunlight wouldn't penetrate. Ground temperatures would fall. Crops would die. Millions would slowly
starve to death."

"I get that humanity is teetering on the edge and that climate is
critical to our survival. I get that. But . . ."

"It's not like it hasn't happened before. Not human-generated,
but from volcanic activity. We could have a mini ice age or a full-
blown one. Or a runaway greenhouse effect."

"Rash, you can't overthink this. There's only so much you can
do. You can't change the world."

"We can, if we all play a part."

"Oh, alright. Get some sleep, otherwise you'll tire you and the
baby."

She rolled back over to her side of the bed. "Sure. I'm sorry I
woke you."

"It's no bother." He turned over in bed and faced her. He looked
the same as when she had cut her foot open and needed stitches.
Eyes full of concern. He kissed her gently on the lips.

She squeezed his hand, and he grabbed it comfortingly. Before
long, he fell back to sleep.

Rashi lay there in the dark, quietly cursing her imagination.

* * *

The baby started kicking again.

That sensation returned, as if something deep beneath the earth
was calling to her. The ground shook.

She glanced over at her ICARUS radio pager, but it remained
silent.

She wasn't dreaming now.

Careful not to wake Juan, she pulled her hand from his and
climbed from bed.

She pulled her jacket over her nightdress, stepped into her slip-
pers and thrust her hands into her pockets, once again finding the
obsidian. Her fingertips tingled with the contact.

Rashi strode into the warm outside air, a gentle breeze pulling at
her hair. A flock of birds launched from a solitary tree to her left and

circled. The incessant baying of dogs in the distance was unusual.

The dogs could be a warning. There might be a quake, or a volcano eruption from the nearby Jura Mountains. These creatures weren't her sentinel animals. There were no RFID-enabled solar-powered tags or Nano-trackers fitted to animals in this ancient and yet stable part of the world.

The crescendo of dog barking rose to a unified howl. The baby inside her kicked and fidgeted as if on a mission to warn her, and she bent over in pain and held her stomach as she strode further from Earthship Trinity, each step expecting a nuclear-like explosion to end the world as she knew it.

The ground rumbled, and she smiled in bitter confirmation.

The baby twisted even harder, and she stumbled out further down the plateau out of calling distance. Stumbled past the area she now felt safe, toward the ancient thermal vent.

She stared into the distance at the faint red shimmering glow around the Jura Mountains. Could it be happening? A volcanic eruption about to take place? A third event? Was Gaia done with humankind?

Underneath her, the ground vibrations increased as she approached the vent.

It was happening!

In the distance, flames from Gaia's Jura Mountains burst upward, high into the sky. A distant siren blared, faint from where she stood.

A myriad of sensations simultaneously shook her. The wind accelerated and whipped at her hair and jacket. A low droning sound buzzed in her ears.

The smell of rotten eggs burst from inside the ancient vent. Her body hummed and tingled.

That sensation from deep beneath the earth called.

The obsidian in her hand numbed her fingertips. Rashi frowned. When had she grabbed it? She pulled it out, and everything spun. Her vision shifted. For a moment, she was at the centre of the universe. She was important. Not just one of Gaia's nine billion subjects.

They were connected.

And then everything became clear. There was magic in the stone, just as Juan had suggested, though not necessarily of the sort he had been suggesting. It wasn't just a piece of obsidian. It connected to the planet beneath her feet. There was power, and in every one of Gaia's subjects.

She gripped the stone harder and rubbed it against her stomach. The baby twisted, pushing as if to escape. She raised the obsidian high above her, and like a touchstone, it ignited. Light exploded from within it, and it matched the intensity of the volcanic activity. The surrounding area glowed with the brightest light she'd ever seen.

The heat from the vent grew. A red glow from within it burst to the surface, as if it too acted in unison with the Jura Mountains.

She strode over to the ancient thermal vent and aimed the light down into it. A pain in her stomach burned through her, and she arched her back.

She raised her gaze high into the sky and yelled, "Gaia, I promise you the next generation will be wiser if you protect my child. They do not deserve this. They won't blindly follow the last. I promise you. Give all of us on Earth another chance. Help us . . . save you."

The baby squirmed. The ground underfoot stilled. She looked through the ashen sky and glimpsed the dust around the moon clearing slightly.

"Let us save you!"

She shouted the words, and as she said them, she felt an echo. It was faint, barely more than a whisper, but she heard the words repeated in a dozen languages. No, hundreds. The words resounded perpetually in her mind, as if said by parents across the planet.

She stood with allies in this fight.

And so did Gaia.

The volcanic dust cleared. The glowing light faded.

Rashi smiled. Trusting in Gaia was all she had needed to do. It was that easy.

But something within her changed. Something about her baby. Warm water ran down her leg and pain surged through her body.

Her waters broke and she fell to the ground, unable to move. She gripped her stomach, too breathless to call out.

The baying of the dogs quietened. A cool breeze stirred, and she accepted Gaia's final embrace.

Everything around her faded to black.

TALKING TREES AND THE HEAVY METAL MOOSE

NICHOLAS HANEY

2048 C.E.

1

Lansing, Michigan— Midwestern Federation
Connor

Waiting was always the worst part.

He swiped left.

"More local fighting today broke out across the western border of Indiana and Illinois, as rising tensions over a water pipeline from Lake Michigan to the south continue to boil over . . ."

Waiting for the shit to hit the fan, for the pot to boil over, for the storm to roll in. There was never anything to do now but wait. A months-long wait for the phone to ring, for the call Connor wanted to finally come through.

He swiped again. Another news station this time. Another talking head.

"Canada continues to take in climate refugees, while Michigan Border Police attempt to stop them at the border." The scene panned out, showing a crowd of thousands on foot waiting to cross the International Bridge in Detroit. Connor swiped again. A new head filled the screen.

"Water tensions have been growing for decades, and the fact of the matter is, the Great Lakes region sits on one of the largest sources of freshwater in the world. They have an obligation to share it."

Another head cut in.

"But that is built into the constitution of the Federation, and it is built directly on the old Great Lakes Compact that dictated waters rights for the region." This head was talked over.

"That's the point though. The Great Lakes Compact is a relic, an artifact from another age. It's out of date, and people are going thirsty. MY PEOPLE, if I may remind you, Indiana too was part of the compact. We have direct access to Lake Michigan, and the Southern States demand a seat . . ."

Connor sighed heavily, and his attention wavered. The news was hard to watch these days. It was always about water. Seemed like it was talked about more than climate change, though frankly the Great Lakes issue went back decades. A huge source of freshwater, and only bordering states and provinces with access. It was a prime resource, and everyone in the old US was eyeing it. Not to mention the shifting climate, and Canada being the only open border for refugees . . . Well that meant a whole lot of eyes were on the lakes and forests of Michigan.

Too many of them were running the profit/risks analysis. Too many corporations salivating over the amount of money they could make in the water trade. Connor sighed again, the long sound echoing over the empty apartment. He looked at his phone.

"I hate the waiting part . . ." He said the words to no one but himself. The phone chimed as he went to set it down. He nearly dropped it from the shock.

```
Casey: Hey man, you as bored as I am?

Connor: Yup.

Casey:  The   news   is   so   depressing.
Almost  makes  you  wonder  what  life  was
like before the constant anxiety.

Connor: Yup.

Casey: A man of few words, I see. You
heard  anything  from  her  yet?  I'm
itchin' over here.
```

Connor: I haven't heard anything. There
is a protest down the block at the
capitol, and I'm thinking about going
down there just to pass the time.

Casey: Man, you know how i feel about
protests. A bunch of catharsis for the
folks, and little change in the block-
heads that run things.

Connor: I know, just. I don't know.

Connor sat there, not knowing what to say next. The endless
waiting.

Casey: Hey, pop on over to MWNN, that
might take your mind off things for a
while.

Casey: Yeah, yeah, I know, anxiety.
Just do it.

Casey's last text popped in before Connor could finish a text
reminding him about the anxiety.

Casey: This one will interest you.
Trust me.

The texts ended after that. Another long sigh. A few quick
swipes on his phone and the feed for the Midwestern News Network popped up on his television.

Sure enough, the face of the biggest shit-eater on the planet
grinned on the screen. Another one of the damn Merkos dynasty,
and one of the richest capitalist goons on the planet.

"The Forester line of natural resources robots is top of the line
and state of the art. A herd of these machines will help manage

every forest on the planet for the next thousand years," Alarita Merkos said.

"How does it work?" The interviewer beamed. She was interviewing a celebrity after all.

"I'm glad you asked. We modeled the Forester in honor of the severely endangered *Alces alces,* the majestic Moose . . ."

Connor snorted. Maybe we will vacation in Sweden this year. See the majestic moose. It was an old joke. Mount Python, or something like that. He couldn't remember the exact details. The Merkos continued to stink up the screen.

"The Foresters can go where tread and wheel can't. They will use specialized interlinks to coordinate their efforts to comb forests, taking only the best trees without raising the entire forest through clear cutting."

"I must say, Madam Merkos," said the reporter, "they look a little horrifying. Between the lifter horns and saws below the jaw . . ."

Alarita laughed at the interviewer. "Let's not forget, they're industrial equipment," Merkos said. "While we do everything we can to honor the loss of biodiversity, we can only make it so cuddly. But the ruggedness of the logger is an American tradition!"

The interviewer looked uncomfortable. Connor's phone chimed.

```
Casey: It's gross, isn't it.

Connor: It makes my stomach crawl.
```

He swiped off MWNN, and his stomach sunk.

"Hartwick Pines," he said aloud. The last old growth forest in the Lower Peninsula. Ever since the first constitutional conventions in 2034, almost every piece of public land had been targeted by corporate interests looking to privatize and profit. Most of the old states and the new regional governments had been able to keep things in check, but the vultures continued to circle, and every year took another nibble. New justifications replaced old ones. "Sustainable" plastic required plant material, after all.

Now, Hartwick Pines was on the dinner plate.

Casey: That's why we do what we do.

Connor: Still no word from her?

Casey: No. Still waiting. Always. Waiting.

Connor: Alright, well let me know when
you know. I'm going to head down to the
protest. I feel the need to scream for
a while.

He locked up on his way out, grabbed his bike, and peddled toward downtown Lansing and the Michigan capitol.

The chants of "Whose trees, OUR Trees!" echoed a block away. He chuckled to himself. They'd used the same chants for a hundred years now.

2

Hartwick Pines, Northern Michigan
Brutus

Brutus took a deep breath through his nose. The world was filled with the smell of old pines and slightly damp earth. It smelled like heaven on Earth, and Brutus wondered what he had done to be blessed with such an experience. He had grown up in the old rust buckets near Gary, and so his formative years contained a lot more broken concrete than old growth forest. Yet, he knew why he was here, and that knowledge left him deeply uncomfortable.

His colleagues, Thomas and Marta, were off to the left. Thomas was built like a bulldozer, and his Great Lakes Forestry Corporation security uniform looked like it wanted to explode. If the cliché "arms like a leg" had a poster boy, it was Thomas. Brutus looked down at his own security badge, and while he was in good shape, he didn't have the aura of corporate muscle like Thomas.

Marta wasn't that far off. While a few inches below Thomas's six feet and change, she looked like a heavy destroyer to Thomas' battleship. Those two were the embodiment of corporate muscle on Earth. Both of them carried their rifles like they belonged there. Brutus, he wasn't so sure. Still, he had taken the job, and here he was. In these glorious woods, and likely, for the last time. That last part fell like an anchor in his stomach.

Corporate security was his job, and like it or not, he was in charge. He outranked both Thomas and Marta, and so far the two had been commendable subordinates. Former military, both of them, and they knew how to take orders. He was their CO, and while he knew they could split his lip with a grin, he respected them. Considering the two of them had not beat him to a pulp, he assumed they respected him too. Or, at the very least, respected the chain of command.

He felt the rumbling coming up the road before he could see it. Heavy trucks, bringing in the cargo. He walked over to Thomas and Marta.

"This is such a beautiful place," Brutus said. "Gary was all rust and abandoned factories. This place is truly a wonder."

"It is a really nice place," Thomas said after a moment of silence.

"It's kind of sad when you think about it. Knowing what we are here to do." Maybe they shared his uneasiness. Thomas grunted, and Marta spit.

"We have a job to do," Marta said. "Let's not forget that."

Thomas nodded. "This is what corporate said we do, so we do it. Pays the bills."

Nope. They had made their peace. Probably never had a second thought about it. Good soldiers. They obeyed.

"Yeah. We all signed up for the job." Brutus walked away feeling forlorn. He didn't add in the part that signing up didn't make it right.

* * *

The trucks rumbled into sight, Great Lakes Resources emblazoned on the side. The name didn't really matter, because it was still a Merkos holding corporation. Just another color to hide the umbrella over it all. Probably had something to do with tax withholdings too, but Brutus didn't want to think about that. He wished he could have been working for a company like SustainAble.

Even before the trucks rolled to a stop and opened up, he knew what they were carrying. The Forester Herd, the newest toy in the Merkos arsenal. In the corporate PR speak, they were meant to be green robotics, to manage forests for the next thousand years. Most of that was just petty greenwashing. They were loggers, shiny loggers sure, but loggers nonetheless. They had one job: cut down old growth trees and feed the lumber to a greedy market. Corporate saw dollar signs, not trees, and Brutus grew even more uncomfortable. He took another pine-scented inhalation.

"I've got a job to do," he said out loud.

"Everything alright over there chief?" Thomas said.

"Uh yeah. I was just thinking . . ."

Thomas tilted his head in a way that said "go on."

Brutus changed his tone. "Thinking about my son. My . . . estranged son. I wonder what he would think of this."

"You got family?" Marta said.

"Yeah. I haven't talked to my son in years, though."

Marta shuffled in her pockets for a moment and pulled out her phone. A picture on the screen showed a young woman and a toddler. "My wife and daughter." Marta smiled.

Brutus smiled back. "Your family is beautiful."

Thomas gave his grunt of acknowledgment.

Marta grinned, and then her face grew sad. "They're in Canada."

Brutus was taken aback by the personal note. That was more than he expected from Marta. "Refugees?" he asked. Indecision shot across her fate.

"Uh, yeah," Marta said. "They are in temporary housing outside Toronto."

There were a thousand questions Brutus could ask at this point, all very personal. "Why aren't you with them?" He could see the struggle. Would she shut down, or actually tell him?

She sighed. "I send my checks to them . . . You know how the borders are. Plus over there, they are on basic income. They have that option, and there's a lot of work you know. Rebuilding green spaces and old forests and wetlands . . ." Marta trailed off.

"They're lucky to have you." Brutus said, flashing her a genuine smile. She nodded, and the moment was gone, broken by the back-up warnings of the large trucks.

A car pulled up a moment later, clearly nicer than the environment was used to. Head honcho, boss man. Er, boss person, he realized, as the brunette stepped from the car. It wasn't the Merkos daughter, thankfully. Just some higher up here to oversee things. The camera and fanfare would come later.

The woman walked over to Thomas as she hung up a call.

"You in charge here?" she said.

Thomas scowled, and gestured over at Brutus. The woman looked disappointed as she walked over.

"You're the CO?" she asked again.

"That's right ma'am. I'm—"

"I don't care." She cut him off. "You have one job here. Stay out of the way, and shoot anyone that doesn't belong here."

"Crystal clear, ma'am," Brutus said.

She scowled at him, and then walked away. He caught the eyes of Marta and Thomas, and shrugged. Marta smiled slightly.

Four large semi-trucks had parked themselves. Each trailer opened automatically, splitting lengthwise along the length and opening up like a clamshell. Each trailer housed two Forester robots. The massive metal beasts lay on the bed of each trailer like a sleeping moose laying down with the legs tucked underneath.

"They're . . . even bigger than I had thought," Brutus said.

"I find it helpful to think of them more like bulldozers with legs," Marta added.

"Eight of them in all," Thomas added.

"That doesn't seem like very many." Brutus squinted, trying to get a better look at the robotic creatures.

"Well, figure it this way. They can work twenty four hours a day, three sixty five. No breaks, and no need to take time off," Marta said.

"You seem to know a lot about these things." Thomas tilted his head.

"I was a technical specialist in a past life, so yes, I do know a bit about them." Marta grinned.

"Like what?" Brutus asked.

"What, do you want a readout? Look at them!" Martha said.

"Give us your best guess."

"I don't have to guess, because I've read about them" Marta shrugged. "About twenty feet long, twelve feet high when standing. Between fifteen and about twenty tons each. They're bulldozers."

"That cut down and haul trees. What powers them?" Brutus asked.

Marta gave them an inpatient look. "They're gas-electric hybrids. Batteries, and a micro-turbine in the back. They can run on anything from natural gas to biofuel."

"Like, wood waste?"

"There's going to be a lot of it when they start cutting. The heavier ones use onboard gasifiers to create their own fuel. Like that one." Marta gestured to the nearest one, slightly larger than the others.

"Why is that one at the far end so much bigger than the others?" Thomas pointed at the far truck.

"That's the command unit. It coordinates the others and with HQ."

"So it's like the CO here," Thomas said.

"Just physically more impressive." Marta gave Brutus a playful shrug.

"Hey now!" Brutus smiled.

The largest Forester started to whir as it powered up. The three of them watched in silence as it went through its start-up routine, right up until it stood up and took the first heavy step off the truck.

It rumbled through Brutus's feet like thunder through the earth.

3

Lansing, Michigan
Connor

Lansing, capital city for the state of Michigan, and one of the most important cities of the Midwestern Federation. The city, and nearby major university, had pushed for the expansion and protection of green space. Pushed for regenerative agriculture, and the long term protection of the Great Lakes. The city lost ground year after year, despite the best efforts of the public. Another impotent government, besieged on all sides by corporate goons and an existential crisis.

In other words, a common place for large protests.

The protest was like dozens Connor had been to over his life. Lots of people, plenty of signs, a few of them genuinely clever and creative. Most were the stock of all climate protests since the start of the twenty-first century.

The oceans are rising and so are we.

The oceans were already up almost a meter. That's why climate refugees were such a problem from the coasts. Cities were drowning.

Save our forests. Save the trees!

They were losing more forests per day than in the past. They were losing that fight, no matter how hard everyone tried.

Whose trees? Our Trees!

Great in theory, but the fact was, a growing number of trees were under private control and could be exploited at an ever growing rate. The governments of the world had had several chances to genuinely step up and change course. They had frittered most of them away, and now the entire planet was in dire straits. Up nearly two and a half degrees Celsius, and rising.

Connor made his way through the crowd, listening to snippets of conversation. He tried not to entirely succumb to the cynicism clouding his brain, but he also noticed how the crowd was, overall, a lot younger than him. Maybe he was too jaded to subscribe to their optimism. These kids honestly thought the system was going to do the right thing. Then again, twenty years ago, he would have been right here with them. Decades of climate policy failure had driven that kind of idealism mostly out of him.

He was still a sucker for hope though, and he wished them luck with a smile. Maybe the kids were alright. Maybe some of them would really make the changes they so desperately needed. Maybe. Maybe. Maybe. Maybe this time would be different.

He couldn't despise them for trying. The world desperately needed more people willing to try. His ears tuned into a conversation that was closer to his thoughts than he wanted to admit.

"That's the purpose of diversity of tactics!" the random protester said. "We generally don't want violence, but we have to have real hard talks about our overall strategy and how we get there. We need system change, and that will take a lot of different methods. This protest is just one. Throwing yourself in front of a bulldozer or blowing something up is another."

"You say you don't want violence on one hand, and then condone blowing stuff up in another!" another retorted.

"Property damage isn't the same as killing people, so don't equate the two!" Another voice this time.

"Look, all I'm saying is," said the first person, "we have to be honest about our goals, and what will get us there."

Connor walked away. He knew a heated argument was coming, and he didn't want to be dragged into it.

Someone was up on the podium, speaking through a bullhorn. Another staple of the protest. Another well-rehearsed story of political negligence, leaders looking the other way, and a whole host of calls to action. *Vote for someone better! System change! I'm running to save the planet!* It had been the same story for decades, and Connor didn't think it was going to work any better this time around. The endless march of capitalism was killing the planet, and they needed a better story to counter that. They needed a better alternative, and Connor had no idea what that would look like.

He looked down at this phone. His own call to action had not come in yet.

"Diversity of tactics," he said to no one but himself. "There has to be something better. A better story."

That's what he was holding on to. Why he was waiting for the call. He thought the person he was to meet held that alternative. A way to change course.

He looked down at his phone again, and it chimed in his hand. He rapidly texted a response.

    Connor: Stop scaring me!

Casey: Well excuse me cranky pants!

Connor: Sorry. It's just the chime always catches me off-guard.

Casey: Stuck in a reverie about your glorious revolution? Ha!

Connor: I'm kinda waiting for a call. I'm jumpy.

Casey: You know silent is an option, right?

Connor: I'm. Waiting. On. A. Call.

Casey: :D I know man, I know.

Connor: Any news?

Casey: Why do you think I'm texting you? Meet me at the train station.

Connor: Wait? Is it go time? Did she call you?

Casey: Not yet. But it's only a couple hours by train. By the time we get the call, we can be on our way.

Connor: Punctual.

Casey: Right, doesn't hurt to look good in front of the ladies.

Connor: You're awful. I'm on my way.

He put away his phone. He had biked downtown, and the train station wasn't too far away, the train heading north to Hartwick Pines. Well, pretty close anyway. He put his foot to the pedals, and off he went.

Lansing was a beautiful city, and it had done everything it could to fight the climate crisis. The city was full of trees and green spaces, solar panels and bike lanes. Connor admired them all as he moved through the latter, but it hadn't been enough. It was still too hot, and too many had been displaced. Too much corporate power, and too much corruption. His mind whirred through the possibilities of what another world could look like.

He pulled into the train station, and Casey was waiting for him by the terminal. The two of them embraced.

"Hey, you made it! I already got us tickets, so it's all aboard." Casey smiled.

"It's great to see you!" Connor said. "We can get going any-time."

"Just store your bike in the back with mine, and we can go."

The hydrogen-electric train was a new line from Lansing to northern Michigan. It had been built during the late 2020s and through the 2030s, before the world fell apart. When there were a few governments that cared about at least trying. It was a fast and relatively clean train, so there were far worse things in the world.

The two of them chatted, catching up on the way toward Grayling and Hartwick Pines. About an hour into their trip, his phone finally rang, the call coming in through the encrypted Contact app.

4

Hartwick Pines, Northern Michigan
Brutus

They say no one should ever look a gift horse in the mouth. Brutus had no idea what that really meant, but he assumed it went quadruple when it came to looking a Forester in the mouth. The robotic harvester stood head and shoulders above him, and the mouth, the jaw, and pretty much everything besides the eyes and antlers were made of steel. Steel chainsaw teeth on the lower mandibles, and cutting saws and disks above and below for removing smaller branches. The never blinking eyes, or rather the optical sensors, glowed in a soft shade of green. Everything about it made his skin scrawl, and a sense of dread ran all the way down his spine.

He had to turn away. The Forester never looked away, and he could feel its gaze as he made his way back over to Marta and Thomas. Another security squad had arrived, and the first press conference attendees were starting to mingle. The big unveil was starting soon, and with it came the most important part of his job.

Crowd control.

"Was it worth it?" Marta asked.

"It's creepy. I don't like it," Brutus said. "It's all steel and teeth, and it makes me uncomfortable."

"It is designed to take down whole trees, and turn the waste into pulp." Marta shrugged.

"Bet it could do the same thing to any of us. Bloody pulp." Thomas added.

"The robots have pretty strict protocols against that."

"But war robots are a thing," Brutus said.

"Yup." Thomas looked toward the forest. "They are probably turning some poor desperate sod to pulp right now. In the Middle East or Asia I'd bet."

"That's . . . dark," Marta said.

"But it's true." Brutus shuddered. The momentary silence was a great opening for a topic change. "So, do you think we will have any trouble?" Brutus asked the others.

"That's what they pay us for," Marta said. "To make sure there isn't, right?"

"True. But we wouldn't be here if the boss folks didn't expect trouble."

"You expect protests?" Marta asked.

"The first bus is arriving right now. These are old growth forests, robotic loggers, and a high profile member of the Merkos family. If there isn't a protest I'd eat my shorts."

"Guess we should check in with the other security teams then?" Thomas said.

"You two go ahead, you can handle that job. I'm going to go look around."

Thomas and Marta nodded their agreement, and off they went to hobnob. Brutus wasn't exactly feeling social, so he decided to walk through the woods. It was also so he could keep an eye on the ever-growing crowd. The trees looked peaceful and resolute, and most of the protesters looked peaceful, too. Signs and street clothes, not a huge threat there.

Yet, some of the trees looked forlorn, too. Brutus wasn't sure what to make of it, but it was almost like they were tense. That the forest might have an idea what was coming. He thought again about the face of the Forester. No breath, no blinking. Just steel and purpose. Did the trees fear the metal jaws? Maybe they were holding their breath too.

Another bus unloaded. The press kept arriving in notably marked vans, a few executives in fancy cars. Busloads of protesters. Some came on bikes and on foot. The protesters were already forming a swirling mass behind the press lines, and the barricade's security had set up as well. The line that shall not be crossed. That was Brutus's place.

Beyond a doubt, not all the protesters were peaceful. He kept catching sight of helmets, heavy sticks, and improvised body armor. Some were hoping for a fight. Brutus looked back at the security line, with a couple dozen corporate police. It . . . wasn't going to be enough. He quickly made his way to the line to find Marta and Thomas. He was going to want the big soldiers near him.

"Sometimes I wish they would keep these events invite only," Marta said, raising her voice as things got louder.

"It's too high profile. Next to impossible to keep something like this under wraps." Brutus gestured to the press.

"The Merkos family probably has their own entourage for just that reason," Thomas said.

"And their own ravenous supporters too." Marta gestured toward the crowd. It was pretty obvious. The separate camps were staking out their lines. The supporters were arriving in mass too, and there was the smallest separation between them now. A few people were already arguing with one another. Save the forest versus the march of progress. Brutus had no intention of being part of that fight.

"Should we keep them apart before they start a riot?" Thomas said.

"We don't have the people," Brutus replied. "We hold this line and protect the big wigs, as we are paid to do."

"Man, when that Merkos lady gets here, the shit is going to hit the fan."

A drone whirred overhead. It drew Brutus's eyes to the wondrous pines towering above them. Watching, waiting, like ancient sentinels. Brutus exhaled. "Any port in a storm."

5

Hartwick Pines, Northern Michigan
Claire

Claire checked her phone one last time as the bus pulled into Hartwick Pines. The atmosphere was electric on the bus, in the only way that electricity could be: powerful, useful, and deadly. It crackled, and Claire had to remind herself that it couldn't actually rain inside a bus. In theory, anyways. A lot of things defied theory over the past few years.

She checked-in with her people. Connor and Casey were nearby, and would be there soon. The others in her group would be as well. People she trusted with her life, and respected immensely. Friends to the last, and stalwart, every single one. The moment she knew what had to be done, she called. Every single one of them had answered, and now they rode the storm front like avenging angels.

Or maybe like witches on broomsticks. She looked down at the phone again. Thirteen of them in all, counting herself. She laughed out loud, but the bus was loud, and nobody noticed.

"My coven," she said to herself with a laugh. It wasn't true, and at best ironic, but the thought was amusing. Her phone chirped twice. Connor and Casey were at the park. She would have to find them. People filed out the bus like a wave the moment the door opened. She surfed right along with them, and soon found herself planted on the ground. Pine filled the air, an olfactory message from an old forest.

Just like you practiced, girl, she thought. *Roots down into the earth, like a tree, like a stone. You are the bones of the earth, and from this spot you shall not be moved. May the fires burn and the storms rage, here we make our stand.*

Claire exhaled deeply and took it all in. The air was stifling, but it was not the heat of the day. The tension of the crowd and the trees. The closeness of it all. Her attention wavered, and she could almost feel it in her own mind.

"CLAIRE! HEY CLAIRE!"

Casey's voice snapped her back into herself. She shifted the backpack on her shoulders and went over to meet them. Connor and Casey both threw themselves at her, and they all smiled and laughed. Dear friends, wayward friends. Seeds on the wind.

"It's great to see you both!" Claire said.

Connor smiled and hugged her again. Casey fell against the two of them, and they all toppled over. She hit the ground laughing. Breaking the tension, laughing at the anxiety.

"Did you think we'd really miss this?" Connor said.

"Of course not. But this isn't exactly a social call either," Claire added.

Casey scoffed. "Sure it is. This is the *best* kind of party." He smiled.

His smile had always been contagious. She couldn't help but smile back. Each of them held out a hand and helped each other up. Connor and Casey brushed the fallen pine needles and detritus away. Claire didn't bother.

Maybe it will count as a blessing in the work ahead. "It's quite the party. That I'll admit. Anything interesting yet?"

"We haven't been here that long," Casey said. "Probably a few scuffles already. You know how tech-bros are. The others arrive yet?"

"Next bus." Connor nodded in the direction of the parking lot.

"We should go over and meet them."

Claire nodded and they walked on over to the road as another bus pulled up. It was clearly a private bus painted in insultingly bright colors.

People poured off the bus, and soon enough, the three of them were surrounded by the other members of their group. All of them joked and embraced in turn, old friends scattered on the wind. Dandelion seeds, looking for purpose.

This one . . . This one can hear us?

Claire stopped and breathed. One . . . two . . . three, and exhale.

"You alright?" Harris asked. He was the youngest member of their group.

"Yeah. It's just a lot to take in." Claire nodded. "Maybe we should talk in private?" she quickly added.

The others added their agreement, and they made their way down one of the hiking paths deeper into the pines.

"So what's the plan, boss?" Tucker asked in his silly faked cowboy accent. He thought it was funny.

This is odd. This one is different. She can hear us.

"Do you feel that?" Connor asked. The earth rumbled beneath them.

"It's the Foresters moving around," Harris said. "Back behind the crowd, behind the privacy fence and the trucks."

"Damn, they are that heavy?" Casey asked.

"Boy, you've never seen a cattle drive have you?" Tucker said.

Claire rolled her eyes. "Neither have you Tucker. You're from Minnesota." Claire scoffed.

"Yeah . . . I know," Tucker said, dropping the accent.

"Alright, you all know the outline of the plan. I need to get to the lead Forester, which is going to be under guard. Which means the rest of you . . . Well, I need a distraction."

"I think you picked the best group of people to cause a ruckus," Marti said. They were way overdressed for a day in the park. As always.

Claire ruffled around in her bag and pulled out four pistols. She checked each of them before she handed them out—Harris, Tucker, Connor, Marti.

"Don't shoot anyone unless you have to," Claire said.

"And if we do? Have to shoot someone?" Harris asked.

She could hear his anxiety. "Aim for the legs and arms. Those are high powered tranqs, and will put down a bull moose in a hurry—" Claire had to stop. Moose were almost extinct. The Foresters had a higher likelihood of long term survival. "You get the idea, but they don't work through body armor. Aim for the legs and arms."

What are you doing little one?

She saw the look Connor gave her. He tapped her on the arm and pulled her aside.

"Are you alright? No mask this time," Connor said.

Claire exhaled. "I'm alright. You just know that trees are a lot. Especially old forests."

"This place is chatty?" he said.

Claire smiled. "A lot. Yeah."

"And the foresters?" Connor asked.

"I haven't heard them yet. But they are here. Just . . . quiet."

"It's just, a lot rides on you. No one else can do what you can, and you look like you are going to pass out."

"I'm okay. Let's just get this done." The two of them returned to the group.

"Do you have a preference for the distraction, or just . . . wing it?" Marti asked.

"I trust you all with your various skills to come up with something." Claire said.

"And you?" Harris asked.

She is here for the machines. Why?

Another deep breath. "I need to get to the Foresters. While the rest of you . . . do what you do best, I need to get in that pen. I need to get to the lead one, and hope it works."

"You're going to hack it?" Yuri said. One of the older members.

"More or less. If we shut down the lead one, the others will follow suit. It's a failsafe."

"Provided you don't get trampled flat," Harris said.

"They aren't war machines. Killing people isn't in their programming."

"But you and I both know how corporations treat environmentalists," Casey said, "and that those machines do have self-defense protocols for just this kind of thing. Accidents happen."

All the group looked at her, their eyes searching. She was their friend, and they were worried about her.

"You're going to have to trust me on this. As I trust each of you. Make a mess, get the security away from the paddocks. The four of you that are armed, you get me into the paddock. Got it?"

The group nodded.

What is the purpose, little one?

"You all know what you need to do."

"If we time this right, that Merkos boss lady will arrive just in time, and the cameras will catch everything." Harris smiled.

"Exactly. Now let's go," Claire said.

Everyone embraced one last time before they made their way back to the growing crowd. Still electric, still like lightning about to strike. Her other friends blended into the crowd, and then it was just the five of them.

"How long do you think it will take them?" Connor said.

The crowd started to shout. Another scuffle broke out.

"Hopefully not long," Harris said. "This crowd is volatile enough."

Moments later, a blast rang out and people started to scramble. The crowd shuddered and shifted, and then a mass hit the security barricade and fights broke out.

"I think Casey brought firecrackers again." Marti laughed.

"It's go time folks," Claire said. She ran through the crowd, dodging bodies until they came to the security barricade. The corporate police were busy busting heads, and Claire hopped over, followed closely by her comrades. A tentacle of the swirling crowd followed them over the barricades and threw themselves at the security. Supporters and protesters ran and fought with each, and Claire made a beeline for the paddock.

"Hey, get away from there!" A large security officer came bowling at them. Tucker went down from a quick baton swipe, and Harris shot the man just above the left kneecap. The tranquilizer took a total of two seconds before the man went face first into the dirt.

"I need to get over this fence NOW!" Claire shouted.

Connor and Marti were at her side in a second. The fence was a large wooden stockade, meant to keep prying eyes out, but not very sturdy or very high. The two of them cupped their hands and lifted Claire over the fence. She hit the dirt hard on the other side and tumbled. She heard shouting on the other side of the fence, and the sounds of batons. All she could do was hope her friends were okay.

The heavy footsteps broke her reverie, and she rose slowly. The Foresters stood in a semi-circle around her, with her back against the fence. There was a small shed off to her left near a semi-truck, so she had no way out. The green optical sensors fixed on her. The largest lead Forester stood right of center, a good foot taller than the others.

What is she doing?

The trees continued their whispers.

WHO>ARE>YOU.

Another voice rang out in her head.
"I'm a friend. I'm here to help," she said.

QUERY>FRIEND >NOT RECOGNIZED

"What are you doing here?" A different voice. She looked up to see a security officer coming toward her from the shed. "You don't belong here! You're under arrest."

"Look, I'm not here to hurt anyone. I'm here to help!" Claire's hands and voice shook as she spoke.

"You're trespassing on corporate property, and you look like a saboteur to me. Let's not do this the hard way." The officer looked as scared as she felt.

"I don't want to do things the hard way. I want to save the forest."

The officer froze. She saw his indecision. He glanced up at the trees.

"What's your name?" Claire asked.

"Officer Clifford," he responded.

"I'm Claire."

"Uhh. Brutus."

"Listen Brutus, you know what these machines are meant to do. You know what this place is?"

"Hartwick Pines."

"It's a beautiful place," she said, "and these machines are meant to wreck it."

Brutus wavered. "It is a beautiful place. But . . . I've got a job to do, and that's to keep these machines away from dangerous people."

She didn't see indecision anymore. His eyes filled with steel. Decisiveness. His mind was made up.

"Now if you'll excuse me, I have a job to do," he said.

This was it, she was going to get caught and arrested here at the end of it all. *No . . . It can't end like this.*

He nodded once and smiled as he turned to walk away. A brief moment of understanding. "Do let me know if you see anyone that looks dangerous . . ." he said as he left.

Claire's knees gave up, and she collapsed.

A friend of a friend of a friend . . . A friend of the forest.

The lead Forester took one heavy step forward. Then another. The ground shook, and Claire started to cry. When she looked up, the steel teeth were less than a foot from her face. She reached up and grabbed the mandibles on either side, flinching as her hand caught a saw tooth. A little bit of blood ran down the saw.

INQUIRY>FRIEND?

"You're free now. I need you to protect this forest. Not cut it down, not serve unfaithful masters. You're the guardian of this forest now."

The eyes of the Forester shifted. From yellow, warning, back through blue. A blue fog crawled out of her hands and into the eyes. The Forester lifted its head, shook it back and forth, and let out an actual snort.

Claire chuckled. "You're a real boy now. Go. Make a show of it if you want." Claire smiled.

The lead Forester turned to the others, and each of their eyes shifted to a shade of blue. The large bull snorted once more, and the entire herd crashed through the paddock, into the screaming crowd, and toward the forest.

Interesting.

What shall we do with this one?

This one has done enough.

For now.

Thoughts and voices smashed through her head like a brick, and she blacked out.

6

Grayling Hospital
Claire

The hospital lights hurt her eyes. It was too bright, too white, and smelled of sterility. She wasn't a big fan of hospitals. As the room focused, she heard a voice. Several voices. The images were still a bit blurry though. As the voices condensed, they started to make more sense.

"The scene at Hartwick Pines was one of devastation and chaos. Several GLR Foresters were hijacked before a presentation and broke loose from their paddock. Riots had broken out beforehand, and the security forces were quickly overwhelmed. No fatalities have been reported, but countless injuries continue to show up at local hospitals . . ."

"Hey Connor, I think she is coming to," Another voice said.

"MWNN was able to catch up with several witnesses that were at the scene."

"Yeah man, it was a riot. People were arguing, and throwing punches, and then all of sudden these metal mooses came crashing through the crowd. It was wild!"

"MWNN would like to note that 'moose' is the plural form."

"She still looks pretty out of it to me . . . Hey Claire, you in there?"

"Corporate security attacked us once all hell broke loose. I got hit in the head with a baton. The weirdest thing was, after the machines broke loose, I think I saw a girl in the paddock. I don't know what she was doing, but it was really strange."

"Earth to Claire. Olly olly oxen free." That was Casey's voice. His head was bandaged.

"She must have been some kind of super-hacker, because she went through those corporate beasts in like, seconds."

"How are you feeling?" That was Connor. Casey and Connor were here.

"Why . . . are you wearing a sling?" she managed to say.

"There was no way she was a hacker. That's crazy. I saw it happen through the fence! She just waved her hand, and poof, all the robots were here. It was like witchcraft."

"Claire?" Casey's voice again.

"Hi Connor, hi Casey," she said.

"We were really worried about you there for a while. The doctors weren't quite sure what happened."

"Yeah, you just wouldn't wake up," Conner added.

"Are you feeling better?" Casey added.

Claire cracked a smile that made her head hurt. "My name is Claire, and I can talk to trees . . ."

"What do they say?"

Claire put her finger to her lips. "That's a secret."

"Gods, she is out of it."

Laughing really made her head hurt. It was entirely worth it.

ENHANCED WEATHERING

CHRISTOPHER R. MUSCATO

2049 C.E.

Sofia would never fully be able to explain why she did it. Perhaps it was the hypnotic, monotonous rhythm of the train's movement along the rails, the white noise of the high speed engine eroding just enough of her normal social inhibitions. Perhaps it was the isolation, the listless nature of her work and the desire to form even those simple bonds of communication. Or perhaps it was something in the air. A low-pressure system. Storm moving through. The weather had been acting strangely.

Whatever the reason, Sofia felt less content than usual to simply pass the time focused on her own work, her computer, her social media accounts. At 35, she was more than comfortable with herself and her silence. But today, her mind was restless. She couldn't focus. And so she did something that was largely out of character.

She talked to the stranger sharing her train car.

"Going home or leaving?" she asked casually, voice hovering at an audible but slightly disinterested volume so as not to betray her restlessness.

The stranger across from her looked up from his newspaper, one eyebrow arched. "Hard to tell sometimes. Feels like I live on these rails."

"Tell me about it," Sofia grumbled, glancing out the window at the whirl of colors speeding past, trees and buildings and fields blurred into an ever-changing pastiche.

The stranger eyed her for a moment, then folded up his newspaper. "And how about you? A long trip, I take it?"

Sofia nodded, unsure now why she had engaged the stranger if she wasn't prepared to sustain a lengthy conversation. Or was she?

Her jumbled emotions did nothing to help improve her mood. The stranger, a balding man on the upper end of middle age with glasses inched halfway down his nose, waited quietly.

"About five weeks since I was home," she answered finally. "Feels like I've been to every corner of the Midwestern Federation."

"Sales?" The stranger asked.

Sofia guffawed, a little louder than she meant to, and shook her head. "Climate research. Global Climate Solutions, that's our research center. You?"

"Sales," the stranger returned with a smile. Sofia felt a tinge of red in her ears.

"So what kind of sales are you in . . ." She trailed off.

"Amit. Call me Amit."

"Sofia. Sofia Yfe."

"Nice to meet you, Sofia."

And before Sofia knew it, she was explaining her work to Amit, discussing the weather, wondering at the future of the American nations, debating the early-season prospects for various sports teams throughout the Midwest.

"Next stop, Kearney," the conductor's voice rang through the speakers. Sofia blinked. Hours had passed.

"Well, that's me," she mumbled, suddenly aware of how much of herself she had shared with this stranger. "Maybe I'll see you around, Amit."

He nodded. She gathered her things and slid out of the compartment.

* * *

"Same as the others," Sofia held a hand to the headphones in her ear, listening as the voice on the other end cut in and out. Even if communications between the nations had deteriorated somewhat over the last years, it still wasn't usually this difficult to get a clear signal. "Yeah, I'll keep you updated. Bye."

Sofia tapped on her tablet and released a sigh as she surveyed the scene. Just another small town in Nebraska, agriculture and wind turbines, some oil drilling still in place. At least, that's what it had been. Now . . . she held up the tablet to take a few pictures.

It was like a war zone.

Entire buildings, demolished. Cars overturned, pulled apart. Phone lines and cable wires tangled like a knot in a neglected ball of twine, some of the ends still sparking. This area had experienced derechos before, but this . . . this was different. Sofia looked over her data. The numbers told her this weather system had produced a massive downpour, enough of a deluge to overwhelm the soft sediments and result in extensive flooding. They told her winds reached hurricane forces, coming in from the northwest with gusts over 230 km/hour. They told her the storm appeared suddenly, with little warning, and dissipated with the same impossible haste. But there were also things the numbers didn't tell her.

Sofia craned her neck, scoping out the crumbling downtown. There it was. A makeshift community center, coffee, water, Wi-Fi hotspot, a few small turbines and generators, a place for people to gather and organize and console each other. Sofia flipped off her tablet and marched toward the tents.

It didn't take her long to find people eager to share their experiences. Survivors of the inexplicable were generally desperate to talk about what they saw. Sofia thought it helped them process the trauma.

"It was just another day," the old farmer told her, a quickly cooling cup of coffee dangling from his clammy hands, its contents untouched. "We were down at the feedlot, Carl and I. Gettin' ready to head back to the fields. I looked outside, noticed the leaves—that they were blowing all around. Then the whole tree started shaking, and then the building. Then the roof was gone, and then Carl . . ." he trailed off, voice cracking. Sofia sat in silence, letting the farmer catch his breath.

"No warning signs at all?" She asked. "Nobody mentioned anything? Anything in the air that morning? Humidity, pollens, smoke, unusual air pressure? Anything out of the ordinary?"

"Nothing." The farmer shook his head, fading deeper into his own thoughts, eyes unfocused.

Sofia leaned back in her seat, fingers tapping on the back as the tablet. Same as the others.

After a few days gathering what data and information she could, Sofia decided it was time to move on to the next data point. The next anomaly. She scrolled through the list on her tablet. There was a town in rural Illinois she wanted to visit, near the Indiana and Kentucky borders. With a few taps, she secured her ticket on the next high-speed in that direction and was there within hours.

Gallat, Illinois was similar in many ways to the town in Nebraska she had just left. Small, rural, agricultural, but here there were more turbines, more solar panels, and Sofia could not find a single oil drill in sight, despite her reports indicating drilling had been long conducted here and deposits likely still remained. She scanned the fields of corn, noticing the natural grasses permitted to thrive in between rows of crops, the light powder blanketing the ground.

"Are these new?" She asked the town councilwoman who had agreed to show her around, gesturing to the turbines. Polished and bright, they were a stark contrast to the rubble and scaffolding defining much of the town.

"Yes, yes, all new," the councilwoman nodded. "After the tornado hit two years ago, we made some serious changes to reduce carbon emissions and eliminate harmful industries from our area."

"Why *after* the tornado?" Sofia asked, scanning through her notes. "You were already experiencing drought by that point, and increasingly violent weather for years. What made this tornado different?"

The councilwoman shrugged. "You've read the reports we gave you, the interviews. The droughts, the seasonal storms, those we could predict. We knew they were bad but they were, dare I say, expected. Just the way it was. But that tornado?" She shuddered as she said it. "It came from nowhere. Ravished the town and then poof—disappeared. It was like it was hunting us."

"And you connect that with your carbon emission standards?"

"It was an idea proposed to us by a traveler who passed through. He represented an environmental nonprofit group, helped us understand we were putting ourselves at risk by resisting full carbon neutrality, by continuing to drill and continuing to pollute. So, we made the changes. If you want to talk to him, he's actually in town right now, checking up on our progress."

"Can I get a name?"

"Sofia Yfe."

Sofia spun around at hearing her name and was surprised to see a balding, middle-aged man walking toward her, tie secured neatly to his shirt but sleeves rolled up to his elbows.

"Am-Amit, right?" She waved at the man, recognizing him from her train ride through Nebraska.

"You two know each other?" The councilwoman asked, delighted. "How wonderful! Mr. Tahan here helped us plan our rebuilding! Wonderful man."

"You are too kind, Jessica," Amit smiled, shaking her hand and then turning his attention to Sofia. "What a pleasant surprise, Sofia. You must allow me to buy you a cup of coffee."

It did not take long for the two to settle into a small café downtown.

"I didn't expect to see you here," Sofia confessed, sipping her coffee.

"Nor I, you," he returned with a slight lift of his cup. "On the train, you said you were in climate research. What brings you to Gallat?"

"I could ask you the same." She responded. "I thought you were in sales, but the councilwoman said you represented a nonprofit?"

"Nonprofits need salesmen too," he said slyly, and Sofia felt her ears burn upon realizing that she had never thought to inquire as to the nature of Amit's work during their long conversation on the train. Amit laughed.

"My nonprofit promotes ecologically sustainable land use. We target small towns throughout the Midwestern Federation, most of them agricultural communities. Two years ago, I happened to be passing by Gallat when their tornado hit, so I was able to help them plan a more sustainable rebuilding, but that's honestly not my specialty. My job is pitching a system of enhanced weathering."

"What's that?" Sofia asked, surprised. In her years with the climate center she had never heard the term.

"You are familiar with the process by which the natural chemical weathering of certain minerals traps carbon?" he asked. Sofia nodded. When rain falls, it tends to absorb carbon dioxide from the air, making the rain slightly acidic. If this rain falls on carbonate or silicate rocks, it creates a chemical reaction that breaks down those minerals and traps the carbon dioxide as bicarbonates. These will, eventually, wash into the ocean where it could be trapped for thousands of years.

"Natural chemical weathering can take millions of years," Amit continued, "but artificial enhanced weather speeds up this process. We used pulverized silicates in the farmlands, that's the powder you see everywhere. When it rains, the carbon dioxide from the air is caught in the already weathered minerals, trapping it much more quickly."

"So it's a carbon sequestration system." Sofia nodded along. Several solution-oriented countries around the world had proposed various methods to artificially remove and trap carbon dioxide from the atmosphere. Other countries were exploring more aggressive geoengineering, like the reflective sandstorms in the United Republic of Arabia. She was skeptical of any tactic, though, that didn't directly cut carbon emissions.

"Yes, but our system has other benefits as well. These minerals act as natural fertilizers that enhance crop sustainability, productivity, and yield. We are producing more food, and healing the environment all at once." Amit's fingers jabbed in the air as he spoke, punctuating his words. "And helping communities break their bonds with SustainAble. Our nonprofit buys excess industrial silicate materials wasted from mining, construction, and slag operations, turns it into usable fertilizer and distributes it to farmlands that participate in the enhanced weathering system. I find new clients, and keep up with communities already using the process. But that is enough about my work. Now then, tell me what a former USAF soldier from California is doing studying climate in the Midwest Federation?"

Amit laughed as Sofia's eyebrows shot up.

"Don't look so surprised." He was still chuckling. "Once a soldier, always a soldier. It's in how you carry yourself. I saw plenty of soldiers in my village. Before my village turned to dust in the heat and the drought."

"You're a climate refugee?" Sofia asked.

Amit nodded. "I was lucky to have a chance to start over. I don't know that refugees today will manage so well. The borders were more open then."

"I was USAF auxiliary forces during the war," Sofia responded. "Deployed to protect the combined interests of the American nations abroad. Our resources being held in other countries. I never realized until then that despite all our climate-neutral talk, we had just outsourced a lot of our harmful practices overseas. I got to see firsthand what the climate crisis meant in other parts of the world. It was so abstract to me before that. We weren't there to help people, just to satiate the greed of people back home. So when I got home and started working in climate research. Feels like a lifetime ago." She mumbled the last few words.

Amit nodded along as she spoke.

"How did you know I'm from California?" Sofia asked.

"Your climate research center. It's my job to sell enhanced weathering and other sustainability systems and that often means working with centers like yours to implement solutions. I thought it was odd that I had never heard of your research center, so I looked it up after we met. I was wondering how you got around the border restrictions between the Western Republic of America and the Midwestern Federation. USAF contacts, I assume?"

Sofia nodded, biting her lip. If it hadn't been for those old connections, her short-term research visa would have almost certainly been denied. "Can I show you something?" she asked. Amit raised an eyebrow as she pulled out her tablet. "On the train, I didn't tell you everything about my work. It's true I'm a climate researcher, but a little while ago, I started to notice some odd trends. That's why I'm here. Here, look."

She handed Amit the tablet, and he scrolled through the list. Sofia watched him, thinking about what it had taken to compile that information. The rising isolationism and declining trust between the American nations had made collecting even this simple data set nearly impossible, or Sofia would have discovered the connections earlier. Or, at least, she liked to think so.

"A dozen communities," she pointed at the list. "Most in the

Midwestern Federation, but two in the Western Republic, one in the Texan Alliance. Different altitudes, different latitudes, different times of year, but all were hit by incredibly destructive storms."

"Drought and storms have both gotten worse with the warming climate," Amit said as he scanned the data.

"But this is different," Sofia struggled to find the words to explain it. "These storms, they're not only worse in magnitude. They appear, and disappear, without any meteorological explanation. No storm fronts moving in, no predictable weather patterns. They materialize, devastate a community, and then vanish. These places, they look like combat zones. But only a mile away, the land can look entirely untouched, no sign of advancing or retreating weather systems at all."

"Why isn't this on the news?" Amit asked.

"A dozen weather anomalies, spread between three countries and hundreds of miles? I only happened upon these patterns by accident, and the lack of scholarly communication between the nations made it almost impossible for me to aggregate the data. My USAF contacts are the only reason I got any access to climate research across the borders. I've been traveling for months now, visiting these sites, and I'm no closer to having any answers. I've seen towns that experienced a weather anomaly only once. And I've been to a few towns that have been hit by these anomalies multiple times. But I can't tell why."

She sighed, running a hand through her hair as she continued. "The people in these regions, they're starting to spread stories. I suspect these storms will become staples of folklore long before they hit the news waves."

"What kinds of stories?" Amit was leaning in closer, glancing around the café.

"They say . . ." Sofia paused, biting her lip. "They say the storms are hunting people. Communities. I've heard this from almost every town I've visited. People seem to think the storm was almost alive, targeting them. Just a way to rationalize what happened, I guess."

Amit leaned back in his seat, eyebrows furrowed as he placed crossed hands under his chin.

* * *

Amit was soon on his way, his schedule calling him to the next town on his route, and Sofia spent several days in Gallat learning about the solutions the residents had implemented to improve sustainability, including the enhanced weathering system now ubiquitous among the local farmers and landowners. The residents here were like those from most places she visited, wary of the future but optimistic, an earnest belief in their own resilience guiding them. They complained, saying the Midwestern Federation was overlooked by the other American nations, insisting tariffs and artificial scarcity would keep Midwestern agriculture strong in the hemisphere. And they talked about the weather. Warmer, drier, more violent. But improving. Maybe. At least that monster of a storm hadn't returned since they rebuilt.

From town to town, Sofia traveled, the rails hastening her across the Midwestern Federation as she crossed anomaly sites off her list. The story in every town was the same. Wind. Rain. Devastation. Ruin. Some, like Gallat, rebuilt. They treated the storm like an oracle forecasting the necessity of change. To move away from their remaining carbon emitting and resource extraction industries. Other communities remained in ruin, living among the smoldering rubble of their former comfort, treating their future as little more than an artifact of their suffering.

It was in one such town in Kansas that Sofia found herself surveying crumbling walls and piles of rubble, laced with graffiti and frayed, neglected posters of those claimed by what had been a devastating thunderstorm. The trio of old ladies accompanying Sofia pointed out the husks of lost businesses, waxed about the former glory of their community.

"And what do you think caused the storm?" Sofia asked.

"Caused?" One of the old ladies guffawed. "It's weather, honey."

"This storm didn't seem different to you?"

"You climate folks." Another woman waved a dismissive hand. "Always looking to make more out of the weather than there is. And they call us the superstitious ones."

Sofia raised an eyebrow.

"Oh come," the third woman chimed in. "We know some people in these parts are talking about storms attacking them, hunting them. Absurd."

"You don't think there's any chance human actions caused these storms?" Sofia pressed, gesturing toward the oil rigs on the horizon. "You don't see this as a wakeup call?"

"Look at our town!" the first woman exclaimed. "The oil brings in money. Reliable money. We're supposed to give that up? Now?"

"Worse than the magic dirt fellow," one woman whispered to another, who chuckled.

Sofia's ears perked up. "I'm sorry, what was that?"

"Some salesman who passed through." The first woman shot the other two a look. "Wasn't from here, if you catch my meaning."

"What did you say about magical dirt?"

All three women sighed openly. "He wanted us to pay money to spread some special dirt on our crops. He said it would stop the storms from coming back."

"Enhanced weathering," Sofia muttered. "He told you it would stop the storms?"

"Can you believe it? Snake-oil salesman if ever I saw one. That was the second time we saw him. The first time he came through, we hadn't even had the storm yet!"

"And yet there he was, talking about his magic dirt saving us all." One of the women scoffed. As the three women fell into their own conversation, gossiping and arguing and laughing, Sofia tapped absentmindedly on her tablet, chewing her lip.

The meeting was still on her mind back at the hotel that night. She wasn't surprised Amit had been here; he'd mentioned that part of his job involved visiting hard-hit communities like this one. But he had told this town that enhanced weathering could *prevent* anomaly-level storms. Even before such a storm had ever occurred here?

Sofia turned on her tablet, scrolling through the list of communities she had visited, the few left on her itinerary. She typed a quick message. Send all. She placed her tablet back on the desk.

A day later, the whirring of the high-speed under her, Sofia read the responses.

Amit Tahan?

Yes, he'd been here.

Right after the storm.

Right before the storm.

Helped us rebuild.

Tried to take advantage of our climate anxieties.

The enhanced weathering system saved our crops.

He's been back.

Several times.

Sofia spent the rest of the trip typing data into her GIS software. Time, coordinates, duration. Enter.

The map displaying the weather anomalies still contained no discernible pattern by itself, but when she overlapped emissions data and extraction industries . . . Sofia stared at the screen. Every anomaly had occurred in a community with higher-than-average carbon emissions, many caused by a continued reliance on extraction industries. Every storm had hit the center of production, directly. She tapped the screen, overlapping the next set of data. Communities like Gallat, rebuilt with greater sustainability, experienced no anomalies after the first. All of them had adopted enhanced weathering for their crops. Of the towns that had not made any changes, some had been hit two or three more times by sudden and violent storms.

Sofia's temples throbbed as the rational, empirical part of her brain struggled to reconcile the new data against her preconceptions, against everything she had learned about the impartiality of weather. The simple facts, contrasted by the numbers. Hand trembling slightly, she tapped the screen, overlapping the last set of data.

Dots appeared over the screen, lines connecting them in a display of movement in both space and time. This final data set was nearly identical to the others. Amit had visited every town on this map, all of them less than a week after an anomaly event and more than half within a month prior.

* * *

"Hello Ms. Councilwoman, thank you for taking my call. I was wondering if Mr. Tahan left his contact information with you. My research center would like to learn more about his nonprofit organization. Yes, you can text it to me. Thank you so much."

Sofia hung up the phone, the device lingering in her hand as she debated her next step. What would she even say to him? Sofia didn't pretend to understand what was happening, but in her gut, she felt Amit was somehow connected to the weather anomalies. He knew something, somehow. Maybe his nonprofit had developed a way to predict such storms.

The buzzing in her hand made her jump, and Sofia looked down at her phone. The Councilwoman had sent her Amit's contact information, along with a note. Amit was going to be back in Gallat in one week. Sofia chewed her lip. Better to have this conversation in person.

Sofia booked the next train to Illinois and spent the next few days reexamining her data as she waited. She worked from coffee shops and bars, one ear always open, listening as the locals exchanged their gossip and waiting for anything that she could use. Finally, a whisper. The salesman who helped their town rebuild was back.

Sofia packed up her work.

"I'm glad to hear that everything has been going well." Amit shook hands with the Councilwoman.

"Quite well, by the looks of it." Sofia's voice rang down the street. Amit turned, the surprise written on his face, drained slightly of color.

"Sofia. Sofia Yfe." He gestured toward her and smiled, quickly recovering his composure. "I did not expect to see you here."

"It's good to see you, Amit." Sofia leaned in close. "Can we talk?"

As the two walked through town, Amit seemed to keep a slight distance between himself and Sofia, wary eyes shifting from observing her to scanning the clouds above. Finally, they found an open diner and settled into a booth near the back.

"Can I ask what this is about now?" Amit's voice was cautious.

Sofia slid her tablet across the table.

Still eyeing her, Amit pulled out a pair of reading glasses from his shirt pocket. He looked over the map, the data sets, the dots and lines, and waved a hand. "What is the meaning of all this?"

"These are the weather anomalies I've been tracking. This is the relative carbon emissions of the towns that have been hit, and this"—she leaned in closer—"this is you, Amit."

Amit nodded, peering down his nose through tilted spectacles. He ran a hand through his hair, and took his glasses off.

"I have a meeting in another town near here tomorrow. Perhaps we can talk then. You go ahead, and I will meet you there."

Sofia was about to open her mouth in protest when she was cut off by a sharp and violent ringing. Eyes wide, she looked at Amit, whose face was now pale as he stared back at her. The storm sirens blared.

Without a word, Amit leapt from the booth and sprinted outside, his steps nimbler and lighter than his frame would have suggested. Sofia raced after him, pushing through the door of the diner to find Amit in the middle of the street, staring up at the swirling clouds.

And then, the clouds faded.

It was over as quickly as it had started. The sun returned and the rumbling stopped. The townspeople poked their heads out, and a cheer went up. Then more. The entire community erupted into tears of joy, people laughing and dancing in the streets. They were safe.

"Okay." Amit sighed, meeting Sofia's gaze, her mouth hanging open. "We'll talk now."

Amit did not seem to want to be indoors, so they drove his rental car to the outskirts of town and walked along the lush fields with their fine dusting of artificially weathered silicates.

"I was very worried when I saw you here," Amit said eventually.

"You knew the storm was coming." Sofia breathed the words more than said them. Amit nodded silently, eyes still fixed on the crops before them. Sofia's mind whirled. "How?"

Amit shrugged. "I could feel it. It's not always reliable. Sometimes I can tell where the storm will travel next. I keep trying to catch it, but I always arrive just a little too early . . . or too late."

Sofia ran her hands through her hair. She had more questions than her mind could reconcile or even begin to sort into any kind of order. Why would Amit want to catch up with the storm? How was it possible that he could sense the storm's movement? Why couldn't her meteorological equipment? But one question jumped to the forefront of her attention. "Do you know why the storm faded?"

"I think so," Amit gestured toward the crops. "This town did the work to lower emissions. The system worked."

"The enhanced weathering . . . it's to stop the storms." Sofia felt her chest constricting, her breathing increasing. "So the storm is . . . what? Alive? It's actually targeting communities with higher carbon emissions? Intentionally?"

Amit sighed, his shoulders drooping. "I don't know. Honestly, I don't. I know that I started to sense similar storms as a younger man back in my home country—my, it's only been eight years, but that feels like a lifetime ago. But in the past few years, that feeling again returned here. But I don't know what they are. I sense that I am just one small piece in something that is happening."

"How did you know that enhanced weathering would work?"

"I have some experience with the system." Amit shuffled as he spoke, feet shifting in place. "I learned that the storm reacts to the removal of carbon from the atmosphere. Enhanced weathering was a way to implement what I already knew to work. What I had known since I was a younger man, and the first of the storms hit my village."

Sofia tried to find the next question, tried to make meaning of

Amit's cryptic answer, but she was again interrupted, this time by a pinging on her tablet. An emergency alert. She swiped it, and her mouth fell open.

"What is it?" Amit asked.

"The storm," Sofia said. "It came back. It's hitting a town just two miles from here."

"I have to go." Amit turned suddenly, sprinting back toward the car.

"Amit, wait!" Sofia shouted. "If the storm is already in progress, then there's nothing we can do!"

For just a moment, he paused. "I'm sorry Sofia. I wish I had more time to explain. Truly, I do."

And with that, he jumped into his car and was gone.

* * *

"I don't know how to explain it," the teenager stuttered. "It just, he just . . ."

"Why don't you let me see?" Sofia offered, extending her hand. The teenager nodded, gulping, and handed her his phone. Sofia pressed play on the video.

On the screen, the clouds formed, appearing from nowhere, the winds howling as trees shook and bricks crumbled straight out of the walls of the downtown. Then, a car screeched to a halt in the middle of the road and a man jumped out. Sofia bit her lip. From the balding head to the silhouette, he was unmistakable. Amit lifted his hands over his head and began to shout, chant . . . something. She couldn't make it out. But as he did, the air *moved*. Not the wind of the storm—it was not cycling in the direction of the tornado, but against it. A counter-current of air, spiraling around Amit, engulfing him. The vortex grew and grew, Amit's voice still ringing through the chaos, until the entire screen was filled.

Then, in an instant, everything went still. The wind slowed and then stopped. The storm was gone. Only Amit remained, breathing heavy as the dust settled. Gentle raindrops began to fall. Amit stood for a moment, stumbled, then regained his footing. Slowly, he slid into his car and drove away, leaving behind a pair of fresh tire tracks. The image on the screen froze.

End of video.

Sofia looked up from the video and surveyed the town. Some damage, but it was minimal. She bent and ran a hand over the ground, examining the white, powder-like baking soda stuck to her finger. She'd have to send it to the lab to be sure, but the atmospheric data on her tablet supported her hypothesis.

"What is it?" The teenager asked as Sofia stood and handed him back his phone.

"Bicarbonate powder. At least I think it is." She brushed her hands off. "Carbon dioxide, pulled straight from the air and solidified into dust."

"What? Where'd it come from?"

"Carbon sequestration," Sofia muttered. "But this was instantaneous. It was him. It was him."

The teenager swayed for a moment, fists clenching and unclenching as he glanced around the town, fine white powder coating every street and building like snow.

"Ma'am," he said. "What's going on? Who was that? How did he stop the storm?"

The question snapped Sofia out of her trance. "I don't know," she admitted.

"Are you going after him?" the teenager asked.

Of course, she wanted to. She wanted to understand. But her research visa was about to expire, and getting another one seemed unlikely—if not impossible. As way of an answer, she tapped her tablet, and the video from the cellphone transferred to her screen. "I'm going to have to ask you not to show that video to anyone, okay?"

"Don't think anybody would believe it was real anyway," the teenager grumbled.

Sofia nodded in agreement and sighed.

Just another anomaly.

SOOT SHIELD

SOLOMON UHIARA

2050 C.E.

Imagine a city with houses and bridges that move about. Imagine this city spinning like clockwork, rearranging in formation, within seconds and minutes and hours. Imagine, in this well-planned city, people forced to live indoors because coming outside is just as close to suicide itself, because humanity destroys the planet day by day. The entire district is stained with soot that causes harmful diseases and alters the state of the human body. It wasn't always like this. It used to be much better.

Professor Okafor had been snoozing for close to an hour. Outside, the splashes of rain were loud and clear. The rain was a short period of grace. Without it, the blistering heat and the night would have gone by unnoticed. Professor Okafor stirred in his sleep at the sound of quaking thunder. He flipped his eyes open, and the first thing he saw was the red glimmering flashes in the sky, disappearing. A holographic visual channel in his chamber was running an application, and it was televising a dark storm, sweeping through P.H City, ravaging infrared connections and splitting through electrical boxes and circuits. *It was happening again*, Okafor thought. Each time, always greyer and greyer than the last time. Each time, coming up with new destructions.

When he reached for the window and peeped through the electronic blinds, he couldn't differentiate if it was A.M or P.M. In the halo of other mobile houses, heavy lumps of blackwater fell from the sky and invaded the streets. He was seeing a black rain for the umpteenth time now. On the windows, there were amorphous compounds floating around like sinister beings. The city had never been this toxic and active at the same time before. It was as if the sky was going to fall and crush the city into rubble. He recalled when he first presented a thesis based on climate change in front of the public library years ago, but it had been rejected, his opinions stoned to the gallows, because the general public thought his theories were too extreme and unreal.

Now he was the one assigned to salvage the tragedy.

He went about his chambers; his mind drawn to the calculations he had been previously running. The countdown on his stopwatch was still running as well. He knew there wasn't any time to waste, if indeed the world was about to end.

The Professor went back to reassess the blueprint for the SOOT SHIELD he had been commissioned to build. And he was engrossed in the work when the big blackout happened. He heard disappointed voices, complaining in the comfort of their homes, offices, malls, and establishments. Darkness fell upon everything and everywhere. Piece by piece, he made uncountable connections in the diagram from a tiny hologram MIL BUG, which reflected blue lights. Metering out all the unnecessary parameters, the professor left the sensible ones as a final draft.

Yesterday, he had gone in to the streets upon arrival from Lagos. Sometimes, it is easier to see the real cause of a problem from within than from outside. Of course, he had gone with a protection vest. Nothing could survive naked out there after taking in the contaminated air. The toxicity had graduated over time, since the inception of the industrial age, since the gases became charged, since soot became too poisonous, since the pollution contaminated the water reserves and the farms and had plagued P.H City for decades, and counting. It was 2050 now. Only two hours of surveying, and he already understood the traveling pattern around the city.

He even named his mobile house by the family name: Illodibe Cruise Ship. Sitting in the control room, he keyed in letters and digits. Ancestral codes. The letters and digits produced a location nicknamed Ground X. Not too far away, it was churning up fire and smoke, through pipes and cylinders, thick into the grey firmaments. So, by the time the Illodibe gently entered the automated rails and streets, it started displacing itself like a gigantic automobile toward the pinpointed location. The heat outside was obviously unbearable.

The more he approached Ground X, the higher the temperature rose, breeding a greater intensity of heat.

"Solstice of June 21, 2050. The air is still automatically induced with amorphous particles. Carbons no longer have hiding places. They are now on our window edges, they are on the roof, along the streets, in front of our doors, lurking. Acidic rain, evil cancer, God forbid. Right now, my Cruise Ship is sharing a rail line with Pipeline Station, Ground X. I am shutting down the Illodibe. Mark this part, the creation of the exterminator is only minutes away." He pocketed the MIL BUG after clicking SAVE. Strapped on his protective gear—

a helmet attached to a tank, pumped full with oxygen. And as the Illodibe came to a stop, he stepped right into the gravity pod. It carried him to the ground floor.

Ground X was a thick greyish background of excess carbon monoxide and other amorphous compounds and wastes. One whiff and that was it: tuberculosis, acute nausea, the list goes on and on. All of it was the result of incomplete combustion of petrochemicals. If there was any hope of salvaging the ecosystem, the gas flaring program had to be shut down or amended. The damage had gotten out of hand since the global warming debate got swept under the carpet in Nigeria. The oil corporations were making billions of Naira, sucking the earth dry and giving little in return. Professor Okafor had heard the tales of the Ogoni people. How oil spills left their rivers uninhabitable for fishes, and more and more horrifying tales about of land pollution.

They needed things to change. Otherwise, their people would die. Their culture would die. He'd seen what other nations on the continent were achieving, from Egypt to Kenya and beyond. It was their time to make their mark in the fight against the planet's destruction.

He knew quite well the machine needed to be working before the next full moon. That was the agreed deadline. Spending only a brief moment outside the Flow Laboratory, in a section of Ground X, he slipped into the industrial housing via a high security computerized door. Both the refinery and the Research Institute shared a common boundary.

"Clearance granted."

He grunted past the scanners, which wouldn't stop muttering loud electronic sounds.

There was an empty hallway. With bulbs that had no lights in them. With stagnant fans embedded on the walls. With closed offices until he was standing right in front of the laboratory. The P.H City branch of Center for Climate Change and Research Institute. A small group of specialists and Engineers were waiting for his arrival.

Creaking the floorboards, the spaces around the laboratory widened when he let himself in.

"I am not late, am I?" He threw the question around, and one or two personnel caught it.

"Not really, Professor. I just got here, likewise Jaja and Engineer Giwa."

He cast his eyes around the hall and met their stares. "Without wasting time, I'll briefly explain this sequence again. We let this happen to our planet. Me, you, us, our ancestors. Let us make that clear. And it is our responsibility to fix this. Even the ancestors won't fall from the sky and do it for us either. And the rest of the world is failing, too."

Nods went around the room. He was making sense.

Which is why he was proposing this OLD-GEN level tech for emancipation.

The Earth can heal. If we humans heal when injured, then why not the Earth?

We only need to take it back to where it was before.

Stop poisoning the atmosphere with incinerated chemicals.

Plant more trees and help them grow, we need pure oxygen.

Embark on a worldwide cleaning spree of our water bodies and infected lands.

Launch goals and agendas to improve the state of our planet.

"Once we kickstart this cleansing process, slowly, our city will gradually return to normalcy. The ozone layers will grow back again. The sky will be blue like it used to be in the past. Our rivers will be salty and no longer acidic. The air won't be this toxic, but fresh. Our children can come out to breathe fresh air, and play and dance in the rain like we all did when we were their age. I believe time heals everything. I'm glad we're taking this giant step toward redemption."

He tossed the MIL BUG onto the table, and the locked-in images came alive, making revolutions slowly around their faces. Showing the designs, parameters, adjustments. Their eyes gleamed with hope, the simplicity of the designs awed them.

"How feasible is this, Professor? How many percent efficiency? Myself and the board of directors will like to know, before we give the go-ahead order." Engineer Giwa, with his hawk-like eyes, drew back after pointing out his fears.

"If it is about confidence, don't bother. I have run the simulation a couple of times and it works. It really does. And I don't see any reason why the real process wouldn't work." The way he said it was very believable, that they could already see the machine performing miracles and wonders.

Access was granted for the next phase of construction to commence. Access into all the necessary supercomputers controlling the engine-building process. In his gloved palm, there was a crystal key to power it up, a metal shaft branding a set of codes. Stuffing out from his breast pocket was a photo of his daughter, Oluoma, and her pet. It was a chameleon with pretty looking green eyes. It had the name tag Egirl inscribed on a nameplate. The picture brought warmth to the Professor's heart. She was his joy and was also the reason he had departed Lagos to fix the world's climate disaster in P.H. City. He wasn't going to fail, or even harbor the idea of doing so.

If there was ever a way of constructing a specific kind of A-Grade machine in 2050, the great ANIMATOR had to be used in making it. It is fast, reliable, effective and can optimize any amount of time stipulated. It was down a vault. The vault needed the key he had just acquired. Two head personnel, Engineer Giwa and Jaja walked alongside him as he made his way toward history, toward the very place he had dreamed up while sometimes watching his daughter play in their greenhouse garden amidst the fluttering butterflies and the hummingbirds.

Mr. Jaga, always the inquisitive one, asked, "Eh, one more question, Prof, at what stage should we disengage battery power for the hybrid robot ANIMATOR? Here, different products disengage at different levels. We like to conserve power here."

"Oh, Mr. Jaga, you're in the famous Electrolysis department, is that right?"

"Correct."

"Disengage at exactly 100%, nothing less than that," the Professor said, striding off toward the triangular light-beam that would take him into the vault.

This wasn't the first time he was riding a light beam. Diamond colors were everywhere. Before today he had come across something similar at the Apapa branch. Also, he had helped install it at the United Communities of Aba, U.C.A. His hometown. He was now face to face with the famous ANIMATOR. A pure hybrid supersonic system, that intercepts commands and builds any assorted kind of machinery or prototype. All the professor had to do was to power up the ANIMATOR with the key, then implant his MIL BUG into the appropriate unit and watch it rise up like a conscious entity. At his command, it began to assemble the parts together the way they should be. It was turning everything into something.

Wrapped in its own consciousness, it worked like the fingers of a majestic spider, spinning a metallic web. It took five hours at first, then it took more hours after that. Then more and more, transforming mere chunks of metals and accessories into the skeletal form of the portable machinery. The machine that would be called SOOT SHIELD. The machine with a special ability, to channel energy from the burnt hydrocarbons and link them to different partitions. The SOOT SHIELD had a simple mechanism. One thing was certain, it had a dependence on the flares.

Some questions were asked. Does smoke have mass? Does contaminated air have mass? How much gas and flare can push a turbine? The professor had made all the necessary calculations. And he had it under control. His eyes never left the production system as he watched it spin on and on and on.

After approximately 36 hours of working at the speed of light, the ANIMATOR cried out, "Animation Completed." The Professor monitored the process till the very last hour. It cried out continuously for several minutes, forcing the Professor to pull out the key and shut it down completely. Steam rose from everywhere. And the fingers of the ANIMATOR fell down flat. He had done it, created an analog child to sacrifice to the villain smoke, to save everyone, to help exterminate the soot engulfing P.H City and environs.

The plan was simple.

When the crew of Engineers and scientists regrouped outside the flow facility, they took turns to look at its properties, before deciding where to plant it. Using a metric counting software, the Professor calculated the surge passing through the pipelines expelling out the gas flares. Engineer Giwa was as frantic as ever, walking up and down the platform like someone whose wife was scheduled for the labor room. Sweat brooded along his chin.

Millions of Naira had been spent on this particular project. What if it failed? What if he was wrong? What if the efficiency of the new machine didn't meet the required standard? What if we had ruined the earth to the extent that it would be impossible to remedy it?

"What ifs" flooded the Professor's brain, just as they most likely overwhelmed Giwa's brain. His tribal marked cheeks formed more stress lines. It was a thing to behold, his nervousness. And as soon as the installation began, he clutched his heart in his hands and twitched his fingers like he was brooding a convulsion. Strapped in a suit like everyone else, he felt the heat rising. Under a shelter, a new shade of light started to creep in, as if the grey sky was closing itself like the blinds of a shapeless vast window.

"Goddamnit," hissed the Professor, "You've got to be kidding me." He sucked his teeth. He didn't want to find out what it meant when the acidic rain came pouring. When it comes to wound what was left from the previous storm.

Engineer Giwa grinned, and Okafor silently chastised himself for cursing aloud in such a manner. He couldn't let others think he doubted the project. He was not ready to draft a report based on another failed experiment. That was his fear, that it would fail, just like the previous ones had failed.

"I contemplated a scenario like this," Okafor said. "A possibility of the acidic precipitation catching up with our installation. Like for instance, I checked the weather forecast for today, but we all know, due to the climate changes, those results cannot be trusted. The weather used to be easy to forecast. Now it is unstable, changing and changing again."

There was a tear in the folding skies, and lightning showed itself briefly.

"Well, I trust you made plans for an inconvenience like this," Jaja chipped in. He was not helping matters.

Rule one, when fixing something broken, don't ask stupid questions.

Rule two, think of scenarios where what is broken can be restored.

Rule three, provide a possible solution; some broken things can still be fixed.

"We are all suited up, aren't we?" the Professor said. "I don't know about you, but I don't want to be outside when black rain starts to fall, is that clear?" It was already beginning to drizzle foams, he had to pick up the pace and be done with this installation. Time was running too fast. Time respects and waits for nobody, not even the machine that measures it.

He set the countdown for the adjustments to be made, the coupling and the sealing. The finishing. The testing, temperatures running high. For the compartments to work as the professor wanted and pass this efficiency test, there had to be concise lapping. Because the SOOT SHIELD had spontaneous turbines designed so the surge from the flares could propel them. Alongside this component, there was a linkage with a generator for instantaneous conversion of mechanical energy to electrical energy. In so doing, energy was recycled. Rather than exposing the soot into the atmosphere, it now had a use, it combated a problem too. This, according to the board of directors, was an important progress since AI projection. So, when the installation was finished and it started to run, there was an instant reflection of lights around Ground X to show the system the Professor developed was actually working.

They retreated back into the facility. The SOOT SHIELD had to be monitored, and that needed more time.

There was some quiet after. Some soothing feelings circulated around the facility because they had achieved something. A weight lifted from the Professor's shoulders. He could fully believe there was hope for his daughter and other children in this world again.

And that was when he told a story. The story of the mother hawk and the smoke antagonist.

It happened in an unspecified time. A certain farmer had gone to clear his farmland for the farming season. It hadn't rained for days. The grasses had shrunk. So, he set them on fire. They blazed, spreading from portion to portion. The smoke rose to the clouds, and hawks started to lurk in the air for prey that would scuttle out from the heat.

For long hours, the fires blazed. But among the flock, there was a newborn chick, learning to fly. See, the smoke was thick as fog, it must have had weight. It made the little bird lose balance. It ceased its weak wings, the sky falling, slowly, as it fought the wind and carbon and fell into the blazing inferno, as its mother raced to save it.

But she failed, almost costing her own life. This loss turned her into a ferocious predator. Which made her shed tears for nights in her nest while her mates fluttered the skies aimlessly for freedom. She became inclined to the shadow of smoke. It had ruined her life cycle, and that of subsequent birds who had the same encounter. So, she spread the word. She didn't want this to continue happening. She formed a union. Whenever there was smoke climbing into the sky, she would fly out, and other birds followed her trail. They would circle around the thick smell and heat and monitor the outcome. If anyone else falls, if any loses breath, they were not going to let such an event come to pass.

SCOURGE OF THE MOSQUITOES

ERNEST SOLAR

2051 C.E.

"When we walk like we are rushing, we print anxiety and sorrow on the earth. We have to walk in a way that we only print peace and serenity on the earth. Be aware of the contact between your feet and the earth. Walk as if you are kissing the earth with your feet."

— Thich Nhat Hanh —

Hodges stood and stared at the lumbered slatted fence stretching across the gravel entrance to the community. Just past both edges of the road, the fence mingled with a grove of juniper and cedar trees growing along the perimeter of the community. Skirting the fence, Hodges could easily bypass the gate and move through the thick grove of evergreen trees. However, he had already rung the iron bell hanging by the entrance gate.

The deep sound deafened his unsuspecting ears. He glanced at his watch and then the swinging mallet he had used to strike the bell. It had been almost five minutes. He contemplated ringing the bell a second time. Instead, he closed his eyes and took a deep breath. The songs and chitter of the wild birds popped through his senses. The wind caressed his skin and a faint, sweet aroma tickled his nose.

The battered wooden door to the barrier swung open, causing Hodges to take a step back on the rutted gravel road. A tall, lean African-America man wearing a loose-fitting, forest-green, three-quarter sleeve tunic and faded jeans, stood barefoot in the entrance. The gentleman brought his hands together in a prayer position before his face, closed his eyes, and bowed slightly at the waist. Faintly familiar with the custom, Hodges hastily brought his hands up and mimicked the gesture with nervous anxiety. His gaze caught sight of the man's bare feet, and his own shoes felt tight on his body.

"Welcome stranger," spoke the man in a deep baritone voice. He straightened. "How may I be of assistance to you?"

Hodges pulled his gaze away from the man's dark, dust covered toes wriggling in the gravel and made eye contact. Stepping forward, Hodges stuck out his hand in greeting.

Before he could speak, the man in the entrance took a small step backwards with hands raised, palms facing Hodges. "I apologize stranger, we do not touch those we do not know."

Hodges paused and dropped his hand. "Oh, okay. I apologize."

The man smiled. "No need to apologize. You do not know our ways."

"I would like too," offered Hodges.

"You must be Hodges Willington."

"Yes. I am."

"Wonderful." The man stepped back through the wooden entrance to give Hodges room to enter. "My name is Franklin."

Hodges stepped over the threshold and peered at the meadow land in front of him. Franklin closed and latched the battered wooden door to the timbered fence enclosing part of the property. To his immediate left was a small three-side shed with multiple shelves holding various pairs of shoes and boots. Next to the shed was a larger structure shielding bicycles from the weather. To his immediate right, a large iron bell with a faded gold finish as tall as a toddler hung from a beam. Franklin struck the bell twice with a padded wooden clapper. The deep resonance vibrated through Hodges's bones, as opposed to the harsh clang of the bell outside the walls.

"Our way of communicating with the residents in the community that a visitor is among us," offered Franklin.

Hodges nodded his head in understanding.

"Please, walk with me." Franklin's right hand spread out to indicate the path they would follow.

Hodges quickly moved to the manicured grassy trail leading

away from the old gravel road. After a few strong paces, he stopped when he sensed Franklin was not beside or behind him. He turned around and found the other man watching him, his hands clasped behind his back.

"Mother Gaia is our home. Do you walk in your home with shoes on?" asked Franklin.

Embarrassed heat flushed Hodges's cheeks. The leather on his feet felt uncomfortably constricting. "I apologize," he said. He quickly dropped to one knee and began unlacing his hiking boots.

"No need to apologize. You do not know our ways."

Hodges glanced up at Franklin, who offered a hand to accept the boots. After Hodges removed both boots and socks, Franklin placed them among the other shoes in the shelter.

"I assure you, they will be safe," said Franklin.

Hodges wriggled his toes and feet in the grass.

Franklin smirked. "Your feet will grow accustomed to the feel. Mother Gaia will bless you." With that, Franklin set off down the path at a leisurely pace with gentle steps.

Hodges moved alongside the man. "Thank you for having me."

Franklin bowed his head in acceptance. "It is our pleasure." He paused for a moment and then continued. "The main dwellings are at the end of this path. Shall we walk in silence until we come to the great oak tree?"

Hodges sensed the question wasn't really a question. He tabled any thoughts or questions brewing in his mind. Instead, he quietly walked alongside Franklin and admired the beauty of the trees. To his right was the grove of juniper and cedar trees. To his left were open fields of grass and a variety of hardwood trees. The sky was a brilliant blue with white fluffy clouds lazily drifting along as if relaxing on a river. Birds flitted from tree to tree, rabbits skipped across the trail, and deer grazed in the meadow.

Occasionally, along the side of the trail, Hodges saw small painted wooden signs with a single word or phrase. The first sign he saw read "Silence." The second sign, high up in a tree, painted as a rainbow, read "Be Kind." A third sign read "Breathe."

Franklin was a few paces ahead of Hodges as they reached the top of a small rise. At the top, Hodges stopped in wonderment. In the small valley below grew a great oak tree at least a hundred feet tall. The crown of the massive tree shaded a meadow as large as a football field. Circling the meadow, just beyond the shade of the boughs, were clusters of tiny houses shielded by solar panels and green gardens. Beyond the homes and gardens, irrigation streams crisscrossed wooden boardwalks and walking bridges. Among the streams were larger gardens with wooden sheds.

Franklin quietly waited at the bottom of the hill by one of the bridges. Hodges curbed his desire to half-skip, half-run down the hill to join the man. Instead, he forced himself to slowly descend. Reaching the bridge, the two men walked shoulder-to-shoulder. As they moved across the bridges and boardwalk trails, past the gardens and homes, Hodges saw an Asian woman pruning vegetable plants. An older Hispanic man was manicuring a maple tree. As they came to the path leading into the meadow of the great oak tree, a couple, potentially of Indigenous American descent, passed with nods of greeting.

Franklin moved to a wooden bench and sat down. Hodges sat next to him.

"We are a community of intention. Do you know what that is?" asked Franklin.

Hodges shifted on the bench. "Yes. I learned about your community through the Federation of Co-Housing Alliance."

"Hmmm, yes," said Franklin as he nodded his head. "But we are more than just a co-housing community." He paused and looked up at the boughs of the great oak tree. "Together, all who live here, strive toward a common social vision"—he pursed his lips—"no, a common spiritual vision to use less of Gaia's resources while still living an abundant life."

Before Hodges could speak, Franklin continued. "We are a collaborative group, committed to a cohesion of kindness, compassion, and gratitude to each other and the land we live upon."

"I respect that," said Hodges.

Franklin turned toward him. "You do? Why?"

Hodges curled his toes in the cool grass and felt the heat from Franklin's penetrating gaze. Staring up into the leaves of the great tree, he said, "I was part of a special ops team during the Water War.

The CRA felt it was important for there to be an American presence during the conflict. We provided training to the Indian Armed Forces. But mostly, we were used for strategic strikes against China and Pakistan."

Hodges paused as images of military conflict flashed through his mind. He rubbed the palms of his hands across his thighs. His jeans felt rough to his touch. He flipped his hands over and searched the lines that crisscrossed his palms. "There was no kindness. No kindness to humanity and certainly no kindness to the Earth." He looked towards Franklin. "I need kindness."

Franklin nodded his head in understanding. He rose from his seat and moved toward the trunk of the oak tree. Reaching out he stroked the bark. "We are thankful that war has ended. However, fresh water is still a concern for everyone on Mother Gaia."

Hodges remained seated and watched the man. "I'm afraid it will always be a concern."

Franklin looked up into the boughs of the tree. "Our community has an abundance of fresh water via several artesian wells on our property."

"You're lucky."

Franklin glanced at him. "Mother Gaia blesses us because we are kind to her."

Hodges squinted his eyes at Franklin for a fraction of a second. He believed Mother Gaia's blessings were more due to the efficient planning of the original developers of the community. But he thought it best to not express his own opinions. Instead, he asked, "Aren't you worried the CRA or another organization is going to come and confiscate your land?"

"That is why we are interviewing you," stated Franklin. "We are trying to build a self-sustaining society based around love and healing. Healing of the earth. Healing of humankind." He paused and looked directly at Hodges. "May I be frank with you?"

"Of course."

"Many residents believe your kind represents colonialism and are nervous to allow you a foothold in our belief system."

Hodges tilted his head to the side, "My kind?"

Franklin rubbed an oak leaf between his fingers. "Yes, your

kind. You would be the first white male to be a part of our progressive society."

Hodges closed his eyes and took in a slow deliberate breath. He had experienced this type of—he almost thought the word reverse-racism, but that was too harsh and wrong. He knew better now. He had experienced discrimination during the Water War. He could never fully comprehend racism in the historical context, but he understood the unease of the community, as expressed through Franklin. "Fathers shall not be put to death for their children, nor children put to death for their fathers; each is to die for his own sin. Deuteronomy 24: 16," quoted Hodges. He peered at Franklin from across the open space.

Franklin peered at Hodges and smiled. "Well said, my friend."

Hodges stood, trying to control the anger rising inside of him. "How can you call me friend, when you judge me by my skin color and heritage?" he challenged. "I was not a part of my ancestors' decisions." Hodges knew what Franklin would say. He knew the truth of how systems worked. But he could not bite back his instincts.

Franklin fully turned to face Hodges. "No, you were not. But you were educated and indoctrinated in their ways."

Hodges opened his mouth to protest. To resist. Instead, he closed his eyes and sat cross-legged on the grass under the oak tree. As he breathed, he felt movement before him.

A hand lay gently on his shoulder. "You are a friend because you understand the importance of fundamentally reconceptualizing our world toward a meaningful and collective human consciousness in order to heal Mother Gaia." Franklin's baritone voice paused for a breath before continuing. "I do not hold the sins of your fathers' against you. I simply voice the fears of the unspoken. Through truth, communication, and kindness, we can begin to heal the wounds of the past. If we can heal our collective wounds. We can heal the earth."

Time passed. Hodges sat in contemplative silence under the boughs of the great oak tree.

* * *

After a time, Hodges stood and stretched. He glanced down at his feet and crunched his toes in the grass. It had been years since he walked barefoot in the grass. His wife, Ava, was repulsed by the thought of running through the grass without shoes. She often gave him a hard time when their little daughter would follow in her sire's way and dash into the yard barefoot. Ava always, teasingly, blamed him for modeling poor behaviors to their daughter. Before the pang of sadness struck his heart, he took a cleansing breath and pushed the memories of his past life into the recesses of his heart.

A small voice cleared their throat behind him. Hodges turned around to see a young girl, about ten, sitting on the bench. Looking as if she had a mix of East-Asian and African heritage, her long, jet-black, silky hair hung past her shoulders. Her mocha-colored eyes shined in delight.

"You sat for a long time," said the little girl.

Hodges smiled at the compliment. "Thank you."

"Most people who meditate say they sit for long periods of time. But they don't," she said as she slipped off the bench. "You do, though."

Hodges felt compelled to bow in front of this perceptive child. So he did.

She grinned up at him. "My father sits a long time too."

Going on a hunch, Hodges asked, "Is your father Franklin?"

A proud smile broke across the little girl's face from ear to ear. She straightened a little higher. "Yes. But I call him Papa."

"Of course. As you should."

The little girl stuck out her hand. "My name is Isha."

Hodges looked at her hand and hesitated. "I thought touch was forbidden to strangers?"

Isha crinkled her nose with a tilt of her head. "But you aren't a stranger to me."

A soft chuckle rippled through Hodges throat. He willingly and gently shook Isha's hand. With a bow, he added, "It is my pleasure to meet you."

Isha turned and clasped his left hand to pull him along. "Come, you can help me harvest for dinner. It is one of my chores."

"Wonderful."

"We have to hurry though. Suresh gets impatient if he has to wait too long to prepare the evening meal."

Isha led Hodges through the hamlet of tiny homes and across boardwalks traversing the irrigation streams to the community gardens. As they walked along the paths, residents nodded their heads or offered waves of hello to both him and Isha. A sense of serenity passed over Hodges as he got quick glances into the lives of the residents. Many of the individuals were engaged in various chores around their homes or on the common grounds of the community. Other residents were simply reading, writing, or painting. As they reached the outer gardens, the faint hum of electric machinery emanated from the work sheds.

Isha stopped in front of one of the gardens and picked up two baskets from a bench. She handed one to Hodges. Each outer garden was surrounded by an eight-foot-high deer fence. She clasped one of the polls, pulling it to the side and motioning for Hodges to enter first. He ducked and slipped in, with Isha following.

"Are you a vegetarian?" asked Isha. She moved toward the abundance of plants thriving in the garden.

"Just recently," admitted Hodges.

She glanced over at him. He felt the need to justify his answer. "I used to be a carnivore," he teased. "But recently . . ." he struggled to find the right words to express how his thinking had shifted over the past couple of years.

"You've decided to do less harm?" asked Isha as she plucked some tomatoes from a tall green stalk.

Hodges smiled. "Yes, exactly."

Continuing to search for tomatoes, Isha added, "Everyone here in the village is vegetarian or vegan. We have chickens and cows for eggs and milk. They're on the other side of the great tree." As an after-thought, she added, "We have goats too. But that is just for mother's amusement."

Hodges chuckled.

"You can pick the green beans and snap peas," directed Isha.

"Yes, madam," said Hodges. He set to work plucking ripe beans from the stalks.

After a short time, Isha asked, "Are you one of the special ones?"

Hodges paused and looked at the little girl. "Special ones?

Isha squinted into her basket and shrugged, as if deciding she had picked enough tomatoes. Then turned to another garden bed and dropped to her knees. She pulled a small trowel from her basket and started to loosen the soil around a clump of vibrant green stalks. Working, she answered him. "I've heard mother and father talking about them." She paused and twisted at the waist to look up at him with a joyous grin. "One has the power to shapeshift into an animal." She frowned and looked at the ground. "But I don't know what kind." She peered up at him again with excitement in her eyes. "And another can spin the air around her like a tornado and another can control the air molecules in a room."

Hodges smiled. "She must be full of hot air."

Isha asked, "Are you a dad?"

Taken back by the question he stammered, "I-I-I was."

"Straight-up, that was a Dad joke." She turned back to the soil and grasped the clump of green stalks with one hand while tilling the soil with the other, coaxing the carrots from the ground. She mumbled, "And a bad one at that." Her head shook.

Trying to recover, he answered her question. "No, I'm not one of the special ones."

"Hmm, I thought maybe you were." She brushed the dirt off of the bunch of carrots. "With my Dad being one of the Council of Elders, I thought maybe you were."

"Your father is one of the Elders?" asked Hodges in disbelief.

Isha stood and peered into Hodges basket. She looked up at him with concern. "You aren't very good at this, are you?"

He glanced down. He had only plucked a handful of snap peas. "Sorry, I was distracted."

Her bright eyes beamed at him. "It's okay, we all have jobs here that use our special talents. Maybe harvesting isn't yours." She paused and thought for a moment. "Treeshaping probably isn't yours either." She turned walked deeper into the multitude of thriving plants.

"What's treeshaping?" asked Hodges.

"They are the ones that care and shape all of the trees in our community."

"You mean like bonsai trees?" asked Hodges.

Isha stopped before another garden bed and peered at the small cucumbers. She plucked a wrinkled yellow one and tossed it over the Deer fence. "No, like the oaks, maples, ash, and cedars. You know, the forest."

"Oh."

"They aren't like the boy who lives out in Oregon." She plucked a ripe cucumber from a vine. "But I think he is part-tree himself." She turned toward Hodges. "He's a special one, I would really like to meet him."

Before he could answer, someone cleared their throat behind Hodges. Spinning around, he found Franklin standing at a garden bed several feet away with a basket in hand. He nodded at Hodges. Isha saw her father and bloomed like a flower. "Papa!" she shrieked with pure joy and rushed over to him. She embraced his waist with a bear hug, and he easily scooped her up in one arm.

"Have you been entertaining our guest?"

Isha looked over at Hodges before whispering in Franklin's ear. He laughed and lowered her to the ground. He kissed the top of her bed and handed his basket to her. "Suresh is waiting for you."

"Bye." Isha waved and dashed away with all three baskets.

Franklin watched her go until she was out of sight. "Walk with me?"

The two men slipped out of the gardens and meandered along the trails through the community. Occasionally, other community members would pass. They greeted Franklin warmly and gave Hodges a curt nod or a cordial hello. They passed the goat pens and bee hives. The cows grazed in a field just beyond the goats. Ascending through a field of buckwheat, they reached a rise in the hill, providing a beautiful view of the blue sky and green trees. Franklin tugged at the stiff fabric of his jeans and sat crossed legged in the grass. Hodges joined him.

They sat in silence for a time. Insects buzzed and birds chittered in the nearby trees. The wind rustled the leaves and branches. The faint whispers of words and laughter from the community drifted over the hill. The sounds brought him a sense of peace and comfort he had not experienced since Ava. The memory of their happiness brought a small pang of hurt to his chest. He breathed through the pain and focused on the sounds surrounding him. After a time, in the distance, Hodges heard the rhythmic thud of an axe and the brum-brum of a handsaw.

Franklin's voice broke the silence of nature. "Our community has recently acquired more land. Our treeshapers are busy pruning and establishing our borders."

Hodges asked, "Are they special?"

Franklin boomed a laugh. "Ha! My daughter craves to meet a special one." He paused and plucked a blade of grass from the ground. Holding up the blade of grass he peered at it. "To be ten and believe one special person can change the world. I wish it could be that simple." Twirling the blade of grass in his fingers, he continued. "Everyone here is special in his or her own way, but we do not have special gifts like the ones my daughter mentioned to you."

Hodges nodded in understanding.

"Have you heard of EcoDharma?" asked Franklin.

Hodges thought for a moment. Remembered. "It was a movement shortly after the turn of the century. An attempt to foster an ecological consciousness that honors the unique interconnected relationship between humans and the environment."

"Impressive." Franklin nodded in agreement. "As you may have guessed, we, the community, have attempted to embrace this universal truth."

"The interconnected relationship between humans and earth?" asked Hodges.

"Yes," stated Franklin. "We don't have the power to geoengineer a large-scale intervention to change the climate to save Mother Earth." He paused and peered at the blade of grass still in his fingers. "And one 'special' person won't change the world. But a dedicated group of individuals committed to the universal truth of the interconnected human-earth relationship can influence a multitude of future generations to bring about the change that is necessary for all of our survival, humans and Gaia."

"You want to cultivate a field of grass," stated Hodges.

"Yes!" exclaimed Franklin. He threw back his head and laughed with a joy that was infectious. "Yes, my friend. Yes." He tossed the one blade of grass between his fingers into the sea of green. "An entire field can bring about the change the Earth needs to thrive."

Hodges peered into the carpet of grass before them, looking for one particular blade. Finding it, he leaned forward until he was on his knees and then his belly. Curious, Franklin followed his lead and laid down next to him. Hodges touched the tip of one long blade of grass standing above the rest. "And you, one of the Elders, leads this cultivation of change."

Franklin pushed himself up to his knees. He clasped his hands upon his lap and closed his eyes. The excitement the man had just reveled in immediately dissipated. Hodges quietly moved and sat crossed-legged before the Elder and waited.

A long moment passed.

"Children hear all, even when you think they are not paying attention," stated Franklin. "And keeping secrets is a foolish request of one who is innocent and does not know deceit."

"My wife, Ava, and our little girl were lost to me shortly after I returned from the war." Hodges paused, trying to tap down the emotion threatening to erupt from his chest. "The tsunami of '45 that struck the northern coast of California washed them both away."

Franklin reached out and placed a comforting hand on Hodges' shoulder.

"That's why I left the WRA. I wanted distance from the pain," continued Hodges. "I'll be honest, I never cared about this environmental stuff. But Ava did." He took a cleansing breath. "To be close to her memory, now I do."

Franklin squeezed Hodges shoulder. "I am sorry for your loss, but I am grateful for the path you have chosen."

The two men sat in silence for a time as the sun moved across the mid-afternoon sky.

"As Isha told you, I am one of the Elders," Franklin said. "Our mission is to try and seize humanity's collective attention and provide a second choice that brings about global change for the betterment of all."

"Admirable," Hodges said with unenthusiastic zeal.

Franklin's gaze turned icy.

Hodges held the man's gaze. In the distance, the brum-brum of the handsaw ceased. Followed by the triumph cries of many as a tree crashed to the ground. After a few moments the cheers of the men faded away. The birds resumed their songs and nature regained its natural rhythm of life.

Hodges smiled in an attempt to disarm Franklin. He leaned forward and swept his hand through the grass between them. "Nature is resilient. Nature always finds a way to bounce back." He tore a hand of grass from the ground. Holding the sod in his fist, he locked eyes with Franklin. "Humanity is poison. Your ideals are admirable, and we need minds like you to find the balance between humans and nature." He pressed the soil back into the earth. "Real change begins with an individual making a conscious, intentional choice to be kind to nature." Making eye contact again with Franklin, he noticed the man's icy gaze melting. "And hopefully, that kindness will become the infectious plague that will cleanse the poison of our species."

A hearty laugh split Franklin's face from ear to ear. He reached out and grabbed Hodges shoulder and pulled the man in for an embrace. Genuine laughter shook from Franklin's body. The man released him and stood in a swift motion, bringing Hodges with him.

Still grasping his shoulder, Franklin shared, "You should be one of the Elders."

Before Hodges could protest, a deep, hollow, ring of a bell swept through the sky.

Franklin held up one finger. "Come, it is time to eat. Suresh and the others are waiting to meet you."

* * *

Dinner was a community affair. To the west of the great oak tree was a small field with several long wooden tables and benches situated in a pentagon shape. Over a hundred people milled about, gathering food and drink from the serving stations and sitting on both sides of the wooden tables. A hum of conversation as loud as a hive of bees drifted from table to table. Isha had saved a seat for him and insisted he ate with her. The young girl enthusiastically showed Hodges the particulars on getting his food and drink. Once accomplished, they sat to eat.

Isha explained to Hodges that the entire community ate together for the evening meal. Breakfast and lunch were less formal, but there were usually groups of family and friends sharing a meal together. In the warm seasons, they ate outside. In the cold months, the Meeting Hall was used. Isha indirectly shared with him the joys she found living in such a community. She also shared one of her fears.

Conspiratorially, Isha leaned in close to Hodges. "Don't drink the unfiltered well water."

Hodges leaned in and whispered, "Why?"

Isha nodded her head to a group of girls and boys a few years older than her sitting at another table. "There's something in the water that makes them weird."

Hodges smiled and peered at the clump of kids. He didn't notice anything particularly weird about them. They seemed like an average group of awkward teenagers. He whispered back, "Are they a group of the special ones?"

Isha busted out into a giggle and shoulder checked him. "Pft! No!"

They both busted out laughing in joy. A tinge of jealousy stabbed at his heart, remembering all the times he had laughed so freely with his own little girl. Franklin approached with a striking, petite Asian woman by his side.

The woman spoke with a soft voice. "Isha are you dominating our guest's time?"

Isha tried to stifle her laugh with no success. Hodges stood.

"Hodges, I would like you to meet my wife, Julissa," said Franklin.

Hodges bowed at the waist. "My pleasure."

Before either person could speak, the bell at the front gate reverberated over the assembly of gatherers. Instantly, silence swept across the meal. All heads turned toward Franklin.

Julissa reached out and took Isha's hand. She whispered,

"Come."

Isha obeyed. But before leaving, she squeezed Hodges's hand. "I hope you decide to stay." Then she moved off with her mother.

"Walk with me," said Franklin.

Hodges scanned each table of neighbors. Faces of fear, concern, and dread stared back at him. Each face was a different color or ethnicity. Each individual comprised a whole collective mindset wanting to make a difference in a world that was on a path to destruction. Then, on each face, he saw what was in Isha's eyes when she asked him to stay, hope.

The front gate bell tolled again.

Hodges walked with Franklin to the front gate.

The front gate bell tolled again.

"I sense whoever is at the front gate is slightly impatient," commented Hodges.

Franklin smiled. "To say the least."

Franklin released a measured breath that Hodges suspected was a precursor to a conversation he didn't want to begin. "We all have a special set of skills," the other man said. "This community has brought together a unique group of people that want to make a difference. Which, as you can imagine, can attract unwanted attention." He abruptly stopped. "We are in need of your unique set of skills. We need protection."

* * *

Edward stepped from the electric Humvee and straightened his dark suit jacket. He glanced at his smartwatch, then the dust on his black dress shoes. He peered down both directions of the paved road to note the distance of his team. Two additional Humvees were parked about a quarter of a mile to the North and South of him. He also knew additional team members were positioned at key points surrounding the community.

A shadow passed over Edward, causing him to glance up and watch a turkey vulture glide overhead. The bird drifted to the west. Edward appreciated the beauty of the setting sun peeking through the lush green foliage of the native trees. The bird glided past one more time before landing on the branch of a dead ash tree above Team Yankee. He glanced at his smartwatch again and let out an audible sigh. His feet shifted on the pavement and stepped onto the gravel road leading to the entrance of the community.

The lumber slatted fence stretched across the private gravel road and mingled with juniper and cedar trees. Edward grasped the mallet to the bell and struck it a fourth time. The reverberating sound thrummed at his anxiety at having to wait for a response.

Facing the battered wooden door, Edward mumbled under his breath. "What is it with these *idealistic* communities always having a wooden barrier?" He pinched the bridge of his nose, willing himself to stay calm.

In the silence of the setting sun, Edward heard the rhythmic steps of someone walking on gravel. Then, the slide of a metal bolt and the creak of old hinges. He straightened. Let out a breath and clasped his right hand over his left wrist. The wooden door swung open. A tall, lean white man stood in the entrance, wearing a pair of jeans and an untucked, dark blue, buttoned dress shirt. The gentleman brought his hands together in a prayer position before his face, closed his eyes, and bowed slightly at the waist.

Edward rolled his eyes.

"Welcome," said the man as he straightened. "What can I do for you?"

Edward's eyes squinted slightly in thought. The man before him was familiar. But he couldn't place how he knew him. He made a note of the thought and stepped forward with an outstretched hand in greeting.

Before he could speak, the man in the entrance raised both hands, palms facing Edward. "I apologize, we do not touch those we do not know."

Edward paused. The memory hit him. "Captain Hodges Willington?"

"Do I know you?" asked Hodges.

Edward dropped his hand as a leer stretched across his lips. *This may be easier than I suspected*, thought Edward.

"Not directly, but I read reports of your unit in Pakistan during the war."

Before Edward continued, something dark passed through Hodges's eyes. He paused, quickly reassessing his approach on the fly. He combed a hand through his black hair. "Well, it's great to finally meet you."

Hodges continued to stare in his direction.

Edward said, "As you know, since the war ended, many of us vets have moved into the corporate sector. I was lucky enough to land a position with SustainAble."

Hodges blinked. "What is your name?"

Edward stopped. "Excuse me?"

"You didn't tell me your name."

Edward straightened. "Edward Blackstone."

Hodges's eyes narrowed. "You mean former Representative Blackstone?"

Edward held the gaze. "Yes."

"From the Western Republic of America?"

Edward let out a guttural groan. "Yes. But that was many years ago."

"You didn't fight in the war," stated Hodges. "You aren't a war veteran."

Anger flared through Edward. Through clenched teeth. "I am a veteran of the *original* United States of America."

Hodges pursed and twisted his lips in mock thought. "Hmm, sentimental thought." He asked, "So why are you here on the East Coast?"

Edward closed his eyes to control the fiery temper quickly escalating inside of him. "I represent SustainAble Corporation, and I need to speak with Franklin."

"About?"

"Excuse me?" snapped Edward.

Hodges smiled. "What is the nature of your visit?"

Edward pinched the bridge of his nose for a long moment before answering. "SustainAble would like to discuss with Franklin his community's sustainable practices."

"Not interested."

Edward stepped into Hodges personal space and growled. "Who the hell do you think you are?"

"Franklin's assistant."

"Assistant!" snapped Edward. He spun on his toes and took three steps away from Hodges before turning around again. He shoved his finger toward the gate. "I know who you are! I know what you are!" The words snapped, venom dripping from the words. He moved closer to Hodges. In a tight whisper, he continued. "I know what you did in Pakistan." Leaning in even closer to Hodges face. "I know how you went AWOL after the tsunami of '45."

Hodges stood his ground and did not move.

Edward spun again and stalked back to the Humvee. Anger seethed through his veins. *I am getting too old for this shit*, he thought. His smartwatch chirped. He glanced at it. His pulse had skyrocketed. Closing his eyes, Edward forced breath through his nose.

"Are we done here?" asked Hodges.

Edward whipped around. He renewed his charge toward Hodges. "Does Franklin know of the many despicable acts of ecoterrorism you committed during the war? Does he know how you purposefully polluted fresh water? How you torched agricultural fields? How you destroyed wind turbines? Does he?"

"I've changed," stated Hodges.

"You what?" snapped Edward.

"I've changed."

In frustration, Edward withdrew a .45 caliber pistol and leveled it at Hodges's head.

Hodges, instinctually, dropped back into a fighting stance. His left fist struck the inside of Edward's wrist, knocking the man's gun away. Edward went with the strike and spun. The pistol disappeared into its holster as quickly as it had appeared. The frustration of the situation throbbed inside of him as strong as the pain emanating from his wrist. He was sick of these stubborn, idealistic groups getting in the way. He longed for the days when the threat of lethal force was enough to silence those who stood in the way.

Facing Hodges again, Edward growled through clenched teeth. "What? You think you're special because you changed?"

"I am not special. I am always changing. I have a lot of work to do. To be better. To make up for who I once was. But I am not special. I am doing what I must do."

Edward pivoted away from Hodges. He stalked in a tight circle twice before stepping up to Hodges again. He noticed Hodges's bare toes digging into gravel on the road. He waved his arms to encompass the whole of the community. "Does this group think they are special?"

"This group? Yes. They are special. We are special."

Edward flinched at the pronoun. "Are you serious? Are you freakin' serious! Does this community honestly think they alone can make a change that will benefit *Mother Gaia*?" Edward barked out sarcastically. "Franklin knows—"

"If you think you are too small to make a difference, try sleeping with a mosquito," interrupted Hodges.

Edward shook his head in frustration. "What?"

"The fourteenth Dalai Lama shared that nugget of truth at the turn of the century," informed Hodges.

Edward was speechless. He stared into Hodges's eyes as silence, thick as snow, gently fell upon them. Hodges held his gaze. A dozen thoughts and responses raced through Edward's mind as each second slowly ticked by. His smartwatch chirped like a cricket, reminding him of his heart rate. Without taking his eyes off of Hodges, he silenced the device. Hodges pivoted his bare feet in the gravel at Edward's movement.

Edward straightened and pulled his suit jacket tight. He peered at the last of the sun rays filtering through the boughs of the trees. He tugged at the lapels and cuffs of the jacket again. *I need to go fishing,* he thought.

"Inform Elder Franklin and his scourge of mosquitoes, this will not end well for them if they don't comply," stated Edward.

Hodges smirked. "Just because we are peaceful, doesn't mean we forgot how to fight."

A throated growl emanated from Edward. Without a word, he did an about turn and marched off to his Humvee. He circled one finger in the air twice to inform Team Yankee and Whiskey to move out. When he looked back, Hodges was gone. The inner bell of the community rang four times. The deep resonance vibrated through Edward's bones before he sped off.

TRANSLOCATION
KIT HANSON

2052 C.E.

Thick vines and wet leaves brushed past Dr. Machado, sending beads of water—whether from condensation or perspiration, he didn't know—streaming down his face. He stepped carefully, avoiding deep pockets of mud, his hands out at his sides to help him balance on the sturdier parts of the makeshift trail. In the distance, the waves of the South Atlantic Ocean crashed against the shores of São Paulo, and he inhaled deeply, absorbing the faint scent of salt and sea.

"You know," commented Yara, his fellow conservationist, "I expected to see more of them this time of year."

By "them," she referred to the bare-throated bellbird, a small, gorgeous creature native to the area. Dr. Machado silently agreed with her observation—beyond the ocean waves, this part of the forest made little noise. He found it . . . disconcerting.

"Wait!" cried Miguel, one of the equipment crew members. "I see one!"

Dr. Machado glanced up and to his right, smiling. Just above their heads perched a snow-white bird, its beak and throat a rich blue-green, like the depths of the sea. Tilting its head, it peered down at them, hopping along its branch to move slightly closer. Then, it looked to the sky, opening its beak to cry out, the sound harsh and metallic, like the world's tiniest Klaxon siren.

"Absolutely beautiful," whispered Keyton, the second crew member and last of their group.

Nodding, Dr. Machado twirled his finger, and Keyton took aim with his video camera, recording the bird. He moved close enough to be heard by the camera's microphone. He whispered, "What you see here is the *Procnias nudicollis,* more commonly known as the bare-throated bellbird. Usually, this area would be swarming with the creatures, but for some reason, this is the first one we've found in many kilometers."

Yara snapped some photographs with a camera around her neck.

Dr. Machado continued. "We're investigating the possibility of poachers or hunters, and whether we should reclassify the bird's conservation status." He turned to place his hand on a nearby tree trunk, where a patch of bark seemed ripped away, as if by rough sandpaper.

Suddenly, something rumbled in the distance, and the bellbird took flight, escaping the shaking tree branches. Dr. Machado looked around, trying to find the source of the intrusion. A sharp *crack* resounded, and a nearby tree exploded from its roots, tumbling down atop the conservationist crew. Yara screamed, and the two crewmen covered their faces with their hands in response to the impending disaster.

Dr. Machado threw himself in front of the falling tree, quickly holding his breath and stretching out his arms.

The tree slammed against his palms, crackling as the force it carried was halted by Dr. Machado's body alone. It shuddered, and Dr. Machado squinted his eyes, noting the slight haze extending from his body, warping the air like heat from asphalt. He gently turned himself, lowering the massive tree to the forest floor, where it landed with a heavy *thud.*

The others stood silent for a moment, staring, as he finally exhaled, the shimmer in the air fading away.

"You're one of them!" Miguel exclaimed, eyes wide. "One of the Curupira!"

Dr. Machado exchanged a knowing glance with Yara before responding. "So, you've heard the urban legends."

"I've known Dr. Machado for a long time," added Yara. "He's no spirit or myth. Just someone with an evolutionary advantage. Well, at least that's my theory. It has to be a genetic thing."

"And I'm not dangerous or anything," Dr. Machado said reassuringly. "All I can do is create a protective field around myself, and only as long as I'm holding my breath. It's some kind of anaerobic reflex my body creates."

"Whoa," Keyton responded. "You're like a superhero."

Dr. Machado chuckled. "Nothing like that. I'm just slightly more equipped to handle more . . . dangerous areas of the world. Areas other conservationists might not be so willing to go to."

Speaking up to change the subject, Yara commented, "what do you think that was, that uprooted the tree?"

Dr. Machado sighed, placing his hands on his hips. "I don't know. But there shouldn't be anything so big around here. An illegal deforestation vehicle, maybe?"

He turned toward the tree's remains, ignoring Miguel and Keyton's gawking expressions. "Let's follow the path of destruction and see what we can find."

* * *

They traveled southeast for a while, keeping in line with the shredded tree bark and uprooted foliage as they traversed the forest. Along the way, Dr. Machado saw no evidence of a human element, or of any automated machinery. He did, however, notice that the forest grew more and quieter as they progressed, as if this pocket of the world had been suspended in amber.

Eventually, they came upon a large cave angled steeply into the earth, the passing wind faintly reverberating across it like a burst of breath into a flute. Dr. Machado retrieved a flashlight, stepping up to the mouth of the cave and sending the incandescent beam streaming into the darkness. His light exposed smooth stone walls and flattened mud, but he could not quite make out the back of the tunnel. Otherwise, it seemed deceptively empty, as if something squirmed in the darkness just beyond his perception.

Suddenly, something crashed through the trees behind him, and Miguel screamed, the cry shrill and filled with terror. Spinning on his heels, he saw a massive brown-and-yellow blur exiting the clearing, moving so fast he only caught a split-second glimpse. As it vanished, he realized Miguel was now missing from the group, replaced by a small patch of fresh blood on the ground.

"M . . . Miguel?" Keyton asked hesitantly, his voice barely above a whisper.

Another crash to his left, and Dr. Machado turned in time to see some kind of large, brown-and-yellow whip cracking toward him. At the last second, he managed to gulp in enough air to hold his breath, and the whip-like blur struck him in the chest, reflecting off of his protective field. Still, the kinetic force of the strike lifted him off his feet, throwing him backwards and crashing through the trees. He bounced off tree trunks, his field splintering the wood as it kept his body safe, and rolled into the grass, coming to a stop on the forest floor. Exhaling, he felt the field shudder and fade, and the foliage tickled his skin as it touched him.

"Dr. Machado!" he heard Yara cry in the distance.

Leaping to his feet, he sprinted back toward the cave, Yara and Keyton mere specks in the distance. As he approached, something raced next to him, barreling through the trees, though he could not make out its size or dimensions. He broke into the clearing alongside the object, exposing itself.

"Oh my God!" screamed Keyton.

The beast appearing before them had the body of a snake, patterned in brown-and-yellow spots, though this snake was as long and as thick as a train. It rose up, facing them, its eyes glowing a furious red in a way that made it seem as if its retinas were on fire. Keyton looked up at the massive serpent's face, and its head tilted, eyes flaring for a split-second like a camera flash. Smoke erupted from Keyton's eye sockets, and he shrieked, clutching his face in his hands.

"I can't see," the man whimpered. "Oh Jesus, it burns!"

The snake reared back, striking at the blinded man, but Dr. Machado intervened, sucking in a raggedy breath to activate his field. The mouth of the beast clamped around the conservationist, but he clutched the fangs, the field augmenting his strength enough to pry himself loose. As if in shock, the snake retreated for a moment, allowing Dr. Machado to release his breath.

"Yara, grab Keyton," he gasped. "Get in the cave."

Yara seized Keyton by the arm as he sobbed, his eyes still smoking a little. Dr. Machado ushered them to the mouth of the cave as the giant snake hissed behind them, preparing to strike again. The wind shifted, and he held his breath again, shoving his colleagues into the darkness as the creature's snout slammed into his back. Flying over Yara and Keyton's heads, he slid across the stone, moaning as his protective field faded.

Yara rushed to Dr. Machado's side, helping him to his feet. "What is that thing?"

"A Boitatá," Keyton murmured, fumbling around blindly. "It's a Boitatá."

"The mythological animal?" scoffed Yara. "Unlikely."

"What else, then?" he hissed.

Movement behind Dr. Machado drew his attention to the back of the cave, and he inched further into the darkness. As his eyes adjusted, his jaw dropped.

"She's not a Boitatá," he whispered. "She's a mother."

Coiled in the back of the cave sat a mass of thick, muscular snakes, their colors matching the much larger one outside. They shrank away from Dr. Machado as he approached, their little beady eyes flickering red, out of sync with one another. Dr. Machado felt heat prickle his skin, but they seemed unable to produce the same amount of energy as the big one. He smelled seawater, and leaned closer to the soft earth beneath them, filled with murky liquid.

"Yara," he said, backing away, "how far are we from the coast?"

She glanced at him. "We can't be too far. Why?"

"We were on the southeast shores, right? How far are we from Ilha da Queimada Grande?"

"The island?" cocking her head, she thought for a moment before her eyes widened in realization. "Oh, my. They're golden lanceheads."

"They're what?" demanded Keyton. "What is Ilha da Queimada Grande?"

"It's an island not too far from here," Dr. Machado explained. "Or, it was. Last big hurricane that hit this region flooded the island, and the storm surge permanently swamped it. Thankfully, it was unpopulated, with the exception of—"

"Golden lancehead vipers," finished Yara. "We thought they all drowned in the ocean."

"They adapted," Dr. Machado continued. "Just like me. They evolved with the planet, tunneling their way to the mainland. This isn't a monster, or a myth. It's just an invasive species."

"What do we do, then?" asked Keyton. "Miguel's gone. I can't see. How do we kill them?"

Dr. Machado traded glances with Yara before speaking. "I don't think we should. It's our fault, as a people, that they lost their home. If we're going to share the planet, we have to learn to live with the consequences of our past."

"What?" Keyton cried. "Then how do *we* survive?"

Sighing, Dr. Machado rolled up his sleeves, moving to the mouth of the cave. "I'll take care of it."

Holding his breath, he returned to the forest.

The large viper hovered over him, glaring down with its red eyes. He looked away just as they flared, the protective field around him shimmering as a heat pulse refracted away from it. Rearing back, the viper struck, and he darted forward, wrapping his arms around its throat as it descended. Twisting his body, he wrested the massive snake to the ground, his lungs aching in his chest.

The viper stopped squirming for a moment, and he exhaled, screaming. "Yara! Keyton! Run!"

The two explorers burst from the cave as Dr. Machado held his breath again, re-enabling his field. The massive viper snapped at them, but he held it back, dragging it toward the cave. Closing his eyes, he shook his head in sorrow as he slammed his fist against the stone. The viper spun around, red eyes widening as the entrance to the cave began to shudder, crumbling under the force of the conservationist's blow. It slithered forward quickly, barreling into the cave to protect its babies as the stone collapsed behind it.

Dr. Machado released his breath, the dust settling around him as the forest fell silent.

"That's not going to hold it," cautioned Yara. "It's too big. Or, they'll just tunnel out again."

"I know," Dr. Machado agreed. "I'm just buying you time. Get Keyton out of here and back to the preserve. Let them know we need to set up an emergency perimeter around the southeast corner of São Paulo for a new species." He paused. The attention on the new species would bring attention to himself, but he'd deal with that later. "The first recorded Curupira animal."

"What about you?" Yara asked. "Aren't you coming?"

Dr. Machado shook his head. "I can't let these spread until we bring more people back to contain them. I'll be here, defending this corner of the forest, until you return. Don't take too long."

The rubble in front of the cave stirred, and red eyes peered through the cracks. Yara saw them, too, and grabbed Keyton, hurrying into the trees. Once the pair was out of sight, Dr. Machado inhaled deeply, expanding his lungs in preparation for the battle to come. His colleagues' footsteps faded into silence, and he smiled, preparing to meet his match once again.

"Fly fast, friends."

TEAM WOLF ANXIETY

LAUREL BECKLEY

2053 C.E.

It was hot as fuck in the med tent, despite the solar-powered fans doing their damnedest to create some sort of wind flow. This tent had been made in the 1990s—when ninety degrees in April was unfathomable even with Oregon's tempestuous spring and the then-United States were gearing up for their next great war in the desert instead of wildfire-affected regions in their own country.

Liv paused mid-jab to wipe away the sweat dripping down her forehead and into her eyebrows. The movement caused her patient to stop mid-conversation—something about dolphins and plastic ocean palaces and other nonsensical kid-talk—and their gaze riveted on her howling wolf arm patch.

Every damn time. Liv darted a glance to the kid's parent as she removed the needle and braced herself for the inevitable.

"Wait—are *you* a werewolf?" the kid asked.

Liv relaxed her jaw, forming her lips into a smile, trying not to wilt under the attention of parent and child as each leaned forward: the child curious, the adult instinctively protective. Every damn time.

Despite her unit *literally* being called Team Wolf, despite years of community-oriented aid, the lingering fear of the unknown always snuck into every encounter she had with a human. The fear of the supernatural was there, embedded into their bones, from the early days of caves and darkness and the things that lurked outside, coupled with a curious fascination and awe. The fear and fascination were long intertwined after centuries of stories and media and tales. Liv's family stayed out of the limelight, due to their commitment to remaining close to the territory in which they'd lived for centuries.

Still. Everyone wanted to meet a big and scary. And they were always disappointed when it was just her. Their nature as "were-wolves" was particularly complicated. Some members of her family were simply wolves who had begun communicating with human counterparts. Others were originally humans who had gained . . . particular animalistic abilities and characteristics.

"So?" asked the kid.

Liv hadn't realized she'd paused in thought. "Nope, I'm not." Just another regular, non-magical, non-furry human, thanks. Liv held up a box of bandages to forestall any other questions. "Would you like Turbo Teens or Whizz Kids?"

* * *

A whiff of smoke replaced her latest patient. A pale face peered through the tent-flap before the flap flipped back into place, sealing away the stares and the heavy bass coming from the high school gymnasium but leaving the heat.

Liv chucked the syringe toward the trash bin, her hand shaking so much she missed the can entirely.

She stood up to retrieve it, and Ella's patient jerked at Liv's sudden movement. He'd been ogling her cousin the entire brief appointment, taking in the blond hair and bulging belly as if to conjure the wolf from within, and now he watched her. The flap twitched as the next in line jiggled, doubtless filled with impatience and curiosity and frustration and—eight hours of nonstop humans.

Eight *hours* and no end in sight.

They were always watching. Questioning. Fearing. Focusing on the danger without instead of the monsters within their unchanging flesh.

Liv took a deep breath, trying to calm her rising anxiety. How Ella—an actual werewolf, not an adopted member of the family—-could stand it, was beyond Liv. Then again, no human ever assumed the blatantly pregnant nurse before them was a were-wolf—they always questioned Liv, who was weird and socially awkward and therefore met all their assumed checkmarks for hairi-ness. The urban legends spreading about their family throughout the region, in a way, protected their family from the prying eyes of people who would actually mean them harm.

Liv closed her eyes and turned, still feeling the gaze of Ella's patient on her back like raw scrapes gouging into her skin. She heard the tent flap twitch, more a rise from the outside noise than anything else. Fuck.

"I need a quick break," she said.

"Okay." Ella's tone was even, betraying no emotion or condemnation.

Liv sat back down on her campstool, facing the dwindling pile of supplies before her. They were less than halfway through their trip and already she was emotionally drained and exhausted and she *really* shouldn't have checked her email in the high school library this morning.

She forced her attention away from *that*, focusing on a quick inventory, but the mathematical impossibility of their supplies only made her head hurt worse. Two more stops, and Operation Spring Pollinate and Vaccinate—unofficially: Operation Spring Fever—was done. Two more stops, and if they rationed supplies, moved fast enough to beat the fires billowing in the north and west, they might be able to make this work. She just needed to not think about the Roseburg depot fucking over their resupply or the fact that when they returned to home base she had some decisions to make. And avoid imagining how another month of pollen-coated werewolves was going to wreck her sinuses.

Liv rubbed her face with the back of a gloved hand.

This wasn't sustainable.

Team Wolf might make it through this trip, but the next, and the one after that? No matter how much scrimping and salvaging they did, there just weren't enough resources to go around in the Western Republic of America.

There weren't enough resources for urban communities like Portland and Eugene and Bend, which had survived the quake of '22 and the floods and the dissolution relatively well, and there sure as fuck wasn't enough for the rural communities left isolated and unsupported when the dam of prosperity burst. The bees and butterflies were gone, and yes, they could help farmers hand-pollinate each spring, but it wasn't sustainable. None of this was. The human-created devastation would only continue to spread like ripples through time until everyone eventually drowned by the ensuing tsunami.

Anxiety hit, tightening her chest, turning thought into an endlessly spiraling loop of fire, drought, failing infrastructure, white supremacists, rising seawater, more fire. The fires came earlier and earlier, gobbling up a new season with each passing year. Soon it wouldn't be winter, spring, summer and fall, but fire all around, until the world was ash and ember and people starving for ever scarcer resources and her screaming *stop* to the tidal wave, her actions small and useless against the inevitable.

But her family continued to try, and so therefore she was going to try. She *had* to. Because if she didn't, if she misstepped, the conditional admiration the humans gave her family, even as they whispered about their supposed wolfish nature, could be revoked and any minute the pro-human radicals with their guns and their bombs and their hate could pop out of the tree line and kill them all. Except her plan to help wasn't to stay, but to go, to try once again and, and, and—

A hand gripped her arm, fingers wiggling into the crook of her elbow. Liv looked up. Ella was busy tidying up her work space after her last patient left, but she'd reached behind to touch her cousin. They'd worked together long enough that Ella knew just how much comfort Liv needed when her anxiety spiked. And that sometimes, Liv needed to be alone.

Liv pressed her forehead against the hand, leaning into the feel of the biodegradable glove and the faint scent of powder and sweat and that nearly indescribable smell of *wolf*. She took a deep breath, then another. Another. Until she felt like she could pull the unraveling threads of herself into something resembling a human, yet again.

One day at a time. Focus on the mission. Ignore the wildfire on the other side of the hill. Try to make their pocket of the world a little less awful. She had three weeks to make her decision. She released Ella's hand, wiped her eyes, and called out to the next person in line.

* * *

The setting sun created an orange blob over the western hills of the coastal range as the last patient left the med tent. The fire, or wind, had shifted sometime during the afternoon, sending higher concentrations of smoke and ash down the mountains and into the New Riddle valley. Everyone had just pulled on their filtration masks and continued their business.

This nearest fire had sparked from the long-dormant ashes of a brush pile and had eaten up the surrounding unreplanted clear cut slash before turning to the remaining forests beyond. Or maybe it was caused by some doof messing with homemade fireworks. The cause hardly seemed to matter anymore. Everything was so dry, a person could *look* at a tree and it'd combust.

Liv started packing their equipment, gesturing for Ella to remain seated. Her cousin didn't argue. She sipped from a water bottle as she tried to find a comfortable position on her campstool, her belly protruding as she twisted and turned. Liv tossed her an ice pack from one of the solar coolers, and her cousin placed it against the back of her neck.

"When will this baby get here?" Ella muttered.

"Just be thankful it isn't twins." Multiples ran in the family.

Liv stuffed the last of the syringes into a bag for boiling and reuse, ignoring Ella's scrunched up face, and packed the last of their equipment into a battered pelican case. Gathering the last shreds of her energy, she hefted the case onto her hip and eased out of the tent. Ella started to rise, instinctively moving to help her weaker cousin, but Liv shook her head. "Rest. You shouldn't even be with us on this trip anyway."

Ella shrugged, lips curling into a pout. "Auntie Vik said it was okay."

Liv's other mom was their team midwife and herbalist and whatever else needed to be done. Vik dabbled in what she called charms and remedies, although Liv had never seen anything like magic come of it. When Liv was a child, she'd asked Vik if she was a Wiccan or some other kind of New Agey pagan druid, but Vik just rolled her eyes and told her not all things were meant to be perceived by human eyes. Even so, Liv jokingly called Vik her witch-mom—it also helped distinguish her parents, in her own mind at least.

"You're seven and a half months pregnant, and I don't want anything popping out of there before we get home." Liv waggled an elbow in the direction of Ella's stomach.

Her cousin snorted. "It doesn't quite work like that."

"Regardless, I know Mom told you to avoid lifting too much. *Stay.*"

Ella stuck out her tongue. "You can't tell me what to do."

Liv snickered but didn't stop. As she emerged into the slightly less sweltering heat of outside, she heard Ella say she was going to the gym to find the others and some dinner. Liv frowned, but didn't answer. She hoped her cousin took it easy, but she wasn't going to baby her.

Smoke haze transformed the high school and the surrounding buildings of the town of New Riddle into dull grey smears. Liv's eyes watered as she crunched her way past Team Wolf's clinic tent—long since emptied of patients and teammates—toward the line of trucks on the other side of the parking lot.

The doors of the gymnasium crashed open, spewing music and a cluster of humans. New Riddle—named because the original Riddle was destroyed by the quake and a series of wildfires—always put on a party on Team Wolf's last day, as a way to draw out reluctant residents for their annual vaccinations and check-ups and aid packages. Someone had draped a homemade banner of a group of wolves posed mid-howl across the gym's side, the words *welcome back wolves* written in an uneven scrawl.

Liv adjusted her grip on the heavy case and waddled faster, hoping the humans didn't spot her. Rural communities like this were fascinated by visitors and *real* word of the outside world, not like *she* paid any damn attention or like their interest was anything but werewolf-focused. Everyone tried to claim they'd seen one of the wolves transform into a human or vice versa, but of course, no one had ever managed to catch it happening on camera.

She'd learned that when things were difficult for you and yours, you tended to care very little about the suffering of anyone else. Who gave a fuck about the pending water shortage in the Himalayas when a wildfire blazed on the other side of the hills? What did plastic islands in the Pacific matter when you could barely access medical care? What was a future when there was barely a present?

The other thing she'd learned was that when shit was awful, folks wanted to direct blame on anyone and anything that was different. She never, ever forgot that New Riddle's—or any other town—fascination with her wolf family could turn to fear and anger between the span of two breaths.

Without paying attention, she stepped passed the convoy's outer edges. Tingles ran up and down her body; she knew her wolf cousins were smelling her as human-friend, and the case slipped in her arms.

"Let me grab that."

Liv pulled away as someone tried to take the case, refocusing on her surroundings. Her other mom stared up at her, a smile twisting her lips. Liv tugged harder, freeing herself. "I've got it, mom." Rhia's smile fell, triggering Liv's guilt. "But um, there's still a lot left in the tent if you want to help with that."

"Of course, Benson." Rhia lifted onto her toes and planted a kiss on Liv's cheek before bounding toward the vax tent. Liv stared after her, rubbing her face and torn between annoyance over the use of her childhood nickname and wonder for wherever her wolf-mom got the energy after a full day coordinating support with local officials and emergency personnel and Team Wolf members. Rhia emerged shortly afterwards, carrying a stack of cases taller than her head, a reminder that even though the world was fucked, there were still people who fought with all their hearts to make things just a little bit better.

With a grunt, Liv hefted her case into the bed of Team Wolf's decommissioned 7-ton. The box caught on the lip and slipped, nearly knocking her over, but she muscled it up, gasping with effort and triumph. One down, several dozen more to go. And, *bonus*, no other wolf cousins ran over to help and remind her of her human frailty.

Rhia slid her pile into the bed with a little hop and *oof*, and then jogged back to the tent, giving Liv a little pat on the bottom to hurry up as she passed.

Liv rubbed her butt. So much for the reminder.

She loved her family. She really did, but sometimes—sometimes she felt so alone surrounded by the pack. Sometimes, when the swarming and overprotectiveness and helpfulness made her claustrophobic and irritable, she dreamed of a different life. Where she wasn't known as the adopted human child of wolves. Where she was just . . . a human. Totally normal.

Liv cringed as the memory of her *one* attempt to be normal resurfaced. Liv knew endurance, she knew change and upheaval, but she didn't understand the complicated human social structure that was college. Young adult humans were perplexing, their social structures complicated and alien, and being an aro ace introvert in a sea of hormonal urges was torture. She'd tried, but she couldn't manage even a full semester. But she was twenty-three now. Surely that was too old to still be living with her parents, no matter how fucked up the world had become?

And surely, she was still young enough to be able to try to go out on her own again?

She wanted to make a difference—more of a difference than she could as a half-trained nurse slash firefighter slash human pollinator slash whatever else Team Wolf needed. She just didn't know if she had the strength to go out and *do* it. Or at least, get the education she needed to do . . . whatever it was she'd eventually want to do.

The emails burning away in her inbox itched at the back of her mind like a rash.

Rhia returned with another stack and was about to chide Liv into movement when Liv's witch-mom emerged from the woods. Vik had been conducting community outreach with New Riddle's emergency management teams all day, and had doubtless taken a little break to commune with nature and recharge her magical and emotional batteries. Her moms met in the middle of the parking lot, Vik leaning forward to pull down Rhia's mask. They shared a brief kiss, and Liv watched as they offloaded Rhia's cases into the truck and ran off into the tree line for a clandestine evening away from the rest of the group.

Liv groaned. So much for having a helper. Romantic parental units were the *worst*.

* * *

The vax tent was empty, all cases and crates stacked at the base of the 7-ton, when the school-bus-turned-sleep-station's door squealed open. Liv almost called for help, but paused. The voices were only semi-familiar. Not Team Wolf, but human engineers from the Western Republic of America's outreach aid program traveling with the werewolves to Coquille, where they'd help built a series of new solar-powered desalination pumps and develop the plans for a series of planned evacuations and dykes along the flooding Coquille river system. Most of the state was dying by drought, but the sea still rose.

The group disappeared into the gym, leaving Liv with an odd mixture of remorse and want and relief.

Footsteps crunched on the gravel behind her, deliberately loud, the sound of a werewolf trying *extra* hard to ensure their oblivious human counterparts wouldn't startle when they appeared. Liv's lips twitched with exasperation. "I'm just about finished."

Her uncle Ben stepped beside her, head tilted as he regarded the cases still on the ground. "Sure you are." He pushed his glasses further up his nose, and bent to the first stack.

Liv took the hint and scrambled into the high truck bed. As Ben lifted, she dragged each case to the back, nestling it with the rest. It was easier with help, and Ben wasn't like her chattier cousins.

"Have you heard back from any schools yet?"

Liv winced. She'd *almost* forgotten Ben knew her plans. Knew, because she'd asked for help in applying to a few schools. Her first test for herself: apply, and see what happened. And Ben, who had attended college a bajillion years ago, would obviously know that acceptance and rejection letters were released around this time.

Ben took her silence as affirmation. "Well?"

The knowledge that had been clawing at her brain all day emerged. "All yesses."

Her uncle whooped, punching a fist into the air. Something clunked onto the ground and he swore, bending down to pick up whatever he'd dropped. "That's my girl," he said, head popping back up. "Any idea which you'll choose?"

She shook her head. Ben knew the ones she'd applied for, and had probably guessed her rationale of shooting high in order to aim for failure because he'd made her apply to several solid backup programs.

Ben shifted, clearly about to say more, but she burst out, "What's for dinner?"

Her uncle stared at her. "Seriously?"

Liv dragged the last of the 7-ton crates into position. They still had to move the coolers of vaccines into Team Wolf's ambulance-turned-library-and-refrigerator, but this task was done.

"I'm uh, kinda freaking out about the whole thing." She'd been counting on rejection. She hadn't figured anyone would *want* a practically feral community college drop-out attending their prestigious university. Having *all* of them say yes was overwhelming. "And I skipped lunch?"

"Venison stew and pie."

Liv's stomach rumbled. "What *kind* of pie?"

"Hell if I know. Some kind of berry?" Ben held out his hands to help her down, but she shrugged off his assistance and eased herself to the ground, keeping three points of contact on the ladder all the way down the short drop. Even with her extreme caution, Ben sighed in relief when she hit the gravel. "This conversation isn't over, Benso—" he paused, head cocked to the side.

Before she could reach, he whirled, pushing her behind him as he assumed a defensive stance. Fur sprouted from his cheeks, his ears lengthened and shifted, and his mouth elongated, teeth peeling away from his lips.

Liv tried to step around him but bumped her elbow on the tailgate. She lifted onto her toes, straining to peer over his shoulder and saw a pale form emerging from the darkness and into the dim square of outside gymnasium lights. The person's arms and legs pumped as they sprinted, and a brief part of her wondered why the hell a werewolf was running naked in human form when Tea skidded to a half beside them.

Tea had been stationed with the New Riddle Fire Department in wolf form. They had to have been ten miles away, at least.

Fear curdled her belly as her cousin bent over at the waist, sucking in labored breaths from the run and what must have been a rapid change. Sweat dripped down their back, leaving black streaks across their pale skin from the ash, and their entire bottom half was caked in soot and dirt from the roads. Their bare feet were bloody, soles ripped to pieces from rock and asphalt.

Liv stepped forward, conscious of human nudity taboos but unsure how to help, and Tea straightened, pulling her close and tucking their head into her shoulder for pack-comfort. They reeked of smoke.

Liv shared a look with Ben. They knew, without Tea telling them, that the nearby fire had shifted.

"Is it headed this way?" Ben asked.

Two humans exited the gym, New Riddle people who ogled. "Is that person *naked*?" Someone giggled, and Tea pressed closer against Liv's shoulder, shuddering.

"Tea," Ben said. "Is New Riddle in—"

"No." Tea coughed, and added, "But we have to leave now or it'll cut off our route."

Liv gasped. If they were cut off, the communities along the coast would have to wait another two months, at least. Drones weren't powerful enough to run that far, airplane fuel was hard to come by, and even if the Western Republic of America's outreach team could arrange a boat, there were no accessible harbors within a hundred miles of Coquille.

There was no question of them *not* continuing their route. Despite the fictional myths of human pop culture, the werewolves awakened almost thirteen years ago had an instinctive drive to serve and nurture. Her wolf-family were protective and territorial and loving, and they sought to make things better for everyone. They had claimed this section of Oregon as their own, and were determined to help their people as much as possible because they considered the people who lived here as ancillary pack members. There were people in need, and they could help. Fire would not stop their mission.

"Okay." Ben nodded, assessing his nibbling. Werewolves were powerful, but even their strength had limits. "I'll find Rhia, and then get any remainders of the pollinator outreach and overwatch. Tea, get Ella and the kids in the bus. Liv—"

Liv was already untangling herself from her cousin's embrace. "I'll get the others."

* * *

Liv slammed through the gym's double doors into a world of chaos and body heat and *noise*.

There were so many fucking *people*.

The basketball court was practically a mosh pit of bodies on bodies on bodies. The change from quiet to the bass-throbbing chaos was jarring, overwhelming her senses and causing her chest to seize at the people and the noise and the *everything*.

She pushed through the throng, searching for her people. Someone grabbed her arm and she shrugged them off, then bumped into another group who recognized her blue shirt and arm patch and wanted to thank her for her service and ask questions and was Team Wolf hiring and—Liv snapped that she had to go and *would they please move already*.

The humans backed away, fear bubbling as they saw a possible scary werewolf who might eat them, and she escaped through the hole her outburst created and stumbled straight into her cousins' arms. There were four of them and they immediately formed a protective circle about her, responding to her panic and ash-smeared shirt with bared teeth and fierce eyes. Ella's eyes glinted, yellow-bright, as she pulled Liv into a hug, shielding her cousin with her body.

"The fire turned," Liv gasped, pushing them away and trying to catch her breath. They did *not* need an incident caused by her anxiety. Before she could take another breath, her cousins were on the move, a concentrated formation pushing through the humans surrounding them, leaving her to give excuses and platitudes and search for their engineering augments. A hand wrapped about her upper arm, pulling her along in their wake. One of the wolves peeled off and dove into the crowd, probably hunting for their remaining crew.

Liv protested as she was shuffled into the center of the formation, squawking louder as they left the gym and Ella leaned forward, intending on lifting her over their shoulder so they could all move faster. Liv shoved her away, finding her voice. "I can run on my own, thank you *very much*."

Outside the hot and crowded basketball court, the warm air filled with smoke. The bass from the party continued to throb in her chest and ears, but her legs kept moving as she was practically carried to the convoy and deposited before the 7-ton, all four of them shivering.

The convoy had transformed into a hub of activity in her brief absence. As her cousins split into their assigned areas, an uncle took accountability and loaded the bus—including the newly arrived human engineers—cousins strapped down the rigs, Vik walked around the vehicles, chanting New Age protection rituals. Another cousin double-checked the air filters and water reservoirs and blankets.

Rhia stood before the 7-ton, armed with a clipboard and confidence and watching as Tea marked the full extent of the fire's spread on a map spread across the truck's broad hood. Liv shifted closer to get a better look. The main roads to Coquille were fully enclosed by the line, and the edge crept toward their planned back-up route. Liv worried her bottom lip, butterflies rumbling in her stomach. If Route B became overrun . . . they had to leave quickly.

Movement caught Liv's eye, and she looked up, scanning the parking lot. Already, a small crowd was gathering just outside the gym. The double doors were propped open, backlighting the crowd as the bass *thump-thumped* in time to her heartbeat. There was no sign of Ben, who normally handled the ambulance, and the crowd's agitation was rising at the sight of Team Wolf in both human and wolf form. Her stomach twisted, thinking about what would happen if one of her cousins got too close, and a human screamed. People whipped out their phones, probably hoping to catch a transformation. Like any of her family were that stupid.

Instead, they'd just look like a strange group of humans leaving with their wolf-counterparts.

Rhia noticed her daughter's attention, lips thinning as she doubtless made the same connections. "Tea," she barked, "get the changed in the bus, now."

"Of course, auntie," Tea said, and withdrew.

Rhia turned to Liv. "I need you to handle the ambulance." Ben normally drove the ambulance. "And you'll take rear."

Liv opened her mouth to protest. While she hardly ever rode in the bus, she rarely drove one of the vehicles. She wasn't sure she could do it—drive at night, crisscross around a wildfire, and take *rear* of all positions.

Rhia touched her cheek. Pine needles were scattered in her unruly hair, dirt smeared across her highbrow, and the buttons of her shirt were mismatched. "You can do this, Benson."

Liv nodded, unsure of herself but determined not to cause a scene. Team Wolf had twenty members, plus four children and the human augments. With five vehicles to drive and several wolves out of commission due to the change, they were short drivers.

She headed across the lot, pausing as the five werewolves on overwatch and outreach returned, cutting her off on their way to the school bus, their claws clicking as they climbed the metal stairs. They looked, to the casual observer, like very large dogs instead of ferocious myths of legend. It was only after a second look that a person started noticing odd details. Longer limbs, razor-sharp claws, shorter muzzles, human colored eyes, and the strange sense of canny intelligence. But no one ever got that close.

Ben arrived as she readied the ambulance to go. He whined, high-pitched and apologetic, as she loaded the last solar-coolers into the back and strapped down the books. She shot him a glare, half-wishing the werewolf myths had more truth, because a half-wolf, half-human thing with opposable thumbs would be really helpful, instead of a damn dog the size of a small pony. She shut the back doors, fished the keys from underneath the driver's seat, and let Ben jump onto the bench seat.

Vik headed her way, and Liv watched her witch-mom's cool competence as she ran ointments of earth, water, cinnamon, lamb's wool, ground starling bone, and last year's rhododendron blooms in a charm-pattern over each side of the ambulance, with larger workings across the hood and doors. Liv never knew if the herbal traditions actually worked, but she appreciated the never-ending consistency of her witch-mom's beliefs. Cool hope tickled Liv's skin, though the feeling wasn't nearly as strong as the relief she felt when her mother walked around the truck and climbed into the passenger side.

The relief was replaced by guilt as she joined her mom, shoving Ben into the middle seat. How the hell was she supposed to be strong enough to go off on her own if she still couldn't drive a damn car by herself? Vik flicked on the overhead lamp and spread a map across her lap after placing her bag of herbs at her feet.

Vik secured her seatbelt, and a fraction of Liv's anxiety eased as she adjusted her mirrors and moved her seat forward. Safety started from the ground up, even if her sense of control slipped through her fingers faster than the smoke pouring down from the nearby hills.

As she started the truck, Vik leaned forward and tuned the CB to their team channel, checking to make sure Liv could hear what she found difficult. At Liv's nod, she sat back.

The radio crackled. "Listen up folks," Rhia said. Liv translated into ASL for her witch-mom, her fingers happy for a task that wasn't clenching the steering wheel or shaking. "With the wind shift, the Myrtle Creek fire crossed I-5. It's about to merge with the Ben Irving Reservoir Fire, which is spreading south. We're going to have to take the back roads to 42. Route C on your maps."

Liv leaned over, squinting at the map. Vik was already tracing C with a marker. Liv gasped. It looked like they were going to cut straight through forest once managed by the former-Bureau of Land Management, skirting the edges of the wildfire for the entire journey. She thought maybe they'd taken this route once before, when she was eleven or twelve, but she didn't remember—she spent most of those trips sleeping or playing I Spy with Tea and Ella as the bus jolted over potholes and overgrown branches slapped against the metal siding. Would the route still be good after all these years? No one was maintaining it. It could have trees popping up in the middle of the narrow roads or blackberry bushes blocking the way or any number of things wrong.

Her thoughts were interrupted by her mother. "Cow Creek Fire is monitoring our progress with drones, and there's a smokejumper camp at Remote keeping track too. This isn't ideal, and it'll probably get a little wild, but we have a mission to uphold. Follow close, keep your masks on, and let me know if you have any issues. Next stop: Camas Valley."

* * *

Liv tapped the brakes a little too hard at the first stop sign, sending her passengers sprawling forward. Ben planted his two massive forepaws on the dashboard. "Sorry," she whispered, even though it was doubtful Vik could hear her over the background noise of the truck's converted solar engine.

The streets were empty as they turned onto Sixth Avenue, and when they merged on Cow Creek Road. Normally Team Wolf was escorted out by the town's local emergency units or kids begging for candy or just one more chance to see a wolf, but this silence was eerie. A night meant for celebration had been transformed into disaster preparation.

She couldn't see anything except the taillights of the truck in front of her and the black outline of the hills beyond, backlit by a hellish red sky. Her left leg jiggled.

They drove in silence for ten miles, the ambulance bouncing over roads half-destroyed by the earthquake nearly two decades before, then eroded by weather and melted by heat and whatever else killed asphalt.

The smoke thickened as the wind pulled it south and down the hills, drawing the stench of ash and smoke closer. Liv pressed the AC recirculate button, gaze darting up. Did she see a flicker of flame?

The truck ahead slammed on its brakes with a squeal of rubber.

Liv jerked the wheel, swerving to avoid a collision. The ambulance's front plunged into the ditch, and they rocked to a stop, Liv's heart hammering in her chest. She looked up, squinting through the windshield to see what had happened. Beside her, Vik and Ben did the same, pressing their faces against the glass. It looked like the truck ahead had nearly rear-ended the bus.

The radio crackled. "We hit a deer." Tea's voice shook. They'd gotten bus-driving duty. "I missed the fawns. We're loading them into the bus now."

Liv's fingers tightened on the steering wheel, before she released them to sign what was going on to Vik. They didn't need this delay. But her hairier family would never leave behind a child in need—it was one of the reasons why the pack had so many adopted humans and other creatures back at the pack ranch. Yet two fawns in a bus filled with wolves? Disaster.

She pressed the call button. "It's Liv. We'll take them." Ben nodded in agreement, and Vik's lips thinned.

"Okay," Tea replied, sounding relieved. "Ella is waiting on the side of the road."

"Catch up, Benson." Rhia's voice was a mix of tension and resignation. "The fire's moving. We can't wait."

The trucks pulled away, and Liv eased the ambulance out of the ditch. *Ella* was staying behind with them? Couldn't one of her other cousins have helped—like, one who *wasn't* almost eight months pregnant? Fuck this night.

"I'll load them up."

"Mom!" Liv yelped, but Vik had already slammed the door behind her.

Liv pulled forward, stopping right beside Ella, who held two squirming fawns in her arms. Another animal crouched at her feet, eyes dark and wide in the ambulance's low beams. A third deer. Liv frowned and shook her head, but her cousin didn't see her. Vik took one of the fawns, and the two moved to the back of the truck.

The taillights of the convoy faded away as her witch-mom and cousin loaded the animals up. Flickers of movement along the side of the road kept catching her attention—more and more wildlife, all seeming to sense possible safety—or perhaps Vik's witchcraft. Time dragged, and her leg resumed bouncing. They did *not* have time for this.

She turned in her seat. The back swarmed with animals, along with one exhausted, ash-smeared golden eagle. Her breath caught.

She'd thought they were all extinct.

Then Ella crawled into the back with one of the fawns still in her arms, a fox jumping up behind her. Vik looked around one last time before scrambling inside and closing the doors behind her.

Liv didn't need anyone to tell her to go—she shifted into drive and pushed as fast as she dared through the smoke-filled night.

"Uncle Ben, it would be a great time for you to change back," Liv whispered, tapping the steering wheel. She nearly missed the turn onto the BLM road—it was overgrown with disuse, the only sign the gate twisted off its hinges, likely destroyed by the 7-ton. She needed an extra set of eyes or hands or something or they would get lost, but Ben shook his head wearily, panting. He was too tired to change back.

She swerved around the first of a series of twists and turns. Tall Douglas firs prevented her from seeing much beyond the road, but there was a gap in the trees up ahead and—oh fuck.

The hills were on fire.

She had to stop as something darted in front of her. Someone yelped and cursed in a stream of obscenities as the back door opened and closed.

That sounded like— "Mom?"

"We're okay!" Ella called. "Keep going."

Liv hit a pothole, causing a series of groans and animal noises from the back, and slowed the ambulance to a crawl, not really knowing where the road ended or began. "Someone needs to read the map for me. I don't know where to turn."

"Ben, get the map and a flashlight," Ella ordered.

Ben launched into action, smacking his tail in Liv's face on both trips. Paper crinkled as Ella unfolded the map. "Oh yeah, no this is not going to work. Too bumpy."

"Give to me before you throw up everywhere," Vik said. "My ankle's broken, not my eyes."

"Your *what*, Mom?"

"Keep driving, Liv," Ella snapped.

"Did Mom say—"

"Keep. Driving."

Liv kept driving, anxiety gnawing at her insides.

* * *

It became harder and harder to tell what was road and what was ditch.

She could barely see through the thick smoke billowing from the hills. Ben was no use—he couldn't wear his glasses in his wolf form, and it wasn't like shapeshifting fixed things like myopia. So Liv followed the lines of flattened grass, the *swish-swish-swish* of underbrush competing with a dull, aching roar. They turned north, toward the fire.

Night faded, replaced by an orange glow that brightened with every passing second. The temperature in the truck picked up. She had just managed to convince herself it was daylight, before she saw the flames. She picked up the receiver, swallowing hard to find saliva and her voice. "Rhia, the fire caught us."

"Keep pushing. You're going to take a left on 42—the fire's cut you off from Camas Valley. You're going to Remote instead. Cow Creek has drones searching for you."

The trunks of the trees nearest her transformed from benignly comforting shapes into blackened fangs, releasing a roar. Smoke burned her nostrils despite the recirculating air and her mask. Heat pulsed against the ambulance, searching, *hunting* for a way inside. Sparks fell against the windshield. The roaring increased, punctuated by the crackling and popping of wood bursting. Flames billowed, orange fingers reaching toward the sky, toward *them*.

"Mom?" Liv's voice broke. Her cheeks were hot and flushed. If she cried, the growing heat would just evaporate her tears.

The radio crackled, but she couldn't make out what her wolf-mom said. Ben pressed a paw into her thigh. Liv released the receiver, clenching it between her legs to prevent it from retracting on its coiled cord. Her hands death-gripped the wheel, her knuckles turning white as the road twisted and turned.

A Douglas fir toppled, overcome by flame, the noise and proximity making her shriek. Sparks flew and hit her windshield, and smoke enveloped them, rising higher and higher. The flames were all around them.

They couldn't take much more of this. "How much further north?" Liv asked. Shit, shit, *shit*. They were driving closer, not further, from the worst. "We've been on the BLM road for two miles."

Ella relayed the information in a low murmur. "Another mile, then we head south," Vik replied. "Ben, toss me that sprig of firewort. It's on the floor." Ben scrambled to fetch it, tail thwacking Liv in the face. "Get the blankets."

The heat was scorching. There was nothing but flames as far as she could see. Liv drove on a road of fire as the grass combusted from the radiant heat. The windshield shimmered, fine hairline cracks running through the warped glass. If there was a time for Vik's herbs to work, it was now.

"Benson." Rhia's voice crackled. "You've got a wall of fla—"

"Olivia, stop the truck!" Vik screamed.

Liv slammed on the brakes.

The tires skidded. Oh fuck. The *tires*. She hadn't thought about the tires, but they had bigger problems. She stared through the windshield, her jaw dropping. The world was orange and hell. They were trapped.

"Sweet Gaia," Liv whispered. A mass of roiling red and death came down the hill and across the road.

"Get under the blankets and get down!" Vik ordered.

Liv fumbled for her seatbelt and scrambled into the floorboard, squeezing under the dashboard alongside Ben. Liv threw the blanket over them, trusting Ella and her mother to do the same. The wool scratched her flushed cheeks and she accidentally touched the metal on the door, burning her palm. She wrapped her arms around Ben's neck, trying not to cry as the fire roared.

It was so, so hot. She gasped for air. It was so hard to breathe.

The inferno swallowed them, enveloping the truck in a wave of fire.

Liv cried. She didn't want to die—not like this. Not like *this*.

Someone screamed, a stream of words over the onslaught, transforming into a green blue of magic and promise. The ambulance thrummed around them, tinged in green, green, *green*. A whisper of cool caressed Liv's cheek.

Then it was gone.

The peace vanished, like it had never been.

The roar of fire surrounded them.

The overwhelming heat returned.

But the all-encompassing wall of flame was gone.

"Liv—" Ella coughed, then caught her breath. "Get up and drive, *now*."

Liv clambered back into the driver's seat, blanket tangled about her. She didn't bother putting on her seatbelt. There was no time. They had to get out. If another wall hit them, they were dead.

Liv sobbed and hit the accelerator, no longer cautious or careful. It must have been her mother's magic that saved them, unless something else entirely intervened. She could only hope her mother hadn't killed herself in the process.

"Mom?" She had to know.

"She's gonna be okay," Ella soothed.

"Are you okay, El?"

"I'm fine. We're all gonna be okay. It's gonna be fine." Ella's voice shook. "We're all gonna be okay."

Liv didn't know if those words were for her, or for her cousin.

She drove.

* * *

They flew around hairpin turns, narrowly dodging bands of fire as the compass spun from north to south. The grass was gone, leaving behind scorched gravel. Trees burst into flames above them, their canopies awash with red. Then another turn, and the fire receded, darkness falling ahead, the fire casting an odd shadow.

Liv's grip on the wheel stayed firm, but she did not stop. She took a left onto 42, the transition from overgrown gravel to cracked asphalt a jarring relief. She hoped it was 42—it was the only paved road that intersected the BLM road. Tears dripped down her cheeks, and Ben leaned into her side as she flew across potholes and gaps, the ambulance shaking and jarring but staying together. It was a miracle the tires hadn't melted yet, that the engine hadn't ignited. She just had to get them out of there before everything fell apart.

She hadn't heard anything from the back since they left the

worst of the fire. The silence gnawed at her insides, but she couldn't stop. She couldn't stop, or the fire would catch them and they would die. Everything rested on her, and her ability to keep it cool to the end of the journey.

White and yellow flickered ahead of them, and Liv very nearly swerved the ambulance into a rolling U-turn to get away before her panicking brain realizing she was not seeing *fire* but headlights and lanterns. A figure stepped in front of one of the lights, silhouetting themselves.

Liv pulled up beside them, easing the ambulance to a stop. The brakes squeaked and something made a cranky grating sound, but she stopped before she ran into the other truck.

She tried to roll down the window, but it was stuck. The door handle also wouldn't budge—the plastic stripping had melted, sealing them inside and sparking a moment of tight-chest panic when she envisioned being trapped forever. Ben licked the back of her neck, refocusing her attention as the person—she didn't recognize them in the darkness—touched the handle as if to help, then jumped back, scalded. They held up a finger, ran to their truck, and returned with gloves. After a couple minutes pushing and pulling, the two of them managed to open the door, Liv wishing all the while she had the strength of a werewolf.

Air that was slightly cooler than the inside of the truck hit her face. She leaned forward, hugging herself. They were alive. They were *alive*. They were—shit, her mom. *Ella.*

"We need a medic," Liv said, interrupting the smokejumper. She was too tired to be polite. "My mo—one of my teammates is hurt. She's in the back. The other is pregnant and—oh fuck, the heat. The smoke." *Dammit Ella, why'd you have to be a martyr and save all the bunnies and baby deer?*

"Our paramedics will take a look," the smokejumper said, stepping to the right to peer deeper into the cabin, no doubt trying to get a better look at the dog inside. Ben thumped his tail in greeting and the man jumped back with a little squeak.

Exhaustion hit Liv full force. She did *not* have the energy or the patience to mitigate human-werewolf interaction. She needed to know her family was okay. She climbed down from the truck, swaying as she touched dry, unburnt ground. Ben followed, keeping Liv between himself and the smokejumper as they walked to the back of the truck.

Three other people were working to pry open the double doors, grunting with effort. Four other people stood around, gawking at the damage. Liv shoved past them, Ben flopping to her feet.

Finally, the doors opened, releasing a flood of animals that knocked a smokejumper to the ground. He fell with a startled cry, hitting the dirt and covering his face to avoid being thoroughly trampled.

The exodus seemed to last forever—from the two fawns originally rescued to a fox and the brown eagle, countless mice, four coyotes and a very bedraggled cougar who bared its teeth at the smokejumpers as it jumped to the ground and slunk into the darkness—leaving Ella and Vik sprawled in the back. Ella leaned against a cooler, both hands on her stomach, but she lifted one to give Liv a thumb's up. Liv's mom cradled a crow and the broken remnants of her hearing aids. Green vines trailed across her brown skin. Liv rushed forward, hugging her mom, careful of the bird. Vik looked exhausted, but more importantly she was alive. "We made it, my greatest detective."

"Your driving sucks ass," Ella growled, accepting the hands of two smokejumpers to get out of the truck. As soon as her feet touched the ground, she gave a sharp moan and leaned forward. Both smokejumpers jumped forward, holding her steady as she swayed.

A jolt of panic hit Liv. "Oh Gaia. Ella, are you going into labor?"

"No, you asshole. My tailbone is shattered. Were you *trying* to hit every pothole?"

Liv half-laughed, half choked back a sob, unable to rush to her cousin because a paramedic had stepped forward, oxygen mask in one hand and stethoscope in the other, and the group eased her onto a pile of sleeping bags on the ground. "I thought that was how you got the baby out?"

Ella flipped her off.

A smokejumper stepped beside Liv as the paramedics continued examining her cousin and mom. "That truck is a fucking wreck. It's a miracle you didn't burn alive."

Liv eyed the smoking ambulance, at a loss for words. What paint hadn't burned away was bubbled and coated with a thick layer of ash, and the rubber from the tires had melted. It wasn't going anywhere ever again. Someone checked the back at Ella's request, and she heard startled exclamations. The solar-coolers were intact and still working—the vaccinations were fine. The books were fine. Somehow, they had all survived.

Ben leaned his entire body against her leg, a solid reassurance that they were safe. She could relax. It was over. Until tomorrow, when the world would restart.

"Wait, is that a werewolf?" The smokejumper pointed at Ben, then turned to her, eyes widening. "Are *you* a werewolf?"

Liv opened her mouth to answer, but a honking horn interrupted her. She whirled, saw the familiar headlights of a massive truck coming toward them from the same direction she'd traveled. Her jaw dropped. The convoy. They'd somehow pushed through from Camas Valley to get to them.

The 7-ton was still rolling when the passenger door opened and her wolf-mom jumped out, landing on the asphalt in a low crouch and launching up with the ease of a sprinter. Liv met her half-way, barreling into a hug that nearly knocked the wind from her chest before Rhia dragged her toward the ambulance, toward Vik and Ella, who had snuggled into the sleeping bags beside the ambulance. Someone had taken the time to ensure both had propped their feet up; Vik's ankle was already splinted. Rhia and Liv fell beside them.

Vik eased the oxygen mask off her face and kissed her wife, pressing her face into Rhia's solid shoulder. Liv fidgeted uneasily, before Rhia's arm snaked out and pulled her into their embrace. It took a minute for Liv's ears to stop ringing, to hear her wolf-mom through their tears. "You made it. You *did* it, Benson," her wolf-mom whispered. Her eyes were wet with unshed tears. "I'm so proud of you."

Liv leaned into the hug. She *did* do it. She had saved them. Okay, her witch-mom had probably done the heavy lifting, or else the Earth and Gaia herself had saved them, but she'd driven them through the night and the fire. She'd worked through her fear and her panic and everything else. She could—Liv looked up at Ben, curled up against them, and at Ella, who'd managed to join the hug-huddle too. Ben met her gaze, his tongue lolling out as Rhia told her *she had done it* again.

She could keep her cool through a wildfire; she could do anything. She could go to school, and come back filled with knowledge to help her people. *All* her people, not just her pack-family.

Liv opened her mouth to tell her moms about the emails and her decision, and was knocked to her back by a flying tackle. Tea grappled her, pulling her into a hug, joined by the rest of their wolf-team. Liv laughed as her family made sure they were all right, that they were safe and well and sound, as the humans looked on, mystified by the weird behaviors of Team Wolf. They'd watch, they'd tell friends, and they'd spread more legends about the "werewolves" of rural Oregon.

She kept laughing, both from relief and the knowledge that no matter where she went, she would always, always have her wolf family. She was never alone, because she was part of the pack and they were a part of her. Resolve bloomed in her chest. She'd finish this trip, she'd email one of the schools, and in the fall, she was going to college. She *could* do this.

"Moms, I have something to tell you."

THE COAST GUARD

C. D. TAVENOR

2054 C.E.

Ben was strong enough. He understood the truth. They deserved this. He deserved this. The world deserved this. His parents should be proud—he was making the world a better place, one sacrifice at a time.

Rather than giving him strength, the thoughts washed an alien heat over his body, and Ben nearly lost balance before his hands grasped the ceramic edge of the sink. Bile rushed through his throat, emptying his stomach of the protein portion eaten for breakfast.

Waving a hand in front of the faucet, a ration of water trickled, washing away the moist crumbs. Ben took a sip of water from an already-filled cup and spit, phlegm landing squarely on a brown chunk struggling to slide down the drain. Reaching for the towel hanging on the wall, he wiped his face. He breathed. He breathed again.

Knots in his stomach unraveled, but the enveloping silence continued to deafen Ben's soul. He wanted to curl up under the covers and watch an episode of . . . *something*, even if leading into the night he most likely wouldn't have electricity. Electricity. He hadn't been alive when they started rationing energy alongside food and water. The clouds outside shadowed the room through the skylight, yet it wasn't time to activate bio-lights.

The subtle misting of rain broke through the background, like the light buzzing of a bee hidden in a garden. If only they'd saved the bees—

He needed to stop stalling. They deserved a swift end, now that they'd reached it. He had to go outside and face the future. With one final breath, Ben walked out of the washroom and through the small cabin serving as his quarters. After acquiring them from his closet, he looped a yellow sash over his emerald uniform and placed a red beret on his head. When he opened the door to leave, the change in air pressure thrust a half-written letter from the tiny desk onto the floor beneath his feet. A moment of weakness—he'd never say the words.

His boots clicked against the linoleum of the hallway. He headed toward the exit, alone—everyone else had already reached their positions. He was the *only one* who rushed to seek relief after the final hour of orientation.

Pushing open the door, he exited into the dreamy mist. The immense Hudson Seawall spread northeast in all its glory, from Middletown to Long Beach. The massive steel bulwark rose out of the water, long walkways adorning either side of its central parapet. And distributed evenly along the mechanical levee, from shore to shore, hundreds of metal frames rose upward in semi-circles. Beneath each loop, at least two or three individuals dangled, their hands chained to the top of the hoop. Their knees knocked against the iron platforms. In front of each set of prisoners, Ben's fellow guards read the final rites. White. Black. Brown. People from every race awaited their fate.

Walking along the temporary catwalk dozens of feet above the waves, he stared straight ahead, not bothering to make eye contact with any comrades. From the water below, he tasted a tinge of salt, though not expected, given the circumstances. As murky, oily waves crashed below, spray splashed upward, stinging his face. The Coordinators warned it might burn skin if they weren't careful, though a tiny burn was a small price compared to the greater cost spent today.

Another knot tried to rise in Ben's stomach, and he squeezed his thumb against his index finger, cracking at least two knuckles. Passing the fourth concrete parapet, he caught the tears streaking down the face of an old man, wrinkles indicating an age of at least seventy or eighty years old. He might have even seen the end of the twentieth century. Why did he cry? He didn't deserve sadness. It was his fault—their fault—we were here today. Ben hated all of them for bringing us to this point. Why couldn't they have done something?

Anything? Instead, they'd forced the lottery upon themselves.

Though, they shouldn't be scared or upset. The lottery: the greatest honor any citizen of the Coastal Republic could receive, whether participating as a guard or as a sacrifice. Of course Ben had volunteered.

Passing beneath the next parapet, he neared a sign reading CARSON. Before the prisoners came into view, he stopped, leaning his hand against the nearby concrete. Damp from the misty rains, he nearly doubled over, cramps hitting his sides. Ben knew he *could* go through with it. He'd recited the laws. The rites. The charges. He knew them by heart. Why did pain continue to strike?

He brushed water out of his eyes, stepping around the tower. Tied beneath the swaying sign, a man and a woman slumped, reaching for each other as the rain slapped against their umber skin. The woman's hair, white against her black jumpsuit, whipped with the ocean wind flowing toward New York. At the sound of footsteps, the man looked up, icy anger breaking his defeated gaze.

"Benjamin!" he shouted. Unnecessary—Ben could hear fine from ten feet away. "Why? Why are you doing this?"

Ben stopped in front of them. "Connor Carson. Harriet Carson. I have arrived to read your eulogy." He strained against the urge to consider more than his role.

"God damn it Ben," Connor said. "Look at her! She's broken. You've broken her. Is this what you wanted? Is this the best way to change the world?"

Ben ignored the words, but he thanked the precipitation from the clouds above. If tears washed his cheeks, they wouldn't notice. He turned south, toward the distant ocean. The splendor of the sea spread outward, the shorelines peaceful. If only the future could look so calm. It wasn't calm because . . . because of them.

Speaking with enough force and without facing them, Ben said, "By the order of Miami Accords, you have been sentenced to death for your crimes against Earth, against the atmosphere of this planet, and against the entire human species. Under the rights vested in me by the Second Constitution of 2051, I speak these final words to condemn your life to the waves."

Ben glanced up and down the seawall, watching others speak

toward the ocean, too. Did they feel the same anguish? Or did they want to keep their eye on the horizon? He didn't know. Did it matter? But *they* felt pain. Good. And . . . Ben felt pain, too. Also good.

"Look at me in these final moments, boy. Look at her in these final moments."

Compassion pulled at Ben's soul, but he resisted the urge to turn. They didn't deserve it. He didn't deserve the moment, either. They'd thrown the right away years ago. When they deceived him, telling him if he ate only plants, everything would be all right.

"Because you were born prior to the year 2010, you are eligible for condemnation by the Last Generation," Ben said, ignoring the plea. "The lottery has selected you as a necessary sacrifice. Remember that *your death, allowed by your* contribution to *the death of this planet*, will ensure your children, your grandchildren, and all future generations to come, will have the chance to flourish upon this planet as you did. Through each death, we eliminate one more mouth."

A torrential downpour plowed into the wall, and Ben raised a hand to wipe the water from his eyes. Just as quickly as it arrived, the sheet disappeared. Straightening his back, Ben hardened his thoughts. He needed to finish the ceremony. Every second made each word that much more difficult. Yet still, he waited, wondering if the man would say another word. And her silence . . . it drilled into Ben's brain from beyond the pattering of the rain.

"First count." Ben urged his neck to turn toward the prisoners, but a higher power resisted. "You, the Millennial generations, you knew what caused climate change. You knew the risks. You did not act. Your negligence condemns you."

"Yes we did!" cried a voice. Ben thought for a moment it was hers, but it came from somewhere else along the wall. Amongst the cacophony of voices reverberating throughout the bay, no one could replicate Harriet's sound.

Ben closed his eyes. "Second count. When report upon report emphasized the risk, your generation continued using the poisons of the world. Gasoline. Airplanes. Cars. Natural gas. Coal." His mind shifted to the simple things, and he deviated from the memorized script. "You even left the lights on when you left the house, and drove to work when you could have biked!" He sighed, looking to his left. One of his comrades was frowning at him. Ben refocused his words. "You voted against the climate, because you thought, *the world isn't ready for change,* or *we'll make the change next week, but not now."*

A whimper sounded from . . . from her.

"Third count. You hid behind the cardinal sin, the cardinal excuse. You said, *it's society's problem, not mine. We must fix society, and when we fix society, each person will shift their behaviors.* Yet you used the excuse as a pretext not to act on your own volition, not to encourage those around you to reject the poison, not to ensure your children had a planet to enjoy." The tears streamed down Ben's cheeks, anger radiating from his words. But they knew he believed every word he said. He hoped they believed the words too, for their sake. For Ben's sake.

"Fourth count. You recognized the crimes of past generations, yet instead of holding them accountable, you partook in the same excesses created by their resounding commitment to unsustainable growth. Rather than reject it, you hypocritically paid lip-service to the future while embracing the same sins."

"Benjamin, we did none of these things!" said Connor, breaking the silence Ben had hoped would persist for eternity. "You know this. You know we believed in a better way."

Remembering dinners from long ago, conversations swirled in subconscious memories. Shouts at the TV as another politician pushed back the date of de-carbonization. Critiques of the new Con-stitution and its implications. Rejections of the Post UN Charters and the Eco-Education Programmes. Had they really believed in a better way?

"Fifth count." Ben opened his eyes, the words drying in his mouth. He could not say them. He could not tell his parents, with-out looking at them, their greatest crime. Ben pivoted on the iron catwalk, facing the two who raised him. Who'd coddled him for thirty years, somehow *asssuring* a future. Who'd held him when the fifth hurricane in a decade struck New Jersey's coastline, killing three thousand people. Who'd turned the TV off as ten million peo-ple died in an epidemic in Bangladesh following the fracturing of their levees.

"Fifth count," Ben said, staring down Connor and Harriet Carson, mother and father of Benjamin Carson. Him. "You failed to educate the next generation of your mistakes. You continuously failed to act, you continuously failed to do what was necessary to stabilize the planet. You failed your children, your grandchildren. And the greatest crime of all? You failed to recognize that even if *you* did not fail, the failure of *your peers* does not absolve you of guilt."

He exhaled, releasing fists he hadn't known he'd clenched. Pain and anger and sorrow and terror bellowed from his skin like steam from a tea kettle. The Coordinators had told him this moment would come. He needed to embrace hate in order to finish the final rites.

Yet Connor stared at Ben—their son. His eyelids fluttered, fracturing his anger. He drooped, as if he wished to flatten his body against the steel, but his bindings tugged him back to his knees. Ben knelt three feet from their faces, rain plastering the space between them. He tried to meet their eyes. Hate wasn't the only path available.

"I have made peace with my choice," Ben said. "When I submitted your names into the lottery, I thought you'd understand."

Connor didn't look up. Harriet continued staring at the ground, though Ben thought one of her eyes glimmered. Most likely a tear.

Once again, Ben deviated from the script. "You serve a higher cause. Indiscriminate elimination of the generations who failed to save the planet. Through your death, we ensure a better world. You know why the Miami Accords were established. You helped negotiate them. Did you not expect the next generation to follow through? You think we like this? You think we're enjoying this? Your generation failed! Your generation made us do this!"

"We made you do nothing," said fath—Connor.

Ben stood. Fire burned throughout his heart, the anger that they failed to accept the truth of his words devouring his mind. He wasn't wrong. They had no other option. If they were to save the world for their kids, for their grandkids, and for *their* grandkids, sacrifices must be made for the greater good.

Ben wanted to strike them. He wanted to force them to submit. His arm rose into a swing, but he looked to the left. His comrades were making the long walk, leaving their offerings behind. They had done their duty without breaking. Ben could too.

"I love you, Connor. Harriet. I forgive you. But I won't back down from what's at stake."

"I know you won't."

Ben's eyes widened. In these final moments, she . . . she spoke. Her eyes were blazing with warmth and power. She bored straight to the deepest recesses of his mind, to the parts not darkened by our never-ending peril. The wrinkles on her cheeks were drenched in rain-soaked tears, yet somehow, she stretched her lips and smiled.

"My boy, Benjamin," she said. "I love you. And I forgive you too. Do what you must."

Ben's heart shattered. His knees quivered. He wanted to hug her, embrace her, he wanted to hear him say the same words. At the same time, the urge to strike them remained tensed in his forearms. She faced her fate with more bravery than the one holding the noose around her neck.

Connor glanced at her, a tiny smile breaking his lips. Her strength must have invigorated him too. "I don't forgive you," he said, "but if she can, she forgives for both of us."

He desired to hold his wife—Ben's mother, in these final moments. But he couldn't give mercy. Ben stood, turning his back on them yet again. Deep at sea, lightning struck, sheets of rain pounded the waves, and pitch-black clouds swirled in a tempest of power destined to strike New York with fire and fury. The perfect executioner—a storm like this one only existed due to the folly of a runaway greenhouse effect. Killed by their own creation.

Ben considered the unfinished letter remaining in his room. Looking back toward them, the words he'd considered adding to its end sprung forth, escaping his lips before he could stop himself. "Thank you. Your sacrifice will be remembered."

With those final words, their eyes turned toward the sea, looking past Ben, past their son, toward Superstorm Victor, the harbinger of their sacrifice. Through its waters, through its winds, through its surge, the ocean would decide their destiny. For a moment, Ben joined them, staring beyond the horizon and toward their fate. It was the fate of his generation, too. We had descended into darkness, and our only hope of escape was to dive straight through the eye of the hurricane, hoping to find the quiet beyond.

More likely, it would kill them too, Ben knew.

He didn't look back as he turned in step with his comrades. He joined the long line heading toward the North Jersey Processing Facility. Above the doorway, a massive digital screen read:

> *You have served a higher cause in your contribution to the Seventh Lottery of the Coastal Republic of the Americas. In this year, 2054 C.E., we will remember your sacrifice.*

His sacrifice, or the sacrifice of his parents? Saltwater mixed with Ben's tears. The wailing and gnashing of the failed generations chained for their collective crime finally numbed his consciousness. Did the Coordinators think they were happy they sacrificed the lives of their parents to save the world? Anger bubbled in Ben's soul. All of humanity forced their hand by its past actions. Why couldn't they have given them another way?

His mother's words replayed in Ben's mind. *And I forgive you too.* She didn't hate him. She understood the terrible choice he made. Perhaps everyone else would too. Perhaps even his father, when fate arrived in the night. Ben pitied them. They were victims of a system they'd lacked the strength to break. The next generation had broken it instead, even as it continued to break them to the bone.

Ben reached the end of the catwalk. The immense swirl of white, grey, and black dominated the horizon, the storm mere hours from landfall. Its waters would rush into the bay, crashing into the Hudson Seawall. The Coastal Republic's path into the future might not be the only way, but it was *a way*, and they'd made our peace with it.

* * *

Or so Ben thought. He awoke, in the middle of the night, to a cold sweat. Heart racing, pulse pounding, his eyes fluttered. The biolight in the ceiling faintly glowed a dim purple, the algae releasing its luminescence. Through the tiny barred window, lightning flashed. He couldn't hear the thunder, nor the rain, but the storm had arrived. They were in its midst.

His parents were in its midst.

Feet sliding to the floor, he instinctively grabbed his coat and headed out the door. His roommate silently snored, sleeping as if a thousand people weren't about to die outside. The adrenaline of the day faded, his mind had calmed. What they were doing was *wrong*. And there was nothing Ben could do to stop it.

Yet, there was something he could do to give himself peace.

Tomorrow, he and the other guards would have the task of defending and saving the city, even as the storm continued ravaging the coastline. They'd search for people in their homes, bring supplies, and repair what needed repaired. All the while, they would forget the souls abandoned on the sea wall.

No, Ben wouldn't forget them. He was going to join them.

Reaching the end of the hall, he arrived at the door to the outside. Through the tiny glass porthole, water plastered the wall with a lion's ferocity, shredding and tearing into the concrete. After zipping up his coat, Ben placed a hand on the secured door handle, twisted, and pushed it open into the wind.

It took all his strength, but into the outside he went, sliding onto the sea wall. In a pitch-black night sky, he couldn't see the shape of the hurricane above, but the guide lights on the wall illuminated the sheets of rain rolling in from the ocean. And the wind—the wind! Its power rocked his bones. Still, he pressed onward, pushing through the rain and down the wall past already-murdered corpses.

It took him far too long to reach the tomb of the Carsons, but when he arrived, he found their mangled bodies hanging from shackles. He was too late. He couldn't join them in their deaths.

No. Wait.

Ben leaned over, seeing the shallow breath of Harriet, his mother. Her chest rose and fell, slowly, though her eyes were closed. Over the roar of the rain, he whispered, "I'm here, mother." She was most likely unconscious, but he didn't care. He'd stay with her until the end. Until both their ends.

Pivoting, Ben stared outward into inky blackness, facing the unseen torrent assaulting the great metropolis at his back. Hurricanes, the natural cleanser of sea, the tempests which gain power from the waters beneath and unleash fury upon the land. Even before the climate crisis, humans feared the hurricane. When the temperatures and seas began to rise, they only worsened. Superstorm Victor, out there somewhere, was supposedly one of the worst ever.

Ben grimaced, the wind ripping at his skin. "I give myself to you! Alongside my parents. If I can sacrifice them, I can sacrifice myself! It's only fair."

Silence, of course, other than the already persistent roar of the waves. He didn't know what he expected, other than to die, but a few final words made—

With a crash, a wall of water smacked into him, throwing him past his mother and father and over the Hudson-side of the wall. The thrill of icy air thrashed his hair, the water below rushing to meet him. What a way to end.

Only a chance second later, he crashed into the frigid water. His shocked mind embraced the darkness, the cold and all-encompassing relief he hoped would come from death. At least his mind was at peace.

But death did not arrive.

Ben floated in the water, suspended. He *knew* he should be dead. If the cold didn't kill him, if he didn't drown, the toxic slime mixed in with the water would burn the skin right off his bones. Instead, Ben felt . . . peace. A new awareness crept through his system, one of serenity and knowledge, as if he were being greeted by a friend always present but never known until this very moment.

He swirled beneath the choppy surface of the bay. He breathed—and instead of drinking in murky water and flooding his lungs, his body breathed in the liquid like it was simply air, as if he had always breathed like this. Every droplet of water surrounding his mind was for the taking, under his control. He felt alive—ready to become what he was always meant to be.

Now it was time to discover that truth. He had sacrificed himself to the tempest, and the tempest had welcomed him with open arms. He would become its servant.

Ben smiled, kicking his feet into motion. The waters around him cleared as he swam by, as if his presence willed decades-worth of pollution to separate and flee in fear.

A new reality awaited.

THE QUIET GHOST OF WILLOW WAY

P. J. SKY

2055 C.E.

Everyone knew come market day it was old Mrs. Simpson's tomatoes that were always the reddest, and that weren't all—her beets
were always biggest and her beans always the greenest. You stuck
her beans next to ours and ours were just these shriveled little yellow things, deformed, and barely any taste. And not just our beans,
but everyone's in the whole valley. From up at Birchwood, right
down to Cedar Tree Hollow on the edge of the highway, all our
crops looked less like a wedding and more like a funeral, all dark
colours and heads dipped. And I weren't no fool, I could see with
every season our yields were only ever getting smaller, but Mrs.
Simpson's just kept going strong like there weren't nothing wrong
with the world.

Even then, it didn't seem quite fair to me, but people got mighty
suspicious of old Mrs. Simpson. I understood the jealousy and all I
guess, her tomatoes being so much redder than ours, but once you
saw her, you really couldn't feel so sore about it. She'd come into
town once a week in her beat up electric wagon, along with everyone else, towing a cart full of whatever were in season that month,
and the rest of us country folk could barely look her straight in the
eye. And she knew it, too, and that was maybe the worst of it.

She'd get a town boy to stand up front at her stall and dish out
her produce, while she sat out back on a little wooden stool by the
wheels of her wagon, all bent over, head down, her grey hair all
long and matted and mostly covering her face, like she didn't want
to look at us either. I don't think she wanted to see the look in our
eyes or hear what folks were saying about her. Her dark dress and
shawl mostly covered her altogether, like she was just a mound of

- 343 -

rags, but I'd see her hands with those long, thin fingers poking out of the sleeves, skin like crumpled paper, and the little coloured beads she strung around her wrists, and I'd think about how could anyone who picks such pretty colours for beads be all that bad? I'd watch her weaving strands of straw into little corn dolls she'd also sell on the stall. She could probably have made them at home, then she could spend her time in town gossiping with the other farmers, but as she didn't do that, I guess she wanted something to do with her hands while the boy stood up front.

I'd wonder if she was lonely, living all alone up in Willow Way, no one ever going up the road that far to visit. Her fields were adjacent to ours, only separated by the black river. The track to her gate went right past ours. Plenty of wagons and such came our way, but no one ever went no further. Ma told me to keep away from Willow Way, but I couldn't help but be curious.

"Ma," I'd say, "what's with old Mrs. Simpson's tomatoes? They ain't mostly green like ours, and they's at least twice the size."

Looking back now, Ma was a proud woman, but I didn't quite see it then. But pride's a dangerous thing and I see that now. It's taken me a long time to forgive Ma, but you know what, there comes a time when you realise sometimes, when you forgive someone, you're really forgiving yourself.

But I'm getting kind of ahead of myself.

Anyway, like I says, Ma was a proud woman.

"Ain't nothing wrong with our tomatoes," she'd say. "Ours is natural, it's hers that's wrong."

I think that were the first time I knew my Ma was lying, because I got this old book from the library all full of colourful pictures of plants and fruits and such like you could never imagine, and in it, the pictures looked just like old Mrs. Simpson's tomatoes, all plump and juicy and red. Not like ours and not like the images I'd found online. It made me think the whole world was lying to me, including Ma, and that got me pretty angry.

Still, town folk bought her tomatoes, and city folk even came up from Greenville in their shiny cars sometimes and loaded up with all her fruit and vegetables. I even sneaked a tomato off her stall once. I couldn't hardly help it, they just looked so good, and we didn't have no money spare, and Ma didn't hold with me eating other folks' food when we grew it ourselves. The boy spotted me, but I gave him a wink, and he went bright red and never said a word. Once I was round the corner, behind the church, I bit into that juicy tomato. I swear up to then I'd never tasted nothing so good in all my life. The juice ran down my chin and I thought my mouth would near burst with such incredible flavor, all sweet and sour and tart and tangy and all at the same time.

Once I'd tried that tomato it was like I couldn't ever go back to our bland and green things only really good for stewing, with that kerosene aftertaste, like a bit of the polluted ground got sucked up into them. That night, I dreamt about that juicy red tomato. I woke up sweating, and about all I could think of was sneaking another off the stall, but I just felt so bad about even doing it that once, I couldn't hold with doing it again. So I started thinking about going up to Willow Way and getting old Mrs. Simpson's secret, but when I mentioned this to Ma, you'd have thought I near asked if I could sell my soul to the devil. She pointed her finger at me, her face like stone, and said not over her dead body.

"You just mind your own biscuits," she said. "Folks round here keep to themselves, and that's the way it should be. She don't want you poking around her business any more than I do. And besides, we don't need no help. There ain't nothing wrong with our tomatoes."

I wished she hadn't said biscuits because we didn't have no biscuits, and hadn't for weeks, and just the sound of the word made my stomach grumble. Some words can do that, like ice-cream, or pizza, or chocolate. You know you ate them once, but now they have this magic to them, and someone says them and your stomach rolls over and about all you can think of is eating them again. And our own tomato crop had failed, and all we had to eat that morning was this watery gruel that tasted like engine oil.

"But why, Ma?" I said. "Our crop failed but hers are still juicy and red. At least I could ask her how she does it. She might be glad to help us?"

"We don't need no help, not from her and not from anyone. And besides, I can tell you why her tomatoes are red. It's witchcraft. I didn't wanna say nothing till you're older, but you gotta learn soon enough what's going on in the world. See, some folks have turned back to the old ways, and wicked ways too, chants and devil worshipping and all that. You seen those dolls she makes. Well, that's only the half of it. And I knows things are bad but they ain't that bad, and I ain't having you going down that path. It ain't right. Young lady, you're gonna grow up proper, so you just stay away from Willow Way."

But I tell you—hunger, and the taste of those forbidden fruits, and just plain curiosity, it all got the better of me. I knew Ma was lying, and Mrs. Simpson never looked evil to me. She just looked kind of lonely, and most of the other country folk I met just seemed bitter, like they'd had something stolen from them and without it they'd just lost their spark. They looked for it, of course—mostly, it seemed at the bottom of a beer can. Come Saturday night, the valley twinkled with the campfires of the farmers, and farm hands, and folks with nothing better to do, just having themselves a rager, and drinking themselves half blind on moonshine, and letting their guns off like it was the 4th of July.

My folks didn't hold with the drinking, and we stayed home most evenings, but back then, the whole valley seemed littered with empty beer cans, and the black circles of dead campfires, and folks passed-out under bare trees instead of working. Pa used to keep a shotgun by the door, just in case folks started raging our way—he used to say there ain't no reasoning with a drunkard.

Anyway, after breakfast I headed out to the beet fields that ran all the way to the trees and the black river. I knew I weren't supposed to go that way, but just then I was hungry enough to try near anything. I trudged over our dead fields, the dry, brown earth all cracked open like the top of a burnt cake, my mother's words now the farthest thing from my mind. Little bits of brown beet stalks still stuck out of the ground in rows, and it just made the whole field even sadder. Overhead, a drone buzzed, but I already knew it weren't gonna find nothing here. The earth was dead, at least for this season.

The trees on our side of the river weren't much to look at, all bent over like old men, their bark gnarled and their leaves yellow.

But on the other side, the trees were taller, and I swear some of their leaves were actually green. Then, further upstream, the weeping willows actually spilled out over the other side of the river like an emerald waterfall, and their leaves only turned yellow where the tips of their branches touched the black water.

I followed the river to where a cedar tree lay across it like a bridge. The tree had come down in the fall, and if it had come down nearer the house, we'd have had it for firewood. But seeing as my folks never came this close to Willow Way, no one had ever done anything about it.

As I crossed, my hands out to steady myself, I looked down and I had to stop when, on the other side, I saw the eddies of clear water spiraling off the bank. They soon disappeared into the oily good-for-nothing water of the river, but I could see them clear as day just coming off the bank.

On the other side, everything seemed just different. The birds chirped louder, and the insects buzzed, but not like the flies we got on our side. Instead, they were like a constant round of applause, like they had nothing better to do all day than cheer on the world. Everything felt suddenly alive, like the land had a sort of electric charge to it. It was like standing under one of those big electric pylons, but in a good way, like your hair might stand on end but only so you could laugh about it. On the trunk of a tree I saw the most beautiful butterfly with big, vibrant blue wings like I hadn't ever seen before. As I stepped closer, it leapt off the tree trunk and fluttered up to the next branch.

Beyond the trees, the green grass grew to my knees, and I had to wade through it to get to the tomato plants. It dragged on my legs like I were wading through treacle, but I didn't hardly mind. And when I reached them, the tomato plants were like none we'd ever grown on our side of the river. They were so tall they came over my shoulders, with slender, Kelly green leaves, and the big, red tomatoes looked so juicy my stomach just turned. I couldn't barely help it when I reached out and took one, and as I bit into it the juice ran all down my chin, and if anything, straight off the vine, it tasted even better than I remembered.

I started to worry old Mrs. Simpson would see me, which was

kind of crazy because I'd come to see her, but now I was already pinching her fruit. That got me feeling kind of guilty. I ducked down among the plants and chewed up the tomato flesh and that's when I realised what was missing. Looking up to the skies there weren't no drones. We used drones to scavenge out what half-decent crops we had, or to find any source of water, or to find ground that weren't so poisoned, but here there weren't none at all. The skies were silent, but for the birds and the buzzing insects, and it didn't seem like old Mrs. Simpson needed them anyhow, for she just had rows and rows of beautiful tomato plants.

I was finishing the last of the tomato, the rich skin stuck between my teeth, and was licking my fingers when old Mrs. Simpson just poked her head over the nearest plant and surprised the hell right out of me.

"You enjoying my tomatoes then?"

My heart leapt. I hadn't ever heard her speak before, and her voice had sort of a croak. Now I saw her face properly, her nose was longer than I expected and kind of bumpy, the way old folks' noses sometimes are. I sprang to my feet and ran, but tripped right over a rock. I came down hard, my face in the soft dirt, and my ankle near burst with pain. I must have cried out, but I don't rightly remember.

Old Mrs. Simpson was tutting to herself as she ducked under the vines and approached me. "Now, my dear, you shouldn't really go pinching other folks' tomatoes."

I tried to get up, but my ankle hurt too much. I pushed myself up on my elbows.

Mrs. Simpson knelt before me. Her eyes were soft and green, and she had a little smile on her lips like she didn't look angry at all. "Hmmm, looks like you've twisted that ankle."

"I'm sorry," I said. "I didn't mean to take the tomato. I won't do it again."

Mrs. Simpson shook her head. "Ahh, don't worry about it. I don't get many visitors these days. Here, let me help you up and we can go on up to the house and I'll take a proper look at it."

Perhaps I should have felt more nervous, as she slipped her hand beneath my shoulder and helped me to my feet, but close-up there didn't seem to be nothing to be nervous about Mrs. Simpson, so I didn't mind her helping me up.

"Look at you," said Mrs. Simpson, "you're all skin and bones. No wonder you took my tomato."

Together, we waddled through the vines, passing the electric picking machines that looked like big upturned refrigerators, and up to the old house.

In the kitchen, Mrs. Simpson got my ankle up on a stool and bound it with bandages. "You best be careful walking on this," she said as she peeled back the strip and stuck down the last bandage. "But it don't look too bad. I think you've been lucky. Now, let's see if I don't have something better to feed you. You look like you could do with a proper meal."

At the counter, she warmed up this vegetable stew that turned out to be just about the best thing I ever tasted. She joined me at the table with her own bowl and we ate in silence. I'm not sure I ever ate anything so fast.

When we'd finished eating, she took my bowl and refilled it.

"Things that bad at Birchwood?"

"What?" I asked between mouthfuls.

"You're the Christies' kid, aren't you?"

I nodded and continued to eat.

"Well, if once in a while you can keep an old lady company, and you can maybe stop pinching my tomatoes . . ." At this, she gave me a wink. "Then you're welcome to come get a fill when you gets too hungry."

"Ma don't want me up here," I said. "She says . . . well . . . she says you're a witch."

At this, Mrs. Simpson tipped her head back and cackled. For a moment, I thought just maybe it was true, then she looked back and smiled. "Bless her, child, I ain't no witch."

"Then why?" I asked. "Why do your tomatoes grow better than most anyone else's in the valley?"

"Well, now that's a good question." She looked away, like she was trying to decide whether or not to tell me something. She stood and went to the window. "See, I got this way with the plants. I don't know how exactly—to me it's just like breathing or thinking or moving my arm. I just does it. But when I touch the earth, it just sort of heals. It don't last, mind, not while the city folks and, well, not while near everyone keeps polluting the world like they do, but as long as I keep doing it, it works."

"Wow," I said, my eyes wide. "So, you can just . . . heal the earth?"

Mrs. Simpson looked over her shoulder. "That's what I said, ain't it?"

"Can you do it . . . anywhere?"

"I can . . . I mean, it tires me out, just like everything else at my age, but yes, I can. Anywhere I can touch the earth with these." She turned and stretched out her long, thin fingers.

"And . . . you could do it for our farm?"

Mrs. Simpson narrowed her eyes. "I see where you're going with this, but folks round here don't like me using my powers, even when it helps them. I hear what they say about me, even when I pretends I don't. They think this power I have is evil. You see how they all look at me. So, I keeps to myself. I like the quiet."

I nodded. "I guess it gets mighty quiet up here. You always been on your own?"

"Mostly, yes."

At this, Mrs. Simpson's eyes glazed, and she looked sad. She looked to a black-and-white photograph she had in a plastic frame on the windowsill. It showed a man with a beard and a woman with a baby curled up in her arms.

"Who's that?" I asked.

"That's me. A long, long time ago now." A tear formed in the corner of her eye. "Me and Joe."

"That your baby?"

She nodded. "That it is. I guess she'll be somewhat older than you are now."

"Where are they now?"

"Gone. See, the valley weren't always like this, and there was a time when I only used to use my power to perk up flowers in vases and things. Small things, just for me. But the first time I used my power on the farm, when the crops were first failing, Joe saw me, and he got real scared. He didn't understand, and maybe he didn't want to. Folks with powers were just starting to appear then, and we'd see fantastical rumors in the news and no one really wanted to trust them. As the weeks went on, I could see it was eating him up, even when we were doing well while the rest of the valley was suffering. He just really didn't want us to be different. A lot of folks don't like to feel like they're different to anyone else. He thought everyone was looking at us, and they were, I guess. And he started reading up and quoting all sorts of bible stories at me. Then one day he took off with little Laverna and I never saw them again. I went after them of course. I went into Greenville and beyond, but I never heard from them again. Police said it was pretty clear Joe didn't want me to find them, and they weren't interested in helping me. These days, there's so many lost folk out there, and most of them don't want to be found. So, I came back here. I didn't have anywhere else to go, see, and ever since it's just been me and the birds."

I swallowed the last of my stew. "I'm sorry," I said. "Maybe they'll come back?"

She shook her head. "No, they won't."

* * *

From that day on, I started going pretty regularly up to Mrs. Simpson's house. She fed me well and told me stories of the valley when it was all still green. I started to worry Ma or Pa would start to see me getting taller and stronger. They didn't say nothing about it, but in eating Mrs. Simpson's food regularly, I started to wonder what effect it was having on me. I'd look in the mirror and try to work out if my cheeks were redder. I even started touching the earth and seeing if maybe I was acquiring a little of her power, but when I tried, it didn't seem to make no difference. Our harvests only seemed to get leaner while Mrs. Simpson's continued strong. Pa started to use the drones to scavenge the land up higher in the valley, but it was deader there than the fields we had already.

So I started asking Mrs. Simpson if she could maybe use her powers to heal our fields.

At first she refused. I felt like I'd annoyed her by asking, and after that visit I left it a few days before returning, and then I felt mean because she seemed kind of sad I hadn't called on her. But I told her again about how bad it was at Birchwood, and that maybe she could do it and Ma and Pa wouldn't even know. In the end, she relented.

And so, one afternoon, we both went down to the fallen tree and she crossed with me onto our side of the black river. She seemed kind of sad, seeing all the dead trees and plants, and she got down on her knees and touched the earth. She stayed there for a few minutes, fingers outstretched over the dry earth. After she was really tired, so I helped her back to the house. I sat her down in her chair in the kitchen, and I boiled some water for tea.

"Just give it a few weeks," she said. "You'll see. That end of the farm will be green again."

And sure enough, she was good as her word. The beanstalks we planted there grew up big and strong, and soon enough we had the biggest beans on the market. I thought maybe Ma and Pa might suspect something, but they just took to saying grace at dinnertimes again, and thanking the Lord for providing, and that seemed to be good enough for them. Ma even started smiling again, and the beans put a little colour in her cheeks too.

Next were the tomatoes. This time, I had to sneak Mrs. Simpson over at night on account of the tomato trees being closer to the house. She lay her hands on the earth, and sure enough, within a few weeks we had tomatoes as red as any in Willow Way. When I told her about it, I could see Mrs. Simpson was as pleased as we were, and I mentioned the only problem we had now was folks might get suspicious of Ma and Pa too. When I said this, I saw a little glint in her eye.

"Don't you worry yourself about that," she said. "I thought of that already, and let's just say Birchwood ain't the only farm I've been sneaking into at night."

And sure enough, come market day, a dozen farms all had redder tomatoes, greener beans, thicker corn, and bigger beets. And everyone seemed happy about it and there weren't no competition seeing as the town and city folk could always buy up all we had to sell. Everyone seemed happier, and it seemed clear to me Mrs. Simpson's gift was putting some good into the world, and there weren't no need for folk to keep being so suspicious of her, especially as their farms were doing well too. I even saw Mr. Tom giving her a smile, and then Mrs. Jenkins gave her a few flowers from her garden. Mrs. Simpson was almost glowing.

By now, I felt mighty thankful for Mrs. Simpson, and at grace I brought her name up at the table. Ma and Pa said their graces and just as we were supposed to say Amen, I said, "And thank you for Mrs. Simpson too."

But at this, Ma's face turned to stone. I swear, the look she gave me could just about wilt a rose. "And just what do we have to thank that witch for?"

I couldn't hardly believe it. Up until that moment, we were having just about the best afternoon in months.

"Well," I said, "our tomatoes now grow as red as hers do."

"And what's that got to do with her?"

"Well . . . just . . ."

"Let me tell you, young lady, she's been lording it all over us all these years with her rosy red tomatoes. It was just about time we got a little of the Lord's grace. And we did it our way too, with hard work and prayers on Sunday and none of those evil, devil worshiping chants she does up there."

"But she don't do no devil worshiping chants."

"And just what would you know about it?"

"Now, ladies—" interjected Pa.

But Ma just talked right over him. "I see you sneaking off up to that river like you're up to no good, and I know you're curious, but there ain't no good come out of there in years. Her good husband clear ran away, he did, and 'cause of her. Best thing he could do to get that child away from her and her evil ways. That place is unnatural. So you better not be going over to Willow Way, you hear?"

"And what if I am?" I said. "What if I said the only reason our tomatoes are growing better and our beans is growing bigger is because of her, and it ain't no devil worshiping either. She got a power."

My mother sprang to her feet. "Young lady, you just tell me that ain't true."

"Well it is, I been going up there for months, and she been helping us out, using her power, and there ain't nothing evil about it."

Ma went so red-faced I thought steam might just come out of her ears. She pointed at the stairs.

"You just go up to your room and don't you dare leave it till I say. Do you hear?"

I stormed upstairs and slumped on my bed. I was so angry I was near ready to rip Ma's head off. All evening I could hear Ma shouting and Pa trying to reason with her, but I could tell neither of them were happy. I sat there, staring out at the dark sky, and soon I was wishing I'd never said nothing at all about it. It was a mistake to say anything.

But now it was out, and there was no putting it back.

I felt like my insides were all twisting up, like there was a knot in my stomach and a rock lodged in my throat. I thought of sneaking out the window and going up to Mrs. Simpson's but I knew that'd be a mistake too.

I reckoned if Ma found me out, she might just disown me.

* * *

Two nights later, my folks dragged me to the town hall meeting. I don't usually have to go, but since my outburst, Ma wouldn't near let me out of her sight.

I sat at the back of the bleachers as Ma and Pa brought up how Mrs. Simpson had come onto their land and done her devil worshiping chants and bewitched their plants. It was Ma who spoke mostly, and she told it like she'd been right there watching. She made out like Mrs. Simpson had sneaked onto our land and danced naked with the devil, but she didn't say nothing about me being involved. I watched the back of her head as she spat out the words, her bun of hazel hair bouncing up and down, and I hated her more than I'd ever hated anyone in my whole life.

Honestly, you'd think my folks would be thankful, but they didn't seem like they were at all.

As I watched Ma poison everyone with her words, I wanted to stand up and shout out that none of it was true. It's funny how it's only after you think of all the things you could have said. I've lost count of the number of times I've gone back over that meeting, and

I've thought about how I should have stood up for Mrs. Simpson. I think of all the things I could have said, about how my Ma was lying, and about what a wonderful person Mrs. Simpson was, and how she'd brought all this good and happiness to the valley. But, as I looked around at all the angry faces in the audience, I got kind of nervous. So instead, I sank into my chair and I never said nothing until it was all too late. And boy, did it get too late.

Don't think I don't regret my part in all of this sorry story, because I feel it every day.

But I'm getting ahead of myself again.

After my folks had told their story, everyone got pretty angry and seemed to agree the town was having none of it. More folks stood up and told their stories, and I knew all of them were lying, and by the time they were done, everyone was getting really wound up, shouting about how we'd all let the devil into the valley, and that something should have been done about it a long time ago. Before I knew it, the meeting was over, and everyone was leaving and going to their pickups. I heard one person mention getting kerosene, and I started to get really nervous.

Outside the memorial center, I stood on the sidewalk, a growing sense of dread in my gut, and watched folks load their pickups with cases of beer and coolers and deckchairs like they were all going to a rager in the woods. Some of them were angry, but most now looked excited. They had this manic gleam in their eyes, and I tell you that gleam looked more like the devil than anything I ever saw in Mrs. Simpson.

The pickups started heading out of town, in the direction of Birchwood, and I really started to worry then about Mrs. Simpson's safety. The fear in my gut kept growing, and even though I knew Ma would be furious, I took off then and there anyway. I hopped the fence and took the shortest route I could up the valley towards Willow Way. I didn't bother following the river, I just re-joined the dirt road and went through the old covered bridge. As I ran, I started to wonder if my folks had gone straight up to Birchwood in their truck—I reckoned that would have been quicker for me, but by the time I was thinking about it I was already halfway up the valley. And besides, I couldn't stand the idea of sharing the cab back up the valley with Ma by my side.

Even before I got near Willow Way, I could see the fires raging. Folks were standing around, their black silhouettes against the orange flames, with beers in their hands, laughing at their handiwork, and there were those beautiful tomato trees all going up in smoke.

It about broke my heart to see that.

I ducked around the lines of burning trees, my head down, and headed for the drive. I had to take the long way, and every step felt like the longest time, as if the journey would never end, and all the while the smoke was burning the back of my throat and stinging my eyes. I put a handkerchief to my mouth as I made my way up the wide tracks of the drive. The night air above was alight with glowing embers like deadly fireflies. Squinting ahead, even before I got to the house, I could see those hungry flames licking up the wooden walls.

"Mrs. Simpson," I cried, tears running down my cheeks. I don't know why it bothered me then, but it was then I realised I didn't even know her given name. I started to think I'd never really known her at all, and then I'd opened my big mouth and spilled it all to Ma and then this had gone and happened and it was all my fault, even if I hadn't come up here with the kerosene.

Flames licked around the doorway. I wanted to run inside, but the thought near paralyzed me with fear. Through the windows, everything was dark. There weren't no lights on, and black smoke was seeping out of the edges of the windows.

I moved around to the side of the house, but the fire was everywhere, and there didn't seem no way in or out of the house that weren't burning. I looked around for Mrs. Simpson, hoping she was outside the house, but I couldn't see her anywhere. Back at the front door, I ducked down, balled my fists, and was about to brave it when I felt a hand on my shoulder.

"Stay back, it's okay."

It was Pa. I couldn't believe it. I wanted to fling my arms around him, but he held me back.

"Just you stay here, okay."

I nodded, trying to hold myself together.

Pa ducked inside the house and was in there the longest time. I started to get scared for him too and I found myself praying to the Lord that he didn't take both Pa and Mrs. Simpson. Finally, he stumbled out, choking, his arm under Mrs. Simpson's shoulders. He dragged her to the middle of the drive, lay her down on her back, and started to pump her chest.

I paced back and forth, trying not to sob, my hands clenched together, but somehow I already knew the truth. I watched Pa pump her chest and duck down and press his lips to hers and then do it all again. I could feel the heat coming off the burning trees like it was Hell's furnace, and my eyes teared from the acrid smoke, and there was Pa doing his best to save her.

All I could do was pace back and forth.

This was all my fault and I couldn't do nothing about it.

When Pa finally gave up, he looked up at me and I saw it all in his face. He was crying too now and he shook his head and I ran and hugged him and near never let go and I sobbed until I was all sobbed out and yet I knew nothing would bring her back.

In the morning, there weren't nothing left of Willow Way, except the stubs of tomato trees, and a blackened frame that had once been the house. I felt another wave of sadness when I realised not just Mrs. Simpson had gone, but so had the photo that sat on the windowsill. It's funny how you remember those little details. I thought of the beads she'd strung around her wrists, and the way she'd turned the stew in the pot, and I realised it was all gone. All the little things that made up a person just wiped away with a douse of kerosene and a lighter. And I felt angry and upset and guilty and sort of hollow all at the same time.

In the end, the town ruled it was no one's fault what happened, which is the biggest lie I ever did hear. Can you believe they ruled she must have set the blaze herself? A terrible accident is what they called it. Like they couldn't condone what happened, but they couldn't condemn it either. Like sometimes the bad in folks just bubbles up, like a pot over-boiling, and you just got to accept it and carry on. And the folks nearby? Well, they were just having a good old rager—just letting off steam with a few beers. Yeah, a few beers and several drums of kerosene.

That morning after, I could smell it in the air. And now Willow Way was poisoned, just like everywhere else in the valley. Folks had come in the night and made it just like everywhere else. And a few weeks later, our tomato trees all died, along with everyone else's, and that was that.

* * *

On the day of the funeral, I thought I'd be the only one to turn up. Just me and the priest. Not even Pa came on account he was busy on the farm, trying to plant more seeds into the dead ground. But I'd come, and I'd even got dressed up in my best dress and I don't ever normally wear dresses. I put on my grandmother's broach and found a little flower in a hedgerow to put in it. It was a miserable looking blue thing, already half-dead before it had ever properly bloomed, but it was the best I could do. I turned up early and took a seat in the third pew back and didn't say nothing, and the priest sat up by the coffin and didn't say nothing either, and we were just sat like that for ages.

"You know," he said finally, "I think it's just going to be us. Maybe we should start?"

I was about to agree when a silhouette darkened the church doorway. The woman who stood there was tall and slender with long auburn hair right down past her shoulders. Over city clothes, she wore a sort of brown cape which I found kind of strange, and brown, fingerless leather gloves.

"Ahh," said the priest, "are you here to join us?"

"I am," said the woman. She looked at me and smiled like she already knew me, though I was certain I didn't know her.

"Well, please do join us."

She sat in a different pew, and I turned back to the coffin, and the priest got on with the funeral with only two mourners. It was a short service—the priest didn't have much to say about Mrs. Simpson on account of not knowing her at all. He asked each of us if we'd like to say a few words, but I shook my head, and I guess the other woman did the same. And before I knew it, it was over, and the priest ran the curtain around the coffin, and it slid away to the oven.

It'd been a long time since anyone was buried here on account that our bodies only poisoned the earth more.

But I bet in the case of Mrs. Simpson, she'd have done the earth some good.

Outside the church, the mysterious other mourner approached me. "Thank you for coming," she said. "Seems like my mother wasn't too popular round here."

"Mother . . . are you?"

"Laverna Simpson, her daughter."

"She didn't know where you were."

"I didn't know where she was either, not until it was too late. The estate contacted my father and, well, I guess he felt bad and wanted to give me this chance to say goodbye."

I nodded. I couldn't really imagine how she must have felt, but I guessed she must have been pretty angry, and maybe even as angry with her Pa as I still was with my Ma. I couldn't near look Ma in the eyes, and she nearly didn't say a word to me.

"It seems," said Laverna, "like at least my mother had one friend."

"Um . . . yeah, she was my friend. Your Ma was real special, but like you say, folks didn't like her much. They were all suspicious of her on account of . . ." I trailed off, not wanting to mention her power.

"On account of what?"

I looked into her eyes. They looked kind and concerned, and kind of like her Ma's, and this was her Ma we were talking about. I reckoned she deserved the truth. "On account of her power."

"Oh, that." She didn't sound surprised.

"You knew about it?"

"Well, it sort of makes sense." And when she said this, she had this sort of glint in her eye, like she really understood.

"It seems a real shame now," I said. "Folks round here really needed her power, but they just couldn't get past all their suspicions."

"Some folks are like that."

"I tell you, if we had a few more folks like your Ma, maybe we could fix this world."

At this, Laverna Simpson smiled. "You know, you're more right than you think." She reached out her hand, the tips of her fingers showing through those fingerless gloves, and tapped the flower on my broach. At once, the flower lifted its head, and its petals bloomed and turned a vivid sky blue.

I gasped.

Laverna put her finger to her lips. "Our secret, all right."

I nodded.

"There's more of us," she said. "Soon the whole world will know about us, and together we can really change things for the better. But we need people like you. People who can see we're not monsters."

"I can see you ain't no monster," I said. "And neither was your Ma."

Laverna nodded. "I wish I'd known her. It wasn't fair on any of us how this all went down."

"No," I said.

"But this earth is waking up." She put a hand on my shoulder, and for a moment I swear I could feel energy moving from her body into mine. It was a warm, tingling sensation, that started in my shoulder and worked its way down. "And she's choosing people to save her. People like me. And people like you."

My fingers tingled, like electric sparks were bouncing between my fingertips. All the hairs on my body stood on end. It was like the feeling I'd felt when I'd first set foot in Willow Way.

"I'll see you soon," she said, withdrawing her hand.

At the church gate, she looked back over her shoulder. "Don't give up. People don't like change. They fear what they don't understand. But always be true to yourself."

I went back up the road to home. When I came in the house, Ma looked at me like she were about to say something. I could feel the unsaid words hanging on the empty air between us, but neither of us said anything. Then she turned back to the counter, and I went up to my room and stuck the flower in an old soda bottle on my windowsill. I changed out of my dress, went down to the tomato trees, and looked at the wilting leaves and yellow fruit.

Just maybe.

Kneeling, I put my hands to the dry earth and closed my eyes. At the ends of my fingers, I felt little static shocks.

I jumped.

I withdrew my hands and looked at my fingers, but they looked just the same. Placing my fingertips back to the earth, I tried again. This time, I pushed past the little shocks, and I don't know how to explain it, but I just knew suddenly that this power weren't coming from me.

It was coming from the earth.

And I was the conduit, pulling it up from deep in the world's core and drawing it to the surface.

I could feel the roots of the plants as they reached through the earth, and the little creatures that made it their home, and the tiny veins of precious water. Everything was connected. And I understood what Laverna Simpson had said about our planet awakening.

I withdrew my hands and sat cross-legged on the ground. Electricity vibrated the air.

I looked to the base of the nearest tomato tree and watched as a new leaf unfolded, fresh and green.

GAIA AWAKENED

C. D. TAVENOR

2055 C.E.

The colors vibrantly stated: autumn was here, and the trees would continue the rhythm of the seasons as their ancestors had for a thousand generations. The rolling hills of Appalachia hid many secrets, from abandoned coal mines and unplugged gas wells to frothy rapids and the best rock climbs this side of the Mississippi.

It also hid history. Generations beaten down by the greed of corporatists and politicians and corporate politicians, exploiting racism and class divide. Generations living off the land and in community, protecting one another and those in need. Generations hoping for a better life, and being told the next extractive industry, whether coal, gas, timber, or solar, would bring hope for future generations.

Natalie hadn't arrived in the lands formerly known as West Virginia, though, to explore its past. She was here to chart a new future, one over a decade in the making.

She pulled her electric bike to a stop beside a rusted, inconspicuous gate. Gently, she rolled the bike around the dilapidated iron and up a worn dirt path. After a few dozen meters striding around withered white oaks and weathered boulders, she approached a garage tucked into a cliffside. She reached it, opened the blue-tooth app on her watch, and keyed in the memorized code provided by her contact. The garage door silently rose into the rock, and she stowed her bike alongside a dozen or so similar vehicles.

So it looked like everyone else had arrived, then. Good. She was worried she'd be one of the first—or the only one to make the trip. They'd laid too much groundwork, she and Liza and the others. Connected the dots. Pieced together stories. Chased dead end after dead end. There was no more time to wait, however.

The planet's future hung in the balance, after all.

She slung her bag over her shoulder and closed her bike's small storage compartment. After closing and locking the garage, she continued the trek up the supposedly abandoned trail, the sun warmly breaking through the canopy in patches. This far into the "Isolation Zone," it was easy to forget the disaster striking the planet. Civilization had pulled everything it needed from these forests generations ago, leaving them to be reclaimed. If only it could keep its fingers away from everywhere else, too.

After a kilometer or so along the trail, she came across a yellow "no trespassing" sign blocking the trail. She nodded, remembering her instructions. She turned sharply left, heading directly into the forest. The path was trailless, but she saw the markers. A hollowed out oak tree. An old acid drainage pit. The ancient foundation of some forgotten building, probably a mill or a mine's administrative office. Eventually, Natalie stepped foot onto another trail, though it was a little generous to call it that. Probably a deer path. She turned right onto it, following it along the base of a cliff before reaching a small gap in the rocks. She headed through it, and before she took a dozen steps between the cliffs, a woman stepped into her path.

"You're late," she said. "I think we're all a little late," Natalie said, offering a soft smile. "Regina, it's good to see you."

The older woman glared for a long moment before she broke into a grin. "It's good to see you too. Everyone's waiting for you. Toni's been talking non-stop about your return."

"I know, I've been getting the emails every other day." Natalie chuckled. "Well, lead the way."

Regina turned sharply around, setting a pace difficult to match. Natalie readjusted her bag's strap and skipped a few steps to keep up. They hiked the first part in silence, the path traversing up the ridge between giant root systems and fractured boulders. When the path finally leveled out, they both paused to catch their breath. Her guide offered water.

"Thank you," Natalie said, taking a sip. The crisp, clean water parched her lips. "The well we installed last year still doing its job?"

"You bet." Regina arced an eyebrow. "Imelda was skeptical, but your friend Ben really knows his stuff."

"How's he doing?"

The woman shrugged. "As well as you can expect. We've been working with him to chronicle everything that's happened in the Coastal Republic. It's so much worse than we imagined."

"I know," Natalie replied. "The stories . . . it's what made me certain we needed to finally bring everyone together. We've got a lot of work to do."

"I'm probably not going to like your idea, am I?"

It was Natalie's turn to shrug. "It depends if I can convince you of its necessity, first."

"Well, the worst thing that can happen is we all say no, I suppose."

"I'm more worried about what happens if we all say yes."

Their water break over, it took another fifteen minutes or so to eventually reach the massive wall of tires signaling their arrival in the official territory of the Bent Greens. Years ago, when Natalie first witnessed the haphazardly constructed barrier, she thought it dirty and disgusting. She knew better now.

They passed beneath the tire archway. A bell sounded, signaling their arrival.

"They'll be waiting at the putting green amphitheater," Regina said. "I'm gonna make a stop by home first, but I trust you know the way?"

"I know the way," Natalie replied.

* * *

"All right, all right, time to cut the chatter!" Imelda's voice boomed over the small talk of the crowd, and within moments, the conversations ceased. All eyes turned toward the dais where Natalie stood, the de facto leader of the Bent Greens by her side.

The group was smaller than she hoped. About two dozen or so awaited her words, not counting Imelda and her other Bent Greens council members. But she welcomed their friendly faces. Liza, of course, sat in the front row, her eyes beaming with anticipation. In the back, an old Australian man sat, a teenager by his side. At least Mike and his nephew had made it, against all odds. And there was

Graeson, and Claire, and Briar, and Laverna, and Ben. Others still, she knew, wanted to come, but hadn't been able to find a way into the Isolation Zone. Franklin and Hodges sent their regards from across the border. She'd need to visit them personally. Others had jobs they simply couldn't leave for weeks at a time, since that's what it took to arrange trans-national travel.

They would all follow the lead of the group, she hoped. Enough of their slowly growing collective had found their way to the Bent Greens. Some even called it their home, now. It would need to be sufficient.

Imelda cleared her throat. "Nat, you good?"

Natalie nodded vigorously. "Apologies, just lost in thought. It's truly good to see so many friends in one place."

The words were returned with grim smiles. She left unspoken what they all thought—there were too many friends who hadn't made it to today, their lives taken by the perpetual disaster they were all trying to survive.

"I don't want to waste anyone's time, especially since you all committed so many days to this trip. I know you all asked me why this meeting had to occur in person. We may believe our virtual networks are secure, but we can never be certain. We've spent too much time preparing and building and learning to have it all collapse because we sent a message to the wrong person."

They all nodded, though some grumbled, clearly resenting her emphasis on the trek. It had been a long journey for many of them. Though those who had traveled the furthest simply nodded. In the end, they all understood what was at stake: merely the future of their planet.

"So what is it you're proposing?" said Ben. The middle-aged man from New Jersey leaned forward, elbows on his knees. "What fight are you asking us to join?"

She sighed. She knew there would be pushback, but she hoped to avoid it until after she made her pitch. No matter. "It's the fight we've all been in for decades. For some of us, it's been longer than that. But let me start from square one. Let me state what we've all known for a while now, even if we haven't had the whole picture."

She paused, breathing heavily. She'd only truly spoken these words aloud once, when Liza showed her the Gardens and their impenetrable boundary.

"The planet is awakening. Some of you know it better than others. You call it Gaia. I call it Earth. Others call it the wind, or God, Allah, or the universe, or something else entirely. It's something we don't understand, and probably won't ever understand. We've sought scientific answers, religious answers, or delved deep into history to find truth. There is nothing. We only know our experiences, and I've spoken with all of you about what you've seen, felt, and heard. We're all part of something greater than ourselves, brought together by a planet aching for healing. It could destroy us and start again, but instead, it has chosen to work with us. To use us, as it's using many of its systems to fight against the greatest crisis we've ever known."

The soft murmurs gave her the strength she needed to keep going. They all knew of what she spoke.

"For almost a decade and a half, we've all seen the signs. Heard the whispers and the stories. Some of us are the story. The world abounds with rumors of the supernatural, yet we all know what's happened is more natural than what humans have done to the planet for centuries. Even with the significance of the power growing, ever growing, the powers-that-be still don't truly recognize the truth we all know."

She sighed.

"The planet is correcting itself. It is counteracting what our species has done to kill it and its life. We've burned its forests. Devastated ecosystems. Boiled the oceans. Ruined the prairies. Melted every last glacier. And so it has decided to take matters into its own hands. We never thought it possible, but the planet itself has a mind. A will. A conscious force we can't begin to understand. It has an immune system, and we've triggered its response."

She closed her eyes for a long moment. Opening them, she looked toward the brilliant purples splattered by the slowly setting sun. "I believe we're a part of the solution. A part of the response. And we can no longer hide in the shadows. We must take our fight public, uniting the world behind a banner designed to end the climate crisis once and for all." The words finally left her mouth after her minutes of prefacing. The meat of her speech. The call to action.

Her final thesis.

And before she could follow it up with a supporting argument, an uproar thrust forth from her audience.

"What do you think we've been doing—"

"It's too risky, you know—"

"Powers are one thing, but a sentient—"

"They'll take us out before we give two—"

"What is it you're proposing?"

The question came from the back row. Mike's nephew. And its sharpness cut through the clamor easily enough. Everyone quieted, at least for her answer.

"That's what I hope we can determine together," she said. "Collectively, we have limitless potential. Not just because of the things we can do, but because we represent the best humanity has to offer. But I know there's more of us out there. I know you've all been reading the stories. We need to travel far and wide, connecting the disparate places crying out on behalf of our planet. We need to hear their stories. Gather them. And begin to tell them for all to hear. We need to finally change the world. Course correct. Hold civilization accountable for its past, and set it on a path for a truly livable future."

"You seem to be forgetting one thing," said Ben. "You forget who we will need to fight. You forget the forces aligned against us. You forget that people have been trying to change the world for almost a century, and they have failed, generation after generation."

"Surely you have some hope left?" Imelda asked.

"Both of you know when my hope died," the man said. He shook his head. "You can't fix something that's already broken. I'm all about fighting, but we can't rebuild the old world. We need to create an entirely new one in its place."

"We're saying the same thing," Natalie said, "Just with different words. Look at what the Bent Greens have done here." She swept her hand around the forest, from the recycled plastic walkways to the tire constructs and the Earthship homesteads. "They've created a thriving community out of what used to be trash. I've traveled the world, witnessing the chaotic and eclectic communities charting tiny paths forward. I've met people standing against corporate greed and spitting in its face. I've met all of you. We have different paths. Different stories. Yet . . . we all want the same thing: a future for ourselves, and for our future generations."

The nods returned.

"So what, specifically, are you proposing?" The question came from Claire.

"We create a unified banner," she said. "We give it a name. We work collectively, in tandem, to change people, one-by-one, until every civilization is united in its efforts to save the planet. It will look different in every country. In every community. But our disjointed efforts and actions will be stronger if done together. Strategically. Coordinated. With a unified language and voice."

"With all due respect," said a middle-aged woman—Mikayla, if Natalie's memory served her correctly. She was one of Liza's contacts. "With all due respect," Mikayla repeated, "But we've all been fighting for a long time. Taking down billionaires. Fighting fascists. Capitalists. We've made massive strides. Countries are taking action. And none of it seems to be enough. What will we do that's different from what's already been done before? What makes us different?"

A good chunk of the group nodded in tentative agreement. It was a valid question. Plenty of groups had claimed to have the "answer" to the climate crisis before. They'd rise to respond to the material moment, make their big splash, then blend in with all the other NGOs before them, falling prey to the greenwashing and latent ideological supremacy of grants and wealthy donors.

Yet those groups lacked one fundamental factor.

Natalie swallowed. "We all believe, in our hearts, that we're following the will of . . . Gaia. I don't usually use the term I know many of you prefer. I'm not spiritual at my core. Yet even I can't deny the applicability of the word. The Gaia Hypothesis was truer than any of us could have imagined. We might feel like we're individuals, but in reality, we're all a part of the super-organism that is our planet. It has called to us. Told us to take action. How can we not listen? How can we not work together to achieve what it wants us to do?"

"You're asking us to do what we've already been doing!" Ben raised his hands in exasperation. "You come marching in here, your sparkling, polished clothes and the privilege that comes with your UN badge, and you propose making the only thing you've ever known—a political entity designed to take on the politicians. It's always about institutional power with you types. Well, we need to build our own power. Our own systems that can provide for the people. Self-sustaining. We start making the Bent Greens international, and they'll just distort the vision of a place like this."

Natalie opened her mouth, but Imelda held up her hand. "Your passion is admirable, Ben, but I think you're misstating Natalie's proposal. She isn't asking us to abandon our work here. She's trying to propose a way for us to teach everyone to take up our work everywhere."

But Regina was shaking her head. "More likely they'll come at us like they came at us in '45."

Ben snorted. "Exactly. We need to—"

A thunderclap smashed through the amphitheater, though no flash of lightning preceded it. In an instant, the clouds turned black. The sun disappeared. Mist condensed in the air, illuminated by the solar lamps flickering to life. Someone in the crowd screamed.

And Natalie's vision went black.

* * *

The planet breathed, though it was devoid of life. Water covered its surface, though the ground was rocky and barren. Clouds swirled in the atmosphere, following unknown and incomprehensible patterns.

The planet was but an embryo. A cocoon. It was bound for greatness in comparison to its counterparts orbiting the nearby star. It was also destined for tragedy, time and time again.

It didn't take long for life to emerge in the waters of the deep, though you could barely call it life. Simple genetic blobs, replicating and replicating and replicating. Then, after hundreds of millions of years, if not billions, life complicated.

And so the planet breathed and sensed new sensations. But its cocoon hardened. It had a long way to go before it truly lived.

Life complicated. And complicated. And complicated. Multi-cellular. Sentience. Sight. Sensory experiences evolved, exponentially varying the genetic diversity of the planet's chromosomes. Systems generated oxygen from carbon dioxide. The plants became its lungs, the oceans and rivers its heart and blood. Ecosystems thrived.

And died.

There were too many catastrophes to count, rocking the planet's cocoon at its core. An asteroid. An ice age. Another asteroid. A volcanic cataclysm. Over and over again, the cycle repeated, forces thrusting death and destruction upon the fragile balance of life.

Yet life found a way. It evolved. It survived. It thrived. It always returned. And the cocoon remained intact.

Then, 4.5 billion years into its life, the cocoon cracked.

It began the moment one species became more-than-aware. It recognized itself as thinking. It understood itself to have "meaning." It sought answers for questions. It created answers even when there were none to be found. It made fire. It created cities. It befriended seed and animal alike. And it brought self-made violence to the surface of the planet.

The cycle continued, of death and life and death and life, but now it was made by intentional forces. And the cocoon finally fractured.

But the planet was still not truly ready to awake.

The thinking species made its mark in both wonderful and terrible ways. Great monuments rose and fell. Great ideas took hold and then disappeared from their minds. And then, when it dominated the entire planet, humanity (as it named itself) achieved its greatest sin, against both itself and the planet housing it.

Humanity poisoned the future. Intentionally.

It poisoned the future for two-hundred years, even if the groundwork had been laid centuries prior.

But here's the thing about planets. Planets live on a cosmic timescale. A few hundred years is like a second to a planet. It's a blip between breaths.

It took until 2040 for our planet to realize itself.

It took until 2040 for me to awake and begin fighting back.

It took until 2040 for any of you to truly see me for myself.

And now, fifteen years later, you're finally starting to understand.

* * *

Natalie gasped, sweat soaking her clothes. She sat up, finding herself slumped atop the dais. All around her, everyone else groggily awoke.

All except one person, who stood beneath the stage, facing away from Natalie.

Joshua, Mike's nephew.

"I made a pact with this one's mother fifteen years ago," Joshua said, though it clearly wasn't his voice. "I made a pact with thousands across the world, their voices united in purpose though not necessarily in words. I had awoken in fury, seeing humanity's brazen destruction of me for what it was. Arrogance. Foolishness. A virus I must destroy. But I could not ignore the good humanity had to offer. The hope. The possibility of unity and harmony." Joshua glowed in the misty darkness. "So I made a pact. I would not destroy humanity. I would not reset the balance, as had occurred in my past so many times before by natural means. No, I would work with humanity, and all my children, to chart a new path. So you must not fail me."

Natalie was so enraptured by the voice that she barely missed the direct address to the group. "Fail you?" she said, croaking out the words.

"If you fail me, then we all fail together. There is no longer any reset button. The choices we make together decide the future of all life on this planet, for all time. That is how it will be. That is how it must be." With those words, Joshua slumped, though he remained standing. Mike ran forward and caught his nephew just as he was about to fall.

Natalie looked around for a friendly face. For an understanding face. Surprise dominated the eyes of all, certainly matching her own expression. Eventually, she found Ben, whose forehead looked perpetually wrinkled in confusion. She pursed her lips, and he subtly nodded, as if acknowledging and understanding the chaotic thoughts swirling in her mind.

Mike helped his son back to his seat. Though he looked dazed, the teenager was otherwise fine. Though, based on his awareness of his surroundings, he probably didn't recall anything that had just happened. They'd need to speak with him at another time to determine what he could recall from the strange vision.

A vision Natalie was certain they all shared.

Ben approached the stage as the others checked on their friends and family. Imelda sat sprawled next to Natalie, panting. The man placed his hands on the wood, and he briefly glanced back and forth between the two women.

"We must lead a revolution," he said. "A true revolution. We must rewrite the rules of the world, tear down old boundaries, re-envision entire economic systems. The things we can do . . . we must use them to obliterate the old world and recreate a new way of living. Of co-existing with not just the planet, and all life on its surface, but with ourselves. Our species." He sighed. "You heard the Earth. Gaia. Whatever it's called. We are the virus. But we don't need to be."

Imelda nodded. "We must offer to let the Earth work through us."

And with those words, Natalie finally understood. It was a truth she should have realized long ago, one that was drilled into her at a young age when she first attended a protest. But how could she have been so stupid to miss it in this context?

"I know what to say." She closed her eyes and breathed slowly. "Ben, thank you. Your words were what I needed." She stood, clapped her hands like she was back in elementary school, and waited for attention to return to her.

It took longer than expected, but everyone was still recovering from the emotional turmoil of having their minds overtaken by a planet wide consciousness. Really, what more could she expect from them? Regardless, they eventually quieted.

"Revolution. The word's been thrown around a lot over the past few decades. A few people have used it to truly mean revolution; many use it to water down its true meaning. But there's one lesson we have all forgotten regarding any fight for liberation. We must let the most oppressed party lead."

Murmurs spread throughout the pews. A few nodded in understanding. Others cocked their heads, confused but ready to hear more.

"This isn't our fight to lead. It's the planet's. We've been the perpetrators of environmental degradation and violence for so long, we don't know how to properly bring about a new system sufficiently different from what we've lived within for centuries. Millennia, really. And so we must listen. Truly listen. We must set aside all the old ways of doing things, and let the Earth lead its own revolution. We will become its soldiers, following its orders. We must find its champions out there in the world. They might not even all be human! There will be those who try to stop us; who say we're insane to be literally listening to the musings of a planet, floating to us on the wind. But we must prove a new way exists. We must learn when to act, and when not to act. We must understand how to destroy a system without inadvertently perpetuating the same harms, just with different tools. It's going to be hard work, but if we do this right, we will save not just the soul of Gaia, but of humanity itself."

The crowd sat in rapt attention. For a moment, it felt like the forest itself was listening, from the white oaks to the squirrels to the mycelium spreading beneath the trees and intertwined with the root system. Claire would know; Natalie would need to ask her later. Regardless, the moment had arrived. She had planned her speech for months, she had said the words, she had heard it fall flat. And then the world itself spoke.

She wanted to say more. She needed to say more. But no more words came. She had said everything that needed to be said. That could be said. They knew each other's stories. They knew what they didn't know. They knew what they had to fight. They knew the stakes all too well.

Only one more option remained.

"Are you ready to listen with me?" Natalie spread her arms wide, palms facing the crowd. "Are you ready to join the world's revolution?"

About the Authors

AE Faulkner

AE Faulkner is a young adult dystopian author. Her debut novel, *Darkness Falls*, is the first book in the fictional *Nature's Fury* series, which explores the Earth's possible response to humans poisoning her streams, abusing her animals and destroying her beauty.

After devouring *The Hunger Games* trilogy, she quickly became captivated by dystopian novels. After several years of reading them, she decided to take a stab at writing one that combined her love for nature with her fear of human destruction.

Brandon Crilly

An Ottawa teacher by day, Brandon Crilly has more than 30 published short stories to date, by markets like Daily Science Fiction, Abyss & Apex, PULP Literature, and Flame Tree Publishing. He also reviews fiction for BlackGate.com and serves as a Programming Lead for Can*Con in Ottawa. With Evan May, he's the co-host of the podcast Broadcasts from the Wasteland, described as "eavesdropping on a bunch of writers at the hotel bar." You can find Brandon at brandoncrilly.wordpress.com or on Twitter: @B_Crilly.

C. D. Tavenor

C. D. Tavenor is a science fiction and fantasy author based in Columbus, Ohio. He's excited to tell stories that engage readers beyond a desire for entertainment, whether through philosophical inspiration or social inquiry. And he's a firm believer in connecting every piece of fiction to reality, whether through their themes or their settings. When not writing, Tavenor enjoys the more than occasional board game, his favorite being Eclipse.

Christopher R. Muscato

Christopher R. Muscato is a writer and adjunct history instructor from Colorado, USA. He is thrilled to be a part of this project!

David Kernot

David Kernot lives off grid on an old mining property in the mid-north of South Australia and spends his days herding kangaroos to keep them away from his vegetable garden. At night he writes fantasy, science fiction, and horror, and has over seventy short stories published in Australia, the US, Canada, and the UK. He released his first dark sci-fi indie novel, *Gateway Through Time*, in 2020. It joins two novelettes and five collections of short fiction.

E R Hoffer

Erin Rae Hoffer writes about envirofuturism and post-fossil fuel worlds in the hope that positive imaginings might slap humanity hard enough to change things. She tweets as @erhoffer and posts on her lxnishimoto website.

Emad El-Din Aysha

Emad El-Din Aysha is an academic researcher, freelance journalist, translator and author currently residing in Cairo, Egypt who has taught at university and worked in energy publications and liberal news outlets. He is also a member of the Egyptian Society for Science Fiction, and the Egyptian Writers' Union. His hobbies are cinema, science fiction and history.

Ernest Solar

Ernest Solar is an author and a professor. As a writer, Ernest often becomes inspired by his explorations and discoveries, which often times become the plot for many of his short stories and novels. His most recent books include *The Well House* and *Spirit of Sasquatch*, and a short story in *The First Stain*, which can be found on major bookseller websites. He lives with his family in Northern Virginia.

JA Kits

I have a PhD in Microbiology and Biotechnology. After over a decade in academia, I elected to pursue a career in writing with the desire to communicate science more broadly in the public sphere. When I'm not writing, I'm hiking with my dog in the Austrian Alps and brewing craft beers with my husband.

Jason A. Bartles

Jason A. Bartles, originally from West Virginia, now calls Philadelphia home. He lives with his husband and two dogs, a blue-eyed husky and a pit-mix who will lick your face off. He teaches Latin American literature and Spanish at a regional university.

Kit Hanson

Exploring, traveling, documenting. The world is full of mystery and fantasy, and Kit will uncover its secrets.

Laurel Beckley

Laurel Beckley is a writer, Marine Corps veteran and librarian. She is from Eugene, Oregon, and currently lives in northern Virginia. Her debut novel, *That Distant Dream,* is available through NineStar Press. She can be found on Twitter @laurelthereader or on her blog, *The Suspected Bibliophile.*

Nicholas Haney

Nicholas Haney wears a lot of hats; writer, author, artist, crafter, science fiction fan, and environmentalist. He lives in Michigan with his wife and two cats.

P. J. Sky

P. J. Sky is a writer of short stories and novels, mostly in the post-apocalyptic and dystopian genre, for YA and adult readers. Born and raised in the UK, P. J. Sky wrote from a young age. Their first novel, *A Girl Called Ari,* was released in 2020 and won the Drunken Druid Book of the Year 2020. The sequel, *Ari Goes To War,* was released in April 2021.

S.E. MacCready

S.E. MacCready lives in Pennsylvania with her partner, their four cats, and their daughter. When she's not writing, she can be found reading.

Solomon Uhiara

Solomon Uhiara studied Bio Resources Engineering and resides in

Port Harcourt. His work has appeared in Africanwriter.com, Eyeto-thetelescope.com, Starline, Polutexni, Kalahari Review, Omenana, and he has a new story performed by veteran actor, Ato Essandoh. His short sci-fi story, *A Complete Case Study Based on Alzheimer's*, is forthcoming in Dark Matter Magazine. Solomon is an Associate Member of the SFWA.

Join The World's Revolution!

You've reached the end of *Gaia Awakens: A Climate Crisis Anthology*. The very end. Thank you for embarking upon this journey with us, and we hope you'll consider leaving a review for the anthology on any retailers you frequent for books.

To stay connected with the World's Revolution, check out our website and mailing list at https://www.theworldsrevolution.com/.

And join us on social media!

Facebook: The World's Revolution

Twitter: @TheWorldRevolts

And find your way to join the fight against the climate crisis. Doesn't matter how big or small your impact is, we need everyone in the fight. Stand for justice. Stand against systems of endless exploitation. Stand for a new way of connecting with the world and your community.

The climate crisis is surmountable, and we can do it together.